P~~r~~

'...tterly beguiling...'
~~Edmund~~ Lupton, bestselling author of *Sister*

'~~Mar~~garet Leroy writes with candour and intelligence,
~~ca~~pturing the menace of suddenly finding the world may
not be at all as you've thought it'
—Helen Dunmore

'Leroy handles...domestic life with the same graceful, precise,
rueful style as [Richard Yates] the late novelist did, though
with a warmer, more hopeful intelligence'
—*Washington Post*

'Engrossing and affecting'
—*Eve*

'Brilliant at portraying the slow, steady disintegration of a
seemingly ordinary life when secrets are unearthed
and dark suspicions spread'
—*Baltimore Sun*

'Powerful and haunting'
—*Daily Mirror*

'What a storyteller Leroy is and what an eye she
has for contemporary life'
—Fay Weldon

'[Leroy's] quiet, self-assured narrative voice delivers tremendous
psychological depth and emotional resonance'
—*Kirkus Reviews*

'Leroy expertly draws a picture of a woman and a family in
crisis and the moral questions one sometimes has to face'
—*Toronto Sun*

Also by
Margaret Leroy

THE DROWNING GIRL
THE PERFECT MOTHER
THE RIVER HOUSE
THE ENGLISH GIRL

THE
Soldier's
Wife

MARGARET LEROY

HARLEQUIN® MIRA®

Harlequin MIRA is a registered trademark of Harlequin Enterprises Limited, used under licence.

Published in Great Britain 2014.
Harlequin MIRA, an imprint of Harlequin (UK) Limited,
Eton House, 18-24 Paradise Road,
Richmond, Surrey, TW9 1SR

© 2011 Margaret Leroy

Originally published in the UK in 2011 as *The Collaborator*

ISBN 978-1-848-45339-5

54-0914

Harlequin (UK) Limited's policy is to use papers that are natural, renewable and recyclable products and made from wood grown in sustainable forests. The logging and manufacturing processes conform to the legal environmental regulations of the country of origin.

Printed and bound by
CPI Group (UK) Ltd, Croydon, CR0 4YY

Margaret Leroy studied music at Oxford. She has written four novels, one of which was televised by Granada and reached an audience of eight million. Margaret has appeared on numerous radio and TV programmes, and her articles and short stories have been published in *The Observer*, *The Sunday Express* and *The Mail on Sunday*. Her books have been translated into ten languages. Margaret is married with two daughters and lives in London.

ACKNOWLEDGEMENTS

My thanks are due to my wonderfully thoughtful and perceptive editor, Maddie West, and the whole talented team at MIRA; I am especially grateful to Kim Young, Oliver Rhodes and Sue Smith, my meticulous copy-editor. Thank you as well to Brenda Copeland and Elisabeth Dyssegard at Hyperion in New York. I am also deeply grateful to my agents, Kathleen Anderson, and Laura Longrigg in London, who are so committed to my writing and who have supported me in so many ways. And thank you as always to Mick and Izzie, who shared Guernsey with me, and Becky and Steve, for so much love and encouragement.

Among the books that I read while researching this story, two deserve special mention—Madeleine Bunting's fascinating history, *The Model Occupation*, and Marie de Garis's enchanting volume, *Folklore of Guernsey*.

'Qui veurt apprendre a priaïr, qu'il aouche en maïr.'
He who wishes to learn to pray, let him go to sea.

—Guernsey proverb

PART I:

JUNE 1940

CHAPTER 1

"'Once upon a time there were twelve princesses…'"

My voice surprises me. It's perfectly steady, the voice of a normal mother on a normal day—as though everything is just the same as it always was.

"'Every night their door was locked, yet in the morning their shoes were all worn through, and they were pale and very tired, as though they had been awake all night…'"

Millie is pressed up against me, sucking her thumb. I can feel the warmth of her body: it comforts me a little.

'They'd been dancing, hadn't they, Mummy?'

'Yes, they'd been dancing,' I say.

Blanche sprawls out on the sofa, pretending to read an old copy of *Vogue*, twisting her long blonde hair in her fingers to try and make it curl. I can tell that she's listening. Ever since her father went to England with the army, she's liked to listen to her sister's bedtime story. Perhaps it gives her a sense of safety. Or perhaps there's something in her that yearns to be a child again.

It's so peaceful in my house tonight. The amber light of the setting sun falls on all the things in this room—all so friendly and familiar: my piano and heaps of sheet music, the Staffordshire dogs and silver eggcups, the many books on

their shelves, the flowered tea set in the glass-fronted cabinet. I look around and wonder if we will be here this time
tomorrow—if after tomorrow I will ever see this room again.
Millie's cat Alphonse is asleep in a circle of sun on the sill,
and through the open window that looks out over our back
garden you can hear only the blackbird's song and the many
little voices of the streams: there is always a sound of water
in these valleys. I'm so grateful for the quiet—you could
almost imagine that this was the end of an ordinary sweet
summer day. Last week, when the Germans were bombing Cherbourg, you could hear the sound of it even here
in our hidden valley, like thunder out of a clear sky, and up
at Angie le Brocq's farm, at Les Ruettes on the hill, when
you touched your hand to the window pane, you could feel
the faint vibration of it, just a tremor, so you weren't quite
sure if it was the window shaking or your hand. But for the
moment, it's tranquil here.

I turn back to the story. I read how there was a soldier
coming home from the wars, who owned a magic cloak that
could make him completely invisible. How he sought to
discover the princesses' secret. How he was locked in their
bedroom with them, and they gave him a cup of drugged
wine, but he only pretended to drink.

'He was really clever, wasn't he? That's what I'd have done,
if I'd been him,' says Millie.

I have a sudden vivid memory of myself as a child, when
she says that. I loved fairytales just as she does—enthralled by
the transformations, the impossible quests, the gorgeous significant objects—the magic cloaks, the satin dancing shoes;
and, just like Millie, I'd fret about the people in the stories,
their losses and reversals and all the dilemmas they faced.
So sure that if I'd been in the story, it would all have been

clear to me: that I'd have been wise and brave and resolute. I'd have known what to do.

I read on:

"'When the princesses thought he was safely asleep, they climbed through a trapdoor in the floor, and he pulled on his cloak and followed. They went down many winding stairways, and came at last to a grove of trees, with leaves of diamonds and gold…'"

Briefly, I'm distracted by the charm of the story. I love this part especially, where the princesses follow the pathway down to another world, a secret world of their own, a place of enchantment—loving that sense of going deep, of being enclosed. Like the way it feels when you follow the Guernsey lanes down here to our home, in this wet wooded valley of St Pierre du Bois—a valley that seems so safe and cloistered, like a womb. Then, if you walk on, you will go up, up and out suddenly into the sunlight, where there are cornfields, kestrels, the shine of the sea. Like a birth.

Millie leans into me, wanting to see the pictures—the girls in their big, bright glimmery skirts, the gold and diamond leaves. I smell her familiar, comforting scent—of biscuits, soap and sunlight.

The ceiling creaks above us as Evelyn gets ready for bed. I have filled her hot-water bottle for her—she can feel a chill even on warm summer evenings. She will sit in bed for a while and read the Bible. She likes the Old Testament best—the stern injunctions, the battles: the Lord our God is a jealous God. Our Rector at St Peter's is altogether too gentle for her. When we go—*if* we go—she will stay with Angie le Brocq at Les Ruettes. Evelyn is far too old to travel—she's like an elderly plant, too frail to uproot.

'Mum,' says Blanche, out of nowhere, in a little shrill

voice. 'Celeste says all the soldiers have gone—the English soldiers in St Peter Port.' She speaks rapidly, as though the words are rising in her like steam. 'Celeste says that there's no one left to fight here.'

I take a breath: it hurts my chest. I can't pretend any more.

'Yes,' I say. 'I heard that. Mrs le Brocq told me.'

Now, suddenly, my voice seems strange—shaky, serrated with fear. It sounds like someone else's voice. I bite my lip.

'They're coming, aren't they, Mum?' says Blanche.

'Yes, I think so,' I say.

'What will happen to us if we stay here?' she says. There's a thrum of panic in her voice. Her eyes, blue as hyacinths, are urgent, fixed on my face. She's chewing the bits of skin at the sides of her nails. 'What will happen?'

'Sweetheart—it's a big decision. I've got to think it through...'

'I want to go,' she says. 'I want to go to London. I want to go on the boat.'

'Shut *up*, Blanche,' says Millie. 'I want to hear the story.'

'Blanche—London isn't safe.'

'It's safer than here,' she says.

'No, sweetheart. People are sending their children away to the country. The Germans could bomb London. Everyone has gas masks...'

'But we could stay in Auntie Iris's house. She said we'd be more than welcome in her letter, Mum. You *told* us. She *said* we could. I really want to go, Mum.'

'It could be a difficult journey,' I say. I don't mention the torpedoes.

Her hands are clenched into fists. The bright sun gilds all the little fair hairs on her arms.

'I don't care. I want to go.'

'Blanche, I'm still thinking…'

'Well, you need to get a move on, Mum. We haven't got for ever.'

I don't know what to say to her. In the quiet, I'm very aware of the tick of the clock, like a heartbeat, beating on to the moment when I have to decide. It sounds suddenly ominous to me.

I turn back to the story.

'"The princesses came to an underground lake, where there were twelve little boats tied up, and each with a prince to row it…"' As I read on, my voice steadies, and my heart begins to slow. '"The soldier stepped into the boat with the youngest princess. 'Oh, oh, there is something wrong,' she said. 'The boat rides too low in the water.' The soldier thought he would be discovered, and he was very afraid…"'

Blanche watches me, chewing her hand.

But Millie grins.

'He doesn't need to be frightened, does he?' she says, triumphantly. 'It's going to be all right, isn't it? He's going to find out the secret and marry the youngest princess.'

'Honestly, Millie,' says Blanche, forgetting her fear for a moment, troubled by her little sister's naivety. 'He doesn't realise that, does he? Anything could happen. The people in the story can't tell how it's going to end. You're four, you ought to know that.'

CHAPTER 2

When Millie is settled in bed, I go out to my garden.

The back of the house faces west, and the mellow light of evening falls on the long lawn striped with shadows and on the rose bed under the window, with all the roses I've planted there that have names like little poems: Belle de Crécy, Celsiana, Alba Semi-plena. It's so quiet you can hear the fall of a petal from a flower.

I remember how this sloping garden delighted me when first I came to this place, to Le Colombier. 'Vivienne, darling, I want you to love my island,' said Eugene when he brought me here, just married. I was pregnant with Blanche, life was rich with possibility, and I did love it then, as we sailed into the harbour, ahead of us St Peter Port, elegant on its green hill; and I was charmed too by Le Colombier itself—by its age and the deep cool shade of its rooms, by its whitewashed walls and grey slate roof, and the wide gravel yard across the front of the house. In summer, you can sit and drink your coffee there, in the leaf-speckled light. The house stands gable to the road, the hedgebanks give us seclusion, we're overlooked only by the window of Les Vinaires next door, where the wall of their kitchen forms one side of our yard. It was all a little untidy when first I came to

Guernsey, the gravel overgrown with raggedy yellow weed: with Eugene away in London, Evelyn wasn't quite managing. Now I keep the gravel raked and I have pots of herbs and geraniums, and a clematis that rambles up and over the door. And I loved the little orchard on the other side of the lane that is also part of our land, where now the small green apples are just beginning to swell; and beyond the orchard the woodland, where there are nightingales. People here call the woodland the Blancs Bois—the White Wood—which always seems strange to me, because it's so dark, so secret in there in summer, under the dense canopy of leaves. But my favourite part of it all is this garden, sloping down to the stream. This garden has been my solace.

I work through all my tasks carefully. I dead-head the roses, I water the mulberry and fig that grow in pots on my terrace. Even as I do these things, I think how strange this is—to tend my garden so diligently, when tomorrow we may be gone. My hands as I work are perfectly steady, which seems surprising to me. But I step on a twig, and it snaps, and I jump, let out a small scream; and then the fear comes at me. It's a physical thing, this dread, a shudder moving through me. There's a taste like acid in my throat.

I put down my secateurs and sit on the edge of the terrace. I rest my head in my hands, think through it all again. Plenty of people have gone already, like Connie and Norman from Les Vinaires, shutting up their houses, leaving their gardens to go to seed. Some like me are still unsure: when I last saw Gwen, my closest friend, she said they couldn't decide. And others are sending their children without them, with labels pinned to their coats. But I couldn't do that. I could never send my children to England without me. I know how it feels to be a motherless child: I will do everything I can to protect my daughters from that. We go together, the three of us, or we stay. I try to look into the future, but it's all a dark blur to me: I can't imagine it, can't see down either path. The boat, the dangerous journey and going to London and sleeping on Iris's floor. Or staying here—everything fine and familiar to start with, everything just as it always was, sleeping in our own beds. Waiting for what must happen.

The shadows lengthen, the colours of my garden begin to recede; till the shadows seem more solid, more real, than the things that cast them. I can hear a nightingale singing in the Blancs Bois. There's a sadness to evenings on Guernsey sometimes, though Eugene could never feel it. When I first came here, he took me on a tour of the island, and we stopped on the north coast and watched the sun go down over L'Ancresse Bay—all colour suddenly gone from the sky, the rocks black, the sea white and crimped and glimmering, the fishing boats black and still in the water, so tiny against that immensity of sea—and I felt a surge of melancholy that I couldn't explain. I tried to tell him about it, but it didn't make any sense to him: he certainly didn't feel it. I had a sense of distance from him, which soon became habitual. A sense of how differently we saw the world, he and I. But I feel bad even thinking such things, of the many ways in which we were unhappy together, now that he's gone.

There's a sudden scatter of birds in the sky; I flinch, my heart leaping into my throat. Little things seem violent to me. And in that moment my decision is made. I am clear, certain. We will go tomorrow. Blanche is right. We cannot just stay here and wait. Terrified by the snap of a twig or a flight of startled birds. We *cannot*.

I go to the shed and take out my bicycle. I cycle up to the Rectory to put our names on the list.

CHAPTER 3

I take Evelyn her tea and toast in bed, the toast cut in exact triangles, as she likes it. She's sitting up, ready and waiting, in the neat bed-jacket of tea-rose silk that she's worn each morning for years, her back as straight as a tulip stalk. Her face is deeply etched with lines, and white as the crochet trim on her pillowcase. Her Bible is open on her bedside table, next to a balaclava that she's knitting for the Forces. She's always knitting. A tired, nostalgic scent of eau-de-cologne hangs about her.

I sit on the bed beside her. I wait until she has drunk a few sips of her tea.

'Evelyn—I've decided. I'm going to go with the girls.'

She doesn't say anything, watching me. I see the puzzlement that swims in her sherry-brown eyes. As though this is all news to her—though we've talked it through so many times.

'I'm taking you to Les Ruettes. You're going to live with Frank and Angie. Angie will look after you once the girls and I have gone…'

'Angie le Brocq goes out in the lanes with her curlers in,' she says.

Her voice is firm, as though her disapproval of Angie's

behaviour gives her some certainty in this shifting, troubling world—something to cling to.

'Yes, she can do,' I say. 'But Angie's got a good heart. You'll be well looked-after. I'm taking you there after breakfast, as soon as I've packed up your things.'

Sometimes I hear myself talk to her as though she were a child. Spelling everything out so carefully.

She looks shocked.

'No. Not after breakfast, Vivienne.' As though I have said something slightly obscene.

'Yes, it has to be straight after breakfast,' I tell her. 'As soon as I've packed a bag for you. Then the girls and I will be going to town to get on the boat...'

'But, Vivienne—that's really much too soon. I don't want to go today. I really don't feel ready. I've got one or two things that I really need to sort out. I'll go next week, if that's all right with you...'

I'm full of a frantic energy: it's such a struggle to be patient. Now I've decided, I'm panicking that we'll get to the harbour too late.

'Evelyn, if we're going, it has to be today. They're sending a boat from Weymouth. But after today there may not be any more boats. It's too dangerous.'

'It's not very helpful of them, is it? To rush us all like this? They have no consideration, Vivienne.'

'The soldiers have left,' I tell her. 'There's no one here to defend us...'

I don't say the rest of the sentence: *And the Germans could walk straight in.*

'Oh,' she says. 'Oh.' And then, with a light coming suddenly into her face, the look of one who has found the answer: 'Eugene should be here,' she says.

'Eugene's away fighting, remember?' I say, as gently as I can. 'He went to join the army. He's being very brave.'

She shakes her head.

'I wish he were here. Eugene would know what to do.'

I put my hand on her wrist, in a gesture of comfort that's empty, utterly futile—because what solace can I offer her when the son she adores has gone? I feel how frail she is, her limbs thin and brittle as twigs. I don't say anything.

I make the girls their breakfast toast. I'm looking around me, aware of all the detail of my kitchen—the tea-towels drying in front of the stove, the jars of raisins and flour. On the wall there's a print by Margaret Tarrant, a Christening present from Evelyn for Blanche—the Christ Child in his crib, with angels all around. It's a little sentimental, yet I like it, for the still reverence of the angels, and the wonderful soft colour of their tall fretted wings that are the exact smoky blue of rosemary flowers. I wonder if I will ever see these things again—and if I do, what our life will be like, in that unguessable future. I say a quick prayer to the angels.

The girls come down to the kitchen, bleary, smelling of warm bedclothes, rubbing the sleep from their eyes. Alphonse sidles up to Millie and walks in small circles round her. She bends down to stroke him, the morning sun shining on her dark silk hair, so you can see all the reddish colours in it.

'Right, girls. We're going,' I tell them. 'We'll get the boat today. It'll take us to Weymouth and from there we'll take the train to London and stay with Auntie Iris. I put our names on the list last night.'

Blanche's face is like a light switched on.

'*Yes.*' There's a thrill in her voice. 'But you could have decided earlier, Mum, then I could have washed my hair.'

'You'll have to pack quickly,' I tell them. 'As soon as you've finished breakfast. You'll need underwear and your toothbrushes, and all the clothes you can fit in.'

I've put out a carpet bag for Millie, and for Blanche a little leather suitcase that was Eugene's. Blanche looks at the suitcase, appalled.

'Mum, you're joking.'

'No, I'm not.'

'But how can I possibly get everything in there?'

London to Blanche is glamour—I know that. We went to stay with Iris for a holiday once—when Blanche was six, four years before Millie was born. Ever since that holiday, London has been a promised land to her, a dream of how life could be, *ought* to be. Once it was a dream of Trafalgar Square, with its dazzling fountains and pigeons, of the Tower of London, of seeing the chimps' tea-party at the zoo. But now that she's almost a woman, it's a dream of men in uniform—resolute, square-jawed, masterful—and tea in the Dorchester tea-room under a glittery chandelier: a dream of cakes and flirtation, with maybe a swing band playing *Anything Goes*. She wants to take all her very best things, her nylons, her coral taffeta frock, her very first pair of high heels that I bought for her fourteenth birthday, just before she left school. I understand, but I feel a flicker of impatience with her.

'You'll have to, Blanche. I'm sorry. There won't be much room on the boat. Just put in as many clothes as you can. And you'll need to wear your winter coats.'

'But it's *hot*, Mum.'

'Just do your best,' I say. 'And, Blanche, when you've finished, you can give Millie a hand...'

'No, she can't. I can do it myself,' says Millie.

She's been drinking her breakfast mug of milk, and her

mouth is rimmed with white. She bites languidly into her toast and honey.

'Of course you can, sweetheart. You're a big girl now,' I tell her. 'But Blanche will help you. Just be as quick as you can, both of you. If we're going to go, it has to be today...'

I watch them for a moment, Blanche with her sherbet-fizz of excitement, Millie still fogged with sleep. We've come to the moment I've been dreading.

'There's one thing that's very sad, though,' I say. 'We'll have to take Alphonse to the vet's.'

Millie is suddenly alert, the drowsiness all gone from her. Her eyes harden. She gives me a wary, suspicious look.

'But there's nothing wrong with him,' she says.

'No. But I'm afraid he needs to be put to sleep.'

'What d'you mean, *put to sleep*?' says Millie. There's an edge of threat in her voice.

'We have to have him put down,' I say.

'No, we don't,' she says. Her face blazes bright with anger.

'Millie, we have to. Alphonse can't come with us. And we can't just leave him here.'

'*No*. You're a murderer, Mummy. I hate you.' Her voice is shrill with outrage.

'We can't take him, Millie. You know we can't. We can't take a cat on the boat. Nobody will. Everyone's taking their cats and dogs to the vet. Everyone. Mrs Fitzpatrick from church was taking their terrier yesterday. She told me. It was terribly sad, she said, but it had to be done...'

'Then they're all murderers,' she says. 'I hate them.' Her small face is dark as thunderclouds. Her eyes spark. She snatches Alphonse up in her arms. The cat struggles against her.

'Millie. He can't come with us.'

'He could live with someone else, then, Mummy. It isn't his fault. He doesn't want to die. I won't let him. Alphonse didn't ask to be born now. This war is *stupid*,' she says.

Suddenly, it's impossible. All my breath rushes out in a sigh. I can't bear to distress her like this.

'Look—I'll speak to Mrs le Brocq,' I say wearily, defeated. It's as though the room breathes out as well, when I say that. But I know what Evelyn would say—the thing she's said so often before: *You're too soft with those girls, Vivienne...* 'I'll see what I can do,' I tell them. 'Just get yourselves packed up and ready to leave.'

CHAPTER 4

I walk with Evelyn to Angie's house, up one of the narrow lanes that run the length and breadth of Guernsey, their labyrinthine routes scarcely changed since the Middle Ages. High, wet hedgebanks press in on either side of the lane; red valerian grows there, and toadflax, and slender, elegant foxgloves, their petals of a flimsy, washed-out purple, as though they've been soaked too long in water. I have Alphonse in a basket, and a bag of Evelyn's clothes.

The climb exhausts Evelyn. We stop at the bend in the lane, where there's a stone cattle-trough, and I seat her on the rim of the trough to catch her breath for a moment. Sunlight splashes through leaves onto the surface of the water, making patterns that hide whatever lies in its depths.

'Is it much further, Vivienne?' she asks me, as a child might.

'No. Not much further.'

We come to the stand of thorn trees, turn in at the track to Les Ruettes. It's a solid whitewashed farmhouse that's been here for hundreds of years. There's an elder tree by the door: islanders used to plant elder as a protection against evil, lest a witch fly into the dairy and the butter wouldn't form. Behind the house are the glasshouses where Frank le Brocq grows his tomatoes. Chickens scratch in the dirt; their bubbling chatter is all about us. Alphonse is frenzied at the sight and smell of the chickens, writhing and mewing in his basket. I knock at the door.

Angie answers. She has a headscarf over her curlers, a cigarette in her hand. She sees us both there, and a gleam of understanding comes in her eyes: she knows I have made my decision. Her smile is warm and wide and softens the lines in her face.

'So. You've made your mind up, Vivienne.'

'Yes.'

I'm so grateful to Angie, for helping me out yet again. She's always been so good to me—she makes my marmalade, smocks Millie's dresses, ices my Christmas cake—and I know she'll be welcoming to Evelyn. There's such generosity in her.

She puts out a hand to Evelyn.

'Come in, then, Mrs de la Mare,' she says. 'We'll take good care of you, I promise.'

We enter the cool dark of her kitchen. Angie takes Evelyn to the settle by the big open hearth. Evelyn sits on the edge of the seat—tentative, as though she fears it won't quite take all her weight, her hands precisely folded.

I put her bag on the floor. A chicken scuttles in and starts to peck at the bag. I keep tight hold of Alphonse's basket.

'I don't know how to thank you, Angie,' I say.

She shakes her head a little.

'It's the least I could do. And never doubt that you're doing the right thing, Vivienne. With those two young daughters of yours, you don't know what might happen.' Then, lowering her voice a little, *'When they come,'* she says.

'No. Well…'

She leans close to whisper to me. Her skin is thickened

by sunlight and brown as a ripening nut. I feel her warm nicotine-scented breath on my cheek.

'I've heard such terrible things,' she says. 'I've heard that they crucify girls. They rape them and crucify them.'

'Goodness,' I say.

A thrill of horror goes through me. But I tell myself that this is probably just a story. Angie will believe anything. She loves to tell of witchcraft, hauntings, curses: she says that hair will grow much quicker if cut when the moon is waxing, that seagulls gathering at a seafarer's house may presage a death… Anyway, I ask myself, how could such atrocities happen here, amid the friendly scratching of chickens, the scent of ripening tomatoes, the summer wind caressing the leaves—in this peaceful orderly place? It's beyond imagining.

Maybe Angie sees the doubt in my eyes.

'Trust me, Vivienne. You're right to want to get those girls of yours away. She's right about that, isn't she, Frank?'

I turn. Frank, her husband, is standing in the doorway to the hall, half dressed, his shirt undone and hanging loose. I can see the russet blur of hair on his chest. I'm never quite sure if I like him. He's a big man, and a drinker. Sometimes she has black eyes, and I wonder if it's his fists.

He nods in response to her question.

'We were saying that only last night,' he says. 'That you'd want to keep an eye on your girls, if you'd decided to stay. You'd want to watch your Blanche. She's looking quite womanly now. I don't like to think what might happen—if she was still here when they came.'

He's looked at Blanche, noticed her—noticed her body changing. I don't like this.

'It would be a worry,' I say vaguely.

He steps into the kitchen, buttoning up his shirt.

'Vivienne, look, I was thinking. If it would help, I could give you a lift to the boat.'

I feel an immediate surge of gratitude for his kindness. This will make everything more straightforward. I'm ashamed of my ungracious thought.

'Thank you so much, that would be so helpful,' I say.

'My pleasure.'

He tucks in his shirt. A faint sour smell of sweat comes off him.

'The other thing is…' I say, and stop. I'm embarrassed to be asking more: they're already doing so much. 'I was wondering if you could maybe look after Alphonse? I ought to have had him put down, but Millie was distraught.'

'Bless her tender heart. Of course she would be,' says Angie. 'Of course we'll take poor Alphonse in. He'll be company for Evelyn, with all of her family gone.'

'Thank you so much. You're a saint, Angie. Well, I'd better be off…'

I go to kiss Evelyn.

'You look after yourself,' I say.

'And you, Vivienne,' she says, rather formally. She's sitting there so stiffly, as if she has to concentrate or she might fall apart. 'Give my love to the girls.' As though she didn't say goodbye to them just before we left. As though she hasn't seen them for weeks.

I pat her hand, and thank Angie again, and hurry back down the hill. I can't help thinking about what she said, about what the Germans could do. I tell myself she's wrong— that it's just a salacious story. In the Great War we heard that the Germans were cutting the hands off babies, but it proved to be just a terrible rumour.

Yet the pictures are there in my mind and I can't push them away.

CHAPTER 5

The streets of St Peter Port are quiet. Some of the shops are boarded up, and there's a lot of litter lying and shifting slightly in little eddies of air. The sky has clouded over, so it has a smudged, bleary look, like window-glass that needs cleaning. It's a grey, dirty, rather disconsolate day.

Frank drops us at the harbour, wishing us luck.

We see at once why the streets were empty: all the people are here. There's already a very long queue of silent, anxious islanders, snaking back from the pier and all along the Esplanade. We go to a desk set up on the pavement, where a flustered woman ticks off our names on a list. She has a pink, mottled face, and disordered hair that she keeps distractedly pushing out of her eyes.

We join the queue. People are sweating in woollen coats too cumbersome to pack up: they take out their handkerchiefs, wipe the damp from their skin. On this clammy summer day, the winter colours of the coats look sombre, almost funereal. Some people don't have suitcases, and have tied up their belongings in neat brown-paper parcels. A bus arrives, and children spill down the steps; most of them have labels carefully pinned to their coats. They have a lost, dazed look in their eyes. Older children officiously clutch at younger brothers and sisters, responsibility weighing on them, clasping at a coat collar or the cuff of a sleeve.

Millie stares at the children. She frowns. She holds very tight to my hand.

Blanche is wearing her coral taffeta dress beneath her winter coat. She unbuttons her coat and runs her hand over her skirt, trying to smooth out the creases in the glossy fabric.

'Oh, *no*, Mum,' she says suddenly.

Her voice is full of drama; my heart pounds, hurting my chest.

'What is it?' I say sharply.

'I think I've forgotten my Vaseline. My skin will get all chapped.'

I feel a little cross with her, that she frightened me like that.

'It doesn't matter,' I say. 'We're all sure to have forgotten something.'

'It *does* matter, Mum. It *does*.'

We stand there for what seems like a very long time. The queue is orderly, subdued: nobody talks very much. Seagulls scream in the empty air above us, and there are many boats at anchor; you can hear the nervous slap and jostle of water round their hulls. The sun comes briefly out from the cloud, throwing light at everything, then rapidly snatching it back; where the sun isn't shining on it, the sea looks black and unspeakably cold. I can't see the boat that will take us to Weymouth—it must be moored out of sight. The only vessel that's moored to this part of the pier is quite a small boat, not much bigger than the fishermen use, tied up where stone steps lead down from the pier to the sea. I wonder vaguely who it belongs to.

More and more people come, with their coats, their suit-cases, their bulging parcels of precious belongings: with the fear that seems to seep like sweat from their pores.

'Will I have my own room at Auntie Iris's?' Blanche asks me.

'No, sweetheart. It'll be a crush. You'll probably have to sleep in the back bedroom with the boys.'

'Oh,' she says, digesting this. It isn't quite what she'd hoped for. 'Well, I don't mind. It might be quite fun, really, sharing a room.'

'What does London look like?' says Millie.

'You'll love it,' says Blanche. She relishes being asked this—she loves being the expert on London. 'The women have beautiful clothes, and the trains go under the ground, and there's a park with pelicans...'

I understand Blanche's yearning for London: sometimes I long for it too, even after all these years away, remembering the thrilling hum of the city, the people so different from island people, so much more vivid and purposeful, the yellow lamplight on smoky streets, the slow brown surge of the Thames. I remember too the sense of possibility—of a world that's freer, wider, more open than this island. I share her excitement for a moment, allowing myself a spark of hope—that there could be good things about this, in spite of the war. A new freedom.

'Can we go and see Buckingham Palace?' says Millie.

She has a Buckingham Palace jigsaw that Evelyn gave her for Christmas.

'I'm sure we will,' I say.

To my relief, the queue begins to edge forward. Then I see that the people at the front are going down the steps from the pier and over a gangplank onto the boat. The small boat.

It can't be. They can't expect us to go in that, all the way to England.

'What is it, Mum?' says Blanche, urgently. She's heard my quick inbreath.

'Nothing, sweetheart.'

She follows my gaze.

'It isn't a very big boat, Mum.' A little uncertain.

'No. But I'm sure it will be fine. I'm sure they know what they're doing…'

She hears the apprehension in my voice. She gives me a questioning look.

The queue inches forward, silently.

In front of me is a solid middle-aged woman. Round her neck she wears a fox fur, which has a glass-bead eye, a predatory mouth, a lush russet tail hanging down. Millie is intrigued: she stares at the fox. A smell of mothballs hangs about the woman; she will have taken her best winter clothes out of storage. Next to her is her husband, who seems rather passive and cowed. You can tell she's the one who makes the decisions.

'Sorry to bother you,' I say.

She turns and gives a slight smile, approving of my children.

'It was just that I was wondering—is that the boat?' I say.

'Well—that's what it looks like,' she says.

She obviously takes trouble over her appearance; she has plucked her eyebrows out then pencilled them carefully in, and her face is heavily powdered. Her hat is fixed with a silver hatpin like a pansy flower.

'We'll never all get on that,' I say. 'They should have sent something bigger. Didn't they realise how many of us there would be?'

The woman shrugs.

'To be honest—excuse my language—but I don't think they give a damn about us, in England,' she says.

'But—you'd think they'd have sent some soldiers. I mean, there's no protection for us. We could meet anything on the journey...'

'We're expendable, let's face it,' says the woman. 'They've given us up for lost. Well, I suppose Mr Churchill's got an awful lot of things on his mind.'

She's sardonic, resigned. I wish I could be like that—perhaps it's a good way to be: not to expect very much, not to struggle against what is happening. But she doesn't have children with her.

She pulls out the pansy hatpin and fans her face with her hat. Sweat has made thin runnels in the powder on her face. She turns back to her husband.

Panic moves through me. Millie's hand is so tiny and helpless in mine: everything feels so unguessably fragile, so opened up to disaster—the bodies of my children, the flimsy little boat. I have to protect my children, I have to keep them safe; but I don't know how to do that. I think of the boat, packed tight with all these people, edging its way across the wideness of sea, all that shining waste of water between us and Weymouth; of the dark secret threat that lurks in the depths of the sea.

I'm scarcely aware of the moment of decision—as though I perform the action almost before I think the thought. I find myself pulling Millie out of the queue, dumping the bags down beside her.

'Stay there,' I tell her.

I go to grab Blanche's arm.

She's startled. She turns to me jumpily.

'Mum. What on earth are you doing?'

'We're going back home,' I tell her.

She ignores what I say, or doesn't hear me.

'Mum.' Her voice is splintered with panic. 'We'll lose our place in the queue.'

'We're going home,' I say again.

'But, Mum—you said we had to go *now*, or we couldn't go at all.' Her eyes are wide, afraid.

Millie tries to pick up her carpet bag, but she's only holding one handle. The bag falls open and all her things tumble out—her knickers and liberty bodices, her candystripe pyjamas, her beloved ragdoll—all her possessions, intimate, lollipop-bright, spewing out all over the grubby stone of the pier. She starts to cry—shuddery, noisy sobs. She's frightened and cross, and ashamed that she made the things spill.

'Shut up, Millie. You're such a crybaby,' says Blanche.

Millie, outraged, sobs more loudly. There's a slight cold drizzle of rain.

I gather up Millie's things and try to brush the dirt off them. Everyone's eyes are on me.

'Mum, you can't do this,' hisses Blanche, in an intense whisper. She's torn—desperate to make me listen, yet mortified at being involved in such a public scene. 'We've got to get to England.'

'The boat's too small. It isn't safe,' I say.

The rain comes on more heavily. Rainwater soaks my hair, runs down my parting, runs down my face like tears.

'But nothing's safe any more,' she says.

I have nothing to say to that.

'And I want to go. I want to go to London.' Her voice is shrill. 'You *said* we were going to go. You *said*.'

I'm trying to gather up Millie's things.

'Blanche, for God's sake, just grow up. This isn't all about you. Can't you think of somebody else for once?'

Immediately I've said it, I regret it. I shouldn't have told her off like that. I have snatched her dream away from her: I know she's upset, and afraid. But the words hang between us, sharp as blades, and I can't take them back again.

I straighten up, put my hand on her shoulder. She shakes me off and stands a little aside, as though she is nothing to do with us. Her face is a *papier maché* mask: it's set and white and looks about to dissolve.

I usher them back, past the queue of people. I don't know how to get home, I haven't thought this through, haven't thought beyond this moment—just wanting to turn my back on the boat, the journey, the treacherous heave and shine of the sea.

We walk along the Esplanade, heading away from the pier. I don't know if there are any buses going to St Pierre du Bois. Maybe all the buses are busy bringing the children here, to the harbour. The mist and rain are blowing in so you can't see far over the water, the horizon edging nearer, everything closing in, closing down. They'll have a wet, choppy crossing.

And then, with a rush of relief, I see a vehicle I recognise: it's Angie's brother, Jack Bisson, in his ramshackle van. Jack works as a handyman; like Angie, he's resourceful, he can fix anything—burst pipes, loose slates, a cow that's struggling to calve. I wave, and he comes to a stop beside us and winds his window down.

'We were going to go and then we decided not to,'
I say.

'*She* decided not to,' Blanche mutters behind me. 'Not us.
Her.'

Jack has quick dark eyes like a sparrow and Angie's warm
wide smile. His bird-like gaze flits over us. He nods, accepting what I've said.

'Mr Bisson—I know it's an awful lot to ask—but I don't
suppose you're going our way? You couldn't give us a lift?'

'Of course I could do that, Mrs de la Mare. Just you hop
in,' he tells us.

He drops us in the lane just above Le Colombier.

CHAPTER 6

We trudge down the lane towards our house. There's no sound but the rustle of rain on the uncountable leaves of the woods and orchards of the valley. Fat drips spill from the branches above us and soak our hair and our clothes, and I want to wipe the rain from my face, but I'm holding two bags and Millie's hand and can't brush the water away. Millie is tugging at me: she says her feet have blisters. All I can think is how much I want to get home.

We come to the wide five-bar gate that opens into our yard. The gate is unfastened. I must have left it like that—not noticing that I hadn't fastened it in our rush to leave. But I'm surprised I was so careless.

I go to the door: it's half ajar. I feel my pulse skittering off.

'What's the matter, Mummy?' says Millie.

'I'm not sure. You two can wait out here for a moment,' I tell them.

'Why?' says Blanche. 'It's our home. And it's raining, Mum, in case you hadn't noticed.'

'Just do as you're told,' I say.

My voice has an edge. Blanche flinches.

I step cautiously into the passage, then into the kitchen.

Fear rushes through me. Someone has been here. Someone has broken into our house. My kitchen is wrecked, the cupboard doors flung open, my pottery jars broken, flour and raisins and biscuits all over the floor.

I call out.

'Hello?'

My shrill voice echoes.

I stand silently for a moment and listen for running footsteps, my heart thudding. But the house has an empty, frail stillness: whoever did this has gone. I step warily into the living room. All my precious music is scattered, the sheets of paper like white petals from some great blossoming tree that a wind has shaken. The cabinet is open, and they've taken some of the china, and the Staffordshire dogs and the eggcups from the mantelpiece have gone.

The girls come cautiously into the house to find me.

'*No.*' Blanche's voice is freighted with tears. 'I told you, Mum. We did the wrong thing. We should never have come back,' she says.

'The Germans are thieves,' says Millie severely. 'I hate them.'

'This wasn't the Germans,' I tell her. 'The Germans haven't come.' I only just manage not to add *yet*. I swallow down the word.

'It *was* the Germans,' says Millie. It's so simple for her. 'They're robbers. They've taken our china dogs. They shouldn't have.'

'No, sweetheart. It must have been someone who lives around here who did this.'

There's the crunch of something broken, splintering under my feet. I kneel, pick up a china shard. It's from one of the flowered teacups I brought all the way from London, that I always kept for best and only used for Sunday tea, because I was scared they might get damaged. Now, I see I was wrong: I should have made the most of the flowery cups while I could.

'I bet it was Bernie Dorey,' says Blanche. 'I've seen him and his gang round here sometimes. He was in the same class as me at school, his family are all horrible. He used to nick my satchel and he never brushed his teeth.'

'We don't know who it was,' I say.

The thought appals me—that somebody was just waiting for us to leave, watching the house and scheming and taking their chance. Seeking a way to profit from the anarchy of war. And I'm upset by the destructiveness of it, all the spilt flour and the breakages, as though it was just a game to them, as though they enjoyed what they did. I hate that.

Blanche is seized with anger—that nothing has happened as she dreamed it.

'You see, Mum? I was right, we should have gone to England. We could be on the boat by now. We could be sailing.' She's furious with me: her eyes are hard as blue flints. 'It's going to be awful here. Worse than ever,' she says.

'We'll be all right, sweetheart,' I say. 'It doesn't matter that much. We can manage without the china dogs, and the silver eggcups were such a nuisance to clean. At least they haven't taken our books...'

'So why do you sound so unhappy, Mummy?' says Millie.

I don't say anything.

Blanche rips off her winter coat and flings it onto a chair. She stares down at herself, at the hem of her taffeta dress, which is crumpled and dark with rainwater.

'Look. It's all *ruined*,' she says.

Her eyes are shiny with tears.

'Blanche—your dress will be fine. We'll hang it up so it doesn't crease. It's only water,' I say.

But I know she isn't talking only about the taffeta frock.

I go upstairs and look around, in the girls' bedrooms, and Evelyn's, and mine. Nothing has been disturbed here; it looks as though the burglars didn't come this far. But I have to be certain. Le Colombier is a big old rambling house, a labyrinth. The many people who have lived here have built onto it over the years: there are rooms leading into one another, twisty passages, places where you could hide. I hunt around everywhere—open up all the cupboards, explore all the secrets and hidden ways of my house. I climb right up to the attics, to the big front attic we use as a spare bedroom, and the little one at the back, that you reach by a separate stair. All is as it should be. At last I come down to the girls again, and send them off to unpack their bags.

I clear up the mess, the shards of china crunching under my feet. A feeling like grief washes through me, and not only because of the things that are broken or lost. This doesn't feel like our home now, since the intrusion: it feels wrong, smells wrong, in that indefinable way of a place where someone unwelcome has been. Everything is falling apart—all the intricate warp and weft of the peaceful life we have lived here: everything unravelling. They haven't come yet, but it has already begun.

CHAPTER 7

I put together a meal with some food that hasn't been touched by the burglars—a loaf of bread I forgot to throw out, a tin of corned beef. After we've eaten, I walk up to Les Ruettes to bring Evelyn back home. Millie comes with me. The rain has stopped and the sky is starting to clear. There are still great banks of cloud that look as solid as far countries, but now between the heaps of cloud, there are depths and reaches of blue. The hedgebanks are drenched, and the air is rich with musky, polleny scents— wild garlic, wet earth, violets. I breathe in gratefully. The foxgloves brush against us like hands, and there are pale briar roses, each holding a drop of clear water. The little ferns that love the damp flicker like green tongues of flame.

As we near the door of Les Ruettes, Alphonse slinks out from behind a glasshouse and circles around Millie, arching, purring resonantly.

Frank le Brocq comes to the door, a cigarette clamped between his lips. He's wearing his check cloth cap; he takes it off when he sees me. A splinter of amusement floats in his eye.

'We saw you come back. Cold feet?' he says.

'Yes. You could put it like that.'

I feel awkward. There's something shameful about

returning like this: it suddenly feels like an act of coward-ice—not a reasoned decision, more a failure of nerve.

He takes a long drag on his cigarette and looks me up and down, in his appraising way that I don't quite like.

'That cat of yours wouldn't settle,' he tells me. 'He kept going back to your house. Cats are like that, cats are territorial creatures. A bit like you lot.' He grins.

Millie picks up Alphonse and wraps her arms around him.

'Did you miss me?' she says.

The cat rubs his head extravagantly against her.

'Look, Mummy, look, he knows what I'm saying. He really missed me,' she says.

Frank stands aside, and we go into the kitchen. Angie is kneading dough on her table; she greets us with a smile. Evelyn is on the settle where I left her, still sitting upright on the edge of the seat.

'Vivienne.' There's a puzzled look in Evelyn's face, as though her life is a knotted tangle she can't begin to undo. 'Well, you didn't take long.'

'We're taking you back home,' I say. 'We changed our minds. We didn't go in the boat.'

'Least said, soonest mended,' she says.

I feel a little surge of unease. She often gives me this feeling now—that the things she say sound normal, yet somehow they don't quite make sense.

I turn to Angie.

'Thank you so much...'

'Don't you worry, Vivienne. I was more than glad to help out... Let's hope you made the right decision,' she adds, a little doubtfully.

'Well, time will tell,' I say vaguely; then think that I owe her some explanation, after everything that she has done for me. 'The thing is—it was such a little boat. And it's such a long way...'

We walk back slowly down the lane. I take Evelyn's arm to help her. A bird calls with a sound like a pot being scraped, and the moist air is cool on our skin. Millie tries to carry Alphonse, but the cat wriggles down and scampers off through the fields, heading for Le Colombier. Millie slips her hand in mine.

'I'm glad we came back home,' she says, her voice fat with contentment. 'I didn't really want to go. It's nice here, isn't it, Mummy?'

'Yes, sweetheart.'

But even as I say it, a little tremor goes through me. Above us the clouds retreat, regroup, creating new shapes in the sky—new countries, new islands.

CHAPTER 8

On Friday I cycle up to town.

The streets are empty because so many people have gone, and some of the shops are boarded up, but otherwise St Peter Port feels much the same as always, calm and orderly in the warm June sunshine—as though the panic of the evacuation hadn't happened at all. I buy a lamb joint, and stock up on coffee and cigarettes and tea. Such luxuries may become rather harder to buy—when they come, when it happens.

I come to Martel's watch and clock shop, where Blanche's friend, Celeste, has been working since she left school. I glance in through the window, wondering whether she's gone, and she sees me and waves vigorously, her glossy dark curls dancing. I feel so happy for Blanche because her friend will still be here. In Grand Pollet, I pass the music shop that belonged to Nathan Isaacs; this is one of the shuttered shops. Nathan left a while ago, before the fall of France, saying that he could see which way the wind was blowing, a rueful smile on his clever, diffident face—talking about it so lightly. I miss him. We grew friendly because of the shop, where I'd often go to buy music. He was a good musician, a violinist, and sometimes I'd play duets with him at one of his music evenings, up at Acacia Villa, his tall, graceful house on the hill.

I go to the library, where I choose a new Elizabeth Goudge, and then on to the haberdasher's to buy more wool for Evelyn. I can't get her balaclavas and gloves to the Forces any more, but at least the knitting keeps her occupied. And I stop off at Boots on the High Street to buy a first lipstick for Blanche—wanting to give her a bit of glamour, something to make her happier, now I have snatched her dream of London from her.

I like chemists' shops. I walk slowly down the aisle, past opulent silver compacts that I could never afford, moving through drifts of perfume-lavender water, and Devon Violets talcum powder, and all the lavish gorgeousness of Chanel No. 5.

The Yardley counter is right at the back of the shop. From here the land slopes steeply, and through the high arched windows you look down over russet-tiled roofs and out across the harbour; you can see the little boats bobbing, and all the glimmery blue dazzle of the sky and sea. Seagulls wheel and cry in the clear air. The day is mellowing now towards evening, the sunlight turning gold. The tomato lorries are parked in a line on the pier—there are still boats to take the crop to the mainland, though I don't suppose this will happen for many more days. Way above the harbour, in the splendour of the sky, I notice two tiny black specks—a couple of planes that are flying there, very high, very far: they look innocuous as birds. I can't tell if the planes are theirs or ours. Frank le Brocq would be able to tell, even from such a distance—he says he often sees German reconnaissance planes. It's a good thing, really, that they fly over, he says: they'll be able to tell that we're defenceless—that there are no army camps or naval ships or anti-aircraft guns here. That we're really not worth bothering with.

I stare at all the Yardley lipsticks, not knowing which colour to choose—maybe the rose-pink, maybe the peach. The simplest choices seem hard now, after all my hesitation about whether or not we should leave—as though I have somehow lost faith in my power to decide. In the end I choose the coral because it will match Blanche's taffeta dress. Then I head back down the High Street: I have left my bike against a wall in the lower part of the road.

'Vivienne! It *is* you!' I feel a warm hand on my arm. 'I called you but you didn't turn. You looked like you were off in a dream...'

I spin around. It's Gwen.

She smiles, a little triumphant—as though I am something she has achieved. Her gaze—chestnut-brown, vivid, shining—rests on my face. Her frock has a pattern of polka dots and little scarlet flowers. It's so good to see her I'd like to put my arms around her.

'I didn't know if you'd gone or not,' she says. 'It was all so sudden, wasn't it? Having to choose?' She dumps her heavy bag of shopping down on the pavement, rubs a sore shoulder. 'So you've decided to stick it out?'

I nod.

'Cold feet, at the last moment,' I tell her. 'A bit pathetic really. We actually got to the pier. Then we went back home, and someone had broken in and stolen some of our things...'

She shakes her head wearily.

'It happened to a lot of people,' she says. 'You wouldn't think it of islanders, would you?'

'It was horrible,' I say.

She puts her hand on my arm again.

'I'm so glad, though, Vivienne,' she tells me. 'I'm just so glad you're still here.'

Her warmth is so welcome.

'Look—are you in a rush?' she says.

'Not at all.'

'We'll have tea, then?'

'I'd love to.'

We have a favourite tea shop—Mrs du Barry's on the High Street. We take the table we always choose—the table right at the back that has a wide view over the harbour. There's a crisp starched tablecloth, and marigolds in a glass vase; the marigolds have a thin, peppery scent. The shop is almost empty, except for an elderly couple talking in slow, hushed voices, and a woman with eyes smudged with tiredness and a baby in her arms. As she sips her tea, the woman rests her cheek against the baby's head. I feel a surge of nostalgia, re-membering the sensation of a baby's head against you—how fragile it feels where the bones haven't fused, and how hot and scented and sweet.

'Gwen—how did you decide?' I ask.

'Ernie wouldn't leave,' she tells me. Gwen and Ernie live at Elm Tree Farm, in Torteval; they have a big granite farm-house and a lot of fertile land. 'Not after all those years of work. "I'm damned if I'll let them take it all away from me," he said.'

'Well, good for him…'

Her bright face seems to cloud over. She pushes back her hair. A haze of anxiety hangs about her.

'How can you ever know what the right thing is? How can you ever know?' she says.

'You can't. I keep wondering too. Whether I've made an awful mistake...'

'Johnnie can't bear it, of course, being stuck here, kicking his heels. Poor kid. He simply can't bear that he was too young to join up.'

'I can imagine that. How he would feel that...'

I think of her younger son, Johnnie—how impulsive he is, how he'd yearn for action. I've always been fond of Johnnie, with his exuberance, his wild brown hair, his restless, clever hands. He and Blanche would play together a lot when they were small—making mud pies and flower soup, or building dens in the Blancs Bois—until at seven or eight, as children will, they went their separate ways. Then I taught him piano for a while, though he often forgot to bring the right music, and scarcely practised at all. Until he discovered a talent for ragtime, which I could never play. He had the rhythm in him, and there was no stopping him.

'But I wasn't going to let Johnnie go to England on his own,' says Gwen. 'Not after... Well...'

She doesn't finish her sentence. Her eyes glitter with unshed tears: the stricken look crosses her face. Brian, her elder son, was lost at Trondheim, in the Norwegian campaign. After it happened, I would panic sometimes when I was with her; afraid of the gaps in our conversations, as though they were cliffs you could fall from, afraid of saying his name. Once I told her: I'm so frightened of reminding you, I don't want to make you upset... And she said, Vivienne, it's not as though you're reminding me of something I've forgotten. It's not as though I don't think of him every moment of every day. The only time I don't think of him is when I'm fast asleep—then every morning I wake up and I have to learn it again. So let's just get on with it...

'I want to keep Johnnie close,' she says now.

I put my hand on her wrist.

'Of course you do,' I say. 'Of course you wouldn't want him to go…'

Perhaps I'm lucky that both my children are girls. When I was younger, I felt I'd love to have a son, as well; but war changes everything. Even the things you hope for.

Mrs du Barry brings our tea. The quilted tea cosy is shaped like a thatched cottage, and the milk jug has a crochet cover held in place by beads. There are cakes on a silver cake stand—Battenberg, cream slices, luxurious chocolate eclairs. I take a slice of Battenberg. We sip our tea and eat our cake, and watch as the sun sinks down in the sky and spreads its gold on the sea.

Gwen sighs.

'Johnnie's such a worry—what he might get up to,' she says. 'He's been a bit wild since it happened. It's not really anything he's done—just what I feel he *could* do…'

'It's such a short time,' I tell her.

'He worshipped his brother,' she says.

'Yes.'

I remember Brian's memorial service—how Johnnie didn't cry; how he stood to attention, his face white as wax, his body so rigid, controlled: making me think of a cello string stretched too tight, that might suddenly break. He troubled me. I know just why Gwen worries so about him.

'He longs to do what Brian did,' she tells me. 'He wears Brian's army jumper. And he's got a box of Brian's things—his binoculars, and his shotgun that he used for shooting rabbits, and his famous collection of Dinky cars that he kept from when he was small. The box is Johnnie's most precious possession; he keeps it under his bed…'

I feel a tug of sadness, for Johnnie.

We're quiet for a moment. It's getting late, and Mrs du Barry hangs the Closed sign on her door. My hands are sticky with marzipan from the Battenberg cake, and I wipe them on my handkerchief. The spicy scent of the marigolds is all around us.

And then I ask the question that looms at the front of my mind—vivid as neon, inescapable.

'Gwen. What will happen?'

She leans a little towards me.

'They'll overlook us,' she says, too definitely. 'Don't you think? Like in the Great War.'

'Do you really think so?'

'Nobody bothered with us, during the Great War,' she says.

'That's true enough. But that was then...'

'I mean, what difference do we make to anything? What use could these little islands possibly be to Hitler?' There's a note of pleading in her voice: perhaps it's herself as much as me that she's trying to persuade. 'Maybe he won't think of us. That's what I hope, anyway. You've got to hope, haven't you?'

But her hand holding the teacup is shaking very slightly, so the tea shivers all across its surface.

She clears her throat, which seems suddenly thick.

'Anyway, Vivienne—tell me more about all of you,' she says. Moving on to safer things.

'Blanche is unhappy,' I tell her. 'She terribly wanted to go.'

'Well, she would, of course,' says Gwen. 'There isn't much here for young people, you can see how she'd long for London. And Millie?'

'She's being ever so brave, though she doesn't really understand.'

'She's a poppet,' says Gwen.

'And Evelyn—well, I'm not sure she's quite right in her mind any more. Half the time she seems to forget that Eugene joined up...' I see the shadow that rapidly moves across Gwen's face, at the mention of Eugene, then fades away just as quickly. I wish I hadn't eaten the Battenberg cake: the sweetness of the marzipan is making me feel slightly sick. 'Sometimes she asks for him,' I tell her, 'as though he's still at home.'

'Poor Vivienne. Your mother-in-law was never exactly the easiest of people,' says Gwen carefully. 'You've certainly got your hands full.'

We say goodbye. Gwen leaves, and I go to the Ladies. I wash the marzipan from my hands, push my brush through my hair, take out my compact to powder my face. My hands have a clean, astringent smell from Mrs du Barry's carbolic soap. Then I go back to the table to pick up my cardigan that I left there.

All the china on the tables begins to rattle violently. There's a roaring noise from outside; at first, I can't work out what it can be, then I think it must be a plane—yet the sound is too sudden, too loud, too near, for a plane. Fear surges through me: if this is a plane, it will crash on the town. Everyone rushes to the window at the back of the shop, which looks out over the harbour. The air seems too thin, so it's hard to breathe.

'No no no no,' says Mrs du Barry. She's standing close to me; she clutches my arm.

We see the three planes that are flying over, swooping down over the harbour: we see the bombs falling, shining, catching the sun as they fall. They seem to come down so slowly. And then the crump of the impact, the looming dust, the flame—everything breaking, broken, fires leaping up, loose tyres and oil drums flung high in the air by the blast. I hear the ferocious rattle of guns. I think, stupidly, that at least there are soldiers here after all, the soldiers haven't left us. Then I realise that the guns I hear are German guns, in the planes. They're machine-gunning the men, the lorries: there's a ripping sound, a flare of fire, as a petrol tank explodes. The men on the pier are scattered, running, crumpling like straw men, thrown down.

Fear floods me. My whole body is trembling. I think of my children. Will the planes fly all over the island, will they bomb my children? And Gwen—where is Gwen? How much time did she have? Could Gwen have got away?

I stand there, shaking. Someone drags me under a table. We are all under the tables now—the elderly couple, Mrs du Barry, the mother clutching her child. Someone is saying *Oh God oh God oh God*. There's a shattering sound as the window blows in, shards of glass all around us in a danger-ous, glittering shower. Somebody screams: it might be me, I don't know. We crouch there, wait for the end, for the bomb that will surely land on us.

Suddenly, amid the clamour, the air-raid siren goes off.

'About time,' mutters Mrs du Barry beside me. 'About bloody time.' I hear the sob in her voice. Her fingers dig into my arm.

The elderly woman is gasping now, as though she has no breath, her husband holding her helplessly, like someone holding onto water, as though she might slip from his grasp. The young mother presses her baby tight to her chest. The sounds from the harbour assault us, the boom and crash of falling bombs, the growl and scream of plane engines, the terrible rattle of guns. More windows shatter around us. It goes on and on, it seems to last for ever, an eternity of noise and splintering glass and fear.

And then at last the sound of the planes seems to fade,

receding from us. I find that I am counting, like you do in a storm—waiting for the thunderclap: expecting them to circle back, more bombs to fall. But there's nothing.

A silence spreads around us. The tiniest sound is suddenly loud. I hear a splash of tea that spills from a table onto the floor: there's nothing but the *drip drip* of tea and the pounding of blood in my ears. Within the silence, the baby starts wailing, as though this sudden stillness appals him more than the noise.

I look down, see that a piece of glass is stuck in my hand. I pull it out. My blood flows freely. I don't feel any pain.

I crawl out from under the table, leaving the other people. Not thinking at all, just moving. I get to my feet and run out of the door and down the High Street and through the arch to the covered steps that take you down to the pier. The steps are dark and smell of fish and the damp stone is slippery under my feet. I have only one thought—to look for Gwen, to see if Gwen is alive.

At the bottom of the steps I come out into sunlight again, on the Esplanade that runs along the harbour past the pier. All the horror of it slams into me. Everything is on fire before me, I can feel the heat of it here, but the fire seems unreal, as though it couldn't burn me. There are bodies everywhere, lying strangely, arms and legs reaching out, as though they were flung from a great height. The lorries are all burning. Tomato juice and blood run together over the stones, and there is grey smoke everywhere—smoke from the fires, and a smoke of dust—and smells of burning and blood, and a terrible rich charred smell that I know must be burning flesh. The body of a man has dropped out of the cab of his flaming lorry—it's an ugly, broken, blackened thing. I hear a cry, and it chills me—it's like an animal blind with anguish, not a human sound. I rub my eyes, which are stinging, as though the sight of the fire is hurting them. Everything is so bright, too bright—the red, the flames, the blood that streams on the stones.

I look up and down the Esplanade, but I can't see Gwen, I don't think Gwen can have been here. I'm praying she got away in time. I walk out onto the pier. Heat sears at my skin as I pass a smouldering lorry. My foot slips in a pool of blood. I have some vague thought that perhaps I could help—I can do a splint, a neat bandage, I know a little First Aid. Yet even as I think this, I know how pointless, how useless, it is—that everything here is utterly beyond me.

I come to a man who is lying on the pier beside his lorry. His face is turned away, but something draws my eye—the check cloth cap on the ground beside him. There's some significance to this, but my thoughts are so heavy and slow.

'Oh God,' I say then, out loud. 'Frank. Oh God.'

It's Frank le Brocq.

I kneel beside him. I can see his face now. At first I think he must be dead already. But then his eyelids flicker. I cradle his head in my hands.

'Frank. It's Vivienne. Frank, it's all right, I'm here…'

But I know it is not all right. The one thing I know is that he cannot live with such wounds—the blood that seeps from the side of his head, the blood that slides out of his mouth. I feel a heavy, passive helplessness: so any gesture, any word, takes all the strength I have.

He's trying to speak. I put my ear close to his mouth.

'Bastards,' he whispers. 'Fucking bastards.'

I kneel there, holding him.

I try to say the Lord's Prayer. It's all I can think of. My mouth is stiff and I'm afraid that I won't remember the words.

But before I get to the power and the glory he is dead. I carry on anyway. *For ever and ever. Amen.*

He's staring at me with empty eyes. I reach out and close his eyelids. Then I just kneel there beside him. I don't know what to do now.

A shadow falls across me; someone is bending down to me. I look up—it's a fireman. Behind him, I see the single fire engine that's come.

'Excuse me,' I say. 'I know you're terribly busy, but this man—he's a friend of mine, Frank le Brocq…'

The fireman's face is white but composed. He peers down.

'I know Frank,' he says.

'The thing is—he's dead, you see,' I say.

'Poor, poor bugger,' says the man. 'You knew him, did you? You knew Frank?'

'Yes.' My voice rather cheerful and brittle and high. 'Well, I know his wife better, really. Angie le Brocq. I was up at Les Ruettes just a few days ago. They were going to take in my mother-in-law, if we had gone on the boat… But then we didn't go of course…'

The words tumbling out of me. This has nothing to do with what's happening, but somehow I can't stop talking.

The man looks at me in a worried way. He puts his hand on my shoulder.

'Look, ma'am, you need to go home. You should go and get yourself some rest. Go home and make yourself a cup of sugary tea…'

'But I can't just leave him here like this…'

'There's nothing you can do,' he says. 'Someone will see to him later.'

I feel he's being obtuse.

'No, you don't understand. I know Frank. I can't leave him lying here. Look at him. It's so awful...'

He gives me a hand and pulls me up. The effort of standing stops the stream of talk from my mouth. I'm shaking so hard I can scarcely stand.

He gives my arm a wary pat, as though I'm some skittery wild animal that he is trying to soothe.

'I mean it, ma'am. You should just take yourself off home now,' he tells me.

I ring Elm Tree Farm from the first public phone box I pass.

Gwen answers.

'Oh, Gwen. Thank God... I wondered...'

'I'm all right, Viv,' she tells me. 'I got away in time. I'm so glad to hear your voice. I've been sick with worry about you...' Then, when I don't say anything, 'Viv—are you sure you're all right?'

I can't answer her question: my mouth won't seem to work properly.

'Gwen—I can't talk now. I have to get back to the girls. But I'm not hurt—don't worry.'

I put down the phone.

When I arrive back at Le Colombier, Blanche's face is at the window. She sees me and runs to the door.

'Mum. What happened?'

Her voice is shrill, her eyes are wide and afraid.

'They bombed the harbour,' I tell her.

'We heard the planes.' she says, in a little scared voice. 'Mum. We thought you were dead.'

Millie is clinging to Blanche's hand. I can tell she's been crying: the tracks of tears gleam on her cheeks.

'I'm all right. I'm not hurt,' I say.

I reach out to hug Millie. She pulls away, stares at my dress. All the colour has gone from her face.

'Mum. You've got blood all over you,' says Blanche, in that small thin voice.

I look down. I hadn't realised. There's a lot of blood on the front of my dress, where I cradled Frank as he died.

'It isn't my blood,' I tell them. 'I'm all right. Really.'

They don't say anything—just stand there, staring at me.

'Look—I'm going to have to leave you for a little longer,' I say. 'I have to go to Angie's.'

I can see that Blanche understands at once. Her face darkens.

'To Angie's? Did they get Frank?' she says.

I nod.

Her eyes are round, appalled.

'But, Mum—what on earth will Angie do without him?' she says.

'I don't know,' I tell her.

I can't go to see Angie with her husband's blood on my clothes. I change, and put my dress to soak in a bath of cold water, swirling the water around to try to loosen the stain. I almost faint as I straighten up, the bathroom spinning around me. My body feels flimsy as eggshell, as though the slightest touch might shatter me. I can't break the news to Angie feeling like this.

I make myself drink some sugary tea, just as the fireman advised. Something has gone wrong with my throat, and it's hard to swallow the drink, but afterwards I feel a little stronger. The girls sit at the table with me, watching over me anxiously.

'Now, will you two be all right?' I say. 'I promise I won't be long.'

'We'll be fine, Mum,' says Blanche.

'No, we won't. I won't let you go,' says Millie.

She comes to stand by my chair, wraps herself around me. I have to peel her fingers like bandages from my arms.

Reluctantly, full of dread, I walk up the lane to Les Ruettes. My feet are heavy, as though I am wading through deep water. I knock at Angie's door, and my dread is a bitter taste in my mouth. I would rather be anywhere else but here.

She opens the door.

'Angie.' My throat is thick. 'Something's happened…'

She stares at my face. She knows at once.

'He's dead, isn't he?'

'Yes. I'm so sorry.'

She sinks down. She's trying to hold to the door post, but her hands slide down, her body collapses in on itself, as though she has no bones. I can't hold her. I bring a chair and pull her up onto it. I kneel beside her.

'I was in town today. Frank was there with his lorry. They bombed the pier and I found him. Angie—I was with him, I was holding him when he died.'

She wraps her hands around one another, wrings them. Her mouth is working, but she can't speak. There are no tears in her eyes, but her face looks all wrong—damaged.

At last she tries to clear her throat.

'Did he—say anything?' Her voice is hoarse, and muffled as though there's a blanket over her mouth. 'Did he have a message for me, Vivienne?'

I don't know what to tell her. I think of his last words. *Fucking bastards.*

'He couldn't speak,' I say.

I take her hand in mine. Her skin is icy cold; the cold in her goes through me.

'He died very quickly, he wouldn't have suffered,' I say.

She moves her head very slightly. I can tell she doesn't believe me.

'Come back with me, I'll give you a meal,' I tell her.

'No, Vivienne,' she says. 'It's so kind of you, but I won't…'

'I think you should,' I tell her. 'You can't stay here all alone.'

'I'll be all right,' she says. 'I just need some time on my own, to take it in.'

'I don't like to leave you,' I say.

'Really, Vivienne. Don't you worry. In a bit I'll take myself over to Mabel and Jack's.'

Mabel and Jack Bisson have four children; their house will be busy and boisterous. But Angie is insistent.

I leave her sitting alone by her hearth, wringing her hands as though she is wringing out cloth.

I cook tea for Evelyn and the girls, though I can't eat anything. Then Blanche helps me bring the girls' mattresses down from their rooms, and I make up beds for both of them in the narrow space under the stairs. This is the strongest part of the house, its spine.

'Look,' I tell Millie, trying to keep my voice casual. 'Tonight you and Blanche will be camping under the stairs. I've made you a den to sleep in.'

She frowns.

'Is it so we won't get killed? When the Germans come and bomb us?'

I don't know what to tell her.

'It's just to be on the safe side,' I say vaguely.

I decide to leave Evelyn in her room—I know I couldn't persuade her to sleep in a different place. And I think I too will stay upstairs: I can't believe I'll sleep at all, and even if I do doze off, if anything happens I'll wake.

I sit at the kitchen table, light a cigarette. I remember that there's some cooking brandy in the kitchen cupboard; it's left over from Christmas, when I put some in my mince pies. I don't drink alcohol often, but I pour myself a glass. The brandy has a festive smell, which feels troublingly wrong for the day, but I feel a little calmer as the drink slides into my veins, all my sadness blurring over.

I sit there for a long time, smoking, drinking, my body loosening, trying not to think. At last I get up to go to bed. As I take the glass to the sink to wash, it simply slips from my hand, falls to the floor, shatters. The dangerous sound of breaking glass triggers something in me: I suddenly find I am weeping. I sob and sob, as I kneel on the floor and sweep up the glittery shards. I feel as though I will never stop weeping.

I check on the girls before I go up to my room. Blanche is asleep but Millie's eyes are wide open; the light is still on in the kitchen, and slivers of gold from the half-open door reflect in the dark of her eyes.

'Mummy, they're going to kill us, aren't they?' she says, in a hissing, melodramatic whisper, so as not to wake Blanche. 'They're going to come in the night and bomb us to bits.'

'No, sweetheart. I don't think they will.'

'Why are we sleeping here, then?' she says.

'We're just being sensible,' I tell her.

She gives me a doubtful look.

I lie awake for a long time. Nothing happens. There are

no planes: all I hear is the creaking of my house as it settles and turns in its sleep, and outside the deepening quiet of the Guernsey summer night, depth on depth of quiet. But my anger keeps me awake. I feel a blind, furious rage—rage against this violence, when there weren't any soldiers here, when we couldn't fight back. I think how they slaughtered Frank like an animal—Frank who I didn't much like, who maybe wasn't such a good man, but who shouldn't have died, who was too young to die, and who died such a terrible death. How they could come in the night and kill my children. How they will walk in, enslave us, take our island for their own.

I sleep for a while, and wake again, with a start, as though something disturbed me. I get up and go to the window. The moon hangs down like a fruit, and moonlight whitens everything. It's so bright there are exact leaf-shadows on my gravel, and the hollyhocks in the flowerbeds of Les Vinaires next door are pale, almost luminous—ghost flowers.

I press my face to the pane. All the anger has left me. There's a cold sweat of fear on my skin. I think—What have I done? We could be in London, in Iris's house. Have I made the worst mistake of my life? Oh, my God—what have I done?

CHAPTER 10

Sunday evening. I weed my garden while Millie plays on the lawn. She tries to make a daisy chain, but her fingers aren't yet clever enough and the stalks keep splitting right through. She leaves the daisies lying there, and plays for a while with her ball, practising throwing and catching. The ball is striped with colours and makes a vivid blur as it falls.

The day cools as the sun sinks down. I pull my cardigan close around me. Evenings can be cold on Guernsey, even in high summer—there's often a freshness in the air, a chill that blows off the sea. A little movement of air shivers the leaves of the mulberry tree, and shadow clots and thickens beneath the elms in the hedge that shield the top part of our garden from the garden of Les Vinaires. The sky is purple as amethyst and streaked with rose-coloured cloud, and I can hear a nightingale in my orchard over the lane, its song spilling out like bright water-drops.

A distant growl of aircraft noise disturbs me. I look up. Six planes are circling in the sky above us. I can see the markings on them. I know they are German aircraft.

The pier is in my mind—the bombing, the shooting, the blood. My heart lurches.

'Millie. Come indoors at once.'

She doesn't move.

'Millie!'

'But my ball just went over the hedge. It was my best ball, Mummy…'

'Do as I say,' I tell her. 'Go to the den we made under the stairs. Go *this minute.*'

'Is it the Germans? Will they kill us?'

'Just do as you're told, Millie.'

I call to Blanche from the passageway but she doesn't seem to hear. I rush upstairs. Music spools down from her bedroom: she's playing Irving Berlin on her gramophone. *Cheek to cheek.* I rush straight in, without knocking. She's standing in the middle of her bedroom floor, startled, slightly shame-faced. I briefly wonder if she's been dancing in front of her mirror, practising moves, as I would do at her age: conjuring up a shiny, scented future, and a louchely handsome partner to hold you close in the dance.

'There are German planes coming over,' I say. 'Go to the den with Millie. Now.'

'But my record…'

'Blanche, just go,' I tell her.

She hears the edge in my voice. She leaves the gramophone, races downstairs. As I follow, I hear the disconsolate sound as the music slows and runs down.

Evelyn is in her armchair in the living room, knitting.

'You should go and shelter with the girls. You'd be safer there,' I tell her.

She doesn't get up. Her sherry-brown gaze flicks briefly over my face.

'There's no need to worry, Vivienne. You always were a worrier…' She speaks so slowly, each word precisely enunciated. I'm frantic with impatience. 'You always did get yourself in a state over every little thing.'

'This isn't a little thing, Evelyn…'

She ignores this, goes on knitting. Her face is still, unmoved, as though nothing I've said has touched her. There's a sound like screaming in my head.

She clears her throat.

'Eugene always says as much. *Worry, worry, worry.*'

I tell myself that she doesn't mean to criticise. That she doesn't really *mean* some of the things she says any more.

'Just come and shelter,' I say.

'I'm not going to hide away, Vivienne. I'm hurt that you thought that I would. Somebody's got to make a stand.'

'*Please*, Evelyn. Just in case something happens…'

'I'm not going to let the Hun move me about,' she tells me. 'Where would we be if everyone did that?'

There's nothing more I can say to persuade her. I leave her in her chair.

I watch the planes from the window. They fly low, towards the airfield, and vanish beyond the wooded brow of the hill. They must have landed. I watch the sky for a long time, as the west flares red with sunset, then deepens to a lingering indigo dark; but they don't take off again.

In the end I tell the girls to come out from under the stairs. I wonder if it has happened: the world cracked open.

Monday afternoon. There's a commotion from outside the door—Blanche jumping off her bicycle, flinging it down. She's been to town to see Celeste. She bursts through the door, her blonde hair shimmering, flying out like a flag.

'Mum, Mum. We saw them. They're here.' She's breathless, the words tumbling out of her; she's flushed and thrilled with the drama of this. 'We saw the German soldiers, me and Celeste.'

'I hate the Germans,' says Millie, staunchly.

'Yes, sweetheart. We all hate them,' I say.

'They're ever so tall, Mum,' says Blanche. 'Much taller than island men. One of them bought an ice cream and tried to give it to me. I didn't take it, of course. It was a strawberry cornet.'

Millie stares at Blanche, a little frown deepening in her forehead. I can tell her opinion of the Germans is being slightly modified.

'I like strawberry cornets,' she says.

'They were very polite,' says Blanche. 'There was one who had his picture taken with a policeman. He said he wanted to send it back home to his wife…'

She pulls *The Guernsey Press* from her bag. We open the newspaper out on the table and read. There are a lot of new rules. There will be a curfew: no islander should be out of doors after nine o'clock at night. All weapons must be handed in… Reading this, I think with a prickling of fear of Johnnie, of his brother's shotgun that he kept in a box beneath his bed: I wonder what he has done with it. The use of boats and motorcars is banned, and all our clocks must be put forward one hour.

As I read, I'm seized by a feeling I didn't expect. It's shame—a dirty, contaminated feeling. That this is happening to us. That we have allowed it to happen. I try to reason with myself, to tell myself that we can live with these regulations, and now at least the girls can sleep in their rooms, because with the Germans here, there won't be any more bombing. But still the shame seeps through me.

I go to talk to Evelyn. I put my hand on her arm.

'Evelyn, I need to tell you something important. I'm afraid that the Germans have landed on Guernsey,' I say gently.

She looks up at me, her mouth pursed and tight. She puts her knitting down in her lap.

'I don't like cowardly talk,' she says. 'We mustn't give in. We mustn't ever give in.'

'I'm so sorry,' I tell her. As though it's my fault. 'But it's happened. The Germans are here. That's what we have to live with now.'

She stares at me. Suddenly, there's a flicker of understanding in her face. She starts to cry soundlessly, slow tears trickling down from her eyes, that she doesn't try to wipe away. The sight tugs at my heart.

'Evelyn, I'm so sorry,' I say again.

I find her handkerchief for her, and she rubs at her face.

'Does that mean we've lost the war, Vivienne?'

'No. No, it doesn't mean that,' I say, with all the conviction I can manage.

Then suddenly her tears stop. She folds her handkerchief precisely and puts it away in her pocket. There's a sudden purposefulness to her.

'We ought to tell Eugene at once,' she says. 'Eugene will know what to do.'

I put my hand around her; her body feels at once stiff and brittle.

'Evelyn—Eugene isn't here, remember? Eugene's away with the army.'

'Well, find him, Vivienne,' she says. 'We can't manage without Eugene.'

She picks up her knitting again; like dandelion seeds on the air, the memory of her sorrow has drifted away.

I change the time on our clocks. Then Blanche and I drag the mattresses back up the stairs.

Once Millie is tucked up in bed, Blanche comes to find me, in her dressing gown and pyjamas. She says she wants me to plait her hair, so it will curl in the morning.

She sits on the sofa beside me, with her back towards me. I start to plait her hair, which is silky and cool in my hands. The lamplight shines on its different colours—caramel-blonde, with pale buttery streaks where the summer sun has bleached it. I love doing this: it's a way of touching that still feels comfortable for her. We don't touch very often now—she's withdrawn from me a little, being fourteen. I breathe in the scent of her—soap, and rose-geranium talc, and the sweet, particular, musky smell of her hair.

'D'you know what it'll be like, Mum?' Her voice rather small and uncertain. 'It'll all be different, won't it?'

I should be able to tell her: it's what a mother should do—prepare her children, warn them. But I don't know, can't imagine. There is nothing I have ever been through that could prepare me for this.

'Yes, it'll be different. Well, a lot of things will be different.'

'Will it be like that for ever?'

She has her back towards me and I can't see her expression.

I don't say anything.

'Mum. I want to know. Will the Germans be here for ever? Is that what it'll be like now?'

'I don't know, Blanche. Nobody knows what will happen.'

'I've been praying about it,' she says.

'Oh. Have you, sweetheart?'

There's a streak of religious devotion in Blanche, that I always find a surprise. We go to church every Sunday; for me, it's mostly out of habit. But Blanche is devout, like Evelyn: she reads the Bible and prays. There's a part of her that's frivolous, loving dancing and stylish clothes, and a part that I only see sometimes, that's reflective, rather serious.

'It's hard, though, isn't it, Mum?' she says now. 'To know what to pray for—with everything that's happening.'

'Yes. It's hard.'

'I prayed that we'd go on the boat, and then we didn't,' she says.

There's an edge of accusation in her voice. I know she's still angry with me.

'Sweetheart—that was a hard thing too. When I had to decide.'

She ignores this.

'And sometimes I pray that we'll win. But I expect the Germans do that too...'

'Yes, I suppose so...'

'Celeste reckons we're going to win the war,' she tells me. 'She told me that. She said we mustn't give up hope. But how can we, Mum? How can we possibly win?'

There are pictures in my mind: Hitler's Victory March up the Champs Elysées in Paris, which we saw on a news-reel at the Gaumont in town. The massed ranks of Nazi soldiers surging onwards, like a force of nature, like a storm or flood—utterly invincible.

I fix a rubber band around the end of her plait.

'You ought to go to bed,' I say.

She stands and turns to face me. With her hair in a plait she looks younger, her cheeks full and flushed, like a child's—like when she was only seven, and still played in the Blancs Bois with Johnnie. Her face is troubled. She turns and goes up the stairs.

The next morning I clean my bedroom. It isn't long since I last cleaned it—I just need something to occupy me. The work isn't very vigorous, but my heart is beating too fast.

My bedroom is a pleasant room. The wallpaper has a pattern of cabbage roses, and there's a taffeta eiderdown on the big double bed, and on my dressing table, all the special things I've collected: a perfume bottle that has a dragonfly glass stopper; my silver hairbrush and comb; a music box that I've had since I was a child. The music box was my mother's. It has an Impressionist painting on it, two girls at a piano in a hazy, pretty room, all the colours running together as though they are melting and wet. It plays *Für Elise*, the sound at once ethereal and clunky, because you can hear the abrasion of all the tiny parts inside. The music always calls up a feeling of sweetness and yearning in me—a window open, a muslin curtain billowing, brown hair blown over a mouth—conjuring up the lavender scent of the past. Just a trace of memory, and a longing I can't satisfy. Playing this music is the nearest I can come to the mother I lost.

This bedroom is at the front of the house; from the window, you can see out over my yard, and the roof and front garden of Les Vinaires next door. I dust the sill, looking out. Connie loved plants, and her garden is full of the loveliest things—honeysuckle, and fuchsias, and Oriental poppies, their colours singing together, scarlet and amber and pink, so vivid, and fading so quickly, just one day in flower and then a bright blown litter of petals over the lawn. But the garden is looking neglected already, grass straggling into the borders, the roses gangly and reaching out over the path, all the neat boundaries blurring and lost—everything grows so fast in high summer. I remember Connie saying, 'Keep an eye on things for me, won't you, Viv?' I feel guilty that I'd forgotten. I ought to try and do something—weed the borders, cut the grass. I tie a knot in my handkerchief to remind me.

A sound comes through my open window—the chunter of an engine drawing nearer down the lane. My pulse quickens. Someone must be disobeying the rules and using a car; whoever it is may be endangering us. I wait to see who will drive past.

But as I watch, a German vehicle draws up at Les Vinaires. Two men in uniform get out. They stand talking for a moment in the profound wet shade of the lane. A little wind ruffles the leaves and the shadows of leaves dance over them. I feel a sense of shock, my heart drumming, to see these invaders standing there, surrounded by the secret gardens and orchards of these deep valleys. Just as Blanche said, these men are tall, much taller than island men. The sunlight glints on their buckles and jackboots and the guns at their belts. They look entirely out-of-place in the leaf-dappled light, amid the cowpats and the potholes, between the hedgebanks with their jumble of leaves and entangled flowers and briars.

They open the gate of Les Vinaires, walk up the path to the door. They seem too big for the garden. I notice that one of them has a clipboard in his hand. There's a bang and a crack as the other man breaks the lock of the door.

Rage surges through me, and a hot flaring shame: that I can't stop them, can't protect Connie's house from them. That I'm so utterly helpless.

In a little while they come out again, and go back down

the path. My rage is blotted out by fear: it's as though a small cold hand is fingering the back of my neck. Angie's words are there in my mind. *They crucify girls. They rape them and crucify them...* What if these soldiers come in here and take our house, as well? They own us, they can do as they wish, they could walk in anywhere—there's nothing to stop them, nothing.

But for now, they drive off.

Later I hear another engine. I rush upstairs to my bedroom, look out over the lane.

It's a different vehicle this time, with four men in it—two in the cab, and two in the back. I watch as the men in the cab get out. One is spare and dark, with a hollow, cynical face, the other is rather broad-shouldered, with greying hair. The second man takes out a pack of cigarettes, taps it to release one, holds it between his lips as he fumbles for his lighter. I notice that he has a ragged pink scar on his cheek. I'm immediately curious. I wonder how he acquired the scar, what happened to him. Perhaps he fought in the Great War: his face has a lived-in look, and there's a web of lines round his eyes—he seems old enough. I wonder what he has been through, what he has seen. How much this injury hurt him.

Then I push the thought away. These men are the enemy: I shouldn't really be thinking about them at all.

The other two men are younger and both have fair hair. I guess they are lower in rank than the men who sat in the cab. They jump down, pull out kitbags. The man with the scar goes round to the back of the vehicle, and holds the cigarette in his mouth as he reaches in for his bag. The man with the hollow face pushes open the gate. All four of them seem more leisurely than the men who came with the clipboard. They look around with an appraising air—almost an air of ownership: and, seeing this, I feel a flare of impotent rage. They're joking, laughing, their gestures expansive, easy. They have the look of men who have come to the end of a journey.

They walk down the petal-littered path between the overgrown borders. The roses snag on their uniforms as they push their way through the flowers; the hollyhocks, pale as skimmed milk, brush against their legs as they pass. I see that Alphonse is sleeping in a pool of sun on the path; it's a favourite sleeping spot of his, because the stone gets warmed there. He's curled in a perfect circle, as though he feels quite safe. As the men approach he wakes, and languidly stretches. One of the younger men crouches to stroke him, makes a fuss of him; the man has the kind of pink, freckled skin that peels in the sun. Alphonse rubs against the man and arches his back ecstatically, so I can see the supple bones rippling under his fur. I feel an irrational surge of fury with the animal—that he's so easily won over, that he isn't resisting at all.

The men go in and don't come out again.

An hour or two later, I'm in my yard in front of my house, picking some herbs for a stew, when I see that the window of Les Vinaires that overlooks us is flung open. I can hear German voices through the window. I can't tell what they're saying—I know only a little German, just the words of some Bach cantatas, from when I was in London and used to sing in a choir. I can't even judge the emotion from the sound of the words.

The thought slams into me—that we will be so exposed. When we are out in our yard, or if our front door is open, the Germans will hear our conversations. I wonder if they will understand us, if they speak English at all. But even if they can't understand us, they will see what we do: whenever I come here to pick some herbs they will see. We won't be able to hide from them.

The day feels unstable, feverish. The outward things—the sigh of the wind in my pear tree, the long light of afternoon slanting into my yard—all these things are just so, just as they should be: yet it feels as though there's something strange on the air, subtle but troubling as a faint smell of scorching, or an insect whine that's almost too high to be heard.

I will have to move these pots that stand beside my door. I will carry them through to the back of the house and put them out on the terrace. There I'll be able to tend them without being seen.

But I stand for a moment, irresolute. Something in me is reluctant. I hear Evelyn's assertion in my mind: *I'm not going to hide away, Vivienne. I'm hurt that you thought that I would. I'm not going to let the Hun move me about.* And in that moment I make my decision. I will leave my herbs and geraniums here—leave everything just as it was. This is the only protest I can make, the only way I can fight this: to live as I have always lived, not let them change me at all.

Millie stares at the cat's bowl of food, which hasn't been touched.

'Where's Alphonse?'

'I don't know, sweetheart.'

'But it's nearly night-time.'

'Don't worry, sweetheart, I'm sure he'll turn up. Cats always find their way home.'

But Millie is unhappy, a frown pencilled in on her fore-head. I think, guiltily, that she's worried because the cat was so nearly put down: she has a new sense of Alphonse's vulnerability.

I read her a story, but she can't sit still. She keeps jumping up and going to the kitchen, looking for him.

'It's the Germans, isn't it?' she says. 'The Germans have taken Alphonse.'

'I don't expect so,' I say.

'I want him back, Mummy,' she says. '*And* I want my ball back. Everything's horrible.' Her face crumples up like paper, and tears spill from her eyes.

I'd forgotten about the ball that she lost in the garden of Les Vinaires.

'Millie, the ball's not a problem. I can easily buy you another one…'

She ignores this. She rubs her tears away angrily.

'Blanche says it's the Germans. Blanche says the Germans eat people's cats,' she tells me. Her voice is shrill with outrage.

'She was teasing you, Millie,' I tell her. 'I really don't think they do.'

But I wonder if Alphonse's absence is in fact the Germans' fault—remembering the young blond man and how he petted the cat. Perhaps he has put out food for him. Cats have no loyalty.

I listen to Millie's prayers, and tuck her up in bed.

'You've got to find him,' she tells me, sternly.

The sky through the living-room window darkens, to a rich cobalt blue, then to night. There's a silver scatter of stars, a slice-of-melon moon. Still the cat doesn't come home. It's well after nine o'clock now. I think about the curfew, but the blackout curtains are already drawn at Les Vinaires, and everywhere is quiet.

I decide I will go out and look for the cat. I know I can be silent, and I'm sure I won't be seen.

My back door isn't overlooked from the windows of Les Vinaires. I go out that way, into the yawn of a black night. I cling to the hedgebank, creep along in the shadows, edge up the lane as far as the track that leads to Les Ruettes. I don't dare call, but I'm hoping Alphonse will hear me—or maybe sense my presence, with that strange sixth sense that cats have.

There's a sudden engine noise behind me. It must be German soldiers, now that islanders can't use cars. I'm suddenly very afraid, my pulse racing, a cold sweat of fear on my skin. I slip through a gap in the hedge, crouch down in the field. The headlights sweep over the hedgebank and pass. I pray they didn't see me. Then I hear the car slow and come to a stop. It must belong to the Germans who have moved into Les Vinaires.

I creep back to my house, and close the door on the night. Relief surges through me that at least I got home safely. Alphonse is on a chair in the kitchen, licking himself assiduously. I curse him under my breath.

I take him up to Millie. Her face shines.

But I can't believe I did this. I think of something that the aunts who raised me were always saying to me, 'Vivienne, you're too trusting. You shouldn't let people walk all over you. You shouldn't be such a doormat… Your soft-heartedness will get you into trouble, one of these days…' I think that perhaps they were right. I've been so stupid, so irresponsible, taking this risk for a cat, just because Millie was a bit unhappy.

★ ★ ★

I'm making my coffee at breakfast-time when I spill a jug of milk. Anxiety must be making me clumsy. I'm on my knees on the kitchen floor, wiping up the spillage, when there's a crunch of boots on our gravel and a rapid knock at our door.

It's one of the men from Les Vinaires, the spare dark man with the hollow face. His uniform, his nearness, make me immediately afraid. And mixed in with the fear, I have a sense of embarrassment, that I'm in my apron, a dishcloth in my hand, that he can see into my kitchen, which is messy with wet washing hung on the rail in front of the stove. I have some inchoate sense that I am letting the side down.

'Good morning,' he says. His English is very precise and measured. I can see him noticing my apron, and the pool of milk on the floor. 'I'm afraid I may have come at an inconvenient time.'

I'm about to say, 'That's all right', the automatic response to his concession. But it isn't *all right*—nothing is *all right*. I bite my tongue to stop myself from speaking.

He puts out his hand. This shocks me. I think how they bombed the harbour when all our soldiers had gone; how they shot at the lorries so the petrol tanks would explode, when the men were sheltering under them; of Frank's burnt and bleeding body. I shake my head; I push my hands in my pockets. I can't believe he thought I'd be willing to shake his hand.

He lowers his hand, shrugs slightly.

'I am Captain Max Richter,' he says.

A sudden fear grabs at me. *He has come here because I went out after the curfew. He saw me.* My mouth is dry: my tongue sticks to the roof of my mouth.

He makes a small imperative gesture, wanting to know my name.

'I'm Mrs de la Mare,' I tell him.

He waits, expecting more, looking enquiringly over my shoulder into the house.

'Four of us live here—me, and my daughters, and my mother-in-law,' I tell him, in answer to his unspoken question.

From my front door you can see into the living room. I notice him looking in that direction; I turn. Evelyn is in her chair, watching everything. He inclines his head, acknowledging her. She gives him a look as barbed as a fish-hook, then lowers her eyes.

'And your husband?' he asks me.

'My husband is away with the army,' I say.

He nods.

'We will be your neighbours now, Mrs de la Mare,' he says.

'Yes.'

'Now—you know the rules, I think.'

There's a hard set to his face when he says this, his mouth thin as the slash of a razor. I find myself wishing that it had been the other officer who came—the scarred one. Thinking that perhaps he'd be less harsh than this man, and less correct and remote.

'Yes,' I say.

'You know about the curfew.'

'Yes.'

My heart races off. I see myself being taken away, imprisoned. And my children—what will happen to my children? I still have my hands in my pockets. I dig my nails into my palms, to try and stop myself from trembling.

'We hope for a quiet life here—all of us,' he says.

'We do too. Of course.' My voice is too high, too eager. I sound naive, like a girl.

'Don't put us in a difficult position,' he says.

'No, we won't,' I say.

His cool, rather cynical gaze is on me. There's something about his look that tells me he saw me in the lane.

'I'm glad we understand one another,' he says.

He lowers his hand towards his belt. Fear has me by the throat: I think he is going to take out his gun. But he pulls something out of his pocket.

'This must be yours, I think,' he says. 'Perhaps it belongs to one of your girls.'

I see what he has in his hand. Relief undoes me, making me shaky and weak. It's the ball with coloured stripes on, which Millie lost over the hedge. A little mirthless, hysterical laughter bubbles up in my throat: I swallow hard.

'Oh. Well. Thank you…'

I stare at the ball. I take it. I don't know what else to say.

'I also have daughters, Mrs de la Mare,' he says.

There's a brief note of yearning in his voice. This startles me.

'You must miss them,' I say, immediately. Because he does—I can tell. Then I wonder why I said that, why I was sympathetic like that. I'm cross with myself—I don't have to make any concessions, don't have to give him anything. I feel entirely lost: I don't know the right way to behave.

His gaze flicks back to my face. I know he can read my confusion. Everything's messy, all mixed up in my head—the fear I feel, the stern set of his face when he talked about the curfew; and now his kindness in bringing back the ball.

'Well, then. Good morning, Mrs de la Mare. Remember the curfew,' he says, and turns.

I close the door rapidly. I feel exposed, in some way I couldn't articulate or define. There are little red crescents in my palms, where I pushed my nails into my skin.

'Vivienne.' Evelyn is calling for me.

I go to her.

'The Hun came in the house,' she says. 'You opened the door to the Hun.'

She's agitated. She puts down her knitting; her crêpey hands flutter like little pale birds.

'Evelyn—I couldn't *not* open the door. The man's living at Les Vinaires now.'

'Fraternising is an ugly word. An ugly word for an ugly deed,' she tells me severely.

'Evelyn, I wasn't fraternising. But we have to be civil. Stay on the right side of them. They could do anything to us…'

She's implacable.

'You're a soldier's wife, Vivienne. You need to show some backbone. If he comes to the door again, don't you go letting him in.'

'No. I won't, I promise.'

'Never let them in,' she says. Ardent. 'Never let them in.' As though the maxim is something to cling to amid all the chaos of life.

She picks up her knitting. But then she puts it down again, looks vaguely in my direction. There's a sudden confusion in her face, a blurring like smoke in her eyes.

'Tell me who that was again—the man who came to the door? Who did you say he was, Vivienne?'

I can't face repeating everything.

'It was one of our neighbours,' I tell her.

'Oh. You and your neighbours.'

She takes up her knitting again.

CHAPTER 11

As darkness falls, I go out into the yard to take some vegetable peelings to the compost heap. Out there, I pause for a moment, breathing in the night air, all the sweet mingled scents that bleed from the throats of the flowers. I can smell the flowering stocks in the borders in my back garden, and the perfume of my tobacco plants, which always seems richer at night. The sky is profound, the shadows are long, everything turning to blue. From the Blancs Bois, where the entangled trees are drawing darkness to them, I hear the call of an owl-shivery, like a lost soul haunting the wood: unworldly.

There's a table-lamp lit in the kitchen of Les Vinaires, and the blackout curtains aren't drawn yet. Lamplight spills across the gravel of my yard, leaching the colours from everything it falls on, so the petals of the geraniums in the pots beside my door are a sickly amber, without brightness. I look in at the window, see the man who is sitting there, at Connie's kitchen table. He's in his shirtsleeves, he has his top shirt button undone. At first glance I think it's Captain Richter, who came to our kitchen door: but then I see it's the other man, the scarred one. The lamplight falls on him, illumines one side of his face. I can see his scar quite clearly, the jagged line of it, the pink, frail tissue that doesn't match the rest of his skin. He seems different from when he came in the vehicle, sitting there alone in the light of the lamp—pensive, less authoritative.

As I watch, he pushes up his cuffs—mechanically, not thinking about what he's doing. His mind is somewhere else entirely. He's reading something—a book, a letter; I can't see what it is, the table is just below the level of the windowsill. I think it must be a letter: only a letter could hold him as this does—for whatever it is, it takes all of his attention. Some new expression flickers over his face: there's something there that displeases him. He frowns; he runs his finger abstractedly over his brow. I think, *This is how he looks when he's concentrating.* Blue smoke from a cigarette resting in an ashtray wraps around him and softly curls and spirals in front of his face. He's alone; and I know he feels alone: he is utterly unaware of me watching him. He has the look of a man who doesn't know he is looked at.

I feel a sudden curiosity about his other life—the life he has when he isn't being a soldier: his home, the people who matter to him. I wonder what it is like for him to be here— with all around him the unfamiliar island night. Landscapes are most themselves, most separate from us, at night: and even to me, who has lived so long in this secluded valley, the Guernsey night can feel a little alien—the cry of the owl so lonely, the dark so dense and deep. I wonder about him—where he comes from, what he longs for. Is he a little homesick, as I was when I first came here? It's a word we use so lightly, but I think of what I learned then—that home-sickness is a true sickness, a longing like grief, for what has been lost or taken away. I can still feel it from time to time, just a trace of that yearning: it comes with a memory of lamplight, of pavements under rain, of the scorched smell of the Underground—all the scents and sounds of London, its humming, sultry energy. I wonder what he longs for.

I stand there watching him. I will him to look up, to look out of the window at me. It's like a child's game—as though I could make him see me, as though he is my puppet. I have the power now, in this moment—just the tiniest sliver of power. Because I am looking in on him, and he doesn't know, doesn't see me.

But he doesn't move, doesn't stir, his eyes are on what he is reading. I slip back into the house. I feel troubled, but in a way I couldn't put into words. As though things are not quite as I thought they were.

I go to bed, but for a long time I can't sleep.

PART II:

JULY - OCTOBER 1940

CHAPTER 12

My mother died when I was three. I remember
how we were taken into her bedroom to say
goodbye—me and Iris, my big sister. The room
smelt wrong. Her bedroom had always had a scent of the
rosewater she wore: but now it held a harsh, sore-throat
smell of disinfectant. And my mother looked strange, somehow blurred, as though her face were made of wax and had
started to melt. I was a little frightened of her. I wanted
to leave the room, to be anywhere else but there. And she
gripped my hand too tightly, and she was crying, and I
didn't like that.

I don't remember much from the weeks and months that
followed—except that for the funeral I had to wear a stiff
black dress that was made of some itchy fabric, and people
told me off for scratching. After my mother's death I was
mute for a while, simply refusing to speak at all: or so I've
been told, though I don't recall that part of it. There's a
fog in my head when I think of those months—I don't remember much at all from those times. Except for the music
box that was mine to keep, that I would play for hours, the
music perfumed with memories of her. And there are little
images in my head of the house where we lived, off Clapham
Common, at 11 Evington Road—a tall, thin, rambling house

that was never quite asleep, that would go on settling and creaking all through the night; and the hidden, enclosed garden with whispery, overhanging trees and the leaves of years piled up under them; and the aunts who looked after us, Auntie Maud and Auntie Aggie, who were kind but weren't my mother, so when they combed my hair it hurt. I always remember that—how they pulled too hard at the tangles, not gently easing out the knots as my mother had done.

I was a nervous, frightened child, frightened of so many things—thunderstorms, and the edges of railway platforms; spiders, even the tiny ones that ran all over the terrace at the back of the house, and, crushed, left a smear like a blood stain; afraid above all of the dark. I was always afraid of the dark. Once Iris and I were playing teacher and pupil. I was five, just a little older than Millie is now—and Iris was the teacher, and was very strict and stern, and she decided I'd been bad, and locked me in the coalshed. It was a concrete shed, no windows, the door close-fitting to keep the coal dry—not even a thread of light from under the door. I remember the darkness, sudden and absolute, the fear that broke over me like nausea, the rapid panicky skittering of my heart. It was so dark I thought at first I had my eyes shut—that they'd been stuck shut somehow—and I put up my hand and found my eyes were open, I could feel the bristly fluttering of my eyelashes. I learned in that moment that there are different darknesses. That there is ordinary darkness—like the night in the countryside, where even on a night with no moon, as you stare things loom, take form; or the darkness of your bedroom—like the flimsy dark of the room I shared with Iris, with the murky amber lamplight seeping in under the curtains. And there is another darkness—a dark so profound you cannot begin to imagine it, cannot conjure it up in your mind. A darkness that blots out all you remember or hope for. A darkness that teaches that all that consoles you is false.

I don't think I was in there for long. Auntie Aggie realised what had happened; scolded Iris, came and unlocked the door. But I don't remember that clearly at all—the moment when she let me out into the cheerful day again. It's the darkness I remember.

How much did that loss of my mother shape the course of my life? Hugely, I can see that now—though it's taken me years to learn this. Now I even wonder if that was why I married the very first man I went out with—whether my decision had something to do with that loss. Wanting to have something settled; longing for safety, wanting to keep things the same—so frightened of change and uncertainty.

I was nineteen when I met Eugene, and still living in the house in Evington Road. I was working as a secretary, in an insurance firm in Clapham. I met Eugene at a church social; he was a bank clerk with the National Provincial bank, living in digs in Streatham that always smelt of broccoli. He'd been excited to move to London, but had hoped for something from it that it had somehow failed to give. He was already longing to go back to Guernsey when I met him. There was a faint mothball scent of disappointment that hung about him, though at first I wasn't aware of it. He was a good-looking man—clear eyes, symmetrical features, sleeked-down hair—a clean-cut face that made him seem much younger than his years. Our daughters have that face as well, that open, candid look. And he was always very well turned-out—his business suits pressed with a razor-sharp edge, his shoes as shiny as mirror-glass. 'He's so *handsome*,' everyone said. 'He looks just like Jack Pickford. Well, haven't you done well for yourself?' There was something reassuring about his effortless, practised courtship of me—the yellow roses, the boxes of New Berry Fruits—a feeling that I could leave it to him, that he would take control, make the decisions. What did he see in me, I wonder? I don't know, can't imagine now—though he would always be very flattering about my looks, my clothes. He knows how to flatter a woman. Maybe my rather French-sounding name reassured him in some way, suggested I would fit in on his island. That may sound rather fanciful, yet people will often let themselves be guided by such things, making a weighty decision because some small hand beckons: I've seen this. Whatever the reason—he couldn't wait to gather me up and bring me back to Guernsey.

But from our very first night together, it wasn't as I'd imagined. I didn't feel the way I knew I was meant to feel. I thought it must be my fault—that there was something wrong with me, something missing. Or, to put it more precisely, something *misplaced*. Because I knew I *could* feel these things—just not in bed with Eugene. I'd see a man—a stranger—loosen his tie, unbutton his cuffs, push up the sleeves of his shirt, and my stomach would tighten, I'd feel the thrill go through me. Or I'd dream a dream in which a man who stood behind me was brushing my hair, and I'd lean against him and feel the warmth of him pressing into my back, and I'd wake in a haze of longing.

Maybe he felt something similar—that sense of something missing. Because we made love only rarely, and, once I was pregnant with Millie, never again. We never talked about it—well, how could you possibly talk about such a thing? Slowly, insidiously, with a little shake of the heart, I became aware that there were rumours. Eugene loved amateur dramatics, and he joined a society that rehearsed in St Peter Port: he had a pleasant, eloquent voice, he loved to play a role. There was a woman there—Monica Charles—who some-times played opposite him. Red hair, an abundant cleavage, pointy lacquered nails; and the plush velvet scent of Shalimar, which she always wore. She was rather outspoken—the sort of woman who seems to use up all the air in the room: she always made me feel somehow small and faded.

Gwen said once—carefully, with a slight anxious frown, not quite looking at me: 'Does it worry you—Eugene being so friendly with Monica Charles?'

My heart lurched. 'No. Why should it?'

'I just wondered,' she said.

'He loves the theatre, he's passionate about it,' I said. Putting the words down with such care, like little stones, between us. 'It's good that he has something to do that he enjoys so much…'

'You're very strong—I admire you,' said Gwen, and moved the conversation on. I closed my mind to what she'd said, careful never to touch on that conversation again—as though her words were sharp things that could cut me.

There was an evening when I took the girls to see him backstage. He'd been starring in *Private Lives* opposite Monica Charles. Millie was two; she was tired out after the perfor-mance, and heavy and warm in my arms. I knocked, he didn't answer, I pushed at the door. The scent of Shalimar brushed against me, darkly velvet, insidious. Eugene was there with Monica Charles. She was standing with one foot on a chair, her skirt bunched up round her thighs: he was easing down her stocking, very slowly. There was a sensuousness in the caressing movement of his hand that was entirely unfamil-iar to me. They looked up, saw me, moved apart. I saw the shock—then all the excuses, forming, hardening, in his eyes. I didn't stay to hear them. Blanche was behind me, Millie was dozing. 'He isn't here,' I said. 'We must have missed him.' I bundled the girls away, I don't think they saw anything.

We never talked about it, just carried on as we were. But something closed in me then, irrevocable as the sound of the dressing-room door that I'd slammed shut behind me. Something was over for me.

Sometimes I've wondered about it—this thing that was so lacking in my marriage—this part of me that it seemed could never be expressed, yet could be stirred up so suddenly, randomly almost, by a dream or a glance at a stranger, or a stranger glancing at me.

I remember a moment from long before, from when I first knew Eugene, when I was still in London. There was a man who looked at me as I walked along the Embankment by the Thames—who turned around to look at me. It wasn't long before the wedding—I was on my way to meet Iris at the Lyons Corner House in Tottenham Court Road. She was going to be the maid of honour at my wedding, and I wanted to show her some fabric samples for her dress. I was wearing a neat navy suit, my high-heeled strappy suede shoes, my best silk stockings, the seams exact, a hat in dusty-pink felt with a petersham ribbon around it. I was a little late for our meeting—probably off in a dream as usual, perhaps with a line of poetry running through my mind—and I must have been flushed from walking in the chill autumn air. The man was older than me, and tall, with a rather worn, lived-in face. He had a serious look, no smile: a look that required something of me, a look beyond approbation or flattery. His glance felt as real to me as the touch of a hand. I felt the heat go through me, the bright thread of sensation passing down through my body, and all around the brown leaves fluttering, falling, the shining river surging: everything fluid, dancing.

I still sometimes think of that moment. If he had asked, I'd have gone with him.

CHAPTER 13

Thursday. I go up the hill to see Angie. I'm wearing one of my two best dresses—the everyday dress that I'd normally wear isn't fit to be seen. It's the one I wore on the day of the bombing, and I've soaked it again and again, but I still can't get the bloodstains out.

This morning there's no sign of the Germans at Les Vinaires: they must have gone to their work already. Though I can't imagine what occupies them: it can't be very strenuous, keeping our island under control. The weather lifts my spirits a little. It's a bright, breezy day, the summer wind smelling of salt and earth and flowers. The hedgebanks are gorgeous with foxgloves and purple woundwort, and the stream that runs beside the lane is overgrown with green harts' tongue fern, little cresses, mother-of-thousands. The thread of water that runs through the ferns squirms in the light like a live thing. Just for a moment I can dream that all is as it always was, that the Occupation hasn't happened.

I've brought Angie a cake, and some blackberry jelly left from last year's batch. Though I wonder if I'm bringing these gifts for myself as much as for her—feeling helpless, needing to feel I'm doing something for her. But she's so grateful.

'Oh, Vivienne, you're always so thoughtful… And don't

you look lovely today? You're a sight for sore eyes in that dress,' she says.

'Oh. Thanks, Angie.'

I smooth down the skirt. As she says, it's pretty: the cotton has a pattern of flowers of many colours, yellow and cream and forget-me-not blue, like a blowing wildflower meadow. I don't tell her why I'm wearing it.

She makes tea for us, in her big brown pottery teapot. Chickens scratch and bustle outside the open door.

'So, have you seen much of them?' she asks me.

I know she means the Germans.

'They've requisitioned Connie's place next door. There are four of them living there now,' I tell her.

Angie snorts.

'Requisitioned? They use all these fancy words, just to confuse us,' she says. '*Stole* is what they really mean… But that's rather close, isn't it, Vivienne? You'll be living in one another's pockets. I wouldn't like that at all.'

'Well—at least they didn't take our house…'

It's her wash day. Her kitchen has a wholesome smell of laundry soap and damp linen. She's nearly come to the end of her wash, she's putting her clothes through the mangle before she hangs them out on the line. I see that she's washing some shirts of Frank's.

'You wouldn't mind if I just finished this off, Vivienne?' she asks me.

'No, of course not.'

She sees me noticing the shirts.

'I thought I'd clear out his clothes,' she says. 'There's plenty of wear left in them. I'm going to give them to Jack, my brother. He's always grateful for hand-me-downs. They're a bit hard-pressed, him and Mabel, with all those children to feed.'

I sip my tea, and watch as she moves the heavy arm of the mangle. Water flurries into the tray that catches the drips, in little spurts that fall in time with the rhythm of her movement.

'So, Angie—are you…?' The words are solid things in my mouth. 'I mean—how is everything?'

She fixes me with her sad, steady gaze.

'Not so good, to be honest, Vivienne,' she tells me, very matter-of-fact. 'But I know I shouldn't complain. So many people have lost someone.'

'That doesn't make it any easier though,' I say.

We are silent for a moment. From outside, you can hear the bubbling sound of chickens, and the bright whistle of a blackbird in the elder tree by her door.

Her appearance troubles me. Her face has an eroded look, as though years have passed since Frank died; as though those years like a river have washed over her and started to wear her away.

'You must say if there's anything I can do,' I tell her, rather helplessly. 'Just anything at all. I could bring you some meals, or something…'

She looks up at me. She pushes her hand through her hair, which is a wiry dark mass round her head—she hasn't bothered with her curlers.

'You've got a kind heart, Vivienne. And—seeing as you've offered—well, there *is* something,' she says. She flushes, a little embarrassed, and I wonder why. 'I need to choose some hymns. For his funeral tomorrow. The thing is—I don't have much book-learning.'

She's telling me she can't read; it surprises me that I never knew this before.

'Just tell me what to do,' I say.

'There's a hymn book in the cabinet in the parlour,' she says. 'I wonder if you could bring it for me? Just while I finish my wash.'

I go to her parlour across the passage. When her house was built hundreds of years ago, this room would have served as the byre—people and animals all sleeping under one roof. It doesn't feel homely like her kitchen. There's a lumbering three-piece suite that's shrouded in dust sheets, and the air is stale, with a thick sweet scent of lavender polish and damp: you can tell she doesn't often open the windows in here. I find the hymn book, take it to her.

'Is there a list of hymns in the book?' she asks me.

I turn to the front, to the contents list.

'Could you read through the first lines for me?' she asks. 'Just to remind me—so I can choose my favourites?'

I read the first lines of the hymns, with a little pause after each, while she considers it, all the time turning the handle, so the water from the mangled clothes splutters down into the tray. She listens scrupulously, with an intent expression.

At last we come to one that she likes.

'There. Stop there, Vivienne. "Rocked in the cradle of the deep."' She rolls the phrase round her mouth, as though it is succulent, like some sun-warmed fruit. 'I've always been fond of that one,' she says.

'Yes. Me too. Would Frank have liked it?' I say.

She considers this.

'Frank didn't think all that much of religion, to be honest,' she says. 'He didn't have much time for religious folk at all. God-botherers, he called them. Bible-thumpers. What he always said was—they're just as bad as the rest of us… But I like a bit of religion myself. I think it helps you through.'

'Yes, it can do,' I say.

'Are you a believer, Vivienne?'

The direct question unnerves me. I think how, right through my life, I've always liked going to church: how I adored the church Nativity play when I was a child—being an angel, with wings of frail muslin fixed to my fingers with curtain-rings, and a halo of Christmas tinsel; how I love the stained glass and the singing; how I can still find comfort in the familiar, resonant words; how I still pray sometimes. But I'm not sure how much I believe now.

'Well, I suppose so,' I say.

The drip of the water seems too loud in the stillness of Angie's kitchen—louder than her voice, which is confiding, nicotine-stained.

'When I was a child, my mother taught me a prayer,' she says. 'The prayer of the Breton fisherman, she said it was. It was the only prayer you ever needed, she said. *Oh, Lord, help me, for Your ocean is so great, and my boat is so small.* That's a good prayer, isn't it? Do you like that prayer, Vivienne?'

I think of waiting at the harbour. Of the little boat that I couldn't trust, wouldn't go in. Of the perilous, shining, unguessable immensity of the sea.

'Yes, I like it,' I say.

She nods.

'I always thought that was a good prayer.' A little rueful smile. 'Except He didn't help me, really, did He? He didn't help me at all. Not this time.'

I leave her wringing out her dead husband's clothes.

CHAPTER 14

I walk home through the summer morning, feeling so sad for Angie, thinking how lost she seems, how much she has aged. Wondering what I can do to help her. I'm not really looking around me: I'm in a trance, abstracted, like when I was a child and didn't come when I was called, and Aunt Aggie would shake her head at me: 'You're such a dreamer, Vivienne. You're always off in cloud cuckoo land. You think too much, you need to live in this world...'

If I hadn't been so preoccupied, maybe I would have noticed the car in the lane: maybe I would have turned in time, and made for the track through the fields, and come home by the back way. But I've almost reached the car before I really take it in. It's not an army vehicle, but a big black Bentley, drawn up on the verge outside the gate of Les Vinaires. I recognise the car. It used to belong to the Gouberts; they lived at Les Brehauts, an imposing whitewashed house near the church, before they went on the boat. The Germans must have requisitioned the car—which, as Angie says, means stealing.

The bonnet is open. One of the men from Les Vinaires is there, the scarred man I saw in the window, peering under the bonnet. I see him too late. I'd have done anything to avoid him, but I can't turn back now: I know it would look like cowardice, and I'd hate him to think I was scared. He's tinkering with the engine, muttering under his breath; then he opens the door, climbs in and tries the ignition—still with the bonnet up. The engine turns once, splutters, dies. He gets out, kicks a tyre, and swears, a rushed volley of German expletives. With a part of my mind, I'm thinking, *Good*—he may have stolen the car, but at least he can't make it go… But I'm frightened too, and the prayer that Angie quoted to me slides into my mind. *Oh, Lord, help me…* I stand there, uncertain, apprehensive. I have to walk past him to reach the gate to my yard. I'm wishing more than ever that I'd thought to come back through the fields.

He turns, sees me. He has a shocked look: he stares, as if I am a ghost or apparition. As though *I* am the one who is out of place, who shouldn't be there. The scented wind blows about us; it billows my skirt, then wraps it back against my body and pushes a strand of unruly hair into my mouth. My face feels hot, I know I've gone red, and I hate this. My heart stutters. I think he is going to shout at me or threaten me.

'I apologise,' he says. His English accent is very good, as good as Captain Richter's. His face flushes slightly, almost as though he's ashamed.

I don't know what to say. I feel stupid, wrong-footed—clumsy, as though I use up too much space, as though my feet and hands are too big for my body.

'That's all right, it doesn't matter,' I say—the automatic response. Then I feel my hand fly to my mouth, as if to stop myself from talking.

He inclines his head in a little bow, and turns and goes into the house.

There's a small scolding voice in my head: You're letting the side down, you handled everything wrong. You shouldn't have said it didn't matter—you shouldn't have spoken at all. *Everything* matters, *nothing's* all right. It comes to me that this will be the shape of it, of our new life under the Occupation: always these troubling, frightening encounters—leaving you feeling that you've transgressed, and given something away.

Later, from my bedroom window, I watch as the scarred man comes out with one of the younger men, the one who has the kind of skin that peels in the sun. The young man has a tool box. He mends the car—deftly, with no fuss. The scarred man climbs in and turns the ignition: I hear the car start up. Through the car window, I can see the ironic smile on his face. The thought ripples in me that I know certain things about him. How he loathes machines, feels they oppose him, will never do his will: how this helplessness makes him angry. How he can lose himself in reading a book or a letter—frowning, running a finger absently over his brow. I know the look he has when he thinks that nobody is watching: how he will light a cigarette and leave it lying there, and roll up his shirtsleeves, doing these things unthinkingly, unaware of what he is doing. This knowledge makes me uneasy. It's as though I am party to a secret that I never asked to be told.

Before the man drives off, he glances up at my bedroom window. Almost as if he knows I am looking, expects me to be looking. My heart thuds. I draw back into my room.

CHAPTER 15

August. The island has never been lovelier, all our gardens lavishly flowering, the sky high and bright, a fresh salt wind off the sea. The Belle de Crécy roses are blooming in my back garden, drowsy with bumble bees, the flowers opening helplessly wide and spreading out their perfume.

Before the war, on such beautiful days I'd have taken the girls to the beach—perhaps to Petit Bôt with a picnic, Millie perched in my bicycle basket. Blanche and I would cycle down the lane that leads to the shore, a lane that is shadowed and secret with branches that meet overhead, and musical with the singing of the streams that run down to the water there; and then suddenly coming out into light at the end of the lane, to the beach that is held between tall cliffs like a jewel cradled between cupped palms, to the sleek wet sand and the glistening jade-green clarity of the sea. Or perhaps we'd go to Roquaine Bay, where the soft sand is perfect for sandcastles, or up to the north, to Vazon, with its wide clean air, all its spaciousness, or to the Forts Roques, the savage black rocks that rise from the water like broken teeth. You could always find a sheltered spot there, a patch of sandy grass where you could spread a rug for a picnic. There'd be crickets, and rock pools with emerald crabs, and delicate tamarisk flowers.

But we can't do these things any more. The beaches are forbidden to us. They're mined by the Germans, in case our army comes to take our island back—something that none of us thinks will happen. Our island is a prison.

Every evening I turn on the BBC news on the wireless, listening with a weight of lead in my chest—the news is all terrible. The Luftwaffe are bombing English airfields. Churchill calls it the Battle of Britain: he says that the Battle of France is over, the Battle of Britain has begun. Evelyn listens with me, though I don't know whether she understands—whether what she hears makes sense to her. Sometimes as she listens her face seems to melt and tears spill over her face. Her emotions are always so near—as though with the passing of the years some defence she had, some outer protective shell, has been scoured and worn away in her.

'That's terrible, Vivienne,' she'll say.

'Yes, I'm afraid so,' I tell her. 'But we mustn't give up hope.'

I don't know why I say that, when I have given up hope myself. Sometimes in the evening we hear the Nazi bombers coming over from France, and then their fighter planes going up from the Guernsey airfield, to escort the bombers over England. When we hear them, I think we all send up a quick, fervent prayer for our aircrews who will meet them— even those of us who'd never normally pray. Will they hold off the Luftwaffe? How long can they hold out against the invasion of England? How long before Hitler crosses the Channel? We know it must happen sooner or later. It's only a matter of time.

Often I think about Eugene—wondering where his

division is, praying that he'll be kept safe. But at these times when I think of him, he feels almost a stranger to me. I tell myself it's because he's so far away now, and because we don't receive any letters or any news of our men. Most women with husbands at war must feel this—the sense of distance, of separation. I don't entirely acknowledge, even in the deeps of my mind, that it was like that when he lived here too. When he'd sit at the breakfast table fenced off behind his newspaper, as though I was nothing to him, as though I didn't exist. When he'd say, We're rehearsing tonight, don't wait up, I could be home on the late side... Sounding so easy and casual, yet I'd sense the sharks darkly circling under the surfaces of his words. When he'd lie in our bed, turned away from me, never touching. I don't admit that we were strangers long before he left.

Millie seems mostly unbothered by the Occupation, though sometimes I hear her reprimanding her ragdoll: 'If you're naughty, I'm going to tell the Nazis. And when I tell them they'll come and bomb you to bits...' But Blanche is still unhappy that we didn't go on the boat. She spends too much time in her room. Mostly she listens to her Irving Berlin records, but one day I go in and she's just sitting there, pulling at a fraying thread on her cuff: not doing anything, staring blankly in front of her. A sudden sadness tugs at me, grief for the things she is missing out on because of the Occupation—dressing up, being taken to dinner, being bought flowers—that whole gorgeous charade of courtship, the gilded time of a woman's life. She worries me. Sometimes I almost wish she were little again, like Millie. When they're small, it's so simple: you only have to buy them a bun or some aniseed balls, and they'll be content.

One day at the end of August, she does some shopping for me, at Mrs Sebire's grocery shop, up on the main road near the airfield. She comes home bright-eyed, hair flying, a smile unfurling over her face: everything about her is smiling.

'Mum. You'll never guess what happened. Mrs Sebire wanted to know if I'd like a job in her shop!'

'What did you say?' I ask her.

'*Yes*. I said *yes*, of course. That's all right, isn't it? She was really pleased. Since her daughter left on the boat, she said it's been a struggle, and she's sure I'll be good at the job.'

'That's wonderful,' I tell her.

It's not what I'd once have hoped for. When Blanche was younger, before the war began, I'd hoped she'd go to the mainland to study—perhaps to train as a teacher. But for now, with everything in turmoil, this offer of work is a gift.

Her face is lit up: her hyacinth-blue eyes dazzle.

'I'll be like Celeste now, won't I, Mum?' she says.

Blanche has always seen Celeste's job at Mr Martel's watch shop as the height of glamour.

I'll miss having her round the house in the day—Evelyn seems so fragile now, so confused, that I sometimes worry about leaving her and Millie together. But it's lovely to see Blanche happy again—and her money will certainly help. We're just about managing for the moment—I have a little money saved, and Evelyn pays some of the bills. But every penny matters.

She starts work on Monday. She gets up early, puts on a crisp gingham Sunday-best frock and some of the lipstick I bought for her. She comes home tired but pleased with herself, with a bag of over-ripe peaches that Mrs Sebire had decided were a little too bruised to sell. We eat the peaches: they are delicious.

'I'm glad you got that job,' says Millie, the sweet juice dripping down her chin.

We are all glad.

Through August, I don't see much of the Germans at Les Vinaires. I tell myself, Maybe they won't bother with us. Maybe they scarcely think of us at all. They want a quiet life here, as Captain Richter said. But I'm wary. I never go out after curfew. When I come back from Angie's, I'm careful always to take the track through the fields. If I'm cleaning my bedroom, I try not to look out into the lane. I don't see the scarred man any more—not in the lane, not in the lighted window. Now, they always draw the blackout curtains early, at Les Vinaires.

The island is filling up with soldiers. When I cycle into St Peter Port to change my library book, I find there are swastikas everywhere, and German newsreels at the Gaumont, telling of Nazi triumphs. There's a lot less food in the shops. I have to queue for bread, and there are no sweets for the girls, and I can't find coffee anywhere. As I walk back to my bicycle, a German brass band starts marching down the High Street, past all the familiar shops, past Mrs du Barry's and Boots. I hate to see this. And yet the sound of it stirs me, as martial music always will, regardless of who is playing it: there's a glamour to it, an urgency, it always makes your heart pound. I find I am walking in time, my body responding to the beat, and this troubles me, as though I am conceding something.

On the way back from town, I drop in on Gwen at Elm Tree Farm.

We sit at her wide scrubbed table. Her kitchen has a scent of baking, so warm and welcoming, like arms wrapped around you. On the table, there are sweetpeas in a white china jug; the flowers are almost over, and the jug stands in a lapping pool of silken fallen petals.

We drink tea, and eat Gwen's home-made *gâche*, which is stuffed with sultanas and candied peel, and has a thin, glittery crust of sugar on top. Every Guernsey housewife makes it, and I learned how when I came here: but my *gâche* has never tasted half as delicious as Gwen's.

I lick the last trace of fragrant sugar from my hand.

'Mmm. That's so *good*.'

'Make the most of it, Viv,' she says. 'There won't be all that much more of that, I'm thinking. I had to queue for the sugar. We'll all have to tighten our belts.'

'Yes, I suppose so…'

I haven't really thought this through—where our food is going to come from. But there are no boats from England, and twice as many people on our island now.

'I suppose they'll have to get in supplies from occupied France,' she says. 'But the Germans will take all the best stuff, you can be certain of that. Anyone with a bit of land is lucky—it's the folks in the town who will suffer… You'll be in clover, Viv, with that nice big garden you've got.'

'Yes. I suppose I ought to start working on it…'

I think of digging up my roses and planting parsnips there. A little sadness catches at my sleeve.

We talk about our children. I tell her about Blanche's job with Mrs Sebire, and the peaches.

'That's a really good place to be working, for the times that are coming,' she says.

'And what about Johnnie? I know you were worried,' I say.

'Oh, well. You know…' She smiles, but not with her eyes.

'Gwen—tell me…'

She gives a slight mirthless laugh.

'You always know what I'm thinking, Viv.'

There's a thread of disquiet wrapped round her voice. Anxiety snags at me. I wait for her.

'The thing is—he spends an awful lot of time with that Piers Falla,' she says.

I feel a rush of relief that it's nothing worse than this. Piers Falla is an odd, awkward lad; I remember him from church, when he was younger and went to Matins with his parents—he doesn't go any more. I think of his face that has the sharpness of a kestrel, his gaze that looks right into you: and his twisted body, the way he drags his right foot. When he was little, he got in the way of a scythe: they said he was lucky to live. I don't understand why his friendship with Johnnie should be so troubling to Gwen.

'He's a funny lad, Piers. To be honest, I don't quite like him,' she says.

'I don't really know him that well,' I tell her.

'He's too intense,' says Gwen. 'He seems too old for his years…'

'I suppose his life hasn't been exactly easy,' I say.

'Well—you've got to feel sorry for him, of course. And I know he's really angry that he couldn't join up. I mean, he tried, but they wouldn't consider him. He's old enough—he's that little bit older than Johnnie. But I think they just took one look at him. Johnnie said he was distraught.'

'Yes. Poor lad. He would be…'

We sit quietly for a moment. A fly crackles against the window, with an ominous sound, like a pan on the stove boiling dry.

Gwen stirs.

'You know what I think, Viv,' she says. 'This Occupation is really hard on the men. The young ones especially—like my Johnnie and Piers, who'd want to be off fighting. I mean, we women just get on with things, don't we? We wash and cook and all that, we still know what we're meant to be doing. But it's terrible for the men, to be invaded like this. To have to just let it happen. Not to be able to do anything about it.'

'Yes, it must be difficult...'

But I live in a house of women: this isn't something I see.

'It's why I worry so much about Johnnie,' she says. 'These young lads wishing that they could fight—all stuck here kicking their heels. It's a recipe for trouble.'

I have a slight sense of disquiet when she says that.

'But—they won't do anything, surely,' I say. 'How could they? It's such a little island—there's nowhere to hide.' I think of the German brass band marching in St Peter Port, of the swastikas, the German presence everywhere. 'I mean—there are so many of them—they're everywhere you turn...'

'You're right, of course,' she says. 'I'm probably being silly. They'll see that, won't they, Viv?'

'I'm sure they will,' I say.

But, cycling home, I have an uneasy feeling—just a flicker of apprehension, like some dark winged thing fluttering in a recess of my mind.

CHAPTER 16

Blanche has laid the table for tea. Everything is immaculate. She's put out the best linen napkins, with the silver napkin rings that she and Millie were given as christening gifts; and there are roses from the garden in a cut-glass vase.

'So what's all this about?' I ask her. 'I mean, it's a sweet thing to do—but it doesn't happen all that often...'

'Don't you like it, Mum?'

'Yes, it looks lovely,' I say. 'Thank you...'

She has an eager, hopeful smile.

'Actually, there *is* something,' she tells me. Her voice a little ingratiating—smooth as Vaseline. 'I wanted to ask if I could maybe go out tonight.'

'*Out*? Of course you can't go out. Not after the curfew. Of course not, Blanche. What on earth were you thinking?' I say.

'The thing is...' She hesitates. 'There's going to be a party at Les Brehauts,' she says. I hear a little uncertainty creeping into her voice. 'Celeste and me have been invited.'

I think of Les Brehauts, the Gouberts' big whitewashed house near the church. It's double-fronted, rather splendid, with wide sleek lawns and abundant borders and whispering poplar trees. Recently, when I've cycled past, I've seen German officers in its grounds.

'So—who's giving this party, exactly?' I say. 'I thought that Mr and Mrs Goubert had gone on the boat. I thought Les Brehauts had been requisitioned...'

Blanche draws in breath, like someone about to dive into deep water.

'The thing is, Mum, it *has* been... Somebody invited us. He said it would be a good evening. There's going to be dancing. You know how I love dancing. What could happen to us exactly?' she says.

'Who is this somebody, Blanche?'

I see her throat move as she swallows. Pink spots come in her cheeks.

'He's called Tomas Kreutzer,' she says.

'Kreutzer?'

'He likes Celeste,' she goes on rapidly. 'He came to the shop where she works. He wanted to get his watch mended.'

I stare at her—not quite believing what I'm hearing.

'So—the *Germans* are giving this party?'

'Celeste says Tomas is ever so polite. Really, Mum. He doesn't agree with the war. He thinks Great Britain and Germany should be allies—because we're so alike. He says we aren't like other races.'

I don't say anything.

'He was going to be an English teacher,' she says. 'Well, there's nothing wrong with that, is there? That's good, isn't it? To want to be a teacher? It's not *his* fault this happened, Mum.'

I'm amazed that we're having this conversation.

'Blanche. You'd be out after curfew. You could be shot,' I say.

'Of course we won't be.' She has all the blithe certainty of youth, when you believe that nothing can touch you. 'Tomas will give us a lift,' she tells me. 'Tomas says it will be fine.' She comes close to me, clasps my wrist with urgent fingers. 'Mum. It's just some boys and girls wanting to have a good time. It's just a party. What could be wrong with a party?'

'*No*, Blanche. You can't go.'

'The thing is—Celeste won't go without me.' She clears her throat. 'I *promised* her, Mum.' She suddenly sees a new argument to try, appealing to the morality of promises. 'I should keep my promises, shouldn't I? You've always said that's important…'

'And what does Celeste's mother say to all this?' I ask.

'*Yes*. Definitely,' says Blanche. 'I *know* she'll say yes. I mean, it's not as though there's all that much fun in our lives nowadays, is it?'

'Blanche. Of course you can't go. I'm amazed you asked. You'd be putting yourself in danger. That's the end of it.'

She can tell now that I'm not giving in. I see the bright blaze of anger in her.

'You never let me do anything.' Her voice is shrill. 'You treat me like a baby.'

'Things are difficult, Blanche. You know that. We have to be careful. We can't just do what we want.'

'I've got a job now, Mum. You can't treat me as though I'm still *three*.'

'Blanche. We're at war, for goodness' sake.'

'It's *your* war,' she says. 'It's not *our* war. This stupid, stupid war…'

'Well, that's what we have to live with,' I say.

I glimpse Millie open-mouthed in the doorway—fascinated, appalled.

Blanche's eyes spark.

'We didn't *have* to live with it.' She's spitting out the words. 'It didn't have to be like this—we could have gone on the boat. It would all have been different if only we'd gone on the boat. I would have a life then...' Bitterly.

It hurts, because there's truth in it. Probably we should have gone. Everyone got to Weymouth safely. Perhaps I was a coward. Perhaps I should have been braver. It all seemed to happen so rapidly—that sudden fork in the road: and you choose one path above the other, and then there's no going back.

'Blanche—I made the best decision I could.' Wanting her to understand—wanting to justify myself to her.

'Well, it wasn't the right one, Mum. What kind of a life is this, cooped up here on Guernsey?'

'I'm trying to keep us all safe,' I say.

'That's all you care about, isn't it? Keeping safe,' she says. Her eyes flare like blue gas-flames. 'You don't care about *living*... You can't keep me shut away here for ever. I've got my own life to lead.'

'Blanche...'

'I hate this stupid, stupid war.' Tears are streaming down her face. 'It was just a party,' she says.

She runs off up the stairs.

Tea is ready, on the immaculately laid table, but Blanche stays up in her room. I knock on her door, but she says, 'Go away.' She sounds as though she's still crying: there's a choke of tears in her voice. I decide to leave her for now, and let her come down when she's ready.

'Blanche isn't here,' says Evelyn.

'She's not feeling well,' I tell her.

I'm glad Evelyn didn't overhear the quarrel; I know if she had she'd be giving me lots of advice: how that girl needs a good talking-to, how I shouldn't put up with her backchat; how children need plenty of discipline, they need to know where you stand.

Millie gives me a conspiratorial look from under her eye-lashes. Tonight, her table manners are perfect; she has a rapt, goody-two-shoes expression. She's relishing this unfamiliar role—of being the better-behaved daughter.

After tea, I read her a bedtime story that tells of a girl who married a creature as ugly as a hedgehog: and at night he took off his coat of spines and became a handsome man. I've always loved this story, but I'm reading mechanically, not very aware of the words. The thing Blanche said is in my mind: *That's all you care about, isn't it? Keeping safe. You don't care about living...* I wonder if she is right—if this is a flaw in me—remembering how when I first came to Guernsey, I embraced the restriction, the simplicity, of life here, content to live in the quiet of these secluded valleys, with my roses and my piano and my poetry books. There has always been something in me that is drawn to seclusion, to life in a small enclosed room. I'm so shy, so wary of strangers—it's as though I need to protect myself against other people, defend myself against them. Yet deep inside I know that a cloistered room, however willingly entered, will soon become a prison.

Blanche doesn't come down as she usually does, to half listen to the story and flick through old copies of *Vogue*.

Once I've heard Millie's prayers and tucked her up, I go to Blanche's door. This time I will walk in and speak to her, whatever she says. I hate it when there's trouble between us.

I'm longing to patch up the quarrel, now she's had time to calm down.

I knock, but there's no answer.

'Blanche?'

I half open the door, say her name again. My voice falls into silence.

I walk right into the room.

Oh God. No.

The room is empty. The clothes she was wearing are in a neat pile on her chair, but the bed is still made, not slept in, her pyjamas under her pillow; and I see with a thud of my heart that her window is flung wide. You could climb out there, and clamber down onto the roof of the shed, and from there down into the garden, and leave without being seen.

I can't believe she's defied me like this. I'm so angry with her; so frightened for her.

CHAPTER 17

My pulse races off: I'm full of a desperate energy. All I can think is that I have to find her, and bring her back and keep her here, where she's safe. Evelyn and Millie are both in bed: I can leave them. The light is thickening already, sepia shadows gathering in the corners of the house, and I remember what Captain Richter said: You know about the curfew. Don't put us in a difficult position... I can see his stern mouth, as thin as the gash of a razor. But I push the thought away. I can walk through the fields to Les Brehauts, and nobody will see me. I will find her and bring her home again.

I cross the lane, walk through my orchard, along the hem of the wood. The air is chill, profound, smelling of autumn coming—of woodsmoke and rot and ripening fruit. On the other side of the wood, the fields belong to Peter Mahy. I walk along the narrow track that leads across his land. The sky is a lavish ultramarine, and the unshadowed parts of the fields are bleached and colourless in the twilight. The rabbits that dart and skitter there are absolutely black, as though they are made of darkness, and shadow laps at the foot of Peter's broken-down barn, like a pool of deep water.

When I come to the field below Les Brehauts, I can hear music from the party, spooling out over the quiet land, like a roll of bright silk flung out. 'I've got you under my skin.' I'm startled that they listen to the exact same music as we do, these people we are at war with. Somehow I hadn't expected that.

Down below Les Brehauts, there's a wrought-iron gate in the hedge that opens into their garden. I look up the long slope of lawn that leads to the back of the house, where there are graceful French windows and a terrace. I slip through the gate, walk silently up the garden between the herbaceous borders; dahlias hang their heavy heads, paled to the colour of milk in the dusk. The perfumes of the garden wrap themselves around me.

I stop at the foot of the terrace. From here I can see in; the blackout curtains have been rather carelessly pulled, and a sliver of topaz brightness falls out over the lawn, gilding each blade of grass it touches. There are moths about, drawn to the radiance; they seem to have a glittery dust on their wings, which glimmers when they enter the light. All around me is the drenching scent of honeysuckle.

I stare into the lighted room. This is the big drawing room across the back of the house. Mrs Goubert used to invite the whole congregation in here after the carol service at Christmas, to eat apple *gâche* and drink mulled wine and talk about island affairs. The room has been utterly changed—the carpet rolled up, all the furniture pushed to the sides, to make a dance floor. On the sideboard there are bottles of claret, and delicate crystal glasses that have an opulent gleam. Several couples are dancing. The men are all Germans in uniform, the girls all island girls. One of the men is winding up the gramophone. Celeste is there, dancing the Charleston with a tall German boy: I imagine this must be Tomas, her boyfriend. Celeste is wearing a dress

that is the rich, extravagant blue of cornflowers; it's made
of some glossy fabric that swings out with her movement
and catches the light. There's a faint gleam of sweat on her
forehead: everything about her is gleaming. For a moment
I can't see Blanche—then I spot her by the piano, which has
been pushed to the side. She's talking to a solid young man,
who is looking at her intently. She's wearing her taffeta dress
and one of her two good pairs of stockings and her favourite
coral necklace, and her lips are very red: she has put on the
lipstick I bought for her. She's holding a glass of wine, though
she isn't used to drinking, she's only ever had a little wine
before, just a half-glass at birthdays or Christmas. Now and
then she drinks the wine in small, hurried sips, running a
finger up and down the stem of the glass. She looks flushed
and scared and happy.

I was going to bang on the door, to march in and take her
home with me. But I don't move, just stand there, staring
in through the glass. I can tell that she's nervous—she's nib-
bling her lip, and with her free hand she's twisting a strand
of her hair. She can stammer a bit when she's anxious, and
I wonder if she is stammering now, and trying very hard
not to. She makes me think of a faun that might startle and
skitter away.

I try to imagine walking in there, to tell her she has to
come home. I see I was wrong, to think I could do that—
that it was *right* to do that. I realise that all the anger and
fear have left me. I feel a little foolish, that I ever thought
such things. I watch her a moment longer; and a feeling
falls over me like a fisherman's net, captures me—a confused emotion, bittersweet, a little like grief, yet not that.
My eyes fill up. I hear her words in my mind: *You can't keep
me here for ever. I've got my own life to lead.* I know what this

moment is—the moment every mother faces. This is when my daughter leaves me—when she steps out into the stream, steps into her own life. And so much about it is wrong: this setting—the Occupation, the war. But it still has to happen. She has to make her own choices now. I know this—that I have to let her go, that I can't stop her, shouldn't stop her.

There's a pause in the music, so all I can hear through the window is the ripple of laughter and talk. Close to my face a moth beats soft, tenuous wings against the glass. In the room, the man beside the gramophone kneels down to change the record. More Cole Porter: 'Night and Day'. More couples take to the floor, though Blanche is still talking to the young man by the piano. I watch the dancers a little longer. If I half close my eyes, the room is just a hectic, glamorous blur, a kaleidoscope of colour. I can't make out the enemy uniforms, all the things that jar—it's just young men and women dancing.

I walk silently back through the darkening meadows, the music singing in my mind. Above me, the moon is rising, and the night wind in the leaves of the wood is one long indrawn breath.

CHAPTER 18

I pass into my orchard between the quiet old trees, whose branches are bending already with the weight of swelling fruit. I am safe at last: no one will find me here. I only have to cross the lane, and I will be home.

It's completely dark now. The moon is high above my orchard. Where the apple leaves are silhouetted against its whiteness, they are black as a rook's wing, and precise as though cut with a blade. I walk on through the soft dark and the scent of apple leaves.

'Mrs de la Mare.'

A sudden voice in the darkness behind me. No footfall.

Just for a moment, I'm so frightened. All the fear that I try to keep tamped down leaps up at me out of the night: all the terror.

I spin round.

'Mrs de la Mare,' he says again.

It's one of the men from Les Vinaires. Not Captain Richter, who told me off about the curfew: it's the other man, the one I saw in the lane, the one with the scar. His face is shadowed, and I can't see his expression. He's standing now, but he must have been sitting on a tree stump when I passed him: that's why I didn't see him. All the detail of his uniform is blotted out by the dark.

'Oh,' I say.

I bite my lip, to stop it trembling. I hope he didn't see my fear. I desperately don't want him to see it.

'You shouldn't be out, Mrs de la Mare. It's ten o'clock. It's after the curfew,' he says.

I think of what Captain Richter said. *Don't make things difficult for us.* I remember the threat in his voice.

'I know. I'm really sorry. But there was something I needed to do,' I say.

I'm shaking. I think—Why is he here in my orchard? Was he waiting for me? These questions frighten me. I force myself to breathe, drawing all the chill sweetness of the night air into me.

'Whatever it was could have waited,' he says. 'There are penalties. You shouldn't forget that.'

I dig my fingernails into my palms, to try and stop myself trembling. I think—Perhaps if I explain, perhaps then he won't be angry...

'I walked over to Les Brehauts,' I say. 'To the party. My daughter's there.'

He doesn't say anything. He waits. It's so quiet that I can hear the distant murmuring of water, from the little stream in the Blancs Bois, and the stream that runs down the lane. And I can hear his breathing, and the quiet click as he clears his throat.

'I walked through the fields,' I tell him, 'and I thought that no one would see.' I won't—maybe *couldn't*—explain what happened: how I went there intending to march in and bring her back home. How something changed in me when I looked through the lighted window. 'I wanted to see what had happened to her. I wanted to know she was safe.' The words come tumbling out; my voice is shaky and shrill.

'Your daughter Blanche?' he says.

'Yes.'

I'm disconcerted that he knows her name, as though it is something he has stolen from us. But of course he must have noticed us, must have heard me talk to her, looking out over our yard from the window of Les Vinaires. The thought of him watching us troubles me. I wonder what else he has learned about us.

The white raw moonlight falls around us; the darkness under the trees is deep, and fretted at the edges with the cut-paper shadows of leaves. I can't see his expression, and I don't think he can see mine. When he turns towards me, his face is entirely in shadow.

'Someone will bring her back. You don't need to worry about her. One of the boys will give her a lift at the end of the evening,' he says.

I feel his eyes on me.

'The thing is—she's only fourteen,' I say. 'I wasn't happy with her going. She shouldn't have gone.' Then I wonder why I said that. Showing him my weakness, that my daughter has defied me. 'I just wanted to see—that she was all right…' My voice trails off, feebly.

'And what did you see, at Les Brehauts?' he asks me.

I think—What did I see? I think of Celeste in her corn-flower dress, with all the shine spilling from it; of Blanche leaning on the piano, flushed, a little scared; of all the young men in their uniforms. Of the loveliness, and all the wrong-ness, of it. All these thoughts are muddled up in my head, confusing me. I don't say anything.

'I hope it wasn't too alarming,' he says. There's a thread of amusement in his voice.

'They were dancing,' I say stupidly.

'Stefan has a lot of gramophone records,' he says. 'Stefan likes Cole Porter.'

I notice the way he calls the man by his Christian name, to me. Not calling him by his surname and rank. It isn't casual: I know that this is some kind of concession he's making.

'Perhaps a cigarette?' he says.

He takes out a packet of Gauloises and offers me one. This startles me. Then I think, If I were in trouble, would he be offering this to me? Perhaps he isn't going to do anything too dreadful.

I hesitate. I know I shouldn't accept anything from him. But here in the dark of the orchard it doesn't seem to matter. It's just a cigarette. My hands are still trembling as I take it, and I know he sees this.

He takes out his lighter and leans in towards me; his face is close to mine. He has a faint scent of the day—of leather, sweat, of the smoky rooms he has been in. He cups his hand against the night breeze. In the flare of the flame, his skin is briefly, startlingly red. I see the knotted veins, the pale hairs on the backs of his hands.

I usually smoke Craven A. I inhale, and cough like a girl. I'm embarrassed.

'It is too strong for you?' he says.

'No. It's all right,' I tell him.

I'm grateful for the taste of tobacco, on my lips, on my tongue. The smoke rises up between us, like breath on a white morning.

'Your husband is fighting, Mrs de la Mare?' he says.

'Yes.'

'I also am married, and I have one son,' he tells me. 'Hermann.' His voice smudges, softens. I hear the tenderness in it. I'm surprised that he's telling me so much. 'He is

fighting. He is in the Luftwaffe. He is seventeen, just three
years older than Blanche.'

'He seems so young to be fighting. I always feel that—
seventeen is so young,' I say.

'Yes, it is young,' he says.

'You must be very proud of him,' I go on, unthinkingly.
It's how you always respond when someone speaks of a son
at war. Then all the crassness of my remark slams into me.
This son of his—the son that he loves so deeply that his voice
is softened as he speaks his name: this son is bombing our
airfields. I feel I have betrayed something. My hand instantly
covers my mouth, as though to stop myself from speaking
treachery.

He's watching me, as if he's trying to read my thoughts
in my face.

'Yes, I am proud of him,' he says. 'We are all proud of our
children, are we not, Mrs de la Mare?'

'Yes.'

He shifts a little. I hear the creak of his boots as he moves,
and the crunch of dried-out apple leaves under his feet. A
bat flits around us, too small to be properly seen, elusive as
a half-formed thought.

'When did you last see your husband?' he asks me.

'He joined up last September,' I say. 'He was home on
leave a few months ago. But I don't suppose I'll see him again
now—until the war is over.'

'You must miss him.'

'Yes.'

I take a breath, as though to say more, then stop. *Do I miss
him? Do I really miss Eugene?*

I feel him reading something into my hesitation. The
silence spills over between us and scares me. I want to, have

to, break it: but I don't know what to say. Nothing feels safe to me.

'These are complicated times,' he says. 'For all of us.'

'Yes,' I say. 'Yes, they are.' Grateful.

The moonlight falls on him briefly, and I can see the scar on his face. A thought sneaks into my head—a startling curiosity, wondering how that scar would feel to the touch. Thinking that, it's as though I can feel it, under the tips of my fingers, the different texture where the skin is frail and glossy and stretched. I feel a jolt of desire—so out of place it makes me breathless, all the wrongness of it. Around us, the streams cry out with a hundred little voices.

'My name is Gunther Lehmann. You should call me Gunther,' he says.

As though we may speak again. But we won't, I tell myself. It will never happen again.

I know he expects me to tell him my name. But I have given too much away already.

'I must go in now,' I tell him.

'Yes. Of course,' he says.

I leave him there with his cigarette, under my apple trees. I feel his eyes on me as I walk across the lane that is shining like a river in the moonlight. My body feels clumsy, strange, as though it's fixed together wrongly. I pass through my gate and, gratefully, into the familiar gloom of my house.

I sit in the kitchen and wait for Blanche. I don't turn on the light, just sit there. The moonlight slides into the room, and the ordinary things look changed, unreal, in its cool whiteness.

After a while, I hear the man's slow footsteps crossing the road, then on around the corner to the gate to Les Vinaires.

I wonder what he was thinking, all the time he stayed there smoking in my moonlit orchard.

At last, I hear a car pull up in the lane. I hear Blanche's cheery 'Goodnight' and the banging of the car door. She comes in, very silently, takes off her shoes at the door, puts them down so softly. She doesn't see me.

'Blanche.'

She turns; she's flinching. It's as though she's afraid I will hit her—though that's something I've never done.

I switch on the light. She blinks, dazed by the sudden brightness.

'You shouldn't have gone—when I told you you couldn't,' I say. 'That was wrong of you.'

She nods. She says nothing. She has a puzzled look. Things are not happening quite as she expected them to happen.

'Was it a good party?' I ask her.

'It was quite nice,' she says carefully. I can smell the wine on her breath, and the hazy scent of French cigarettes that hangs about her. Her gestures are loose and fluid, her eyes very bright, her lips and teeth stained mulberry-dark with the wine. 'It felt a bit funny, talking to the German boys,' she says.

'Yes,' I say. 'Yes. I can see that it would.'

'Though I think you could get used to it,' she tells me. 'After a while, you wouldn't think it was odd.'

I don't say anything.

'I met a friend of Tomas', his name was Karl,' she tells me. 'He comes from Berlin. It was sad, he told me how his little sister died. It was in a bombing raid. He showed me her picture and I couldn't believe she was dead. She had little pigtails...' She moves her hand over her face, cautiously, as though her features might surprise her. 'He was trying not to cry when he told me,' she says.

'Blanche—you are never to go out again without telling me,' I say.

'Yes,' she says. 'Yes, I know. I'm sorry.'

'I need to know where you are. If you want to go to one of those parties again, we'll talk about it.'

'Yes,' she says. 'Yes, of course.'

She turns to go—anxious to reach the safety of her bedroom while I'm still conciliatory.

I take Evelyn her morning tea and toast. She's sitting up in bed, waiting, in her tea-rose silk bed-jacket, her back as straight as a reed. She has an air of triumph: there's something she's longing to tell me.

'Someone came in late last night. A little bird told me,' she says.

Immediately I imagine that she saw me and Captain Lehmann in the orchard. Guilt washes through me. But I tell myself—I *had* to talk to him, I had no choice. I can't afford to alienate him, when he's living next door: when he has so much power over us. I'm about to explain this to Evelyn, but she has more to say.

'Someone came in late. I heard the car in the lane… I'm not surprised you look worried, Vivienne.'

She's talking about Blanche. I feel a rush of relief. Evelyn's room looks out over the lane: perhaps the car would have woken her.

'Blanche went out,' I tell her. 'There was a party. She's young, she needs to get out.'

'I hope she wasn't doing what she shouldn't,' she says.

I smile at the old-fashioned phrase.

'I'm sure she wasn't,' I say. 'She went with Celeste, her friend. You know how Blanche loves dancing…'

Evelyn is quiet for a moment. Then her eyes seem to glaze over. The thread of the conversation has slipped from her grasp.

'Someone came in late,' she says, looping back.

'Yes. But everything's fine,' I tell her.

'It's all such a muddle. It's so confusing, Vivienne. I don't like it being confusing.'

'Try not to worry,' I tell her.

She picks up her teacup. Her hand is unsteady: the tea in the teacup trembles.

'What are we coming to, Vivienne? Where will it end?'

To that I have no answer.

CHAPTER 19

Later, when I'm out in my yard, I glance across to my orchard. There's something lying on the tree stump that dazzles in the morning light. I cross the lane to investigate. It's Captain Lehmann's cigarette lighter, lying there, catching the sun.

Immediately, I worry that someone will see it—one of my daughters, or Evelyn, or someone walking past in the lane. That they will find it, and know it was his, and wonder what he'd been doing here, on my land: that they will work the whole thing out, the conversation, everything. I can't just leave it lying here and wait for him to come back for it.

I pick it up. The metal has been warmed by the light of the sun—it's almost burning on my skin. When I look at it shining in the palm of my hand, I have a sudden memory of his presence, vivid and immediate. I see his right hand holding the lighter, his left hand cupping my cigarette, sheltering it from the night air that might threaten to put out the flame. I half imagine I can smell the faint scent of his closeness. I can see the grace in his gesture, the veins that show through his skin.

I put the lighter in my apron pocket. I tell myself I will

take it round to Les Vinaires, and give it to one of the men there so they can return it to him. That some time soon I will do that.

But I don't.

CHAPTER 20

There's the cheerful jangle of a bicycle bell in my yard. It's Johnnie, jumping off his bicycle, grinning when he sees me.

'Morning, Auntie Viv.'

He always calls me Auntie, because our families are close.

He follows me into my kitchen. He's whippet-thin, with unruly hair and his mother's vivid eyes, brown as conkers. Every time I see him he seems a bit more of a man—a shading of stubble on his chin, his shoulders a little more square—yet his face is still the trusting, curious face of a child.

He has a bag of potatoes for us. He dumps them on the table and pushes his hair from his eyes. There's a breezy energy about him.

'Present from my mum,' he says.

'Your mum's an angel,' I say.

I offer him coffee, though there's only a scraping left in the tin.

'Water will be fine,' he says.

I bring him a glass: he gulps it gratefully down.

'So how are things at the farm?' I ask him.

'We're breeding rabbits—that's the latest. You should try

it, Auntie... My mum isn't all that keen on bumping them off, though,' he says.

'Just don't ever tell Millie,' I say. 'She doesn't approve of eating things that have fur. She'd be appalled at the lot of you...'

He grins, his nose wrinkling. I love how he looks when he smiles.

'My mum told me Blanche has a job,' he says.

'Yes—at Mrs Sebire's.'

'She's like a cat, that Blanche,' he says. 'She always lands on her feet.'

There's a sliver of admiration in his voice.

'I hope so.'

There's a splash of September sun on us. Happiness opens out in me, with my kitchen full of sunlight and warmth, and Johnnie here at my table—his vividness, his wide white smile, his hair falling over his face.

'So—Jerry been giving you any trouble, Auntie Viv?' he asks.

I nearly tell him about the Germans next door, but something stops me. It's not important, I think; there's really no rush, I'll tell him some other time.

'No, we're fine here,' I tell him, vaguely. 'It's so secluded here. You're not very aware of it all...'

His fingers are moving in restless jazz rhythms across the top of the table, as though he's at a keyboard: Johnnie can never keep still.

'I'll tell you one thing for free, Auntie. We won't take it lying down, me and my mates. We won't let them walk all over us. That's something you can count on, I promise,' he says.

The thing that Gwen said enters my mind—how the

young men have been left without any way to be men. A chill moves over my skin.

'But what can you do?' I ask him. 'There are so many of them—they're everywhere. What on earth can anyone do?'

'There's always something,' he tells me. 'Maybe just a small thing. You've got to do what you can. That's what me and Piers think.'

I remember what Gwen had said about Piers. *He's a funny lad. He's too intense. He seems too old for his years...*

'I don't really know Piers,' I tell him.

'Piers has got brains,' he tells me. He lowers his voice: there's a thrill of conspiracy in it. 'Piers is clever... Piers has a lot of ideas. He's got this scheme for painting V-signs, like they're doing on Jersey. V for Victory. We're sneaking out after curfew, putting V signs all over the place.'

'But what good will that do?'

'It's all about morale, Auntie.'

'Well, just you be careful,' I tell him. 'You know how your mother worries about you...'

He shrugs but doesn't say anything. A frown slides into his eyes. I sense that I've let him down in some way: that he's disappointed in me, because I don't share his excitement. I'm just another disapproving adult—not quite his friend any more.

'Another thing, Johnnie—I hope you've got that shotgun of Brian's well hidden,' I say.

There's a fragility about his face at the mention of Brian: a translucence.

'There's no way I'm going to part with that. But I won't let them find it,' he says. A little stubbornly—not quite answering directly.

I have said something I shouldn't have said. Anything touching on Brian is locked away inside him, in a secret room, marked No Entry.

'Johnnie, I mean it—about being careful,' I tell him.

He makes a slight gesture, flicking something away.

'We're going to do our bit. Make some trouble for them. You do what you have to do, Auntie Viv,' he tells me.

'But you could end up in prison. Or worse.'

He ignores this. I can tell it isn't real to him. He leans towards me across the table, his clear, eager eyes on my face.

'Tell you what, though, Auntie. I'm pretty disappointed in some of the islanders,' he says.

I find myself looking away from him—just not quite meeting his gaze.

'They're pretty spineless,' he goes on, 'some of the folks who live here. Giving Jerry a bit too warm a greeting, if you ask me. Putting out the Welcome mat.'

I see myself talking to Captain Lehmann in my moonlit orchard. I can't imagine why I did that—what kept me there all that time. I feel a hot surge of guilt. In the pocket of my apron, pressing against my leg, I can feel his cigarette lighter that I somehow haven't managed to take back to Les Vinaires.

'Still—there are plenty of us who've got the right idea,' says Johnnie. 'We need to give them a bit of bother. Until we win the war.'

We're silent for a moment. The words hang in the air between us—glittery, rainbow-coloured, but weightless, ephemeral as soap bubbles blown around on the wind. *Until we win the war.* I think of all those newsreels we've seen, of Hitler's army surging through Paris, like some unconquerable flood. I imagine them marching into London, see the lava flow of them—up the Mall to Buckingham Palace, on to Hyde Park Corner and Marble Arch. I can see it so clearly. They've come here to our islands, they've come the first step of the way—just walking in so effortlessly. This is Britain's future—a future of Occupation. This is what we will all have to learn to accept...

'Johnnie.' I hear the catch in my voice. 'Do you truly think we can win? In your heart of hearts? In spite of everything that's happened?'

He fixes me with his warm dark eyes—so trusting, a child's eyes.

'Of course I do, Auntie. You'd better believe it. The British are never defeated. And till we win—well, me and Piers, we're going to do what we can.'

I look at him as he sits at my table, the syrupy sunlight falling on him. He's still just a boy, urgent, reckless. I remember him at six or seven, playing with Blanche in the woods: how he'd climb the tallest trees, showing off, so desperate to impress her. And mostly that's how I understand this fighting talk of his—that it's just a boy's bravado—and especially since his brother died. That he's seeking to live for Brian—to be bold as his brother was bold. It's how he shoulders the burden of being the one who's left alive.

But just occasionally I wonder if Johnnie has something that I don't have. Sometimes when he's with me I could almost believe we could win.

'Well, I'd better be going, then, Auntie.'

'Lovely to see you, Johnnie.'

I follow him out to my yard, which is full of wind and sunlight, a few yellow leaves from my pear tree cartwheeling over the ground. Summer is sifting down into autumn.

Soon, everything will be falling apart in a last brave flurry of brightness.

'You know what annoys me, Auntie?' says Johnnie, getting onto his bike. 'The way you hear folks saying that they're glad it isn't any worse—that Jerry's so polite to us—that it isn't as bad as they thought. Some folks are almost *grateful*... But you know what I think, Auntie Viv? They haven't even *started* yet. Folks think this is it—that this is how it's going to be. But what I think is it's only just beginning.'

I open the gate and he cycles off, lurching all over the lane as he turns around to wave to me.

CHAPTER 21

The next day I make my final cup of coffee, scraping the last trace of powder from the bottom of the tin. The coffee is very dilute: it's really just hot water with a faint brown colour. I take it to the table outside my door. I'm going to pretend it's the real thing.

It's another lovely September morning. There's a haze of cloud softening the sky, and all around me the slow dance of autumn—the weaving flight of lazy insects, leaves spiralling down from the trees. The dew has just dried from the nasturtiums that grow up the walls of my house; their flowers glow scarlet, orange, saffron in the sunshine. Flimsy, dusty sparrows peck near my feet, unafraid; birds are always so tame on islands. Through the open door, I can hear Millie playing. I have put her dolls' house out on the kitchen table for her: it's a rather lovely old toy that used to belong to Iris and me, with glittery candelabra and scraps of watered silk on the walls. She's singing a breathy, tuneless song as she rearranges the little dolls in the rooms. I let the peace of the moment settle on me like a blanket. For a moment, it's as though the Occupation hadn't happened.

There are footsteps in the lane. A pigeon breaks out of the pear tree, with a sound like something torn. I look up.

Captain Lehmann is at the gate to my yard; he has his hand on it, to push it open.

'May I?' he says.

My heart pounds. I know I have to say no. I shall tell him I want nothing at all to do with him: that our talk in the dark of my orchard was just an aberration—I wasn't myself, I was frightened for Blanche, it should never have happened at all...

'Yes, all right,' I tell him.

He comes in, closes the gate quietly behind him. He stands in front of me, looking down at me thoughtfully. There are three other chairs, but I don't invite him to sit—though this makes me feel uncomfortable, it seems so impolite. Sitting, I'm very aware of how big he is—aware of his rather heavy body, and how he's so much taller than me. But he looks different in daylight—less imposing than in my moonlit orchard. His head is close-cropped, so you can see the strong shape of his skull; his hair is pale grey in the sunlight. I wonder how old he is—perhaps ten years older than me.

Anxiety seizes me, not knowing why he's here. Have I done something wrong or broken some rule? I remember yesterday morning with Johnnie: how openly we were speaking. What if the Germans overheard? Was the door closed when we were talking? I was careless. I didn't think to check that the door was properly shut. My heart skitters off.

Captain Lehmann clears his throat.

'I came to tell you that we have coffee,' he says.

'Oh.'

He smiles at my startled expression—a slight crooked smile.

'Max brought some back from France—too much. It is

very good coffee—coffee beans. Perhaps you would like some for your family?'

I think of the coffee, imagine how good it would taste. Made from beans, the French way. I used to make coffee in that way sometimes, back before the war. I love good coffee. I imagine the rich roasted smell, the kick as the caffeine slides into you—the world around you becoming more vivid, more sharply defined.

I shake my head.

'It's kind of you to offer, but no, I can't take it,' I tell him.

I hope I've got the balance right—that I'm courteous, but clear. From now on I will do everything correctly. Johnnie has reminded me how to behave.

Captain Lehmann doesn't say anything. The silence stretches out between us and panics me. I have to say something, anything.

'I mean it. I can't take it. It wouldn't be right,' I say again. But perhaps I'm protesting too much.

He looks at me with a little quizzical frown. The light shines searchingly on him, on all the detail of his face—the lines in his forehead, the jagged scar on his cheek. His eyes are the dense, rather melancholy grey of woodsmoke.

'But I think you like coffee,' he says.

I'm intrigued, in spite of everything.

'What makes you think that?' I say. Then know I shouldn't have asked—I shouldn't have given him anything, shouldn't prolong this conversation.

'I have seen how you bring it out here to your table in the sunshine,' he says. 'How you wrap your hands round the cup. This is a special moment for you. A peaceful moment…'

I try to shrug—dismissing this. Though it's true.

'And that, I think, is not good coffee,' he says, pointing to my cup, his frown deepening. His expression makes me smile, I can't help it: he has such a disapproving look, as though my coffee is an affront to him. 'That is just coloured water.'

'I'm used to it,' I tell him.

He shakes his head, almost sadly.

'But you could do so much better than that. Why not?'

His words hang in the air between us.

'No. Really. I don't want it. But thank you...'

I'm willing him to go, but he just stands there, looking at me.

I shouldn't have smiled. I try to make my face very stern, very sure.

'Captain Lehmann. I mean it. I don't think we should talk like this. I don't think it's appropriate...'

But I can't finish my careful speech. He moves rapidly towards me: the words dry up in my mouth. For a brief, alarmed moment, I think he is going to hit me. Then I see that he is swatting a wasp from my sleeve.

I half stand, dodging the wasp, knocking against the table. My apron snags on a nail, and the things in my pocket tip out—a couple of clothes pegs, one of the dolls from Millie's dolls' house; his silver cigarette-lighter. We watch as the lighter falls and lands with a small, clear crunch on the gravel. In the sudden stillness between us, the sound is shockingly loud.

My face is burning.

'Well, Mrs de la Mare,' he says, with a kind of mock-gravity. 'That is mine, I think.'

'You left it in the orchard.' My voice sounds high and

naive. 'I was going to return it. I was going to bring it back to Les Vinaires…' The words spilling out of me.

I pick up the lighter and brush off the dust and place it on the table. I can't quite hand it to him. In the silence all around us, I can hear the tiniest things—Millie's breathless song from the kitchen, a sparrow light as a leaf that lands on a branch of the tree. I can still feel the place where he touched my sleeve, the thin flame running over my skin.

He is about to say something, but then thinks better of it. He reaches out and takes the lighter. He isn't smiling, but there is something pleased about him.

'Good morning, then, Mrs de la Mare,' he says, and leaves me.

I realise that the coffee that I have made tastes horrible. I take it into the kitchen and tip it away down the sink.

CHAPTER 22

It's darker in the evenings now. I draw the curtains ear-lier, turn on the lamp. Shadow reaches out its fingers from the corners of the room. I read a new story to Millie, from our fairytale book. We sit on the sofa together, and Blanche sprawls on the floor with her magazines, and the lamp spills its light across us, bright as petals that fall from a flower.

The story tells of a soldier who is returning home from the wars. I think of the tale of the dancing princesses that I read to Millie the evening before we nearly went on the boat: in that story too there was a soldier coming back from a war. In fairytales, there are always wars, and men who go off to the battlefield: and then—some of them, the lucky ones—who make their way back home. I think about this, as I read: how in these stories, war is a given, a part of the condition of life, like the ageing and eroding of the body, like stormy weather. War is what men do—and the reasons are never explained. And to return from a war is a protracted, testing journey: the soldiers have epiphanies and encounters with the uncanny as they return from the battlefield, as though the things they have suffered open them up to the unseen.

Millie is pressed against me. I hear the slight wet sound as she sucks her thumb. She's looking at the picture; it shows a soldier walking up a simple storybook road that winds with perfect symmetry towards blue distant hills. You can't see the soldier's face, yet you can see how weary he is, so profoundly weary of war: you can read all his longing for a quiet life. It's written there in his hunched worn body, the way he trudges along.

Millie has the hypnotised look she always has when I read to her, scarcely blinking.

'The soldier's like Daddy, isn't he? Daddy's a soldier,' she says.

'Yes,' I say.

'Where is he?' she says.

I wonder how real her father is to her. She was only three when he left.

'I don't know where he is exactly, sweetheart. We don't get news any more, because of the Occupation. But I'm sure he's thinking of us, wherever he is.'

'*All* the time, Mummy? Is he thinking of us *all* the time?'

The question hurts, with a dull familiar ache, like when you press on a bruise. I'm sure Eugene thinks fondly of his children; but if he thinks of a woman on Guernsey, I know it isn't me. But I'm always so careful in these moments—careful never to hint that there was anything wrong between us. Careful never to let our unhappiness show in my voice.

'I'm sure he thinks of us all the time,' I tell her.

I read how the soldier shares his last crust of bread with a beggar, and, to thank him for his kindness, the beggar gives him a magical sack; how the soldier boldly captures Death in the sack. The soldier is at first triumphant and celebrated by all. But he later comes to regret what he did: because now that Death is conquered, there is no escape from this world, and the hordes of the weary old surround him, accusing, yearning to die. There's a picture of Death, with a white bald head and narrow slitted eyes, yellow like a wolf's eyes.

Millie pulls her thumb out of her mouth. She's frowning slightly, pensive. Her wet thumb shines in the lamplight.

'But nobody wants to die,' she says.

'Maybe if you're very old.'

'Like Grandma? Does Grandma want to die?'

'No, I'm sure she doesn't. I mean—much older than that… I think perhaps that very old people can start to feel rather tired…'

But my voice doesn't sound very certain. Perhaps the story is wrong. Perhaps it's as Millie said, and nobody wants to die.

I read her the rest of the story, thinking of the soldier. I see him so exactly: but not as he looks in the book. Well, maybe in some ways like the picture—the tattered clothes, the trudging step, as he follows the long and winding road that will bring him back to his home: but in my mind the face of the soldier is Captain Lehmann's face.

This makes me feel uneasy: as though even the thoughts in my mind are betraying me.

CHAPTER 23

October. The Luftwaffe are bombing London. They fly over every evening: there's terrible devastation. Londoners are sheltering in the Underground at night, with singsongs to keep their spirits up. Morale is high, we are told, in spite of all the destruction. I'm so afraid for Iris and her family.

Through the early days of October, we don't see much of the German soldiers next door. Captain Lehmann has disappeared. Sometimes when I'm out in my yard, I seem to hear footsteps behind me, and I turn, expecting to see him there, resting his hand on my gate, looking at me with that look he has—courteous, and perhaps a little amused. But there's no one. Or I'll be cleaning in my bedroom, and I'll hear a car in the lane, and I'll look cautiously out of the window—but it'll just be one of the other men who live there.

It's a relief, in a way. I don't know how it would be if we met again. A hot embarrassment washes through me, even imagining such a meeting. I tell myself—Perhaps he's on leave. Perhaps he's even been posted elsewhere. Yet when these thoughts enter my head, I feel a quick surge of something like anger. How could he go without telling me? Why didn't he say goodbye? And then I think—Why on earth would I expect that? Where does this anger come from? I have no right to this feeling. He owes me nothing.

One day I leave Millie with Evelyn and cycle down to St Peter Port. The shelves in the shops look emptier now, but I manage to find a joint of pork and some bread. At the ironmonger's, I buy broad bean seeds and a tray of winter cabbage seedlings. I know it's time to dig up my flowers and plant my garden for food.

I've arranged to meet Gwen for tea. When I get to Mrs du Barry's, she is there already, at our favourite table at the back of the shop, where we sat on the day of the bombing. It seems an age ago now. I ask how she is, and she says she's fine, but I wonder whether that's true: she's wearing a pilled old cardigan, and she hasn't put on her lipstick, and she seems too thin, her bones too clear in her face. I know I must look much the same—we're all shabby, tired, resigned now.

Mrs du Barry brings tea and biscuits; the biscuits are made with potato flour, but she still has proper tea. We drink gratefully, sitting in companionable silence, looking out over the harbour, at the red-tiled roofs, the water, the seabirds lifting into light, all the glitter and sparkle and white wings over the sea; and the enemy warships at anchor, and the soldiers on the harbour road. I know we're thinking the same thing— How could this happen *here*?

'We hear them marching at night sometimes,' she tells me. 'Along the main road. Marching and singing at the tops of their voices. It gives you a chill. It's like they're saying—*We'll show you who's in charge here*... After that, it's hard to get back to sleep... But you must be less aware of all that, down at Le Colombier.'

'Yes, I suppose so. It's still very quiet down there... Though there are German soldiers at Connie's place next door.'

She's half opened her mouth to take a bite of her biscuit. She's suddenly still, her biscuit poised in her hand. Her eyes widen.

'What—at Les Vinaires?'

'Yes.'

'Oh. I didn't know. You never mentioned it before.' She frowns.

I feel all the heat in my face.

'They keep themselves to themselves,' I say.

'I can't believe you never told me,' she says.

'They're very quiet. To be honest, we're not all that aware of them,' I say.

I'm not quite looking at Gwen; I look past her out of the window, where in the clear air the other islands look close enough to touch. I think—Why did I say, *to be honest*? I read somewhere that it's what people say when they're not quite telling the truth.

'It must be a pain though,' she says. 'You must feel they're constantly keeping an eye on you. I mean—there's that window in Connie's house that looks out over your yard…'

I feel that I'm lying to her. Or, if not exactly lying, keeping part of me concealed. I hate this.

'I suppose you can get used to anything,' I tell her.

I tell myself—that whole strange thing with Captain Lehmann, those awkward, halting conversations—it's all in the past. I'll never see him again. So it's stupid to feel so guilty—as though I've done something wrong.

'And how are the girls? How's Blanche?' she asks me. 'Enjoying Mrs Sebire's?'

'Yes. Though I think she still wishes we'd gone on the

boat… She went to a party at Les Brehauts. It was German soldiers and island girls.'

'Oh,' says Gwen, digesting this.

There are little sharp lines between her eyes. Something unsaid floats past me. I feel a slight shift between us, like a weed growing up between stones.

Then she shrugs, and the moment is passed.

'Well—young people need a social life.' I know she doesn't approve, but she's making allowances as it's Blanche. 'It *is* hard for them—with half the island men away, and all the shortages, and no new clothes in the shops… Look, I brought you something.' She pulls a piece of paper out of her bag—a recipe she's written out for macaroni cake. 'This doesn't taste all that wonderful, but it fills you up,' she says.

I thank her, too effusively. I think we're both relieved to move the conversation on.

The shop bell jangles; we turn as two people come in—a German soldier with a Guernsey girl. I know the girl by sight—she was in the same class as Blanche at school. She has a heart-shaped face and hair the colour of barley-sugar, and unlike most of us, she's put her make-up on—peach frosted lipstick, pale powder. She has a delicate sheen. When they sit he reaches over the table and takes her hand between his.

Gwen shakes her head.

'How can she?' she says, almost under her breath. 'How *can* she?'

I don't say anything.

'I mean—being polite is one thing. They're human beings too. And I can just about understand Blanche wanting to go to that party. I mean, let's face it, young people need to get out…' She's trying to find the place to draw the line: wanting to show where she stands, to say—This is all right, but *this* is unacceptable. 'But *that*... I just don't understand it. It's going too far. I mean, when all's said and done, we're at war with them. They bombed us. I just don't see how she can possibly live with herself.'

I don't say anything.

I think, What would Gwen think if she knew—about me and Captain Lehmann? But there's nothing to know, about me and Captain Lehmann.

'Viv—are you sure you're all right?' Her eyes are searching my face. 'You don't seem quite yourself,' she says.

'I'm fine, Gwen. Honestly.'

I prop my bicycle against the wall of my house. My fingers are stiff and numb from clutching the handlebars: there's a cold edge to the air today, hinting of winter's coming. I rub my hands together, feel the sting as the blood rushes back.

I'm relieved to find that nothing has gone wrong in my absence. Millie is playing upstairs and Evelyn is fast asleep in her chair. I empty out my bicycle basket on the kitchen table—the bread, the pork, the tray of seedlings—feeling a brief sense of triumph that I can still feed my family. Behind me, the front door is open onto the yard.

A shadow falls across the floor behind me. I turn, step into my passageway.

'Good afternoon, Mrs de la Mare.'

Captain Lehmann is standing on my doorstep.

I have a sudden shock of recognition—as though I've half forgotten his face in the time he's been away.

'I haven't seen you around,' I say. Then think—That suggests I was looking for him, was too aware of his absence. I feel the blood rush to my face.

'I have been on leave. I went to Berlin,' he tells me.

'Oh.'

I think of the Berlin of the newsreels—the Berlin of the

military parades, of Hitler's speeches—at once preposter-
ous and chilling. And at the same time, I wonder about the
people who wait for him in Berlin—his wife, his son—feeling an intense, illicit curiosity. These thoughts from different
universes co-existing, colliding, in me.

'I have some chocolate,' he says. 'I bought it on my way
back, from a chocolate shop in Cherbourg.'

He holds it out. It's Suchard milk chocolate, in a wrapper
of cornflower blue with gold lettering. Even the look of it is
so glamorous. I imagine how it would be as you unwrapped
and ate it—the delicious crackle of silver paper, the rush of
sweetness in your mouth.

'Take it. It's for you,' he says.

I shake my head. I think I can smell the chocolate faintly
through the wrapping. Or maybe it's just that intense imagi-
nation that comes when you're feeling deprived—when for
afternoon tea you had tasteless biscuits made from ersatz
flour. My mouth fills startlingly with water, I have to swallow. He watches my throat, I know he can see this.

I blush. I feel a kind of shame.

'I think you like chocolate, Mrs de la Mare,' he says.

'Everybody likes chocolate,' I say vaguely.

'So why won't you take it?' he says.

'Thank you, but I can't,' I say. I'm speaking very quietly,
so as not to wake Evelyn. It makes our conversation seem
more intimate than it should. 'I told you before—when I
wouldn't take the coffee...'

'But it's such a small thing, surely—to say no to some
chocolate.'

'That's all I can do—small things,' I say. Remembering
what Johnnie said. *There's always something. Maybe just a small
thing. You've got to do what you can.*

'Mrs de la Mare—no one will die because you took a very small gift from me,' he says. 'Nothing is being put at risk here.'

I don't say anything.

He's standing a little too close to me. I remember how he swatted the wasp from my sleeve: and thinking that, I feel it again—the bright flare of sensation in me.

'And you have taken a cigarette from me,' he says. 'What is so different now?'

'I shouldn't have taken the cigarette,' I tell him.

His grey pensive gaze is on me.

'If you won't take the chocolate for yourself, you can give it to your children. Would that make you feel a little less guilty?' he says.

I put out my hand and take the chocolate.

He gives a slight sigh—as though he is pleased, relieved. I try not to think about this: why my concession matters, why it is so important to him for me to take this gift.

CHAPTER 25

I take the chocolate into the kitchen. I open up the paper, breathe in its scent for a moment. I break two pieces from it that I will keep for myself, and put them aside on a saucer. I decide to give Millie and Blanche their portions after tea, so they won't be too hungry and gobble it up, so they'll make the most of it.

That evening, when our plates are empty, I go to the cupboard, bring the chocolate in.

'I've got something for you,' I tell them. 'A treat.'

'It's chocolate. I can *smell* it,' says Millie.

The girls watch intently as I take off the blue outer wrapper, unwrap the silver paper. There's a tantalising rustle.

'Where did you get it, Mum?' says Blanche.

'I got it in town,' I tell her.

'But I thought there wasn't any chocolate anywhere,' she says. 'That's what Mrs Sebire's been saying.'

'I was lucky. I managed to find some,' I say.

I break the chocolate into three. I hold some out to Evelyn, but she shakes her head.

'I won't have it, thank you, Vivienne. Chocolate doesn't suit my digestion…'

'That's awful. Poor Grandma,' says Millie.

I give the girls their portions.

'Make the most of it. Eat it slowly,' I say.

Though they don't, of course.

When they've finished, I divide Evelyn's portion between them. The girls thank her politely, and eat their second helping.

Millie's mouth is darkly stained with chocolate. She licks her lips elaborately and gives a little sigh. She lifts her face, the evening sun lighting her skin and her eyes.

'I like chocolate, Mummy. I want to have chocolate all the time...'

'Millie, you're so greedy. You'd only get fat if you did,' says Blanche.

'I want to be fat,' says Millie. 'I want to be fat like a pig.' She sticks out her chest and makes big fists of her hands. 'I want to be fat like a *walrus*.'

'You don't even know what a walrus is,' says Blanche.

'I *do*. I *do* know. It looks like this,' says Millie.

She blows out her cheeks to make a big bloated face. Blanche reaches over and pinches Millie's face with two fingers, and Millie lets out a little bubble of breath. Both girls find this very funny, and the room is briefly festive with laughter, as though our lives are normal again, as though the war isn't happening.

A bud of gratitude opens out in my mind—gratitude to Captain Lehmann, for making my children's eyes shine, for filling our house with laughter. I try to push the thought away: I will not let myself think that.

Blanche stops giggling and wipes her eyes with her hand.

'D'you remember when we had chocolate whenever we wanted?' she says, yearningly. 'When there were shelves in the shops with those big glass jars full of sweets? When there was sherbet and fudge and liquorice?'

There's incredulity in her voice—as though she finds it hard to believe in this now, to remember.

'Sweetheart, it'll happen again,' I tell her. 'I know it will. We'll have all those good things back one day. This won't go on for ever.'

Blanche shakes her head, as though she doesn't quite believe me.

'Can I have the silver paper to press?' she asks.

I give it to her. She runs her fingers over it, smoothing out the creases. She likes to collect silver paper: she will press it between the pages of one of her Chalet School books.

Evelyn frowns at me. She has a tense, strained look—the look of someone struggling to touch a thing that's just out of reach.

'Where did you get that chocolate, Vivienne?' she asks me.

'Like I said, in town,' I tell her. But I'm not looking at her.

Evelyn's mouth is small and tight, as though she finds my answer somehow unsatisfactory.

'Chocolate doesn't suit me,' she says again. 'It doesn't suit me at all.'

When everyone is in bed, I open the kitchen cupboard and take out the two pieces of chocolate I was keeping for myself, briefly wondering why I'm doing this, why I've chosen to eat it secretly. I put the first piece in my mouth, feel the surge of sweetness through me. It's smoothly velvet, melting on my tongue; the taste, after months of bland food, is somehow exotic, hinting of the Tropics, of abundant plantations and warm starlit nights. I eat it slowly, hold it in my mouth for a very long time.

CHAPTER 26

Sunday is a beautiful day; and in the afternoon Blanche sits out in the garden, catching the last of the autumn sunshine, wanting to top up her tan. Millie is playing gymkhanas, with the garden broom as a horse; she's wound hair-ribbons through the bristles, and she's galloping round a pile of grass-clippings left from when I last mowed the lawn. I watch them for a moment through the living-room window.

I play the piano for Evelyn—a Chopin Nocturne that she likes: it's gentle, rather elegaic. For myself I love his Mazurkas the best—they're rather harsh and sad, with a streak of wildness in them: but Evelyn finds them too strange. For a while I'm lost in the music—the whole world settling around me and rearranging itself, everything fluid, perfected.

'That was very nice, Vivienne,' says Evelyn politely, when I've finished.

There's a sudden shriek from outside.

'*No*, Millie! You *beast!*'

I go to the window. Blanche has jumped up. There are lawn clippings stuck in her hair: as I watch, she spits out blades of grass. Millie is watching her sister, at once aghast and thrilled. While I was wrapped up in the music, she must have crept behind Blanche and tipped grass all over her head.

'You stupid little idiot!' Blanche is furious. '*And* I've only just washed my hair… I've had enough. I'm going to *slaughter* you,' she says.

Millie runs off, shrieking. I open up the French window, go out to intervene, but they're too quick for me. Blanche disappears round the side of the house, chasing Millie. I hear the crunch of their feet on the gravel, then a thud, a silence, a scream.

Evelyn shakes her head.

'Trouble's coming, Vivienne…'

Blanche rushes in to find me. She looks worried.

'Mum, you'd better come.'

Millie has tumbled on the gravel. On her hands, the grazes are shallow, but there's a nasty gash on her knee, ragged, dirty, bleeding profusely.

I put her in the bath to try and clean out the cut. Normally I'd have put salt in the bath to disinfect the wound, but salt is very precious now. The gash still has a dirty look; there's gravel stuck in the broken skin that I can't get to wash out. I know the wound needs antiseptic. I pick up the bottle of TCP, but Millie's face dissolves.

'No! It'll hurt! Mummy, no!' Her shoulders shake with sobs.

I can't face holding her down. I tell myself that the cut will probably heal just fine anyway.

A knock at my bedroom door wakes me, dragging me up out of sleep. I turn on my lamp and go to open the door, my body slow and lumbering.

It's Millie. Her wet face shines in the lamplight; her lashes are clotted together with tears.

'Mummy. My leg hurts.'

I put out a tentative finger to touch her knee. The skin has a hot, inflamed feel. Millie cries out at my touch. I'm so cross with myself: I should have been firmer, and disinfected the cut.

'I'll take you back to bed,' I say, 'and we'll think what to do in the morning...'

I'm restless. I can't get back to sleep. After a while, I get up, and listen outside her room. She's still crying, but I decide to leave her. The sobs sound drowsy; I know that soon she'll sink down into sleep and it's better not to disturb her.

In the night the weather breaks, and the rain is there in my dream. I dream that there are gaping holes in the roof of Le Colombier, and the rain has come in, and my entire house is flooded. I wade slowly through my living room, which is knee-deep in water, and lit by a pure, chill aquamarine light. Things from my life float past me on the shining flood—my poetry books, dolls from Millie's dolls' house, my mother's musical box. They're all drenched with water, ruined, but in the dream I view all this with equanimity: the depredations of the flood water don't concern me at all—the way it stains, rots, devastates. I just let everything drift past me. I take a kind of voluptuous pleasure in not struggling any more, in giving in to what must happen.

In the morning, it's still raining, with a heavy pewter sky.

As Blanche goes to work, she turns towards me in the doorway, sweeping her hair back, tying a chiffony scarf round her head. Her skin is golden from yesterday's sun and she smells of rose geranium talc. The rain hisses on the gravel behind her, and patches of standing water gleam, giving back the grey metallic shine of the sky.

'Mum, is Millie all right? I heard her crying,' she says.

'I'm not sure,' I tell her. 'I'm rather worried about that cut on her knee. I probably ought to try and get the doctor to call.'

But I'm reluctant: I don't really want to leave Millie. And it would take an age to contact him. I'd have to cycle up to his house and hope that he or his wife were there; or I could try and ring from the nearest phone box, which is almost as far.

Blanche is frowning, her blue anxious gaze on my face.

'Well, you will if you're worried, Mum, won't you? Promise me you will.'

'Yes. Of course.'

Something at the edge of my vision makes me suddenly turn. The window at Les Vinaires is open. I see something in the darkness of the room beyond the window—a paleness that I can't make out—a face, or the sleeve of a shirt. I feel a quick impotent rage. I hate this—the way the men who live there know the most intimate details about us. As though the Occupation entitles them to see straight into our lives.

Blanche's eyes glitter with tears.

'It was my fault, wasn't it?'

'No, of course not, sweetheart. You were both just fooling about. It's just unlucky she fell on the gravel.'

'I shouldn't have got so cross,' she says. 'But you know what she's like, Mum, don't you? She looks as though butter wouldn't melt in her mouth. But she can be such a pain in the neck...'

She walks off, pulling her gabardine close around her; though it's raining hard, and I doubt the coat will keep her dry for long.

CHAPTER 27

There are footsteps on the gravel, and a knock at the door. My heart thuds. But it isn't who I thought: it's Captain Richter, his black hair plastered slick against his skull by the rain.

'Excuse me, Mrs de la Mare, but one of us overheard you talking.'

Fear has me by the throat. Have I done something wrong—broken some rule that I didn't even know existed?

His clever dark eyes are on me.

'One of us heard you say that your daughter was hurt.'

His voice is emollient as lanolin: he has seen the fear in my face.

I look at him uncertainly.

'I was a doctor, Mrs de la Mare, in my other life—before…' He opens out his hands, makes a small, rather helpless gesture that seems to encompass everything—the war, the Occupation, all of it. A gesture that says there are no words for these things.

'Oh,' I say.

I try to imagine him as a doctor—no uniform, no gun. It's hard to do.

'Would you like me to examine your daughter?' he says.

I don't say anything.

'I worked as a surgeon, at the Rudolf-Virchow Hospital in Berlin.' He smiles slightly. 'Though I'm sure that surgery won't be necessary…'

When he came here before, he warned me about the curfew. I remember his stern look, the razor-thin line of his mouth. Now he's offering to examine Millie. I'm unnerved, wrong-footed: I don't know how to be with these men.

I hesitate. But then I remember how Millie sobbed in the night.

'It's her leg,' I tell him. 'She fell on the gravel. I'm worried it might be infected. Why don't you come in?'

In that moment, as I invite him into my house, I have a sudden queasy sense of misgiving. As I turn, my passageway looms at me—claustrophobic, oppressive, the shadowy walls pressing in. An urgent voice comes in my head, scolding me, outraged, appalled. *What on earth do you think you are doing? This man is your enemy. You're trusting him with your daughter, but he isn't on your side…* But I can't go back now.

Millie is on the living-room sofa, her sore knee propped on a cushion. She looks up as we go in; in spite of the pain, her face is bright with curiosity.

He kneels on the floor beside her.

'Millie, my name is Max. I am a doctor,' he says.

She gestures extravagantly at her knee, enjoying being a patient, enjoying the drama of this.

'It hurts,' she says.

He examines her, touching the skin around the gash, bending her knee. She flinches away from his touch. A splinter of doubt swims in her eye when he hurts her, and I have an urge to rush forward and pull her away.

'So how did you cut yourself, Millie?' he says.

'It was Blanche. She chased me,' she says.

'My daughter also likes chasing and running,' he says. 'And teasing her big brother...'

He must have seen everything that happened from the windows of Les Vinaires. I feel a little surge of hostility towards him.

But Millie is at once intrigued.

'How old is she? Does she fall over?' she says.

'She is six. And, yes, she does fall over.' His voice softens, talking about his daughter. 'She is always running and rushing. She cannot be still...'

He stands up, turns to me.

'The cut is infected, as you thought,' he tells me. 'She needs medicine.' He takes a brown glass bottle out of his pocket. 'These are called sulphonamides. They will help her fight the infection. Are you willing for me to treat her?'

I nod.

'Millie, can you swallow pills?' he asks her.

'Of course I can. I'm four and a half,' she tells him.

He hands me the bottle, explains how she should take them. He says goodbye to Millie. Above us, I can hear Evelyn creaking around in her room; I'm praying she won't come down just yet. I take him out to the door.

I think about him being a surgeon; and somehow that makes sense to me. A surgeon would need to be rather distant and dispassionate—and I'm aware of a kind of remoteness in this gloomy, cynical man. He's an observer, someone who watches from the margins—separate, withdrawn, but seeing everything.

'Do you miss your work in Berlin?' I ask him. Feeling a sense of social obligation—a need to be polite, now I am indebted to him.

'I miss it very much.' His expression darkens; his face has a hollowed-out look. 'But many people are missing things in these troubled times, as we know. The ones who make the decisions have other plans for our lives. As always.'

I'm startled. Should he be saying this, to me? Is he criticising Hitler? What do these men, these soldiers, really think about the war?

'It is like that for all of us,' he says. 'None of us can be where we would want to be…' Then he shrugs slightly, backing off from that moment of revelation, as though he's a little embarrassed that he has given something away. 'But in the circumstances, we consider ourselves fortunate to be here, on your beautiful island,' he tells me. 'We are, all of us, grateful… Though I imagine you view our presence here rather differently.' He has a clever, self-deprecating smile.

'Thank you so much for your help,' I say.

I open the door, glance nervously up the lane, to be sure that no one can see him coming out of my house. He turns and leaves me, stepping fastidiously between the puddles in the gravel. The rain has stopped now; the dark fallen leaves are shiny as leather with wet.

I wonder who told him that Millie was hurt, who it was heard us talking. Was Captain Lehmann watching our house? Did Captain Lehmann send him?

Evelyn comes to find me in the kitchen. She's frowning.

'One of them came here, didn't he? One of the Hun. I heard him.'

'Don't worry, Evelyn. Everything's all right,' I say soothingly.

'Why did he come here, Vivienne?'

There's an air of agitation about her. She makes little

fluttery gestures: you can see the fine bones in the backs of her hands, like harp strings.

'He's a doctor,' I tell her. 'He came to have a look at Millie's knee.'

'You shouldn't let them in here, Vivienne,' she says.

'Evelyn—he was only trying to help.'

'Well, maybe that's what he told you... You can't trust the Hun,' she tells me. 'The Hun is full of deceit.'

'He offered to examine Millie. He was kind,' I say.

I decide it's better not to tell her about the pills he gave us.

She shakes her head.

'The Hun is always slippery. We don't want the Hun in our house,' she says.

She goes through to the living room, takes her knitting out of her basket. I fetch a blanket for her legs. She's so frail. She feels the cold all year.

Through the window, I see that the weather is clearing rapidly: the seam of the sky is split apart and bright blue light pours through. More leaves have been torn from the trees in the storm: the world looks different—opened up.

Evelyn is still upset.

'You shouldn't have let him in, Vivienne.'

'Well, it's done now,' I tell her. 'And you really don't need to worry. I can't imagine why it would ever happen again.'

I pick all the fruit on my land. The apples I store on cardboard trays in the shed, and I bottle up the plums from the plum tree in my garden, but the Comice pears from my yard we eat at once—they won't keep. Millie refuses to eat the skins, and I peel and slice the fruit for her: the grainy flesh is oozing with syrupy, viscous juice.

The wind is blowing from the north, and birds come in on the wind, making their way to the warmer lands where they will pass the winter. Our island lies on one of the main migration routes in Europe, a route that leads south down the western fringe of the land. At night you can hear the fluting calls of waders in the darkness, and sometimes the crying of geese, like lost souls, harsh and desolate.

A day comes when a sudden storm blows in from the sea. I'm cycling home from Elm Tree Farm when cloud masses and boils above me. There's a sound like many people running in the lane, and a rustle along the hedgebanks, and then the rain streaks down. I'm instantly drenched—I've left my raincoat behind. I curse the unpredictable weather of these islands, feeling that crossness familiar to every housewife— when you've left your washing on the line and now you're far from home, and all your hard work will be wasted.

My bicycle slows, and grinds on the ground. I can tell my

front tyre has gone flat. I get off, swearing under my breath. It'll take me an age to walk back, and Millie and Evelyn are on their own, and I don't like to leave them for long. I push my bicycle down the road, start out on the lengthy walk home. A German truck passes me, driving straight through a puddle, so water plumes up and splashes me—all over my face and my front. This feels malicious, deliberate. My dress and cardigan are sodden, and water seeps into my shoes. I feel so tired, suddenly—exhausted, dragged down by it all: by Evelyn, querulous, losing her mind; by Blanche, still angry with me because we didn't go on the boat; by the Occupation, the shortages, and all the rain-soaked washing on my line—these things muddled up in my head, all utterly beyond me.

Another vehicle approaches. *Damn*. I turn my face away as it passes, not wanting to get splashed all over again.

I hear the car stop, then reverse. I glance up. A familiar black Bentley, gliding back towards me. Captain Lehmann is driving. He stops the car beside me, and leans across to the passenger side and winds the window down. My heart slams around like a tennis ball in my chest.

'Mrs de la Mare. May I give you a lift?'

I can't imagine how messy I look. My hair is plastered to my head and across my face, in rats' tails. Water runs along my parting and drips down onto my nose. I push the wet hair out of my face. I try to shake my head, but I can't quite manage it.

'You have a puncture, I think,' he says. 'So why not let me help you?'

'I can't do that.' But my voice doesn't sound very sure.

'Why can't you do that?' he says.

I don't want to think why he's being so insistent, when of course he knows my answer perfectly well.

'I really don't think I should,' I say. 'You know, with the war. With the Occupation and everything.'

He doesn't say anything. He watches me, as I hesitate. I feel he will wait for ever.

'Anyway—my bicycle...'

'You could leave it here,' he tells me. 'I can send one of the boys to pick it up.'

'But you must be busy, you must have things to do...'

Though as always I'm baffled imagining what those things might be.

I see a slight smile in his eyes when I say that: as though he knows I am conceding something.

'Nothing that can't wait,' he says.

'And you weren't going that way...'

'I can easily drive to your house,' he says.

'I really shouldn't...'

He reaches across the passenger seat and pushes open the door.

I find myself padlocking my bicycle to a tree. I take my handbag out of the bicycle basket, and climb into the Bentley that used to belong to Les Brehauts. I ought to be angry, that Mr Goubert's car was requisitioned, I ought to say no to this lift; but I feel so tired and cold and wet, and it's such a long way home.

Captain Lehmann is looking at me—at my dripping hair, the goose-pimpled flesh on my arms, my wet clothes sticking clammily to me.

'Mrs de la Mare. You are shivering. You should borrow my coat.'

'I can't do that,' I say.

'I think you should. You don't want to get pneumonia. Especially when you have people who depend on you,' he says.

That, at least, is true enough.

When I don't say anything, don't protest, he reaches round to the seat behind him. He takes his coat and wraps it round my shoulders, pushing it down between my body and the back of the seat. His nearness shocks me. He slides his hand under my hair in the nape of my neck, easing out my hair where it's been caught under the coat collar. He does this scrupulously—not missing a single strand, but scarcely touching my neck, just grazing me with his fingertip. His skin is warm against me. I can hear his breathing; I'm sure that he can hear mine. Neither of us says anything.

He starts up the car again. The coat is long, it rucks up at the small of my back. But it's warm and close on my shoulders.

'This is kind of you,' I tell him. As formally, politely, as I can. My voice has too much breath in it.

He shakes his head slightly, as though denying that this is kindness at all.

'How is Millie?' he says.

'She's fine now. Thank you for asking…'

'Max came to see her?'

'Yes.'

'I thought that Max would be able to help her,' he says.

'Yes. Thank you.'

The thought ripples in me that he wants me to know this: he wants to tell me that he was the one who sent Max. He knows that nothing would draw me to him like his concern for my child. This thought makes me feel happy, in a way that I don't want to look at.

I turn from him, stare out of the window. It's a long time since I saw Guernsey from the inside of a car. The storm is passing over, the world filling up with colour: the drenched grass a startling feverish green beneath the white of the sky, wet rowan berries shiny as a woman's lipsticked mouth. The windows steam up with our breathing, so the countryside blurs, its colours running together, as though this land is insubstantial, about to dissolve. He winds his window down a little, so the cool air will clear the window-glass.

He is silent for a while. The scrape of the windscreen wipers fills in the silence between us. The damp brings out the smells of things—the wet wool of my cardigan, the musk of my wet hair. I turn slightly towards him, watch his heavy, solid body, the way his hands move on the steering wheel. I remember the feel of his fingertip on the back of my neck—warm, terrifying. He's driving very slowly.

'So—the chocolate,' he says. As though he is continuing a conversation we've had. 'Did you eat it yourself or did you give it all to your children?'

'I ate some of it,' I tell him.

'And did you like it?' he says.

I remember the melting sweetness of it—the portion I kept for myself.

'Yes. It was delicious…'

'Even though you were so reluctant to take it?' he says.

I don't look at him, but I hear the smile in his voice.

'I didn't say no because I thought I wouldn't enjoy it,' I say.

The words hang there between us.

The wind is tearing the clouds apart. Light pours over the land, everything lit up, sparkly. He wipes the mist from the inside of his window with his sleeve. The colours of the countryside dazzle—the copper and bronze of the turning leaves; a field of tawny dandelions, leggy as girls. We pass a fabulous vine that tumbles over a wall, its leaves all the colours of flame, but soft.

'This landscape is like a watercolour,' he says. 'I would like to paint this landscape.'

I'm immediately intrigued.

'You're an artist?'

'I wouldn't presume to call myself that,' he says. 'But I like to paint when I can. Just for my own pleasure.' He hesitates for a moment—as though searching for the right words to express what he feels. 'I find it good to leave my daily life behind for a while...'

I recognise that impulse—when you crave a safe place, a haven. Like me with my piano and my poetry books. But it isn't quite what you'd expect a soldier to say.

'Art is not my profession,' he says. And then, when I don't ask, 'I was an architect, before the war.'

I'm surprised, as I was when Captain Richter told me he was a doctor. I never think about these men having other careers. I try—and fail—to conjure up an intelligent question to ask.

The sky is clearing rapidly now. Ahead of us, against the blue splendour, there's a great bank of dark cloud that looks completely solid—like a far country, like the rounded storybook hills in the tales I read to Millie. He doesn't say anything more, but it doesn't seem to matter. I feel so happy, here in the car, in his coat—feel a rash, impulsive happiness, which rushes through me, floods me. I can't control it or deny it or push it away.

At the bend in the lane, by the cattle-trough, there's a dark shape under the hedge—a woman in a headscarf, walking her dog. I recognise Clemmie Renouf, who I know a little from church. She's looking straight at the car; her keen gaze seems to seek me out. I feel a judder of fear. I tell myself she can't possibly see, through the blur of wet on the glass. But I wish this hadn't happened.

We're nearly at Le Colombier now.

'I could drop you at your door. But if you prefer I could leave you round the corner,' he says.

'Yes. That would be better really.'

He stops the car some way from my gate.

'If you give me the key to your padlock, I can send Hans Schmidt to pick up your bicycle,' he says.

I take the key from my pocket and drop it into his hand, careful not to touch him.

'Thank you for the lift,' I say.

'My pleasure, Mrs de la Mare.'

I take off the coat and fold it and put it down on the seat. I'm so lonely, so cold, without it. I open the door of the car; I have my back towards him.

'My name is Vivienne,' I tell him.

'Vivienne.' He repeats my name gravely, carefully, as if he might damage it if he spoke it too roughly. 'Thank you.' As though I have given him something.

I step out of the car. The world is bright and beautiful, a spidery water-dazzle all over the lane, water drops spilling from all the trees as innumerable as petals. But the wet air chills me. All I want is to be back in the warmth of the car with him again.

That night I dream about him. In the dream he's holding me close—just holding me, no kiss, no sexual touch, just his body pressed entirely against me, wrapped so close around mine, as you might hold someone you loved after a long separation. In the dream, this is the most natural thing—how things are meant to be. But when I wake the dream appals me.

CHAPTER 29

'I've been sorting out some of Frank's things,' says Angie.

There's a pile of books on her kitchen table. *Mr Middleton Talks About Gardening*; *Three Men in a Boat*; a book of Guernsey tales.

'These were all Frank's,' she tells me. 'They're no use to me now, Vivienne. I'm not like you or him. I've never been one for book-learning, like I told you. So I thought I'd give them away, to people who'd put them to use...'

She hands me the book of Guernsey folktales.

'I know how your Millie loves her stories,' she says. 'And I thought she might like this book.'

It has a calfskin binding. I open it; and the pages release an old-book smell, a scent of dust and mould. I flick through. The typeface is old-fashioned, decorative, the initial letter of each tale wrapped round with trailing leaves. A pressed flower serves as a bookmark; though it's paper-pale and dried-out, I know from the shape that it's restharrow, a creeping plant with pink petals that grows everywhere on the island, on any verge or clifftop or patch of unmown ground. I've always liked its name—that idea that its loveliness makes the harvesters stop in their tracks.

'Thank you. Millie will love these stories. Both of us will,' I tell her.

She has made a kind of coffee by infusing roasted parsnips. It's rather bitter, but drinkable—as long as you put the memory of real coffee out of your mind. We sit and drink quietly at her kitchen table.

She still has a white, frayed look. When I ask her how she's keeping, she smiles a small rueful smile.

'Not so bad, Vivienne. Mustn't complain,' she tells me.

'If there's anything I can do…' I say.

Angie as always is practical.

'Well, you could help me shuck some peas, Vivienne, while you're here,' she says.

She takes peapods from her vegetable rack and dumps them on the table. She puts out two bowls, and I pull a heap of pods towards me. For a while there's just the snap of the pods, and the neat, percussive sound of peas falling into the bowls, and through her open door the scratch and bustle of chickens and the whisper of the countryside. A dark lacquer of sadness seems to spread across the room.

After a while, she clears her throat, but she doesn't look in my direction.

'You know, Vivienne, I hated Frank sometimes,' she says. Very matter-of-fact, almost as though she's replying to a question I've asked. 'The thing is, in the drink, he couldn't keep his hands to himself. Did you know that, Vivienne?'

I'm a little shocked that she's talking about this in such an open way.

'I'd wondered sometimes,' I tell her, carefully.

'Well, you're very sensitive, Vivienne, you do notice things,' she says. 'You notice what people are feeling… So when he was in the drink, I had to watch my P's and Q's. I had to sit there just like a good little girl, or he would give me a beating... But now he's gone I miss him to distraction. Love's a strange beast,' she tells me, shelling the peas.

'Yes, it is,' I say.

'He could be two people. Two different people. That's odd, isn't it, Vivienne? And one of those people was like a stranger to me... Sometimes I think, Did I really know him at all?'

I think of that terrible moment when I looked into Eugene's dressing-room—the moment when I saw him with Monica Charles. I think of the sickness, the insect-creep of that knowledge on my skin: seeing my marriage wasn't at all as I'd believed it to be. The parsnip coffee has left a bitter, burnt taste in my mouth.

'I know what you mean—how you could feel that,' I say. 'How you could wonder how well you knew someone...'

Outside, the leaves of the elder tree rustle. They're drying out with autumn; they have a harsh, sibilant sound.

'He was a good man really, in spite of it all,' she tells me. Speaking slowly, exactly—choosing her words. 'A very hard worker, which is what you need in a man. And I miss having a man around the place—well, that's the natural order of things, isn't it? To have a man about the house. I used to hate him sometimes and now I miss him something cruel... What I've learned, Vivienne—you should always be grateful for every gift life gives you.' She splits open a pod with a crisp little snap. 'Cherish what you have,' she says, as the peas rattle into the bowl.

I walk back to Le Colombier, feeling a tug of sadness because of the way she has changed. She's so quiet now, so reflective. But when Frank was alive she'd always be talking, talking. She'd be full of news and gossip: she knew so many old tales, and she loved to describe the superstitions old people still believe in. The scrape of the undertow on the shingle, when heard inland, presages rain. Whistling on board ship calls up a wind and so is seen as unlucky—for you may get a greater wind than you want. Births happen more readily with the flowing tide, and deaths with the ebb—for life comes in with the flood, and goes out with the fall of the water.

She especially loved to tell about the Guernsey witches, who long ago met at Le Catiorac, a headland out to the west. There's a dolmen there—a prehistoric tomb. The witches would dance there naked, as witches do, she'd say; and they'd curse the monks who lived across the water on Lihou Island—Guernsey's holy island, just off the western shore. It was rather a startling picture: the ferocious naked women, cursing and railing into the wind—for there's always a wild whistling wind on the headland, at Le Catiorac. I took the girls there for picnics sometimes, before the Occupation, when Millie was only three, and Blanche thirteen. The dolmen fascinates children. There's a shadowed space under the stones and nothing grows in their shade—it's like a cave, a child would scarcely need to crouch down to enter there. Though I used to prefer the girls not to go in under the stones: I don't really believe in the malevolent power of witches' curses, but there's a feeling about the place that's not entirely benign, in spite of the prettiness of the flowers that grow there—cranesbill, and blue flax flowers, and pink columbines in summer. Sometimes at low tide we'd cross the causeway to Lihou Island. There are no monks there now, no one lives there: it's rather a bleak place—black rocks, grey water, black seaweed on pale sand. The girls would dart off, poking around in the rock pools, and on the way back I'd always be telling them to hurry—the tide comes in so rapidly, you could easily be cut off. There was always an urgency to those walks: always that fear at the back of your mind, that the water might overtake you.

CHAPTER 30

Evelyn calls out to me from the living room.

'Vivienne? Is that you, Vivienne?'

She's in her armchair, with her knitting. I go to her.

She gives me a stern look.

'Clemmie Renouf dropped by when you were out,' she says. 'She brought the parish magazine.'

'Did she?' I say, everything sinking in me.

'Clemmie Renouf told me something I didn't want to hear.'

My heart pounds.

'She saw you in a car, with the Hun. She said it was definitely you.'

I briefly wonder if I should deny it. But how can I?

'It was one of the German officers from Les Vinaires,' I tell her. 'He saw I had a puncture. He gave me a lift.'

'Clemmie Renouf said you were smiling,' says Evelyn.

'Evelyn. That isn't a crime,' I tell her. 'The man gave me a lift. It was raining. I'd only just left Gwen's place—it's an awfully long walk back. I needed to get home to you and Millie…'

'A great big smile,' she says.

'He wanted to help. It's just a question of human decency,' I say.

'Yes, it is,' she says. 'A question of decency.' Speaking slowly, freighting the words with significance. 'And Clemmie said another thing. She said you were wearing his coat. His *army* coat. Tell me it isn't true, Vivienne.'

Oh God.

'Clemmie can't have seen properly,' I tell her. 'Like I said, it was pouring with rain. The windows were all misted up.'

But I feel terrible that I'm lying to her.

Evelyn pulls her back very straight. Her eyebrows, thinly pencilled in, are lowered in a frown.

'You were letting the side down, Vivienne. Eugene wouldn't stand for it.'

'We live together,' I tell her. 'It's such a little island. We have to find a way of getting along.'

She shakes her head.

'He wouldn't let it happen. Eugene always knows what's right...' Her voice trails off. Her gaze flickers suddenly round the room. Doubt creeps into her voice. 'Vivienne—where's Eugene?'

'Evelyn—Eugene's off fighting, remember?' I say gently.

Her face has that opaque look, like a pane of glass misted over. A question gathers between her eyes, in a delicate sketching of lines.

'Is he, Vivienne?'

'Yes. Look...'

There's a framed photograph of Eugene on the mantelpiece. I took it with my Kodak camera, just before he left. He's in uniform, and staring straight at the lens, and there's a seriousness about him—a recognition that this is a solemn moment. Though I don't know if he really felt that—I'm no longer sure that I ever knew what he felt. Perhaps even in this moment he was acting—projecting an appropriate solemnity, playing the part of the resolute soldier going off to war.

'Here he is—just before he went off with the army,' I say.

'Oh, Vivienne. He looks very smart,' she says.

'Yes, doesn't he?'

'When did this happen?'

'It happened last autumn,' I tell her. 'Just before the outbreak of war.'

'Oh. Oh. Did it? You know, Vivienne, sometimes I don't remember things very well… So Eugene's gone to war, you say?'

'Yes. We're all very proud of him…'

'He's *gone*, Vivienne?'

Panic flares in her voice. Suddenly she starts crying. Her tears arise so suddenly—a minute ago she was angry, and now the tears come. It's as though her emotions are all too close to the surface—her feelings raw, like broken skin, so the slightest touch can hurt her. The tears make glistening snail-tracks in the powder on her face. This is so terrible for her—that she keeps forgetting he's gone, and then has to learn the pain of it all over again.

I wipe her face, as you would with a child. She slumps in her chair: she looks small and lost. I put my arm around her.

'Everything's all right. Don't cry.'

All the anger has left her—she's spent, wrung-out, now. I feel so guilty that I upset her and made her cry. I feel so guilty about everything.

CHAPTER 31

I'm working at the bottom of my garden, in the part of our land that leads off round the back of Les Vinaires. There's a low hedge between our gardens here, and a little gate in the hedge. I'm digging up part of the lawn to make a vegetable patch. It's hard work. Millie was with me to start with—digging with a kitchen spoon, collecting worms in a jar—but now she's gone off to play in the house. She's left the jam jar on its side, and the captured worms have found their way out and are secretly gliding away. The sun is warm on my skin: in this sheltered corner, summer seems to linger. There are still a few flowers blooming— an autumn-flowering clematis in my hedge; dahlias, dusty pink, drooping their soft heavy heads; a few of my Belle de Crécy roses, peeling back their silks, and smelling so sweet they leave an ache in you. Bees fumble in and out of the throats of the flowers.

I've stopped for a moment, breathing heavily, resting my weight on my spade, when a shadow falls across me. I jump.

'Vivienne.'

I turn.

Captain Lehmann is there. He's come in through the gate

in the hedge. I notice how my name sounds different in his mouth—foreign, almost glamorous.

'You startled me,' I tell him.

'Yes. I saw that. I'm sorry,' he says.

He's always apologising to me.

Today he has a purposeful look—the air of someone who is about to go and do something important. He looks entirely wrong in my garden: he has the random, displaced quality of someone met in a dream. His presence here makes the whole day feel a little unreal: dreamlike.

'You have a beautiful garden,' he says.

'Thank you.'

I brush the earth from my hands. I'm wearing a baggy old jersey of Eugene's that's rather hot for the day. I can feel the sweat on me—under my arms, on my face. I tuck an unruly damp tendril of hair behind an ear. I feel messy and dishevelled—he's immaculate, cool, remote from me.

'This flower is beautiful,' he says. He gestures towards the clematis that is growing up through my hedge. The flowers are a rich cream colour, the stamens red as garnets. He reaches out, touches a petal; I watch his finger moving across the open, vivid bloom. There's a slight catch in my breath: I wonder if he hears it.

'You like gardens?' I say. 'You have a garden at home?'

He shakes his head.

'We have no garden, in Berlin. We have only a balcony. My wife has some pot plants there, and a bird in a cage.'

An entire little picture is conjured up by his words. I think: This is what he was seeing in his mind's eye, when I glimpsed him reading a letter through the window in the evening—his wife, the balcony, the bird in the cage.

'It sounds very nice,' I say. Polite: helpless.

He shrugs slightly. His eyes are on me, his gaze grey as woodsmoke, requiring something of me.

'I would prefer to have a garden,' he says.

I feel my face burn. The smell of my roses licks at us like the tongue of an animal.

You can't see this part of the garden from Evelyn's bedroom, or the living room. But I feel intensely uneasy—thinking how appalled she'd be if she glimpsed us standing here, when she's already so suspicious of me. Wondering if she could possibly see us—if anyone can see us. I turn my back towards my house, as though that makes me safer: like an infant who hides her face in her hands and believes she can't be seen.

'Have you always enjoyed this—to grow things?' he says.

'Yes. Even when I was a child.' I clutch at the lifeline of something that feels safe to talk about. 'Just the fancy stuff—not vegetables. I used to spend my pocket money on packets of flower seeds...'

'When you were a child...' he says. He smiles, as though the thought pleases him.

'I loved the drawings on the packets,' I tell him. 'I remember buying Love-in-a-Mist because I liked the name and the picture.'

The minute I've said it, I'm so embarrassed, because of the name of the flower. But he has a perplexed look—not understanding the words.

'There's a plant that we call Love-in-a-Mist,' I tell him.

Talking about it, I remember it suddenly, with such clarity. Standing in front of the rack of seeds in the ironmonger's off Clapham Common, choosing the packet with its enticing blur of blue-petalled flowers.

'But they never came up like they promised,' I say. 'I'd have such high hopes, then I'd just get a few ragged plants that didn't ever flower… I've learned to grow flowers since then, of course.' The words tumbling out of me: I can't stop. I feel drunk, light-headed, and there's an unpleasant cold trickle of sweat down my back. 'But I'm going to have to change, of course—I'm going to have to dig half of them up and plant something we can eat. I should have started already, probably. But it's difficult—I really love my flowers…'

'Yes, I can see that,' he says.

'The thing is—I'm not very practical,' I tell him. 'It would be useful now, with the shortages and everything, if only I was more practical, if I was a different kind of person. I suppose I wasn't really designed for such times…'

He smiles slightly, but I see a kind of sadness in his eyes.

'There are very few of us, Vivienne, who were designed for such times.'

He's silent for a moment. I hunt desperately in my mind for something else to say, but after my outburst there's nothing left in my head. I feel as if I am underwater—it's the damp on my skin, the watery surge of the wind in the trees in the hedge: the way I can't breathe.

I hear the slight click as he clears his throat.

'There was something I wanted to ask of you, Vivienne. A favour.'

There's a different tone in his voice; he's hesitant, unsure. Hearing this, I feel my mouth dry up.

'You may remember I told you I like to draw,' he says. 'I wanted to ask if you would sit for me.'

I think—That was why he seemed so purposeful, coming in through my garden gate. *I* was his purpose. I don't say anything.

'I'm sorry, I shouldn't have asked,' he says.

He's retreating rapidly. I can tell he is a proud man.

'No, no, it's not that,' I say.

'It was wrong of me.'

'I didn't mind you asking. Really.'

He takes a step away from me, everything in him withdrawing.

'Good afternoon, then, Vivienne,' he says.

He's distant and formal again. He turns to go back through the gate.

I swallow hard.

'It would have to be…' My throat feels thick. My voice is very quiet.

He turns quickly back towards me.

I'm not looking at him. I'm studying my hands, the staining in the lines of my palms, the black crescents of earth in my nails.

I try again.

'It would have to be when Millie and Blanche are asleep. It would have to be late. Maybe ten o'clock?'

I can feel his eyes on me, can feel the warmth of his gaze.

'Thank you,' he says.

I don't dare look up as he leaves me.

CHAPTER 32

I hear the softest knock at my door. I let him in.

'Vivienne.' He says my name rather slowly, as though he doesn't want to let go of it. Around us is the gentle quiet of the slumbering house, where everyone else is sleeping.

I take him through to the living room. He looks around, and I suddenly see the familiar room through his eyes. For a while now, only women have lived here: and I see how feminine it is—all the lily-of-the-valley chintz, the tasselled tie-backs, the dahlias in a white jug. Everything draped and flowery. He seems too solid, too male, for this place.

He has a drawing pad and pencils in a leather case, and a bottle of brandy, which he holds out to me. It has a French label. It looks expensive.

'This is to say thank you,' he says.

It seems an age ago that I tried to refuse his gift of chocolate.

I take two brandy glasses from the china cabinet—the only ones that weren't smashed on the day we nearly went on the boat. I put them on the piano. He pours the brandy. As he hands me my drink, he touches his glass to mine; the bright, assertive chink of glass is loud in the silence between us. I gulp at the brandy, and feel it warming me through, feel my edges soften.

He's looking at my bookshelves.

'You have many books,' he says.

'Yes.'

'So who do the books belong to? Are they yours or your husband's?' he says.

'Mostly mine. Eugene didn't much like reading.' I've used the past tense—I'm not sure why I did that. I wonder if he will notice. 'I brought most of them from London.'

'Could you lend me a book, perhaps?' he asks me. 'To help me practise my English?'

It's one of those moments, again—wondering where I should draw the line. But I can't refuse him this, when I invited him in—to draw me, to drink brandy.

'Which one would you like?' I ask him.

'Which is the best book here?' he says.

I smile.

'That's an impossible question,' I say.

He waits.

My gaze moves over my shelves. I take down one of my favourite books—a volume of poems by Gerard Manley Hopkins. Then reflect that this wasn't at all a sensible choice for someone who isn't a native English speaker—the language the poet uses is rather eccentric and strange.

The book falls open where there's a ribbon bookmark—at a place where I have so often opened it before.

'May I?' he says.

I hand it to him.

'You can correct me,' he tells me, 'if I read it wrong.'

He starts to read, quietly, carefully, stumbling slightly over the words.

'"I have desired to go
Where springs not fail,

To fields where flies no sharp and sided hail
And a few lilies blow…"'

He pauses, looks up at me.

'*Sided*? Is that a real word?' he asks me.

He has that rather affronted look, which always makes me smile.

'Kind of. But it's an odd way to use it,' I tell him. I feel stupid that I chose such an inappropriate poem. 'Maybe that wasn't a very good choice. He's quite a difficult poet…'

'No, Vivienne, it was a very good choice,' he tells me.

He turns back to the page.

'"And I have asked to be
Where no storms come
Where the green swell is in the havens dumb
And out of the swing of the sea…"'

The silence after he's spoken seems to hold onto the words, as you might hold water between your hands: just for an instant, a precious moment, before it all leaks away.

'Did I read it right?' he asks me then.

'Yes. Yes, you did.'

But his reading has brought a kind of yearning sadness to the room, a desolate feeling. I don't know where this comes from.

'I like that poem. That is a beautiful poem,' he says.

'That was always my favourite,' I tell him, trying to push away the sadness, my voice bland, ordinary. 'We studied it at school.'

'How old were you when you read this poet at school? Fourteen, fifteen?'

'Yes. Something like that.'

He smiles, as though the thought pleases him.

'What were you like, at fourteen?' he says.

I don't know how to answer.

'Like everyone else, I suppose…' Then feel he deserves something better than this—more precise. Because I remember exactly what I was like—I hated being fourteen. 'Well, no. That's wrong. *Not* like everyone… I was always being told off, for looking out of the window in a dream. For not concentrating. And I was horribly shy, a bit clumsy, all elbows and knees…'

His eyes rest on me—warm, interested.

'I used to envy the other girls. The shiny ones. The ones who seemed poised and perfect,' I say. 'There are always those girls—you know, the ones whose stocking seams were always straight, whose hair was perfectly waved.'

'Yes. There are always those girls,' he says, shrugging a little. As though he knows exactly what I mean about the shiny girls. As though they don't really interest him. I feel a sudden light happiness, which I know I shouldn't feel.

'You can borrow the book if you want,' I say. 'So you can practise your English.'

'Thank you. Thank you very much.'

He rifles through the pages, flicks back to the title page. I see him look at the place where I have written my name. *Vivienne Mary Collier*: then *Collier* crossed out, and *de la Mare* written in. He runs his finger across the writing, as though he expects it to have a different texture from the rest of the page. As though he thinks he will learn from it—from the feel of my name on his skin.

He puts the book in the pocket of his jacket.

'Thank you, Vivienne,' he says again.

I feel all the intensity in his gaze. I turn from him.

'Where do you want me to sit?' I ask, keeping my voice light, casual.

He gestures towards the sofa. I seat myself, suddenly self-conscious, pulling down my skirt, and awkwardly arranging and rearranging my legs. He sits opposite me on a chair. He takes out a pencil and rests the drawing-pad on his knee.

'Where should I look?' I ask him.

'If you could turn a little to your left…' he says.

I turn.

'Like this?'

'Yes. That's perfect. So the lamplight will fall on your face.'

To start with he's mostly looking at me, just now and then marking the paper. He holds up his pencil, squints, works out the proportions of my face. It's disconcerting to be looked at so intently: I'm glad I'm not quite facing him, that I don't have to look in his eyes.

'So—exactly how still do I have to be? Am I allowed to talk?' I ask.

He smiles slightly.

'Yes. For the moment,' he says.

But then I can't think what to say, can't think of anything intelligent.

'Have you always liked to draw?' I ask.

The question is too obvious; it makes me sound stilted, naive. But he answers it very seriously.

'Not always. I drew all the time as a child, but then of course life intervened, as it has a habit of doing. I began again a few years ago, when I reached forty. I longed to have some time that was just my own. I thought—If I don't do this now, I never will.'

He must be in his mid-forties now. I feel how old we are, both of us: how much we have seen.

'Getting older is strange,' I say. 'It isn't at all how you think it's going to be...'

He looks at me quizzically.

I'm not sure quite why I said that. I try to explain.

'I'll soon be forty myself,' I tell him. 'Yet sometimes I feel as if I'm still waiting for my life to begin...' I'm speaking slowly, working out exactly what I mean. 'I spend so much time waiting. Waiting for Millie to start at school, so I'll have a bit more spare time. Waiting for Eugene to come back home...' I hesitate—wondering if I mentioned Eugene because I felt I *should*: not sure if I feel that, if I miss him. 'Waiting for the war to be over... But life doesn't wait— it trickles between your fingers, trickles away... Does that sound stupid? I'm sure it sounds stupid...'

'No, it doesn't,' he says.

'Do you ever feel that? Well, no, you wouldn't, of course. Men's lives aren't like that, are they?'

'Maybe not,' he says.

'Sometimes I've envied that—the way men's lives are more about doing than waiting. Sometimes I feel as though the real things are passing me by. As though I've been pushed to the margins of life... Sometimes I've even envied Eugene—going off to fight.'

'Maybe war isn't quite as you imagine,' he tells me. 'Much of war is waiting. Much of it is feeling life trickling away...' He has a slight crooked smile. 'Though it has its better moments...'

He looks up at me; he's stopped drawing, the pencil poised over the page.

'Vivienne. I'm drawing your mouth now, so you will have

to be quiet,' he says. He looks down at the paper again, marks it. 'I'm just tracing in your upper lip now.'

I'm suddenly very aware of my mouth. My face is hot. There's a new little pulse at the side of my mouth, which I didn't know was there. I wonder if he can see it.

He stares at my mouth and draws in silence. I'm aware of the tiniest sounds in the room, a moth that beats at the lampshade, a log that sparks in the grate: they seem crystal-clear and dangerous to me.

At last he puts his pencil down.

'You can look at it now,' he tells me.

I get up, go to him. He stands, puts the drawing down on the piano for me to see. I sense a slight nervousness in him—that he cares what I will think.

'It's rough, it's just a sketch,' he says.

But I see he is being self-deprecating. It isn't rough: it's all there, very precise. I can tell he sees me clearly—the mole on my chin, the frown-lines coming in my forehead, my way-ward hair that escapes from the hair-grips and curls around my face. As though he sees me as I am. In the drawing, my mouth looks big and I know that's true, though I don't like it: I envy women with neat small mouths that look like little buds. I think maybe I have been wrong about him—maybe he doesn't really admire me at all. I would have welcomed a little flattery.

'It's very accurate,' I say.

'Some of it, perhaps,' he says. 'But I haven't drawn this part quite correctly.' He touches the paper with one finger, traces out the line of my cheek on the page. 'I tried, but I couldn't capture it. This part of your face is very lovely. This curve.'

He takes his hand from the paper. He reaches out to my

face and moves his finger very slowly along the curve of my cheek. His touch takes all words from me. We stand like that for a moment, his finger on my skin. His heat goes right through me.

He lowers his hand, steps back from me. I can't bear him moving away like that, can't bear the distance between us.

'Can I keep the picture?' I ask him. Wanting to hold onto something of the evening, something of him. My voice seems to come from far away.

He's surprised: pleased.

'Yes, of course. Yes.'

He hands it to me.

'I ought to go,' he says. 'Thank you.'

'Your brandy?' I pick up the bottle.

'Keep it. It's for you,' he says. 'But may I come and drink it with you again?'

'Yes… The day after tomorrow—you could come then…'

He gives a little sigh when I say that, as though something is settled. Yet the words mean nothing—it was all decided when he touched me.

Afterwards I hide the brandy at the back of the cupboard, where nobody will see it, and I tuck the drawing away in one of my poetry books. I can still feel the place where he moved his finger over my face, as though my skin has come alive.

CHAPTER 33

I take out the book that Angie gave me.

'This is a present from Mrs le Brocq,' I tell Millie.

She presses up against me on the sofa. Her hair needs washing: I breathe in its sweet, complex scent.

'Well, read me a story, then, Mummy,' she says.

I open the book.

She frowns.

'There aren't any pictures,' she says.

'No. We'll just have to imagine them…'

The sprig of restharrow is still held between the pages. Millie takes it and holds it lightly between her finger and thumb.

I turn to the first story.

'"There was once a man from Guernsey who took the boat to Sark…"'

Millie is immediately pleased. A smile unfurls over her face.

'We've been there, haven't we, Mummy? We've been to Sark,' she says.

I remember how we made the boat trip, one summer day before Eugene left, before the war began. We took lettuce and Marmite sandwiches and home-made lemonade. Sark is a small peaceful island, with no motor-engines, no cars—a place of deep, dreaming lanes between overhanging hedges, of lovingly tended gardens lavish with flowers; and there are great seabird colonies there, on reefs and islets offshore, on L'Etac and Les Autelets. The birds rise in the air like a white smoke, and the noise of them reaches a long way over the sea.

Millie is attentive—proud that the story tells of a place that she knows.

I read on.

"'The man was an excellent marksman, and planned to do some shooting, to put dinner on the table. He sat on the cliffs above Havre Gosselin, and saw a flock of wild duck that flew in a perfect circle, and seemed untroubled by the sound of his gun…'"

Millie has a pensive look.

'D'you think they weren't proper ducks? D'you think it was really magic, Mummy?'

'Yes. I think so.'

She sighs with pleasure, content that this is a tale of the uncanny. She strokes the pressed flower absently over her face.

"'When the man returned to Guernsey, he went to see a white witch—a *sorchier*—for advice…'"

I'm about to explain, but Millie nods, familiar with the word.

"'The *sorchier* told him to shoot at the duck with a special bullet—a bullet of silver, marked with the sign of the Cross. So the man took the boat back to Sark and sat on the cliffs above Havre Gosselin. In the bright, still air beyond the edge of the cliff, the ducks flew in their perfect circle. The man shot his silver bullet, and the bullet hit one of the ducks—just catching its wing, not killing it."

"'On his way back home in the boat, the man noticed a girl among the other islanders—a girl who was pale and shaken, with a terrible wound in her hand…'"

Millie's eyes shine. She knows about the kinds of things that happen in such stories—the dazzling metamorphoses, the things that are not as they seem.

'That was her, wasn't it, Mummy? The girl was the duck he shot at. The girl could do spells and could make herself into a duck…'

'Yes, I think so,' I say.

But I'm only half listening to her. The story stirs me in some way that I couldn't explain or express. I see the scene so vividly—the little boat, grey sea, grey sky, the girl's black, black hair and her white racked face: how she shuddered with pain, and the bright blood dripped from her hand.

I turn the page.

"'The man knew she was the duck he had shot, but he looked at her and said nothing. And for many years afterwards, he kept silent—speaking of what had happened only on the day of his death…'"

Millie is thoughtful.

'He was sorry, wasn't he? He shouldn't have shot her. That's why he didn't tell anyone…'

I think about that moment, when they looked at one another, these two—the girl with her forbidden magic, the man who had wounded her hand. Did she understand then, when he looked at her, that he wouldn't tell, that he would keep their secret?

This moves me, in the story—the complicity between them.

PART III:

OCTOBER 1940 - SEPTEMBER 1941

I take rainwater from the water butt that is meant to be good for your hair. I wash my hair and curl it. When it's dry I shake out the curls; my hair smells fresh, of the countryside, from the rainwater I washed it in. When I've finished the clearing up after tea, I put on my best navy dress. It's made of silk shantung, and the dark gleamy fabric has a prismatic sheen, like oil on water. I look at my face in the mirror of my dressing table. It's a three-way mirror, reflecting into itself, and my many reflections recede from me, all bright-eyed, flushed and scared, as though I contain a multitude of eager, anxious women.

Blanche comes into my bedroom in her pyjamas, to say goodnight.

'You look nice, Mum,' she says. 'You haven't worn that for ages.'

There's a question under her words.

'I just felt like putting on something nicer,' I say.

'That dress is ever so pretty,' she says. 'You could go dancing in that. You don't really look like somebody's mum any more...'

She looks at me wistfully—perhaps a little enviously. Then she turns away from me, running her finger over the music box, the blurry Impressionist picture of two girls at a piano.

'May I?' she says.

'Yes, of course.'

She winds the handle. The music sounds like the chiming of many tiny bells—chill and silvery as ice or glass. Blanche sways slightly, in time. Almost any music will make her start to dance—even *Für Elise* on a music box.

I feel a pang for my daughter. It should be Blanche who's dressing up, not me. It's the special time of her life—she should be going to dances, being courted.

'Blanche. You never went to another of those parties with Celeste.'

'Like the party at Les Brehauts, you mean?'

'Yes. Aren't they happening any more?'

'Oh, yes, I think they still have them,' she says.

'I don't mind if you want to. Really. As long as you're safe. As long as you get a lift home.'

'I'm fine, Mum.'

'But you seemed to enjoy it when you went...'

There's a frown pencilled in on her forehead.

'Well, it was fun at the time,' she says. 'I liked the dancing. But I prayed about it afterwards, and then I decided it wasn't the right thing to do...'

'Oh. Did you, sweetheart?'

It still startles me—this streak of religious fervour in her.

'The thing is—they ask you out, the German boys,' she says. 'But that wouldn't be right, would it, Mum? To have a German boyfriend?'

This surprises me. I didn't know she thought this.

'Well, that depends,' I say vaguely.

'I wouldn't want to do that,' she says. 'And you wouldn't like it either, if I did that.' Her gaze is on me, blue as summer skies. There's such clarity in her.

'Well, obviously there are people who wouldn't approve. But if he seemed a good person...' My voice trails off.

'But you can't tell, can you really?' she says. 'I mean, you can't be sure.'

'What about Celeste?' I ask. 'Is she still going out with Tomas?'

Blanche nods.

'She likes him a lot,' she says. 'I really don't think she should, though.'

'Does she know what you think? About it not being right?'

'Yes, of course, Mum. We talk about everything, me and Celeste. We don't have secrets,' she says. 'But she says I'm wrong, she says he's not like the others...'

'Well—maybe she's right—maybe he *isn't* like the others...'

The music from the music box slows as it comes to an end, and you can hear the clunking and whirring of all the tiny parts inside. Blanche closes down the lid of the box.

'I still wouldn't do it,' she says. 'What I think is—how can you ever really know someone? How can you ever be sure what they're like?'

'But don't you think you can tell—if someone is a good person? Even if they're on the opposite side in a war?'

She gives me a doubtful look, as though I just don't get it.

Once the girls and Evelyn have gone to bed, I sit in the kitchen and wait for him. Shadow heaps up in velvet folds against the walls of my room, and doubt creeps into me.

Blanche's words are in my mind. *How can you ever really know someone?* I see it all so clearly now: that this was a wild, irrational notion—rash, impulsive, all wrong. And as I sit there in the shadow, I make my decision. I shall tell him that he can't come in—that I have changed my mind. Because our relationship is wrong for so many, many reasons. He will understand; or at least, he won't be surprised. Perhaps I should take off my shantung dress, put on something more workaday. Perhaps I should blow out the candles that I have lit upstairs in my room…

I hear his knock. My heart lurches. I go to open the door.

He doesn't quite smile at me. I see at once that he too is nervous, and this touches me: I know I can't tell him to leave. I have already chosen my path: I can't turn back now. *Choose* not to turn back now.

'Vivienne…'

I love the way he says my name—slowly, like a caress.

He comes in, stands in front of me in my passageway. I feel a flicker of desire at his closeness—but more diffuse, more ephemeral, than the desire I felt before, when he ran his finger down my face: just a thread, a whisper.

I turn and lead him up the stair, intensely aware of all the people who are asleep in this house. I show him where all the creaks are, murmur to him where not to tread on the stair. My heart beats fast, like a thief's. I am a thief in my own house.

I open the door to my room and usher him in. I close the door behind me, turn the key in the lock. The sound is eloquent in the quiet between us. I turn around to face him, my body pressed to the door.

I'd expected to feel self-conscious, even ashamed, in this

moment—as he stands there in the candlelight, looking and looking at me, as though he will never look anywhere else. Yet an absolute joy startles me: that we are here together. I have a sense of infinite freedom, in this little room—that we could do anything here—in this place where the war doesn't come, behind this shut door. When he takes me in his arms the joy floods me, and the sense of his infinite preciousness— running my fingers across his face, feeling the bones beneath the close-cropped skin of his head: as he moves his hands all over me, possessing me with his touch.

Before, with Eugene—years ago, when we sometimes still used to make love—I was always somehow outside it, withdrawn, observing myself. Looking down from the ceiling, remote, untouched, removed: split in two—part of me doing, part watching. But here, now, all of me is present in every touch, every caress: I'm intensely aware of the hardness of his body, the scent of his skin all around me, his mouth exploring my mouth; and the movement of his hand on me, so I am shaken and shaken, as though I am falling apart. He puts his hand on my mouth. 'Shh,' he says. 'Shh…'; and then him inside me, my body wrapped all around him: hiding myself in him, hiding him in me.

Afterwards we lie together, quietly. I open my eyes, and see that my room is just the same as before—and this astonishes me. I feel as though I have travelled a great distance or entered a different country.

His uniform is lying on a chair. The sight jars, reminds me of all that I've chosen to put from my mind. I look away; I tell myself—all that is part of another life, his life when we are apart. It says nothing about who he really is, here with me in this room.

He kisses me, his mouth just grazing mine.

'Thank you,' he says.

I feel a sudden light happiness. It seems so strange that he should thank me, when he has given me so much.

I lie with my head on his chest, listen to the quiet beat of his heart. He has his hand in my hair. For a while, we say nothing: but the silence is the sweetest thing. I hadn't known that sex could take you to a place of such peace.

And then I hear the sound I dread—footsteps, and someone trying my handle, and then a knock at my door.

'Hide under the covers,' I tell him.

I wrap my dressing gown round me, unlock the door.

I'm so afraid that it's Blanche—that she will look past me into my room and at once understand everything: why I was wearing my best shantung dress, the conversation we had. But it's Millie, in her candystripe pyjamas, her feet big and ponderous in her knitted bedsocks. Her eyes are wide and staring but I don't know what she sees; her face is dazed, unfocused.

'Mummy, there are bees. There are bees in the house.' Her voice thin, shrill, brittle.

She's still living her nightmare. The reflections of my candles are held in her eyes, in tiny immaculate images.

'No, sweetheart. It's just a dream…'

'They're in my bed, Mummy!'

I crouch down, hold her. Her heart pounds against my chest, as though her heart is my heart. There are smudges of blue shadow round her eyes.

'There aren't any bees,' I tell her.

'Mummy, there are bees in my hair. I can hear them… I ran and I ran but I couldn't escape.' Her voice is a thin bright juddery thread.

I stroke her hair.

'It's just a dream,' I tell her. 'There's nothing to be frightened of.'

'Can't you hear them buzzing?' she says.

I take her back to her room. Guilt washes through me. I wonder if this is my fault, that she is troubled like this. Did she see something, hear something? I listen carefully, make an extravagant show of looking in every corner, to prove there are no bees. Then I sing her to sleep. I don't think she saw Gunther. But the sense of peace has left me, its smooth still surface fractured, splintered into a thousand glittery shards.

When I get back to my bedroom, he has dressed.

'Is she all right?' he asks me.

'Yes. She's asleep now. I don't think she saw anything...'

He takes me in his arms.

'Vivienne. Will we do this again? I would love to see you again, my dearest. Would you want that?'

His questions flood me with happiness.

'Yes. Please...'

But Millie's nightmare has troubled me. I feel the enormity of what we have done—of what we are planning to do.

'Gunther. Can we really do this without anyone knowing? Can we really keep it secret? It has to be completely secret—from Evelyn, from the girls. From everyone...'

'We'll be very careful,' he says.

I take him down to the door. I watch him as he leaves, walking across the gravel: walking back into his other life. There's a silver spill of moonlight over my yard, so bright he casts a shadow.

I go back to my room. My body, my damp bed, smell of him. I'm missing him already.

CHAPTER 35

We work out the rules. I leave a signal for him—an empty flowerpot on my doorstep, to let him know that it is safe, that everyone is in bed here. If he does come round to my house, it is always exactly at ten; if he hasn't arrived by quarter past, I go up to bed on my own.

I have lived for so long in a house of women: I'm astonished to have a man again in my bed, so grateful for the warm weight of his solid body, the subtle scent of his skin, his difference. Astonished too by the way I am with him—when I always think of myself as being so shy, so reserved. Yet with this man I will do anything—open up, be shameless: as though I have a different body when I am with him; as though I am changed by his nearness.

After we have made love, we will always talk for a while, me with my head on his shoulder. In the gentle light of my candles, the room will seem secret and separate—a cave in a forest, a boat on a shifting sea. You can hear all the creaks and stirrings of the old house settling down to sleep, as a boat will creak at anchor.

He will take two cigarettes, light one for him and one for me. Mostly we talk about the past—which is safer than the present.

'What were you like when you were a child?' he asks me. 'Tell me about your childhood.'

He blows out smoke. The peacefulness of the moment laps around us. I love to see him here, in my bed, loving the things I know about his body: the patterning of hair on his chest, the way his spine shows through his white skin, the cords of his wrists, a kind of grace in his gestures; and the startling smile that will suddenly light up his face. He feels familiar to me already—as though he is part of me, as though I have always been waiting for him.

I tell him about Iris, about growing up in London in the tall, thin house with the hidden garden piled up with the leaves of all the years; about the aunts who brought us up.

'My mother died very suddenly, when I was three,' I tell him. 'She had pneumonia.'

He doesn't say anything. He puts his arm round me, pulls me close. He waits.

I'm remembering. It's suddenly so vivid to me; I can smell the chill, antiseptic smell of the sickroom. There's an ache that seems to rise like dough in my chest.

'We were taken in to say goodbye—me and my sister,' I tell him.

I find I am starting to cry. As though the hard shell that protects me has been softened by his presence. I haven't spoken about this grief for years.

He wipes the tear from my face with one warm finger.

'You were so young,' he says quietly. 'To have to face such a thing.'

It's all there in my head, with a sudden, troubling precision.

'The room smelt funny and she looked strange. She didn't look like my mother any more... I've learned since, how—when you go to see someone who's ill, sometimes you *know*, you can tell… You know that they will die soon. You can tell, they look different.'

'Yes, I have seen that,' he says.

'I suppose I saw that in my mother,' I say. 'Though I had no way of understanding it.'

He strokes my hair. The touch, the rhythm, soothe me.

'That was very difficult for you,' he says. 'For your mother to die when you were still so young… I have felt from the beginning that there was something hurt in you,' he tells me. 'Something withdrawn, reserved. Waiting to be drawn out. Even from that very first time I saw you in the lane.'

'Did you? Did you really think that, even then?' I say. 'Tell me…'

Afterwards, I am glad that I told him about my mother. I don't understand why this should be so consoling; but it is. As though telling him has freed me.

At night, our intimacy seems completely natural to me—as though it is all intended, how my life is meant to unfold. But sometimes I'll see him during the day—in the requisitioned Bentley, or with the other soldiers, perhaps laughing with Hans Schmidt or Max Richter, in that loud, rather raucous way that men will laugh with other men, and he'll seem so utterly separate from me, and the realisation of what I am doing slams into me.

I'll think, What is he like with those other people—those enemy soldiers—doing whatever they do to keep our island under control? Do I really know him? What does it mean to know someone? And whenever I think this, I'll hear Blanche's voice in my mind: *How can you ever really know someone? How can you ever be sure what they're like?*

One day I ask him.

'What are you like when you're not with me?'

He smiles a little at my question.

'None of us knows that,' he says, lightly. 'How could we? That is a problem for everyone. We never know what the person we love is like when they aren't with us.'

'No, of course, but...we aren't *everyone*...' My voice fades.

He can tell that his answer didn't quite satisfy me. A new seriousness comes in his face.

'My darling, that is a very difficult question. You would need a philosopher to answer that question,' he says.

I wish he'd be clearer.

I lie on my side, looking at him. On the dressing table behind him, the dragonfly on my perfume bottle is lit up by the candlelight, so it looks as though it's burning. His face in profile is featureless, black, against the fiery wings.

'I know so little about you really,' I say.

'What do you want to know?' he says.

I hesitate. My head is a tangle of questions, and I can't pull out the right one. I retreat to something safer.

'Tell me about Germany,' I say. 'I've never been there.'

'Some of Germany is beautiful,' he says.

'Tell me about the beautiful parts,' I say.

'Bavaria is beautiful,' he says. 'My wife's uncle lives in Bavaria. We would go there in the summer—before the war, before it all began. There is no air like the air of those forests. The pines, the smell of juniper. There is no silence like that silence...'

I try to imagine them—those great forests, the scent of juniper and pine. I'm ignorant, like a child; I know so little of the world.

'Berlin presses down,' he says. 'All the big buildings, and people living on top of one another. I don't like to spend too long there. I like to go far away. Not to have to think about things…'

I remember the poem I chose for him. *I have asked to be/ Where no storms come.* Perhaps it wasn't quite such an inappropriate choice as I'd thought. Perhaps there was a kind of rightness to it.

'I like to draw and paint there, in Bavaria,' he tells me. 'To set up my easel on the mountainside. To have a whole day of quiet there, with my charcoal or my paints… There are moments when you don't have to try—when there is no struggle. You are there in the place where you should be, and everything flows like water, the scene forming under your hand…'

I think how everyone has a dream that sustains them: a thought that begins, *When the war is over…* And for him the dream is there, amid those forests and that silence. That is where he has left a part of himself—on a mountainside in Bavaria, with his easel and his brushes and his little tubes of colours; with the scent of juniper and the silence.

I say this to him.

'That is where you would be now—if you could choose,' I tell him.

He is quiet for a moment.

'No, Vivienne,' he says then. He turns to look into my face: there's such intensity in him. 'You see—maybe as you said, you know so little about me. Of all the places that I could choose, I would be here, in this bed.'

There's a letter on my doormat, in an envelope that has no name or address. I wonder who dropped it off here, and why they didn't stay to speak.

I open the envelope. There's a single sheet of paper inside it, folded in half. I open it out. The room tilts around me.

The message is made from newsprint letters cut from *The Guernsey Press* and glued down on the paper. The letters are crooked, at drunken angles, as though stuck down haphazardly, all in a rush: but the message is horribly clear. *'Viv de la Mare is a Jerrybag!!!'* The harsh words scream out at me.

I put the letter down quickly on the hall table, as though the touch of it could hurt, as though it could sear me like acid. But I know I can't leave it lying there, where anyone could see. I pick it up again and take it through to the living room and screw it up and throw it on the fire. The paper opens out as it falls, and catches light, a red line of flame running round it. As I watch it flares and blackens and collapses into ash. I can't think—don't want to think—who could have sent it.

The floor creaks behind me as Evelyn comes into the room. She sits carefully in her chair and pulls her knitting from her basket.

'Something's burning,' she says. 'What's burning there? I can smell it. Something's burning in the grate.'

'It's nothing, Evelyn,' I say. 'Don't worry.'

'Who's burning a letter?' she says.

She can see the charred paper in the grate. I poke the fire, break up the ashy fragments. Even now it's completely burned I still see it in my mind's eye. The skewed newsprint letters, the ugly words. *'Viv de la Mare is a Jerrybag!!!'*

'It's not a letter,' I say. 'It's nothing. Just an old drawing of Millie's.'

I suddenly wonder how Evelyn knows it was a letter. Did she see it on the doormat? Did she see the person who brought it, from her bedroom window that looks out over the lane? But I can't ask if she saw anyone, can't find out who left it here, because I've already told her that there wasn't a letter at all.

She starts on her knitting. Her fingers move briskly, her knitting needles make a quick stern sound: like a reprimand.

'Something's burning,' she says again. 'I can smell it. I don't like that smell, Vivienne. Something's been thrown on the fire.'

'Shh, Evelyn. Everything's all right.'

She's quiet for a moment. I think—What will happen to me? How many people know, and who will they tell? I imagine how people would condemn me if they knew about my love affair; I think of the stares, the coldness—how Evelyn and Gwen and even my children would turn away from me. It's hard to breathe. I'm worried that Evelyn will see all my guilt and my fear in my face.

She stops her knitting suddenly, the needles held downwards in front of her. Her hands are loose: the stitches start to slide. I move towards her, worried that her knitting will unravel and upset her.

'Where's Eugene?' she says. 'Where's he gone?'

'Eugene isn't here, Evelyn. You know that.'

'Oh.'

I press her hands round her knitting needles. Her skin is cool and papery—it doesn't quite feel like flesh. She starts on her knitting again.

'Where's Eugene?' she says again, after a while. 'I want to kiss him goodnight. *Somebody's* got to.' She gives me a rather flinty look.

'Evelyn. Eugene's away fighting. He's being very brave,' I say.

'Was the letter from him? Did you burn his letter?' she says.

'No, of course not. Why on earth would I do that?'

'He doesn't write to us,' she says.

'No, he can't. You know that. I'm sure he wants to, but he can't. The letters can't get through. Not with the Germans here. There's a war on, Evelyn, remember.'

'A war. They say there's a war. They always say there's a war on,' she says. 'But I don't see any fighting round here. Rather the reverse in fact.'

The smell of burnt paper is faint, just the slightest trace on the air—yet it seems to hang around for a very long time.

Later, I walk up to Angie's. There's a raw, wet wind, the last tattered leaves being whipped from the trees in the lanes. The letter is there in my mind; I can still see it so vividly— the crooked letters, screaming out, full of accusation and rage. I think, *Am I that ugly thing?* Everyone I pass in the lane, I think, Was it them? Did they send it? The island feels hostile to me—as though it has spewed me out and pushed me away. As though I am not wanted here.

CHAPTER 37

One night, when we are in bed, I touch the scar on his face. It feels very soft beneath my finger, like a small child's skin.

'So how did this happen?' I ask him.

For a moment he doesn't speak. As though his mind is full of words, and he can't choose the right ones. His eyes are a dense grey, like the smokes of autumn gardens.

'This was my stepfather,' he says.

I'm startled. I wasn't expecting this. I thought the scar must be from some war injury, from the Great War.

'Your stepfather?'

'He hit me, and I fell on the stove,' he tells me.

'You haven't told me about your stepfather,' I say.

I think how he keeps himself hidden: how he has taken a long time to tell me this part of his story. Our revelations have been unequal: he knows so much more about my childhood than I know about his.

'My own father died when I was six, and my mother married again. My stepfather was a difficult man. He was a pastor. Everyone admired him, but at home he was cruel,' he says.

I try to imagine his stepfather—cool and stern and righteous.

'How terrible for you.' My voice sounds paltry, thin—as though my words are too easy, not weighty enough.

'You learn to keep quiet,' he tells me. 'You learn to keep out of the way—to do what you are told to do…'

'Of course you would,' I say gently. Not wanting to intrude on his thought—wanting him to go on talking.

'I have thought about this very much,' he tells me. 'When you are small, you think, *My stepfather is right, surely? Maybe I am a bad child. If he says it is so, it must be true.* When this man is so powerful, and you are dependent on him, you have to believe he is right.'

He takes a long drag on his cigarette. I have my head on his chest. I hear how his heart speeds up as he talks, like somebody running away; though his voice is slow and full of thought.

'But then, as I grew older, I knew that wasn't so. I came to understand that my stepfather was a cruel man.'

'He sounds very cruel,' I say.

He shifts a little, moves a few inches away from me in the bed—as though my closeness distracts him from the thing he needs to say. I lie on my side, watching him.

'There was a night when he started to hit my brother. Before that night, it had always been me that he hit. It was for the smallest thing, some water spilt on the floor. He blamed my brother, and beat him. I should have defended my brother, knocked my stepfather down. I was big enough then, I was eleven, I was big for my age, I could have fought him. But I didn't.'

I hear the catch in his voice. I can feel how raw this still is—the shame still vivid for him, still present.

'He started to beat my brother, and I did nothing. I just remember hiding under the stairs. Hearing the blows. I covered my ears with my hands, but I still heard the sound of the beating. A blow in the silence of a house is a very loud thing.'

His voice is even, measured; but I sense the distress that lies under his words.

'You see—I am not such a good man, Vivienne,' he says.

I shake my head.

'It was such a long time ago,' I tell him. 'And you were only a child. Eleven is still very little. How could you possibly have stopped him?'

'I know what I was thinking then.' His voice is very quiet. When he turns towards me, I can feel his words on my skin, but I can only just hear him. 'I can remember it now. *While he hits him, he won't hit me...* That is what I thought,' he says.

'You were only a boy. What choice did you have?' I say again.

CHAPTER 38

December. I have lit a good fire in the living-room grate, and we sit on the hearthrug and have our story by the light of the flames. Alphonse is sleeping beside us, his curled-up body moving with the rhythm of his breath, and the room has a friendly smell of warm wool from the clothes that are drying on the fireguard. Outside, rain lashes the window: there's a storm blowing in from the sea.

I read from the book that Angie gave us; about a ghostly funeral that winds its way down the lanes; about a reef in Rocquaine Bay that is haunted by an unnatural beast, whose roar can be heard when storms approach; about the old road that runs between St Saviour's and St Pierre du Bois, a road that is known as La Rue de la Bête, where lonely travellers have met a supernatural creature.

Millie sighs with pleasure.

'I like ghost stories, Mummy. But Blanche is really frightened of them.' She grins smugly.

Blanche's mouth tightens briefly.

'Millie, you talk a load of nonsense,' she says.

Blanche is sewing—letting down the hem of one of her skirts. She's growing so fast at the moment, growing out of her clothes, her limbs gazelle-like and angled, so she seems at once gawky and graceful. She holds up her needle to thread it: it has a brief dangerous glitter in the light of the fire.

'Read me another one,' says Millie.

I read about Portelet beach, where at dusk you may meet a little hunched woman all wrapped up in a shawl, who is said to be searching and searching for the son she has lost.

'Is that *really, really* true?' says Millie.

'No, sweetheart. It's just a story…'

There's no sound in the room but the stir of the fire and the rush of rain at the window. A log in the grate collapses inwards and sends up a fountain of sparks.

Millie frowns.

'Why do people tell ghost stories? If ghosts aren't really *real*?'

I wonder what to say. I could give her the obvious answer—Because the people who first told the stories believed that ghosts were real. But then Millie would say, Well, maybe they were *right*, Mummy—and I don't want to mislead or frighten her.

'I think they do it because they're afraid of the dark,' I tell her.

'*I'm* not afraid of the dark,' she says.

'No. But lots of people are. I was very afraid of the dark when I was little…'

I remember the time that Iris shut me in the coalshed. How I had my eyes wide open, but there was only darkness. I shudder even now, thinking of it.

'*I'm* not, Mummy,' she says. 'I'm nearly five, and I'm not afraid of the dark.'

I move the clothes round on the fireguard, so the warmth will reach the damper parts. Raindrops are blown down the chimney and hiss and spit in the flames. The cat shifts and yawns and burrows more deeply down into sleep.

I turn back to the storybook, turn the page.

There's a story that tells how some island people have fairy blood—the blood of fairy invaders. These fairies came from their far-off homeland and over the sea in boats, which were craftily made, with spells woven into their sails. As the fairies drew nearer and nearer to land, the boats became smaller and smaller, until when they finally beached them, the boats were tiny as pebbles or the delicate bones of a bird. The fairies were beautiful creatures—both men and women—looking human, but lovelier; and sometimes they fell for island people, and married and set up house with them. But however happy they were on Guernsey with their loved ones, they were obliged to return eventually to their homeland—under a contract written in blood that could not be disobeyed. Sooner or later they had to leave the people they loved and sail away.

'Is that the end of the story?' says Millie.

'Yes. That's all the book tells us.'

She frowns. The fire shuffles softly; tiny flames red as poppies dance in the dark of her eyes.

'I don't like the ending. It's sad. It's not a good ending,' she says.

And I think just for a moment that, yes, that was sad, and how could you live, not knowing when the one you loved would leave you. And then think that it's always like that.

CHAPTER 39

One day I ask about his wife: I feel an intense, feverish curiosity about her.

'What is she like? Could you tell me something about her?' I ask boldly.

'Ilse?' He hesitates. 'How do you sum up a person? She keeps the house well. She holds everything together.'

Ilse must be a strong woman. I can sense that.

'She gave me safety, for a while,' he tells me.

'Yes,' I say: understanding how that would matter to him—to have a safe place, a place to retreat to. That need is one that we share.

'And she is a good mother to Hermann. But it was a difficult birth, with many complications. She decided she would never have another child. That part of our life is over for us. It has been over for a long time.'

I feel a quick illicit happiness, when he says that: because it takes a little of the guilt away from me. Then feel guilty again, that I felt that.

'Show me,' I say. 'You must have a photograph. Show me.'

As he pushes back the covers, goose-bumps come up on my arms. It's chilly in my bedroom tonight: a bitter wind rattles the windows, and the candle-flames dip and tremble in the draught that sneaks under the door.

He goes to the pocket of his uniform jacket, pulls out a photograph, brings it to me. It shows the three of them together.

It's unnerving—this image of his other life that I know nothing of: his real life. His life of family, country, duty, obligation. I am looking in on a story that has nothing to do with me.

The first thing I notice is how much younger he looks in the picture—how the years since this was taken have written on him and marked him.

'You seem so young in the picture,' I say.

He smiles a rueful smile.

'You mean, I look much older now,' he says.

'I suppose I do…' I reach out my hand and trace out his face, the strong bones under the skin. 'But I love the way you look now…'

Then I turn from him, stare at the other people in the picture.

Ilse is small, with high cheekbones and faraway eyes. Her hair is pale—maybe blonde or grey—and coiled in a plait round her head. Her expression is diffident, earnest: I picture her lying awake in the night-time, worrying, weaving the disparate strands of her family's life together—struggling to make it all work out; adding everything up. Their son is maybe twelve in the picture, and very fair and freckled; he has his mother's expression, eager for approval. He is wearing some kind of uniform.

Gunther watches me as I study the photograph—trying to read what I think.

'We would have very much liked to have another child,'

he tells me. A little yearning creeps into his voice, when he says that, and I can tell that this has been a source of sadness for both of them. 'But life doesn't always give you what you want,' he says. His eyes on me. 'Well, most of the time it doesn't.'

I turn back to the photograph, feeling the heat of his gaze.

'He looks too young to be in uniform,' I tell him.

'We have a movement for young people—the Hitler Jugend,' he says. 'Hermann was very keen to join. He did get very involved. I was not entirely happy.' His face is still, contained, giving nothing away. 'My wife was happy, but I was not happy. They go too far,' he says.

'So why did you let him join?' I ask.

'You have to be careful, you don't want to step out of line,' he says. 'And before Hermann joined the Hitler Jugend he was a wayward boy. He kept bad company. The movement gave him a sense of purpose. My wife says that is good, that life is nothing without purpose… My son is in the party now.'

I feel a little shock of cold. *My lover's son is a Nazi.*

'So you couldn't stop him? You think they go too far, but you couldn't stop him?' I say.

He shakes his head.

'It would be unwise to do that,' he says, carefully.

I think of the things we have heard—of the burning of synagogues, Jewish businesses stolen, the broken glass, the insults, the beatings on the street. I don't say anything.

But he hears my unspoken question.

'You have to understand this, Vivienne. We couldn't go on as we were. Germany was on her knees. The Depression was terrible for us. Our world was made of hunger and emergency decrees. We had nothing.' He's not looking at me any more: he's staring into the darkness in the corners of the room, as though he can see those years spooling out again in front of him. 'The habits you learn then stay with you. Ilse still has her biscuit-bag—a bag for broken biscuits and crusts that hangs on her cupboard door: nothing could be wasted. Something had to change,' he says. 'At first we welcomed Hitler. We felt that his arrival was like a glimmer of hope. Before Hitler, we didn't eat: once Hitler came, we could eat... But there is much that they do that seems wrong to me,' he tells me.

'So—if you could choose, you wouldn't fight this war?'

Then I wish I hadn't expressed it like that. I'm putting words into his mouth.

'Which of us would choose war? To have our lives torn apart like this?' There's an edge of anger in him, that I could even ask the question. 'But I would never say that anywhere else but here. You have to think always of the safety of your family,' he says.

I think what I said to him before—when he told me how he was beaten, how he should have fought his stepfather: *What choice did you have?* I think, What choice do we have, any of us? But I can't answer that question.

He puts the photo away in his pocket and gets back into my bed. I can hear the wind howling around my house, like an animal, hunting, predatory: how it seeks to find its way into my house through the least little fissure or crack.

CHAPTER 40

February. Johnnie comes with a gift for me, all wrapped up in brown paper. He puts it down on the kitchen table and starts to peel off the layers; inside, there's greaseproof paper, which is red and shiny with blood.

'There you go, Auntie. A present for you,' he tells me.

It's a whole dead rabbit. Gwen has skinned it for me, so you can see the pale mauve flesh, but it still looks very rabbit-like. Once, not so long ago, I found the sight of dead animals saddening. Now, I'm just thinking how I will cook it, with some sprigs of thyme and rosemary; how rich the gravy will be, how very good it will taste. Though I wouldn't want Millie to see it.

'Your mother's an angel,' I say. 'But are you really sure you can spare it?'

'Don't you worry, Auntie. Those rabbits breed like—well, you know what they say.'

I make him a cup of parsnip coffee. I've learnt how to do this—grating the parsnips, roasting them just the right length of time, till they are a rich brown colour like wood shavings, then infusing them. It's better than nothing, but it always has that burnt taste.

'Don't feel you have to drink it if you don't like it,' I tell him.

But he drinks it rapidly.

The clear white light of early spring spills all over my room—that searching light that shows up the dirt where you haven't cleaned for a while, all the cobwebs and dustballs you missed in the dull veiled days of winter; and it falls all over Johnnie, his vividness, his restless hands, his eager nut-brown eyes. I watch him drinking his coffee, and think how fond I am of him.

'So what have you been up to, Johnnie? Still painting V-signs?' I ask.

He doesn't answer at once. In the silence between us, I sense something shifting, rearranging itself.

His throat moves as he swallows.

'I wanted to tell you, Auntie. We've got a new thing going, me and Piers Falla,' he says.

But he doesn't sound very buoyant, and he isn't meeting my eye.

'He was going to come here, Piers was,' Johnnie tells me.

There's something halting in his voice. I don't understand what he means. I can't imagine why Piers would want to come to Le Colombier.

'I told him not to,' he says.

Alphonse slinks into the kitchen, lured by the smell of raw meat. He circles the table, mewing loudly, then crouches, poised to leap up. I grab him, put him into the hall, slam the door on him. He scratches at the door and wails: the sound is unnerving, half human, like some uncanny hybrid thing.

'You see, the point is, Auntie…'

Johnnie isn't looking at me. He puts out one hand in a small helpless gesture, and knocks his coffee cup over. The dark sludgy liquid left at the bottom spills out. He straightens the cup, but he doesn't notice the spill.

I know I should get a wet cloth: but my legs are suddenly shaky and I don't trust them to work.

'The thing is…' His gaze slides past me. 'The thing is… there are women on Guernsey who are doing what they shouldn't. Being a little too friendly. Letting the side down. You know what I mean.'

He flushes—all over his face and his neck, a flush as bright as strawberries.

My heart starts pounding. I wonder if he can see its pounding through my blouse.

'I'm sure there are.' My voice casual, light, as though this is nothing to me. 'Men and women together—you know how it is.'

Then I wish I hadn't said that. I hear the whine and scratch of the cat on the other side of the door.

'We've had a few tip-offs—we know all their names, where they live. We aren't going to let them get away with it, Auntie,' he says. 'We're going round painting swastikas on their houses. To show them we know. Show them they should be ashamed.'

'Johnnie. What good will that do? You'll only get into trouble.'

'You do what you have to do,' he says.

It's what he told me before. But there isn't that bright certainty that I used to hear in his voice.

'Have you told your mum and dad about this?' I ask him.

'Not exactly,' he says.

I think—*So why are you telling me, Johnnie?* The unspoken question hangs in the air between us. The words seem so solid, like tangible things—you could put out your finger and touch.

Johnnie is studying the table, as though a secret were written there, some code in the grain of the wood.

'Piers says—he says there are rumours about you, Auntie.' His voice so quiet I can only just hear. 'About you and one of the Germans at Les Vinaires. Piers wanted to paint a swastika here, on the wall of Le Colombier. I said, no, of course not. I said of course he was wrong.'

But there's a question in his voice.

A pulse is hammering in my throat.

'Johnnie—you shouldn't listen to rumours.'

'Auntie. He says that you were seen in a car with one of them,' he tells me.

I feel a rush of relief—that this is all he knows.

'Oh, *that*,' I say. 'Well, that's true enough. The man gave me a lift. It was raining. I had a puncture.'

He glances up at me. He has a bleak, desolate look.

'It was raining, and I needed to get back to Millie.' I hear the pleading note in my voice. 'Her grandma isn't so good at looking after Millie now. Her grandma isn't quite all there… I don't like to leave them for long…'

He's still looking at me so sadly, as though I have disappointed him. I hate this: I want to be good in his eyes. I don't want to lose his respect. He doesn't say anything.

'What use would it have been, to walk all the way back in the rain?' I'm protesting too much; but I can't stop. 'I don't see how that would help anyone…'

He shakes his head a little.

'You shouldn't have done that really, Auntie. It wasn't sensible. People could jump to the wrong conclusions,' he says.

We are edging towards safety.

'You're right, it was a really bad idea,' I say. 'But it was raining so heavily…'

He lets out his breath in a little sigh, as though he has decided to accept what I've said.

'I told him,' he says. 'I told him you'd never dream of doing anything that you shouldn't. I said, You do realise, this is my Auntie Viv we're talking about.'

We sit silently for a moment. The smell of the raw, bloody meat is sickening. Nausea rises in my throat and I try to swallow it down.

'So who spread the story?' he asks me. 'That there was more to it than that?'

'I don't know, Johnnie.'

'Is there someone who's got it in for you? Someone who wants to get their own back for something they think you did? Someone with a grudge against you?'

'Not that I know of.'

He's still waiting. Waiting for a lifeline—something to haul him in to shore. I have to give him more than this.

'But of course there might be,' I say. 'There might be someone with a grudge. You know what island folk are like. People do hold grudges round here.'

'That's probably it, then.' Persuading himself. 'Somebody with a grudge against you, Auntie.'

'Yes, I expect so.'

'I told Piers you weren't like that,' he says. 'That you'd never let the side down. I said, She's my *auntie*…'

When Johnnie has gone, I scrub and scrub at my kitchen table, but I can't get out the stain from the coffee he spilled.

CHAPTER 41

This is how it is, for a long time. This is my life now. I grow accustomed to secrecy, to hiding, to the life I share with Gunther when we close the door on the war, on the world, and lie together in my bed, in the soft shuddering light of my candles. Sometimes I think of the story I read to Millie, just before the Occupation—the story of the dancing princesses, who at night went through their trapdoor and down all the winding stairs and through the grove of golden trees to a secret, separate world. This life begins to seem almost natural to me. Now he will stay with me most of the night, and leave my bed very early, when the first white fingers of morning reach into the room. I feel such peacefulness, falling asleep in his arms. Sometimes I find myself thinking, This is how marriage should be.

Often I am afraid—that another letter will come; or that one of Johnnie's eager friends will paint a swastika on the wall of my house. I worry that someone who suspects me will whisper to Evelyn or Blanche, will tell them about me and Gunther. And when I think that, I feel how fragile everything is—how my whole life here could be torn apart. Sometimes, I'll hear the letter-box snap, and I'll clamp my lips together to stop myself crying out. But there are no more anonymous letters.

One day when I'm walking to Angie's, I pass a big old oak that leans out over the lane. In the corrugated bark of its trunk, lovers have carved their initials with a penknife: VS, FL, the letters intertwined. Just for a moment, I feel such a pang of envy, for couples who live an everyday life: who walk hand in hand in the lanes and leave indelible marks of their closeness, who can express their love in such an easy, ordinary way. Nothing furtive or hidden.

All this while, the war seems distant from me. There are the shortages, of course, the restrictions, the curfew: but I'm not so aware of the power of the Germans, the way they govern our lives, here in my hidden valley, with my family and my lover. Gwen at Elm Tree Farm still hears the German soldiers in the night, marching and singing their martial songs: owning our island, owning the dark; but you can't hear them here, in the peace of these deep lanes. I concentrate on the daily things. I tell myself this is what matters—to care for my children and Evelyn, to bring us through this somehow.

I worry most about Evelyn. She seems to be losing weight, however much I cajole her to eat. She often has a blurred look in her eyes, as though everything is obscure to her; as though her life seems like the back of a piece of tapestry, and she sees, not the pattern, but only the frayed ends and knots.

One day she's knitting in the living room; she looks up as I go in.

'And who are you, my dear?' she says, pleasantly. 'Who are you? I don't think we've met...'

I know it's because her mind is going: but I'm still un-nerved.

'Evelyn. I'm Vivienne—remember?'

But she doesn't.

'Vivienne,' she says thoughtfully. 'Such a pretty name.'

I think how she's nicer to me when she doesn't know who I am. The thought depresses me.

I go to put my hand on her sleeve, with some inchoate thought that my touch might remind her that I'm her daughter-in-law and bring her back to reality. She stares at my hand on her arm, surprised, a little disapproving—as though I have been too intimate. I snatch my hand away.

'You must let me get you some tea, dear, after you've come so far,' she says. 'You're so good to come and see me. I think there's some *gâche* in the larder…'

'Evelyn. This is where I live. I'm Eugene's wife,' I say.

She stares at me, shocked; she raises her thin, arched eyebrows.

'No, I don't think you are, dear.' Her voice is cold and clear; and stronger, as though her certainty gives her energy. 'You're wrong there. You see, Eugene never married. He has the highest standards.'

There's nothing I can say to that. I leave her sitting there.

Five minutes later she calls for me.

'Vivienne. I've dropped my glasses, and I can't seem to see where they've gone. Could you be a dear and find them for me?'

As though the strange little incident never happened.

Because she's so frail now, Evelyn stops going to church. She's too weak to walk there any more, and the service tires her too much. I arrange for the Rector to come and give her Communion at Le Colombier. I decide I will stay home with her. But Blanche still goes to Matins, and sometimes takes Millie too.

'Mum—why don't you ever come to church any more?' she asks me.

'I don't really like to leave your grandma,' I say.

Her eyes are on me, blue as summer.

'But it's not just that, is it?' she says.

I hesitate. Perhaps she's right—perhaps Evelyn is just an excuse.

'To be honest, I'm not sure how much I believe now, really,' I tell her. 'With the war and all the suffering.'

'But you could still come, Mum. You don't have to believe all of it.'

'I don't know...'

I wonder if my reluctance is partly because of Gunther; when he is so precious to me, yet everyone at church would think this love of mine was wrong—and wrong in so many many ways. I remember Johnnie's visit, hear his words in my head. *There are women on Guernsey who are doing what they shouldn't. Letting the side down. You know what I mean...* I can hear his tone when he said these things—all the contempt in his voice.

'Anyway—the war and suffering must be for a purpose,' says Blanche. 'That's what the Rector said. It must all be part of God's plan. There must be a purpose to it.' As though this is simple and clear to her.

'I'm not sure, sweetheart...'

I'm happy she has this certainty—envy it, even, that she can find some kind of order in all that's happening in the world, all this terrible anarchy. But I don't share it.

I polish my pictures and photographs. I wipe them with a damp cloth, then buff the glass with screwed-up newspaper, that always gives a good shine. I clean the Margaret Tarrant print in my kitchen, the Christ Child surrounded by angels with vast, soft, fretted wings. In the living room, I pick up the photo of Eugene. I haven't cleaned it for a while—the glass has a blue pallor of dust. I stare at the picture, move my finger across it, as though the feel of the glass against my skin will somehow make him real to me. His image in my mind is losing its definition: sometimes I have to look at his picture to remember his face. I stare at the photograph, trying to learn him again. Pushing away the secret, the thing that I try not to think: that he's become so remote to me—someone to whom I have little connection at all. That to think of being in bed with Eugene is like a betrayal of Gunther. That Gunther is my real husband, the one I am meant to be with—and my marriage a distant, unreal thing: an old formality, without substance.

'That's my boy,' says Evelyn, watching. 'My darling boy.'

'It's a lovely picture,' I say.

I clean it fastidiously, wipe every single speck of dust from the frame. As though that could make him clearer to me.

There's a story in Angie's folktale book that tells how a traveller once arrived in Guernsey and beached his flimsy boat between L'Erée Bay and Perelle.

'We've been there, Mummy. I know where Perelle Beach is,' says Millie. Her eyes shine. It always thrills her when her story is set in a place that she knows.

Blanche glances up from the *Vogue* she's reading.

'I don't like that beach. It's creepy,' she says. 'At low tide it's nothing but stones.'

Blanche is right—it's a desolate spot, all grey pebbles and

the churning sound of the sea, a fitting setting for some untoward thing to happen.

The story tells how the stranger was accosted by a fisherman, who boldly asked who he was and why he had come. But the stranger wouldn't tell his name or the name of the country he came from—just said, *'J'vais cheminant.' I go wandering.* The wanderer settled on Guernsey and married an island woman; he never revealed his origins, but remained a mystery to the day of his death.

'So she never found out who he was?' says Blanche. 'That must have been awfully strange.'

The story stays in my mind. I wonder what it was like for that woman—to marry someone of whom she knew nothing at all. Yet how much do we ever know about those we love or even marry—their history, where they come from, what has made them who they are? How well did I really know Eugene? Even knowing his mother, his island, the walls of his childhood home, I can think of him and it's as if he's a stranger to me. How well do I know Gunther, who is so often in my bed? I think how this question once troubled me—how I asked him about it, pressed him: *What are you like when you're not with me?* Yet it troubles me so much less now. Perhaps I've learned that a lover will always come to you out of the mists of the sea, beaching his boat on your shores for a while, yet still in some sense mysterious. To love is to give yourself to the unknown. What other choice do we have?

CHAPTER 42

The days lengthen. There's a fresh spring wind that rummages through my orchard, ripping at the blossoms, so beneath the trees the ground is drifted with a sleet of white. I tend my vegetable patch. I earth up my potatoes; I put up hazel peasticks for my peas and runner beans, and cover them over with nets to protect them from the pigeons. I hoe round the vegetables regularly—weeds grow so fast in spring. I pick lettuces and radishes, and plant out the sprouts and cabbages that I have been growing from seed. I start keeping chickens. I buy the pullets from Harry Tostevin—Rhode Island Reds, with chestnut plumage and furtive orange eyes. Johnnie helps me build a run at the bottom of the garden, where our land turns a corner round the back of Les Vinaires. To my surprise, I find that I really enjoy the chickens: I like the ripple of sound they make as they bustle and chatter and fuss, love collecting the eggs that are softly brown and nestle warm in your palm. Millie helps me with the eggs and gives the chickens extravagant names taken from her storybooks—Rapunzel, Cinderella. Angie gives me a lesson in how to prepare one for the table, how to pluck it and gut it. Bread is rationed now—but I know I can feed my family, and this gives me a full, warm, satisfied feeling.

In May, we hear that there has been a terrible air-raid on London: they say that over three thousand people are dead. I'm so afraid for Iris and her family. I think of the horror of the bombing of St Peter Port—think of that happening every night, all around you. Of the people caught in the firestorms; or sheltering in the Underground, hearing the devastation above them, wondering with every bomb that falls—Is that my house? Going out with the All Clear to see their world destroyed. Blanche's eyes fill with tears when she hears the news. 'Those poor, poor people,' she says.

I walk up the hill to see Angie. It's a breezy May morning, wet washing snapping on clothes-lines in all the gardens I pass, and notice a powdery, nostalgic scent on the air, where the tight cones of buds on the lilacs are loosening and letting out their perfume.

Angie isn't quite meeting my gaze. She pulls at a thread on her sleeve.

'There's something I want to tell you,' she says. 'So you'll hear it first from me.'

I wonder what is coming.

'It's Jack—my brother,' she says. 'No one's told you anything, then?'

'No, Angie. Why would they?'

She clears her throat.

'The thing is—he's doing some work for *them*. You know what I mean.' Her voice is ragged and secretive. 'He's working up at the airfield.'

'Well, we all have to get by somehow,' I say.

'He's not proud of it, to be honest. But he has to feed his little ones.'

I hear all the pleading in her voice—how desperately she wants me to be forgiving, not to mind.

'Of course he does,' I tell her. 'Of course that's what matters the most.'

'He's got those four growing children, and hardly any land. Don't think badly of him, Vivienne.'

'Of course I wouldn't think badly of him,' I say. 'We all have to find a way to get through. All of us.'

But she doesn't seem to hear me. Perhaps she misreads my expression, seeing some uneasiness in my face: though I'm thinking of myself, not Jack. But the thing I could tell her to comfort her is the one thing I can't say.

'I know there are some who'd condemn him. There are nasty words for people who do what Jack is doing,' she says. 'And to be honest you can understand it. When you hear the news from London—it's the worst thing in the world to feel that someone you love has *helped*.'

I don't say anything for a moment. I'm not quite looking at her. *Someone I love has certainly helped.*

'I wouldn't condemn him, Angie. Really.'

But something about me troubles her: she isn't reassured.

Sometimes I see the other Germans in the garden of Les Vinaires, when I'm working in my chicken run, where the hedge is low and we can see into each other's gardens. Hans Schmidt, the pink-faced, fair one, seems to be the gardener—though all he does is to cut the grass and prune an occasional branch. When he is out there working, Alphonse will sidle up to him, and Hans will make a great fuss of him—kneeling down to him, rubbing between his ears—so the cat will purr and arch ecstatically.

On warm days, Max Richter will sometimes sit out on the lawn with a book. It makes me uncomfortable—in spite of all his kindness when Millie was hurt. He is a watcher. I know he misses nothing.

If he sees Millie in the garden, he will wave to her over the hedge. One day when she is skipping and I am feeding the hens, he calls to her.

'Millie, let me show you something.'

She goes to him. He reaches his hands across the gate towards her. His hands are loosely clasped together, and I see there is a butterfly fluttering between his folded fingers.

'This is a beautiful creature,' he says.

'It's called a butterfly,' she tells him, slightly superior.

'And does this butterfly have a special name?' he asks her.

He parts his hands a little—just enough to let Millie see. Millie peers between his fingers. The sunlight glints on his boots, and on the gun that shows at his belt.

'That's a Painted Lady,' Millie tells him. 'They come all the way from Africa. My mother told me.'

'It's a pretty name,' he says.

'Once I saw a Jersey Tiger,' she says. 'They have tiger stripes on their wings.'

'You have beautiful butterflies on your island,' he says.

She frowns slightly, watching his hands.

'You must be careful not to hurt it,' she says.

'Yes, I will be careful.'

'Do you have butterflies where you come from?' she says.

He smiles.

'Yes, we have butterflies,' he says.

They look at it for a moment longer, their dark heads

bent together, his hair close-cropped, hers loose and messy and falling over her face, the sun shining on them. I watch them, and think of all the people dead in London, all the wrenching grief, all the innocent lives ripped apart, and I can't put it all together, can't make any sense of it.

'I think you should let the butterfly go now,' says Millie. Rather reproving—like an adult speaking to a child. 'They don't like to be trapped like that. Wild creatures don't like to be trapped.'

'Yes, you're right, of course,' he says. 'But I've been careful not to hurt it.'

He opens his hands. The butterfly flits lazily away. Millie goes back to her skipping.

Later I hear the girls talking.

'I saw you,' says Blanche. 'I saw you talking to that German next door.'

'He had a butterfly. He showed me,' says Millie.

'Grandma will tell you off if she sees you speaking to Germans,' says Blanche.

Millie shrugs.

'Grandma didn't see us,' she says, limpidly. 'And anyway, that's not a German, that's Max.'

June. When Gunther comes to my door one night, I see that something has changed. He must have been drinking heavily. His eyes are too bright, his hands clumsy; a smell of alcohol leaks from his skin. And there's something in his face, something used-up, defeated.

Usually we go straight upstairs. But in the passage, he pulls me to him, forgetting where we are. His kiss is urgent, as though he wants to hide himself in me: he tastes of drink, his skin is clammy. I'm desperate to get him up to my room. I pull him towards the stairway, worried that he will stumble and that Blanche or Millie will wake.

In my room, I lock the door, turn to face him, afraid.

'What is it? What's happened?'

My first thought is for Hermann, his son. I feel a fear that chills me through—that something has happened to Hermann.

He doesn't answer at once. He pulls off his jacket, his belt. He sits on my bed, takes off his boots, his gestures heavy, slow, a frown deeply carved in his forehead.

'The Führer has declared war on Russia,' he says.

His voice is freighted with significance—as though he expects me to grasp at once all the many things that flow from that. But I don't know the meaning of this news—for the war, or for him, or for me.

He moves his hand across his face—uncertainly, as though his own features are unfamiliar to him. He looks up at me then, that unnatural glittery brightness in his eyes.

'We had hoped it would be over soon.' His voice a little slurred. 'But what happens now? I don't know... Max says we will lose the war now.'

'Max says that?' I'm amazed.

'Max says what the hell he likes. Max believes in no one. Max has never believed that those in charge know what they are doing,' he says.

'But why—why does this mean that Germany will lose the war?' I say.

'The war in Europe goes well for us,' he says. As though he's unaware of the abyss between us, when he says this. 'It is the act of a madman to open another front in the East. And Russia...' He shakes his head, as though there are no words that can express what he means. 'Russia has defeated many armies,' he says.

'Oh,' I say.

To me all this seems so far away—another planet. Russia to me is fabulous, violent—almost savage, remote: the Tsar and his family slaughtered; Tolstoy and Tchaikovsky; the gorgeous coloured cupolas of St Basil's in Red Square. I think as so often how little I know about the wider world.

'They say you cannot imagine the vastness of it,' he says. He moves his hand vaguely—as though helpless to suggest that vastness. 'Cornfields and then more cornfields—on and on, to the horizon—and then more cornfields beyond that. And forests, endless forests and swamps. And Russia's armies are limitless... And in Russia, they have winter...'

I tell myself I should be glad, because Max has said that the Germans will lose the war. This should make me hopeful. But Gunther's news has filled me with dread, and I don't know what this means.

PART IV:

SEPTEMBER 1941 - NOVEMBER 1942

CHAPTER 44

In September, Millie starts school at St Peter's up in the parish square.

She wears her blue Viyella dress that has tucks around the bodice, which I will let out as she grows, and her pigtails are tied with red ribbon. Her bar shoes used to belong to Blanche, but I've polished them till they look new.

The playground is full of children, the ones who are starting today pressed up against their mothers, the older ones milling around, playing marbles or hopscotch or jacks. Some girls are doing handstands against the wall of the school, their full skirts billowing out like the petals of over-blown flowers. I remember how Blanche cried and protested when first she went to school, how she was terrified of the playground, not wanting to let go of me, so I had to peel her fingers like sticking plasters from my hands; but Millie just looks back at me briefly and then walks boldly forward, stepping out into the stream of her future in the shiny bar shoes.

The house feels different without her. Even when she was quiet I always knew she was there, as though the air were charged by her vivid, purposeful presence. I keep busy; I get through my tasks much quicker than I did when she was at home. I scrub my kitchen till it gleams, I pick the last of my runner beans, I bottle the plums from my plum tree. They're good fruit for bottling—Victorias: they keep their rich rose colour even when they're cooked, and all day my kitchen is fragrant with their winey, opulent scent. I'm pleased with what I've achieved; but I miss her.

At home time, I wait outside the school with all the other mothers. I know a few of these women from when Blanche started at school, though that was ten years ago now—some of them have big families, or a gap between children, like me. There's Susan Gallienne, tall and slender and stylish: she has a classy pallor and her hair is cleverly waved. There's Vera Hill, who runs her household with army-camp precision: a bracing scent of carbolic soap hangs about her. There's Gladys Le Tissier, who has six children, and an air of being always slightly distracted—as though everything happens too quickly, and things race past and she struggles after them, calling for them to wait for her. We greet one another, tell our news, promise that we'll meet up.

The school doors open; the children spill out. Millie comes running up to me, flushed, rather dazed by all the newness of everything. One of her ribbons has come undone and is flying out like a little flag as she runs. I bend to hug her. She smells of school—of wax crayons, chalk dust, apples. The smell fills me with nostalgia—for best friends and playground conspiracies, for skipping games and whispered secrets and fingers smudged with ink—all the school things.

'Sweetheart. Did you have a nice day?'

She nods vigorously.

'*I* was good,' she tells me. 'But Simon had to stand in the corner. Miss Delaney made him. He put a wriggly worm down Annie Gallienne's blouse.'

'Simon Duquemin?'

'Yes,' she says. 'Simon Duquemin.' She rolls the name

around her mouth, as though it tastes especially good, like a stolen caramel. 'Simon is *seven*.' As if this were a major achievement, and worthy of respect.

The next day, as we walk home from school, she talks about Simon again.

'Simon got the slipper,' she tells me.

I remember Blanche talking about the slipper: it's not really a slipper at all, but an old plimsoll that Miss Delaney keeps in the drawer of her desk. She beats the children with it if they're very badly behaved. All the children are afraid of it.

'But, Millie, it's only the second day of term. I thought you'd all still be on your best behaviour...'

'He had to bend over the desk,' she says. 'He said it didn't hurt him, but I think it did. I think he was trying not to cry.'

The countryside is mellowing with September, autumn's gold gloss on everything. The first bright leaves are falling, and rustling on the tarmac. They sound like stealthy footsteps in the quiet of the lane.

'So what did Simon do—to deserve the slipper?' I ask.

'He was very naughty,' she tells me. 'He was sitting behind Maisie Guerin, and he stuck the end of Maisie's pigtail in his bottle of ink.' Again, there's that thread of respect in her voice. 'Mummy, I want to play with Simon.'

This worries me: Simon Duquemin sounds a little wild. But Millie is insistent.

So the next morning, I speak to Ruthie Duquemin, his mother, as we wait in the playground. I only know her by sight. She's a pale, rather anxious woman, with a mist of fair hair round her head, and eyes of a startling clear green, like the hart's tongue fern in the hedgebank.

'I was wondering—would Simon like to come and play with Millie after school?'

Her smile is spacious and kind.

'Yes, I know he'd love to,' she says. 'He seems very taken with Millie.'

Simon knocks at our door. He has white arms blotched with freckles, his mother's exuberant hair, and a suspicious expression. He peers past me into the passageway.

'I've come for *her*,' he says.

Millie has changed out of her school clothes into her oldest frock. She takes an old satchel of Blanche's: I've put a jam jar in it, with string tied round it for fishing, and an apple to eat. As I say goodbye, it's as though her feet won't keep still: she hops from one foot to the other like a dancer. Her eyes are sunlight-on-water.

'Don't go too far. And be sure to come back before dark…'

My words fall into silence. They're over the lane already, and through the orchard and into the wood, their clear voices trailing like bright streamers behind them.

I tidy my kitchen. I stack up the Kilner jars full of plums on the larder floor. It's good to see all that abundance, the heavy glass jars that are filled with rose-red fruit. I wash my kitchen floor, though really it doesn't need it. As the tree-shadows lengthen and reach like grasping hands across the lane, anxiety creeps up on me and I long to have her safe home with me. It's the first time she's ever played out.

But well before tea-time, Simon brings Millie back to our door, and heads off up the lane to his house. Millie bursts into the living room, where I am doing the darning and

Blanche is brushing her hair. Millie is muddy, dishevelled, pink with happiness. She smells of bracken and sunlight.

'Simon climbed to the top of a tree,' she says.

'Boys are such show-offs,' says Blanche, pausing in her hair-brushing. She's counting the strokes, bent forward, her bright blonde hair hanging down; each day she tries to do a hundred strokes before bed.

'Well, I hope he didn't expect you to climb up there, as well,' I say to Millie.

'He was looking for an old woodpigeon's nest,' she tells me. 'I was meant to catch him if he fell out. And then we made a den in the wood. We were hiding from bombs. The bombs killed everyone but they didn't hit us… And then we were *soldiers*,' she says.

She shoots a pretend gun at Blanche.

'Honestly, Millie. Girls don't shoot. You ought to know that,' says Blanche.

She straightens, swings her hair back over her head. She looks at herself in the over-mantel mirror, posing a little. Light shimmers on the river of her hair.

'Simon really likes me,' says Millie, boastful. 'Simon says I'm really not like a girl at all.' As though this is the highest praise.

After that, Simon plays with Millie most days after school.

One evening, she comes home tense and breathless and thrilled.

'We made an army camp in Mr Mahy's barn,' she says.

Peter Mahy's barn is just beyond my orchard, on the track through the fields that I took when I went to Les Brehauts. He doesn't keep it well. He scarcely ever goes to it: he stores his old farm machinery there now he can't get the spare parts.

There's a rickety stair to the hayloft, where the children could climb and fall through.

'You must be very careful when you play there. You mustn't play on the tractor. And you mustn't go in the hayloft,' I say.

'We were *very* careful, Mummy.'

'You're all out of breath,' I tell her.

'That's because we got chased,' she says.

'*Chased*, Millie? Who chased you?'

'Mr Mahy's dog,' she says. 'His dog is very nasty. We went back past the farmhouse and he chased us up the lane.'

I know the dog—he's a big Alsatian, rather bad-tempered. This worries me.

'What were you doing, to make him chase you?' I say.

'Simon threw a stone at him.'

'*No*, Millie. That's a very bad thing to do.'

'Simon isn't bad. It was a very little stone.'

'He shouldn't have done that,' I say.

'It was little as a leaf,' she says. 'It was really, really tiny. Like this...'

She holds her finger and thumb together: between them, just the smallest sliver of air.

'I don't care how little it was,' I say.

I feel a niggle of doubt: there's a streak of wildness in Simon, something that just doesn't care what adults tell him to do. I worry what he could lead her into.

'You must never do that again, either of you,' I tell her.

'*I* didn't do anything. I promise, Mummy,' she says.

CHAPTER 45

With Millie at school, I have a little more freedom—though I don't like leaving Evelyn on her own for very long.

One afternoon in November, I cycle up to town. I buy bread and meat and onion sets, and change my library book. I manage to find a few balls of knitting wool for Evelyn, and I buy some powdered carravita from Carr's in the arcade; it's made from seaweed and you can use it as a gelling agent. *The Press* had a recipe for a jam that you can make from turnips; it didn't sound very inviting, but I thought I would give it a try.

As I cycle homeward up the hill, I pass Acacia Villa, where Nathan Isaacs used to live—where I'd sometimes come to music evenings, before he went on the boat. I remember those evenings—a little opulent claret to drink, a fine fire burning in the grate; playing Beethoven's Spring Sonata for violin and piano. He especially loved Beethoven. He was a wonderful violinist—a much better musician than me; and there's something about the violin—the silken flow of it, the way it soars and sings—that can make the piano seem a little pedestrian. I wonder how Nathan is now. He said his cousin's house in Highgate was rather full of relatives: I hope it isn't too boisterous for him; I hope he has a room where he can play his violin. The villa always looked elegant, a shiny lion brass door-knocker on the green-painted front door, the front lawn sleek, with flower borders. But it's grown shabby, run-down, without him. The flowerbeds are a tangle of docks and dying blonde grasses; and the brown-paper heads on the hydrangeas rustle and lisp in the wind. The salt air pushes my hair from my face, and a sudden sadness clutches at me for the way the world is changing, so much torn, uncared-for, destroyed.

As I pass the front door, two men come out. I can tell they're not island people. They're thin, and their clothes are ragged, and they're speaking a language that's strange to me—not German, which I recognise now. They look rather desolate and lost, their shadows falling in front of them, jagged and thin as winter branches. I can tell that they're shivering. Today you need a good woollen coat, with the wind that whips off the sea. It's unnerving, to hear this unknown language on our island. I wonder who they are, why they're here, in this place so far from their home.

The light thickens so early now: it's getting dark already. Seagulls cry. Winter is coming.

That night, when Gunther is with me, when we lie to-gether in the peace of my bed, I ask about the men I saw.

'There were some people in St Peter Port. In a house called Acacia Villa, where I used to visit, before…you know, before all this… They were foreign—not island people. Not German. They looked really thin and they didn't have warm enough clothes…'

Something tenses in him when I say that; I see a little hardening in the muscles round his mouth.

'The Führer wants to fortify these islands,' he tells me,

carefully. 'He is very proud of his conquest. The fortifications are nothing to do with us.'

'What d'you mean, they're nothing to do with you?'

'It's a different organisation—the Organisation Todt. They're bringing workers in to build defences around the islands.'

'Bringing them in from where?' I think of the language I didn't recognise.

'Holland, Belgium, some of them. Some are from Poland and Russia. They're prisoners of war or volunteers. Some are building camps to live in… Don't worry about it,' he tells me, smoothing my hair from my face. 'Let's leave the war outside. Let it be just you and me here…'

But later, in the darkness, he abruptly starts awake. His sudden movement wakes me too. He trembles, and the trembling passes into my body. He must have been stalked by some fear in his sleep, some night terror. I've blown my candles out, but the moonlight leaks through my curtains and falls on his face, on his eyes. He stares at me, yet looking through me, as though he doesn't see me. The sweat on his forehead gleams in the chalky light of the moon. He frightens me.

I stroke his arm, trying to bring him back to the present.

'Gunther. There's nothing to be afraid of. Everything's all right. This is Vivienne. My darling, you're here with me, remember?'

He stares.

'Gunther…'

His face shifts.

'Oh,' he says. 'Oh. Vivienne.'

He rubs his hand over his face, becomes himself again.

I wonder what he saw in his dream. But he doesn't tell me, and I don't ask.

I walk home from Angie's through the darkening evening. The sepia air is still, no wind—a thing that rarely happens on Guernsey; a single brown leaf traces out slow spirals as it falls. The world feels empty, hollow, and the shadows are purple as damsons. A sadness seems to come on the countryside with the fall of the dusk. Above the pale earth and the black trees the sky is the dark blue of ashes.

I move through the intricate long shadows of the poplars in the hedgebank, past the land that belongs to the Renoufs. I see that Joseph Renouf has put a scarecrow up in his field, that stands in a pool of damson shadow. It's cleverly constructed, made of scraps of wood and twigs, and dressed in tattered cast-offs. My footsteps are loud and echoey in the silence of the lane. There's a cold smell of night coming.

I walk on. But something about the sight disturbs me— something that doesn't make sense. A shiver of leaves behind me makes me suddenly turn. Fear fingers the back of my neck: the scarecrow has moved to a different place in the field. All the little hairs stand up on my skin. I can see the scarecrow's face now—I see that he is a man. I don't know who he is, or what he can be doing there, in the empty sepia dusk in Joseph Renouf's field. I worry that he will see me: I worry he might be dangerous; but he seems quite unaware of me. He is utterly intent on something he has in his hand that looks like an old cabbage stalk. As I watch he thrusts it against his face, gnawing furiously at it.

I wonder what can have happened—that a man has been reduced to this, to eating a thrown-out cabbage stalk. Has he escaped from a locked ward somewhere? Has he lost his mind?

Before I turn the corner, I look behind me again: but the tattered man has vanished, as though he had never been there. As though I conjured him up from some dark place inside me.

The nights are drawing in, and Millie and Simon can't play out after school. Sometimes she goes up to his house, and sometimes he comes down to ours.

When they're playing together around the house, it's all too much for Evelyn.

'My head hurts. Such a racket,' she says. 'So many comings and goings.'

I tell them to be quieter, but my warnings just slide off them.

Evelyn overhears them singing in German—'*Stille Nacht, Heilige Nacht*': they've been learning German Christmas carols at school. She raps her knitting needle on the arm of her chair.

'Stop that at once,' she says.

Millie flushes.

'Sorry, Grandma.'

For myself, I think it's good that they're learning German: we may face a long future of Occupation, and if they can speak the language they will be better prepared. Though I'd never say that to Evelyn.

'Evelyn—they learnt it from Miss Delaney. It doesn't mean anything,' I tell her.

'Well, that's where you're wrong,' says Evelyn. 'Of course it means something. The Hun may have come to Guernsey, but we're not letting him into our house…'

I turn from her, my face hot.

I send them to play in the small back attic, where they can't be heard. Evelyn settles back to her knitting. I don't see the children again till I call up the stair for Simon, to tell him it's time to go home.

'Did you have a good time, sweetheart?' I ask Millie, after he's gone.

She nods vigorously.

'Simon was a varou,' she says. 'He had fur and very big teeth.'

I ask her to repeat this—I don't recognise the word.

'A *varou*, Mummy. *You* know. *You* know what a varou is.'

'No, I don't.'

She gives me a dubious look, as though she can't believe my ignorance.

'A varou looks like a man—except by the light of the moon. Then…'

She puts back her head and gives a shivery wolf-howl.

'Oh. A *werewolf*,' I say.

'Yes, of course. The varou bit me. Look.'

She holds out her arm, rather proudly. I can see the fading white toothmarks. I'm appalled.

'Millie—you shouldn't let Simon *bite* you.'

'Don't worry, Mummy. There wasn't any blood.'

'I should hope not.'

'Anyway—it was just a game. It was only pretend. He isn't one really,' she says.

'No—well, of course not.'

'But shall I tell you a secret, Mummy?'

I nod.

She pulls my face down close to hers and whispers in my ear.

'Simon knows where there's a real varou,' she says.

'Millie—werewolves aren't real. Not *ever*.'

She ignores me.

'*This* varou is real,' she says. 'The varou I'm talking about.' Her mouth is very close to me: I feel her moth-breath on my face. Her whispery voice is dramatic, intense. 'He prowls down the lane that leads from St Pierre du Bois to Torteval. He has a barrow full of parsnips that he pushes along. And he likes to eat bad children.'

There's a thread of fear in her voice.

'Oh. And how does Simon know this exactly?'

'His big brother told him,' she says. 'It's really true, Mummy.'

'No, sweetheart. It's just a story.'

She shakes her head, emphatically.

'Simon's big brother knows lots of things,' she tells me. 'Simon's big brother made a biplane from cartridge paper and glue. It can really fly. Simon showed me…'

I feel angry with Simon, and Simon's big brother, for frightening Millie like this.

Johnnie comes to see me, with a jar of apple chutney from Gwen, and a bag of spinach, just picked. We sit at my kitchen table and drink some mint tea I've made. He's never said anything more about the swastika scheme, but there's an uneasiness between us now, and this saddens me. There's something reserved in his eyes; and small awkward gaps in the conversation—a sense that there are treacherous places that we have to tiptoe around: hidden channels of dark water.

To fill in one of the silences, I ask him about the men I saw at Nathan's house.

'They'll be workmen from Holland and Belgium, the ones you saw,' he tells me. 'They're bringing lots of workers in from the continent. Hitler's building a ring of concrete all 'round the island,' he says.

It's as Gunther told me; and I ask what I couldn't ask Gunther.

'But *why*, Johnnie? It doesn't make any sense. It's like they really expect the RAF to attack; but nobody thinks that's going to happen. Nobody thinks that Churchill is bothered about us at all. We're just a little island...'

Johnnie shrugs.

'Well, that's what they're doing,' he says. 'That seems to be Hitler's plan. Those workmen you saw in St Peter Port—they don't get treated so badly, they get a bit of a wage.'

I think of the men I saw—how thin they were, how the salt wind made them shiver.

'They looked as though they were treated quite badly enough,' I tell him. 'They looked as though they didn't eat.'

He shakes his head. There are little lines between his eyes, precise as if cut with a blade.

'It's worse in the work camps—far worse. You know—like the camp they've been building up on the hill near the cliffs. Up above Les Tielles.'

I remember how Gunther said that the workers were building camps to live in.

'I didn't know,' I tell him. 'I never go that way.'

'The men are there to fortify the clifftop. The camp up there is a brutal place. They scarcely feed them at all.'

I remember the man I glimpsed in the dusk in Joseph Renouf's field.

'I saw a man in a field,' I say. 'He was very thin. I think he was eating a cabbage stalk. I thought he was just a scarecrow, till he moved and I saw his face.'

'He was probably from the camp,' says Johnnie. 'Those men are really wretched. They're from Poland or Russia, most of them. They're like slaves, the people who work there, treated like slaves. Worse than slaves. They beat them…' A shadow crosses his face. 'I've seen a man hanged from a tree there. The body was hanging for days.'

A shudder goes through me. I don't say anything.

'There are Algerians too, and gypsies. You should go and see for yourself, Auntie. You ought to know what's happening here on our island,' he says.

'Yes. I probably should…'

But I'm only saying that because it's what Johnnie expects me to say. The thought of going to the camp appals me. I think—What good would it possibly do to go and see for myself? It's all too big for me. I can't change it, none of us can, it's all beyond us, we can't stop it from happening… Yet my reluctance still shames me. I know that it's a weakness, that I feel this.

'No man should be treated like that,' says Johnnie. 'You hear things, don't you? Things people say—that they must be there because they've committed some terrible crime. Florrie Gallienne at church was saying that. But what could any man possibly do, to deserve such punishment? We're looking into it, me and Piers. We're going to do what we can do…'

The mention of Piers unnerves me.

'Johnnie—what can you possibly do? It's this great war machine—you can't stop any of it.'

He ignores me.

'In Jersey they've started already. They're setting up a network to help some of the workers escape,' he tells me. 'Safe houses and so on.'

This seems extraordinary to me.

'But where would they go to?' I ask him. 'None of us can escape. There's no getting out of these islands… We're all just stuck here now…'

'They live as islanders,' he tells me.

'Until when? Until the war is over?'

'Until we win,' he says.

January. Stormy weather. Up on the hill at Les Ruettes, the windows are crusted with salt, though you're still a mile from the sea there. It's a struggle to keep my house warm enough: there's a wind like a knife that cuts through closed windows and doors. We all have chilblains.

I wait with all the other mothers in the playground. Everyone looks a little more shabby, a little more darned. The wind rattles the ivy leaves on the wall of the school behind us.

Here too the talk is of the slave-workers.

'Have you seen all those poor workers they've brought in to do their building?' Gladys is frowning. 'They must treat them terribly badly, they look half starved,' she says.

'They must be so cold in this weather,' says Ruthie Duquemin, Simon's mother. 'They sleep in those horrible camps, and they only have rags for their clothes.' She shivers, as though she can feel their coldness in her own body.

'But they're all prisoners, aren't they?' says Susan. Unlike the rest of the mothers, she's made a bit of an effort: she's wearing powder and lipstick, and she still has an easy elegance, even in her threadbare coat. 'So they must be criminals, mustn't they? They've all done something. They must have committed some crime.'

'It's still pretty awful, the way they treat them,' says Gladys. 'It isn't humane.'

Susan pulls her coat closer around her.

'What we have to remember is—we don't know the whole story,' she says. 'They must have done something serious, to be treated as badly as that.'

I remember what Johnnie said—*What could any man possibly do, to deserve such punishment?* But I don't say anything.

'And they look so unhealthy,' says Vera. 'They're probably riddled with lice.' Her face is pinched and tight, clenched against the icy wind.

There's a murmur of agreement.

Susan clears her throat briskly.

'It's awful for them, obviously, but the truth is, they could be infectious. They could be spreading diseases. To be entirely frank, we could do without them on our island. We've got enough to put up with already,' she says.

'Poor wretches,' says Ruthie, Simon's mother. 'It's not their fault they're here.'

She has a troubled look: there's a frown in her fern-green eyes. I know she's upset by the conversation. I ought to join in and support her: but I can't work out what to say.

'You've got to feel sorry for them,' she says.

I start to say something, agreeing; but my voice is sucked in by the wind, and Vera speaks above me.

'But what can you do? I heard about this woman on Jersey.

She took one of the slave-workers into her house, and the Germans found him there.'

'What happened?' asks Gladys.

Vera says nothing for a moment. The wind in the ivy leaves behind us makes a cold hard sound.

'I heard they shot her,' she says.

A little charge runs round the group, an electric current of fear. No one says anything for a moment.

'People who do that kind of thing make trouble for everyone,' says Susan. 'Putting the rest of us at risk.'

Vera nods.

'There's nothing we can do. We just have to knuckle down and get on with our own lives,' she says. 'Look after the people that we're responsible for. I mean, it's sad for them and all that—but it's nothing to do with us. We've got our own lives to lead…'

I'm about to speak, when the school bell rings for the end of the day. The women turn towards the building, the children flood out of the door. Millie rushes up to me and I bend down and she flings her arms around me. I breathe in her scent of wax crayons and apples, and the musk of her hair.

'Did you play with Simon today?' I ask.

'Yes, of course. He's my *friend*.'

We ease back into our ordinary lives. But I feel a small hot flicker of shame that I didn't manage to speak.

I walk up the hill to Les Ruettes with some of the turnip jam I made with the carravita I bought. There are snow-drops in the hedgebanks, meek suppliants, hanging their heads, and you can smell the sweet vanilla scent of winter heliotrope, but spring still seems a distant promise. Above me, rooks roll and tumble like torn black rags on the white rushing stream of the sky.

It's chilly in Angie's kitchen; her fire gives out only a thin, paltry warmth. The wind rattles the elder against her window; the sound seems too significant, as though someone is out there, someone who wants to get in. Cold air creeps under her door and makes little swirls and eddies in the dust and dead leaves in the corners, that haven't seen a broom for weeks—though before Frank died, her kitchen was always gleaming and immaculate.

She's grateful for the turnip jam.

'Really, you shouldn't. You're too good to me, Vivienne.'

She looks older, haggard, a fine graph-paper of lines round her mouth and her eyes. I ask how she is and she shakes her head a little. Usually she'll say something cheerful—*Not so bad, Vivienne. Mustn't complain...* But she fixes me with her sad clear eyes.

'It's over a year now,' she tells me. 'I should be getting over it, but I'm not. I miss him so much, it's killing me.'

I put my hand on her arm.

'A year's such a short time,' I tell her, 'when you've lost someone.'

'I don't know, Vivienne. I feel I need to pull myself together. I mean, it's not as though it's just me. Thousands of folk are going through this...'

It's quiet between us for a moment. I think of all the things that she used to tell me about—the strange old things she still half believes in, the stories of the islands: about the fairy settlements that are connected by underground roads; how the body of a drowned man thrown up by the sea demands burial; how the flower of the hawthorn should never be brought in the house. But now she is often silent—as though words don't come so easily to her, as though she has to dredge them up from some deep place inside her.

I tell her about the man I saw in Joseph Renouf's field.

'I've seen them too,' she tells me. 'They seem to let them out at times—I think they must turn a blind eye. They let them scavenge on the farms. That way I suppose they don't have to feed them so much.'

Her lips are chapped and bleeding. She dabs them with a handkerchief.

'They're treated so badly,' I say.

Something dark moves over her face.

'It's even worse on Alderney,' she tells me. 'Jack told me. Jack's doing some work on Alderney now... Well, I explained to you, Vivienne. He has to make ends meet, he has all those growing children to feed...'

I wonder what on earth the Germans can want with Alderney. It's such a small, bleak, windswept island, with hardly any good soil.

'What's happening there?' I ask her.

'There aren't any islanders there any more,' she tells me. 'Everyone went to England. Jack found a dog running wild—it had to be shot, poor little thing...'

'But what do the Germans want with the place?'

'They're building bunkers on Alderney, and the camps are worse there,' she says. 'Jack told me. There are four camps there, and the men there are starving, he said. The men have high voices, they make a sound like birds... People do, when they're starving, Jack told me. I didn't know that. Did you know that, Vivienne?'

I shake my head. Chill fingers of air reach out into the room. The elder tree knocks at the window.

'The ones who work there are beaten, they're treated like animals,' she says. 'Worse than animals, even... Jack told me this thing, and I can't get it out of my head.' She leans in close; her breath, secretive, nicotine-scented, brushes my face. 'There was a man,' she says, 'who fell into the concrete-mixer there, and the Germans wouldn't stop the machine, and the man was buried alive. Jack saw it happen. He told me...'

That night, I ask Gunther about Alderney.

'People say... People talk about Alderney,' I tell him. 'A friend of mine told me...' I clear my throat, which is suddenly thick. 'She said that people are starving there. There are rumours, of bad things being done. Do you know what's happening there?'

His face is shuttered.

'There are work camps on Alderney,' he says. 'They're nothing to do with us. It's as I told you, Vivienne. It's the Organisation Todt.' He strokes my hair. 'Darling—let's not worry about them. Please. Don't bring them into this room.'

He doesn't know, I tell myself. It's nothing to do with him.

CHAPTER 46

The weather changes. We wake to white sunlight and washed blue skies. There's a froth of blossom in my orchard, and in the grass beneath the trees a scattering of pale windflowers. The evenings lengthen, so Millie and Simon play out for a while before tea. There are glossy lacquered celandines in the hedgebanks, and narcissi, sherbet-scented, dance in the fields. The Blancs Bois shakes and shivers with birdsong.

Angie tells me there are mushrooms—big meaty chanterelles—in Harry Tostevin's fields near the top of the cliff. So one Saturday I leave Evelyn and Millie, and cycle up to the clifftop. The air smells of the changing seasons, carrying the green fresh scents of pollen and sap and the coconut smell of the flowering gorse, and it's so warm I don't need a cardigan. The grasses sway in a light wind, as though a hand is stroking them. Up at the top of the lane I can see the shine of the sea, and from here the waves seem tiny, the water scarcely moving at all. My body is fluid, easy, in the warmth of the sun. I think of Gunther: the thought ripples in me that in spite of everything I am happy.

I leave my bicycle lying where there's a gap in the hedgebank. It's muddy here, the damp earth sucks at my shoes. I find wonderful chanterelles, in hidden ditches and shadowy, damp hollows under the hedge. In the shadows the dew hasn't dried yet, and my shoes and the cuffs of my blouse are darkened with wet. The mushrooms have a rich, earthy smell; I fill my basket with them. I'm planning how I shall cook them, with a knob of butter I've saved. I feel my mouth filling with water as I think how good they will taste.

I'm vaguely aware of something approaching, troubling the peace of the day. A distant disturbance, a man's voice shouting. As the voice comes nearer, I hear that he's shouting in German. The shouting draws rapidly closer, and I hear the sound of many footsteps tramping down the lane. I feel a resentment—that something should intrude on the peace of my morning. I have an instinct to hide, but I've left it too late, I just stand there. I watch as a gang of workers passes in the lane. There are about a dozen of them. They must be going to the clifftop, to build Hitler's ring of concrete that Johnnie told me about. Their appearance appals me. They are dressed in rags and their bones stick out through their skin— their collarbones, the bones of their wrists. They shuffle, not lifting their feet, and their backs are hunched over, pressed down, as though they carry some terrible weight. There are two guards, who have different uniforms from the soldiers of the Wehrmacht, the grey uniforms we are used to—these are brown, with swastika armbands.

I watch them pass. My heart is loud in my chest.

One of the prisoners is limping. As I watch, he stumbles, falls. He's left behind; he tries to get up but he can't—he's too weak, too hurt, perhaps. One of the guards turns, goes back to the fallen prisoner. My first stupid, innocent thought is that at least he will help the man to his feet. But he's shouting something in German—you can tell he's cursing the man. The prisoner struggles to get to his feet, but falls back, helpless. The guard stands over him, hits him with the butt of his gun: hits him again and again, so I hear the sound of it, the gun hitting flesh, hitting bone: it's far too loud in the silent lane. The man on the ground moves slightly, puts his arm over his face in a small hopeless gesture of self-protection, but then his arm falls away. Bright blood leaks from his mouth. The guard lowers the gun and wipes the butt on the grass. I tell myself he will walk away now: perhaps the man could still live, perhaps when the work-gang has gone I could go to him and help him... But the guard takes a step back and starts to kick the man's head, kicks it open: I hear the sound of the crack of the boot on the skull. There's a lumpy red seep from the wound that I don't want to see or to think about—but my eyes are fixed there, and I can't drag them away.

I have a quick impulse to run to the guard, to stop him. I even take a few steps towards him, but something pulls me back—the thought of my children and Evelyn, the people who need me to care for them. A tremor goes through my body. I stand there, trembling, torn. The guard looks up, sees me, shrugs. He doesn't care that I'm there, that I'm watching everything he does. He's casual, he has no guilt. He kicks the man on the ground again, goes on and on kicking, long after the man on the ground is utterly still, the heavy boot breaking the broken head.

The blackbirds carry on singing, the flowers are holding up their vivid heads. I can't understand why the countryside looks just the same as ever, all bright with gilded springtime. This brightness seems an outrage to me.

The guard walks off, leaves the dead man lying—as though he is nothing, worse than nothing. I vomit into the ditch.

CHAPTER 47

I prop my bicycle against the wall of my house. My hands are shaking, my whole body is shaking.

Millie is playing in the kitchen. She doesn't look up at me, she's intent on her play.

'See, Mummy, it's a wedding.' The dolls from her dolls' house are in a procession across the kitchen table. 'I'm going to have a wedding,' she says. 'I'm going to marry Simon. I'm going to wear a big fur coat with purple roses on.'

There's a splash of yellow sun on her, and all across my kitchen.

I put the basket of mushrooms down on the table.

'Ooh. Mushrooms. I love mushrooms. When can we have them?' she says.

I try to answer her, but my mouth won't seem to work properly.

Millie looks up at me then. She frowns.

'What is it?' she says. 'Are you cross that I'm going to marry Simon?'

'No, sweetheart, it's nothing to do with that.'

'Your face looks funny,' she says.

'Does it?'

I can't say—Don't worry, it's nothing to do with you: can't begin to form the words.

'Mummy, tell me.' She's worried. She gets down off her chair and comes to wrap her arms around me. 'Tell me what the matter is. Mummy, did you hurt yourself?'

'I just need a moment on my own,' I say. 'Could you give me that, sweetheart?'

She takes her arms away from me. She stares at me. There's a frightened look in her face. This is something that I have never asked for before.

'Perhaps you could play in the garden? Just for a moment?' I say.

She goes, but keeps turning to look back at me. Her eyes are wide and alarmed.

I sit at my table. The dark, earthy scent of the mushrooms is filling me with nausea. The thing I saw replays in my mind: I can't interrupt it or make it stop. I hear it, see it, so clearly: it's more vivid, more real, than the things around me in my kitchen—Millie's scattered dolls on the table, the ranks of jars on my shelves. All these familiar, substantial things seem flimsy to me, unreal.

Shame washes through me, a bitter hot shame—that I didn't rush out and plead with the guard, didn't grab his arm and implore him to let the man go: didn't do anything. I go through it over and over: I tell myself—Of course I couldn't have stopped him. I'm a helpless, defenceless woman, and I have my family to think of, my family who depend on me. He would have hit me too, or shot me, or had me put in prison, if I'd done that. I made the right decision… But knowing I couldn't have stopped him doesn't shield me from feeling the shame. It's as though by witnessing this terrible thing I have shared in the guilt of it: that it has become a part of me.

And as I replay it all in my mind, I think again and

again—Why did the guard go on kicking, after the man was still? Perhaps because he was seized with uncontrollable anger and rage? Yet he didn't *look* angry. He looked untroubled—casual, even. As though he went on kicking the man simply to be efficient, to make quite sure he was dead. Being thorough—believing this to be the right thing to do: that he was a guard and his job was to beat the prisoners, and what he did was nothing out of the ordinary. Or maybe it was that the cruelty had its own momentum: that he simply started killing and saw no reason to stop. Maybe there is no explanation that makes any sense—nothing but that blind unthinking cruelty.

I sit at my kitchen table for a long time. At last, Millie comes and tugs fretfully at my sleeve.

'It's dinner-time. I'm *hungry*, Mummy.' Her voice high-pitched, aggrieved. 'And I want to play with my dolls...'

I get up, and carry on with the things that have to be done, moving slowly through the rooms of my house as though I am wading through deep water.

But later that day I go back to the lane by Harry Tostevin's field. Not for any clear reason: it's just some inchoate sense that I owe this to the man that I couldn't protect. The body has been taken away. It's all just as it was before, as though nothing ever happened here.

I cycle slowly back through the flowering land and all the brightness of springtime. I have my eyes wide open, but all I can see is the dark.

CHAPTER 48

I sit on the bed. I've planned what I will say, but now I'm with him the words won't come. In the shivery light of my candles, the cabbage roses on my walls are absolutely black, and tremble as though they are shaken by a secret, silent wind.

He's turned a little away from me, taking off his clothes. His face seems made of shadow.

I clear my throat, which is suddenly thick.

'I saw something,' I tell him.

Perhaps he hears the shake in my voice. He stops undoing his shirt. He waits.

'I was picking mushrooms up near the top of the cliff, and I saw this thing that happened. Where there's a break in the hedgebank, on Harry Tostevin's land. Harry has a farm there... I saw something in the lane there. I stood in the field and watched it.'

I don't know why I'm giving him all these irrelevant details. Perhaps it's a way of putting off the thing I have to say.

He stands there, his shirt half undone, his questioning gaze on me.

'I saw a terrible thing,' I say. 'I saw a guard kill a man—

one of the men in the work-gangs. Just because the man fell over. He beat him and kicked him to death.'

Gunther's eyes are on me, trying to read me.

'I'm sorry you had to see that,' he says, carefully.

'It's not that I saw it—it's that it happened at all,' I tell him.

He chews his lip, as though he's struggling to find the right words.

'Bad things happen in wartime. You must know that,' he says then.

'But he did it so casually—as though it didn't mean anything.' My voice is shrill. 'As though it was just part of his day's work…'

Gunther clears his throat.

'Vivienne,' he says quietly. 'It is very easy to kill. To start with, maybe not so easy. But after a while it is very easy to kill. Maybe that shouldn't be so, but it is.'

I don't ask how he knows this.

'You mustn't think about it,' he says. 'You must try not to dwell on it.'

But all I can see is the man who was beaten to death—how he raised his arm so helplessly against the boot, the gun; the seepage from his broken head. He is there between us. He will always be there between us.

'I can't just *decide* not to think about it,' I say.

'I know you probably blame us, but it was nothing to do with us,' he says.

'How can it not be to do with you?' I hear the sharpness in my voice: you could cut yourself on it. 'You're part of the German army…'

When I say it baldly like that, I suddenly think of what I am doing: loving him, giving so much of myself—all the love I could never give Eugene. In this moment, I see with absolute clarity how others would judge me for it. And might be right to judge me.

He shakes his head.

'No, Vivienne. It's a different organisation. Like I told you—it's the OT. They're in charge of all the fortifications and the work camps. We're not responsible for them. We can't control what they do.'

'There must be *something* you can do,' I tell him. 'You can't just let this happen. This savagery.'

'Vivienne—we can't stop it, we have no power to stop these things.' He sits beside me, reaches out towards me. His touch is urgent: he holds my wrist too tightly, his fingers dig into my skin. 'We have to think of our families, of the people who depend on us, who need us to stay alive for them… If you protest they send you to the Russian Front,' he tells me.

'How do I know that you're not just saying that?' I ask, in a little shred of a voice.

My throat feels sore, as though saying this has hurt me.

He looks startled, that I could suggest such a thing—could accuse him of lying to me. Seeing this offers me just a crumb of reassurance. He drops my wrist, stands, turns away.

'It's happened already,' he tells me.

'When? What happened?'

'One of our officers protested about the treatment of the prisoners. He was down at the harbour when one of the prison ships came in. They sent him there, to Russia,' he says. He's speaking very quietly: I can scarcely hear him. There's something new in his voice—a jagged splinter of fear. 'It's Hell on earth, in Russia,' he says. 'It's a death sentence.'

I wish we had more news, more understanding, of the war: I know so little.

'Why? What's happening there?' I say.

'We came very close to Moscow,' he says. 'But then winter came, and many were frozen alive.'

'Oh,' I say.

'There are men on this island who've killed themselves rather than be sent there. Or tried to break their legs in a fall so they couldn't fight any more.'

'I've never heard of that,' I say.

'There was one incident only last week. It happened in St Peter Port. A man threw himself from a wall and died. You have to believe me. This is the trap that we're in... There's nothing we can do,' he says.

'There must be something,' I say again. But sounding less certain.

He hears the concession in my voice. He kneels in front of me, takes my hand and holds it between his—carefully, as though I am very fragile: as though if he moved too suddenly, something might break.

'I'm not a hero, Vivienne,' he says. 'I want to come through this war alive. I want to see my son again.'

I remember what he told me about his stepfather—how his stepfather beat him. I think of what life has taught him. Keep your head down. Don't protest. If you keep quiet, perhaps they will come for someone else, not you.

'Yes, I know that,' I say. 'I understand that.'

I let myself be reassured. I tell myself—He has no choice, he can't stop it. It's what I want to be told—that it's nothing to do with him, that it's all beyond him...

He sees the change in me. He puts his hands to my face. I feel his heat go through me.

'My darling—can't we leave all this the other side of the door?' he says. 'Can't we forget the war for a while? It's just you and me here…'

But it isn't. Not any more.

CHAPTER 49

A few days later, I'm busy in my kitchen when I hear a sound of rattling and clinking from the living room. I go to see what is happening.

Evelyn is on her knees in front of the china cabinet. The glass door is open; she's taking out the china piece by piece, and laying it down on the carpet—all the cups and plates from my flowered teaset that survived the break-in.

'Evelyn, what are you doing?' I say gently.

She turns, gives me a stern look.

'Someone's coming, Vivienne. We want to be ready,' she says.

'Who's coming, Evelyn?'

'*You* know, Vivienne.' Conspiratorial—as though this is a secret. 'Careless talk costs lives,' she says. 'But we want to be prepared.'

'Evelyn—no one's coming. It's just the four of us here— you and me and the girls.'

I kneel down beside her. I put my hand on her arm, hoping my touch will bring her back to reality. She shakes my hand off.

'We have to be ready,' she tells me. 'Someone has to keep an eye on things.'

She reaches into the cabinet, takes out another cup. She

holds it close to her face, studies its intricate, formal pattern of flowers and ribbon and leaves, with a puzzled look. Then, it's as though she loses interest in it—her hand goes suddenly limp. The cup slips from her fingers, falls to the floor, shatters. At the sound of breaking, a shudder goes through her.

She peers at the broken pieces, as though they are nothing to do with her. She picks up a flowery shard and stares at it, trying to make sense of it.

'Someone broke a cup, Vivienne,' she says, austere and disapproving.

'I'll see to it,' I say.

'Someone's in trouble,' she says.

'It doesn't matter,' I tell her. 'No one's in trouble. You should just sit down now.'

I help her to her feet and into her chair.

'But we can't just sit here and twiddle our thumbs,' she says. She's a little breathless: the movement has exhausted her. 'We have to get out the tea things. We might not be ready in time.'

I know I have to humour her.

'We'll be ready,' I tell her.

She picks up her knitting. Her sherry-brown gaze glides vacantly round the room.

'Someone's coming,' she says. 'You mark my words. Someone's coming.' But she sounds less certain now.

I go to find the dustpan and brush, to sweep up the broken pieces.

When I come back she's almost asleep, her breathing slow and laboured, her eyes closing: you can see how her eyelids are netted with tiny lavender veins. I take her knitting from her, and wrap her blanket round her knees.

CHAPTER 50

J uly: the school summer holiday. Millie plays with Simon through the long lazy days of summer, going off after lunch each day, taking the old school satchel with an apple in; bringing it back full of treasures—a milk-white pebble, a twig to make a catapult, a silky indigo feather from a crow. She's thin—both girls are far too thin—but her skin has a flushed, healthy look. She has permanent scabs on her knees, and grass stains on her dresses, and a cocoa-powder spill of freckles on her nose.

There's a day when she doesn't come back when she should. Tea is ready on the table, and the shadow of my pear tree reaches out over the yard, fingering the wall of the house. I go to the gate, peer anxiously through the orchard and into the wood—fearful that Simon may have led her into some new mischief.

But at last she comes rushing in, waving to Simon who is running off up the lane.

'Millie, you're late. I was really worried.' I'm cross, because she frightened me. 'Next time, you're to come back earlier. If this happens again, I won't let you play out any more...'

My admonition slides off her.

'It was really fun, Mummy. Me and Simon played in the barn.'

'Mr Mahy's barn, you mean?'

'Yes. I *said*, Mummy.'

I think of Peter Mahy's barn—the rickety ladder to the hayloft, and all the old farm machines. I don't really like her playing there.

'You must be careful when you play there,' I tell her. 'You mustn't go up the ladder.'

'We didn't. We were *very* careful,' she says.

'And I hope you stayed well clear of Mr Mahy's dog.'

'We went like this.' She walks across the room elaborately on tiptoe. 'The dog didn't even *see* us.'

When tea is over, and Evelyn has gone to her room, and Blanche is on the sofa, re-reading one of her favourite Angela Brazil books, Millie comes to the chair where I'm sitting with my darning. She puts her arms around my neck.

'Can I tell you a secret, Mummy?' she says. 'A big, big secret?'

She smells of the outdoors, of apple-green days, of pollen and leaves and warm bracken. I feel the touch of her dark silk hair on my skin.

'Yes, sweetheart.'

She whispers in my ear, a melodramatic stage whisper.

'There's a ghost in Mr Mahy's barn. We saw a ghost,' she tells me.

A little judder of anxiety goes through me. She's six: she should be able to tell what's just imagined by now.

'Millie, listen to me. It's fun to play make-believe sometimes. But ghosts aren't really real.'

'Yes, they are. You can see them.'

'No, sweetheart. They're just stories—like witches and all the things in our fairytale books.'

She gives me a dubious look.

I feel guilty. I've told her too many fairy stories, encouraged her to believe in all sorts of imagined things. So when Simon talks about werewolves or ghosts—like when he told her about the varou that haunts the lane to Torteval, that gobbles up bad children—she believes him.

'Witches are just stories. But my ghost is real,' she says.

'No, sweetheart. Ghosts are just stories too.' I remember how I explained it before, when I read to her from the book of Guernsey tales. 'They're stories that people make up because they're afraid of the dark. Simon's been teasing you again.'

'No, he hasn't,' she says. 'I saw the ghost with my *own eyes*.'

She points to her eyes with an air of triumph, as though this is conclusive proof.

'Mum,' says Blanche, 'why does it matter so much? She's only a baby really. Babies believe in *everything*. Babies believe in the *tooth fairy*,' she says, with fraudulent tenderness. She puts down her book, gets up, gives Millie an extravagant hug. 'Who's my ickle baby?'

'Blanche—leave her alone,' I say. 'Don't be horrible.'

Millie wriggles away from her sister.

'You're *all* horrible. No one believes me,' she says. Her voice blazes with impotent anger.

She squeezes her eyes tight shut, but tears leak from her eyelids.

CHAPTER 51

I work hard at my vegetable garden. My carrots don't come up, and my lettuces get blackfly, but I pick runner beans, and radishes, and peas so sweet you can eat them straight from the pod; and the chickens are mostly laying well. I still have some flowers in my garden—the ones I couldn't bear to dig up: and my Belle de Crécy roses are blooming beneath the living-room window, drooping their big soft heads in the warmth, opening helplessly wide, releasing their candied, ravishing scent.

Our lives become more constricted. There are new laws and regulations: we read about them in *The Guernsey Press*. Civilian wirelesses have been banned: the Germans are searching people's houses, and if you have kept a wireless, they will send you to prison in France.

Everyone grumbles: it's so frustrating to be deprived of news.

But Johnnie is encouraged.

'It's because the war isn't going so well for them now,' he tells me. His eyes gleam, brown and bright as autumn. He doesn't tell me directly—but I suspect they have a wireless hidden somewhere at Elm Tree Farm. 'They don't want us to know. It's all about morale, Auntie.'

Johnnie amazes me—the way he can find reasons for hopefulness in anything.

The pattern of our days changes a little. Blanche rarely listens to our story in the evenings now. After tea, she likes to go up to Celeste's house, where she and Celeste will lie on the bed and flick through their copies of *Vogue*, dreaming kaleidoscope dreams of the future—a future gorgeous with pearls and lipstick and ruby-red suede court shoes.

'Mum, you'll never guess what Celeste told me,' she says one day, her voice quiet, full of secrets. 'Her mum has hidden her wireless. She hasn't handed it in.'

This immediately worries me. What if she's hidden it in the house? What if the Germans found it? If the Germans came and Blanche was there, would Blanche be blamed as well? Nightmare scenes spool out in my mind, with a horrible vividness—Blanche and Celeste arrested, and sent away to prison.

'But, Blanche—that's terribly dangerous, surely.'

Blanche grins.

'Not where she's keeping it,' she says. 'She hides it in a coffin at Mr Ozanne's.' Mr Ozanne runs the funeral parlour. 'Well, they're not exactly going to look there, are they?'

So now it's Blanche who keeps us up to date with the war. We hear about the battles in the desert in North Africa; and in Russia the Germans have crossed the River Don and are advancing on the great city of Stalingrad. I'm not sure that Johnnie is right: I can't find much reason for hopefulness in any of this news.

I make some bean-flour cake with runner beans from the garden, using a recipe from the parish magazine. You dry bean-pods in a slow oven, pass them through a mincer, sift them and mince them again until they've all been turned into flour. You seem to need a lot of beans for very little flour. Then you rub fat into the flour and mix it up with milk and a little honey and sultanas, and bake it in a cake tin. The process seems to take for ever. Before the war, the girls loved the times when I took out my big yellow bowl to make cupcakes or sponges; they'd help me stir the mixture, and loved to scrape out any uncooked mixture left in the bowl and to eat it as a luxurious treat: then later we'd make icing, blush-pink with cochineal, and Millie was always thrilled to hear how the colour was made from crushed spiders. But neither of them is interested in the bean-flour cake.

We have it for tea, after a plateful of vegetables from the garden, boiled potatoes and peas and cabbage. The cake is bland and rather grainy.

'It tastes like sawdust,' says Millie.

'You don't even know what sawdust tastes like,' says Blanche.

'I do. I *do* know. It tastes like this,' she says.

Blanche shrugs.

'Don't listen to her, Mum. It isn't that bad, really… Well, not when you're famished, anyway. There are days when I feel so hungry I could eat my hair,' she says.

I know what Millie means. The cake is a bit like blotting paper: it seems to soak up all the moisture in your mouth. Perhaps I was impatient and didn't mince the beans for long enough: you chew and chew, but it takes a long time to go down. But at least it's filling.

Blanche pushes her plate away, and gives a little sigh.

'Sometimes I dream about food,' she says. 'I had a dream about jam roll—that lovely steamed roll you used to make, the one with strawberry jam in. I could taste the jam in

the dream… And sherbet—sometimes I dream of sherbet…'
Her voice is yearning, nostalgic. 'And toffee crumble and
liquorice and humbugs and peppermint sticks…'

'*I* had a dream about treacle pudding,' says Millie, not to
be outdone. 'With a big, big dollop of custard.'

'What about you, Evelyn?' I ask her. 'Do you dream about
food?'

'I don't know really, Vivienne,' she says. 'Though I do like
a good roast dinner. When will we have a good roast dinner
again, Vivienne?'

'It's difficult,' I tell her. 'But I'll see what I can do.'

'What do you dream about, Mum?' says Blanche. 'What
was your best food ever?'

I think of that first bar of chocolate Gunther brought
me, the velvety smoothness on my tongue, the rush of
sweetness.

'I like jam roll as well,' I tell her.

When we've finished our tea, there are four slices left of
the cake, and I put them in my food-safe. It's in the coolest
place at the very back of my larder; it has a wire-mesh door,
to let in the air and keep out the flies. I keep food that has
to be covered there, and my butter and milk. We'll finish
the cake tomorrow.

The next evening, Blanche does the ironing while I make
a vegetable stew. I have spread my ironing blankets on the
kitchen table for her; you can hear the hiss of the fabric, and
the friendly smell of hot clean linen fills the room. Blanche
irons one of her pin-tucked blouses, then shakes out the
fabric and folds it, very exact. She's meticulous: I know that
she'll be a much better housewife than me. She will put the
blouse on after tea, to go up to Celeste's house.

When the stew is simmering, I go to the larder to fetch the slices of bean-flour cake.

'*No.*'

The plate is empty.

'What is it, Mum?' says Blanche, alarmed.

I'm briefly afraid that my mind is going—that I'm becoming confused like Evelyn, forgetting things that I've done.

'I thought there was some of that cake left. I *know* there was,' I tell her.

There's an edge of rage in my voice. I feel a sudden surge of self-pity, my eyes filling up with hot tears. I try so hard, work so hard: and then *this*—after all the effort I put into making that wretched cake, growing the beans, and cooking them, and all the mincing and sifting. I know it's the sudden, helpless anger that comes from being always a little too hungry, always tired. I try to push it away from me.

Blanche looks at me warily, afraid she is being accused.

'Mum, you know it wasn't me, don't you? You know I'd never do that.'

'I'm not blaming you,' I tell her.

'I know how careful we have to be, with the war and everything,' she says. 'I know we can't just eat what we want.'

'Really, Blanche, I know it's not you. It's just odd, that's all. I don't understand it,' I say.

Millie, hearing our urgent voices, slips into the room.

'What's the matter, Mummy?' Her eyes are wide and curious.

'It's the bean-flour cake. It's gone,' I say.

'But nobody liked it,' she says to me. 'So why do you look so upset?'

'I just don't understand what's happened...'

Briefly I wonder about Millie. But she had really hated the cake. Then it enters my mind that someone might have broken into our house. That whoever broke in on that long-ago day when we nearly went on the boat—Bernie Dorey, or whoever it was—has come back and raided our larder. Though even as I think this I know it's a crazy notion. No one has broken into our house; and nothing else has gone.

CHAPTER 52

I walk up the lane to Les Ruettes. It's a languorous August day; the meadows are drowsy, hazy, with summer, and there's a carnival of colour in all the gardens I pass—hollyhocks that are the dense, delicious colour of clotted cream, strident orange day lilies, yellow damask roses tumbled over an old granite wall—and the air is rich with mingled scents. Just for a moment I don't believe in the war.

We sit outside Angie's kitchen door, in two fold-up chairs she has put there. A warm breeze caresses our skin and ruffles the leaves of the elder, whose branches are heavy with berries, black and enticing as liquorice. I wonder if Angie will pick them for wine, as she used to do when Frank was alive; but perhaps she won't have the energy, perhaps she'll just leave them to drop.

She has her knitting basket.

'Would you help me ball this wool up, Vivienne?' she asks me.

I hold out my hands, and she stretches a skein of wool between them and starts to wind the wool into a ball, expertly, very evenly. In the whispering elm trees around her farmhouse, hidden woodpigeons are idly turning over their song.

There's something new in Angie's eyes, something veiled and remote.

'You seem very quiet, Angie,' I say, hesitantly.

She smiles a small rueful smile.

'You notice things, Vivienne, don't you, now? You're right—there's something on my mind. Something Jack told me,' she says.

I feel a flicker of apprehension.

'He's still working on Alderney?' I say.

She hears the uneasiness in my voice: she misinterprets me, thinks I don't approve.

'It's good money, that's the thing, Vivienne. You mustn't blame him,' she says.

'Of course, I understand that,' I say. 'I don't blame him, Angie.'

'There are some that say he shouldn't do it,' she says. 'He's had a lot of trouble for it—people who think they can tell other people how to behave.'

'Well, people love to find fault,' I say.

'We all have to find our own way,' she says. 'And the money's so much better than he could earn on Guernsey. It's hard to turn down, with all those little ones to feed. He can't bear the children to go hungry...'

'No, of course not,' I say.

She stops winding the wool for a moment, nestling the ball of wool in her hand, as though it is a fragile thing that has to be protected. I lower my arms, which are starting to ache. When she speaks again her voice is hoarse and hushed and secret: I have to lean a little towards her to hear. A slight movement of air shivers the leaves of the elder tree.

'They sent Jack diving down in the harbour,' she says. 'They've got an anti-submarine boom there, in Alderney harbour. Jack says it's like a big net. It had got all tangled up, they needed Jack to sort it out... Well, there's nothing he can't turn his hand to. He's good at diving, is Jack...'

Her face is very close to mine: her warm breath brushes my skin.

'He said the water was full of bones. Bones and rotting bodies. He can't sleep now, he told me.'

A thrill of cold goes through me. I don't say anything.

'They kill the poor wretches, they beat them or maybe they die at their work, the terrible work that they have to do, and they tip them into the harbour. It's all death down there, Jack told me—death and bones. All skeletons, and the bodies that the crabs and lobsters were eating. He can't get a wink of sleep at night for seeing the bones.'

We ball up the rest of the wool in silence.

CHAPTER 53

Johnnie comes to see me, with a bag of potatoes and some of Gwen's clover honey, and I show him round my garden. He lingers by my chicken run, looking over my chickens with a critical eye.

'Tell you what, Auntie. That one's a goner.' He points to one of my chickens that's been lurking in the corner, looking dejected, not eating. 'I bet it's got worms or a tumour.'

'Yes, I'd noticed,' I say.

'Looks like it's getting pecked by the others,' he says. 'There'll be carnage, Auntie. Chickens can be vicious. You need to get a move on. I'll do it if it would help.'

'Thanks, Johnnie. I know you would. But I'm going to do it myself. It's like you once told me, remember? You do what you have to do…'

His nose wrinkles up as he smiles.

'Well, Auntie, I'm impressed. I didn't know you had it in you.'

I'm happy when he says that: I like impressing Johnnie.

I give him a jar of my bottled plums for Gwen. He rides off, wobbling perilously, the glass jar rattling in one of the paniers slung from the back of his bike.

I choose a time when Millie's out playing—not wanting her to see. The chicken is tricky to catch. I don't like the feel of it on my skin—at once feather-soft and scratchy, and each time I think I've caught it, it fights its way out of my hands, as though it senses its imminent fate. The other chickens squawk and make a lot of frantic noise. Finally I corner it. I hold it in my left hand, grasp its head with my right. I close my eyes as I do it, hear the neat snap of the bone. Its wings go on flapping even after its neck is broken, and I feel a little rush of nausea, that I swallow down. Then finally it lets go of life and is limp and sad in my hand.

Later, I pluck it and gut it, the way that Angie taught me, feeling a quiet satisfaction that I have learnt to do all these things.

I roast the chicken with some of the potatoes Johnnie brought.

'Mmm,' says Blanche, when she comes home from work. 'That smells more like it. That smells *good*.'

'We're having a proper meal tonight,' I tell her.

She gives a knowing grin.

'Rapunzel?' she says. 'She's been looking rather peaky.'

'I'm afraid so.'

'Don't worry, I won't tell Millie,' she says. 'I know she doesn't like eating things that have names.'

I thicken the pan juices with a little bean flour I have left, to make a rich, dark gravy. I lay the table properly, with napkins, the silver napkin rings, and some of our best china. I bring the bird to the table. The smell of the succulent meat hangs in the air like a benediction, and fills our mouths with water.

'Here we are, Evelyn. It's that good roast dinner you wanted,' I say.

But Evelyn is staring at me. Her mouth is narrow, disapproving.

'Why are you carving, Vivienne? Carving's a man's job,' she says.

'It's a woman's job if there isn't a man here to do it,' I say.

A frown moves over her face and away, ephemeral as a trail of smoke.

'Mum—we ought to say Grace,' says Blanche.

So I ask Evelyn to say Grace for us, and she clears her throat, pleased to be asked.

'For what we are about to receive…' She hesitates, her face mists over. The girls join in and help her finish the prayer.

"May the Lord make us truly thankful."

We have such a happy meal-time, full of laughter and talk—like Christmas, like a festival. It's so wonderful to feel satisfied: there's a kind of peace that only comes to you when your stomach is full.

Evelyn puts her cutlery contentedly down on her plate. Her lips are shiny with grease. She blots her mouth decorously on her napkin.

'We ought to have chicken more often… Why don't we have more chicken, Vivienne?' she asks me.

'Evelyn—we have to be very careful with our food,' I say.

'When Eugene was here we had a roast meal every Sunday,' she says.

'But now there's a war on, remember?' I say.

'Oh,' she says. 'Oh. Is there, Vivienne?'

Once Evelyn has gone to her room, I clear the table. I put the remains of the chicken carcase in my food-safe. I'll make a good filling stew with the scraps of meat that are left, and boil the bones with sage and onions for a nourishing soup. It's so good to know where our next few meals will come from.

I sit in the living room, with my darning basket. Blanche is staying in tonight; she has one of Celeste's magazines. She rifles through the fashion pages, gazing at the glossy, imperious women in the photographs, yearning after their ruched satin gloves, their flirtatious little veiled hats.

'Look at this, Mum. It's so lovely…'

It's a Schiaparelli evening gown, extravagantly backless, clinging caressingly to the hips, then flaring full to the floor. I tell Blanche a story I once heard about Schiaparelli—how she made a hat like a birdcage, with canaries inside.

Blanche giggles.

'Mum—you're having me on.'

'No. It's true, I promise.'

Millie is kneeling on the floor, playing with her dolls' house. The gilded light of evening falls into our room, and the scent of lavender floats in, and a drift of rich, lingering perfume from the roses under my window. A sudden pride opens out in me like a flower in the warmth of the sun—pride in what I have achieved here: keeping my family fed and safe, my girls still smiling. I think, We are surviving. Somehow—in spite of everything—we are getting through.

Millie is busily rearranging the little dolls in the rooms.

'I saw the ghost again,' she announces, out of nowhere. The words fall into the quiet room like pebbles dropped in a pond, sending ripples through its stillness. 'Ghosts are very, very scary.'

She has her head down. Her hair is untied, and swings forward and shadows her face.

Blanche exhales noisily.

'For goodness' sake. Not that again,' she says.

'They are, too,' says Millie.

Blanche raises her eyebrows. Millie can tell she isn't being taken seriously.

'They *are*,' she says again.

She fiddles with one of her dolls, trying to make it stand up, but the doll keeps tipping over. She bangs the doll on the floor. She's cross: there's a slight frown etched in her face.

I feel that familiar niggle of worry about Millie—that fantasy seems too vivid to her, that she can't always tell the difference between make-believe and what's real. I kneel beside her and hold her head in my hands, wanting to get her full attention. Her face is very close to mine. I see the gold flecks that swim in the dark of her eyes.

'Millie—there aren't any ghosts. Ghosts don't exist. There's nothing to be frightened of.'

'But I'm *not* frightened. I'm not afraid of anything. I'm six now, and I'm not even afraid of the dark.' She slips like water from my hands. 'The ghosts are very, very scary, but I'm not frightened at all. But *you'd* be scared,' she says to Blanche.

Blanche shrugs. She flicks on through her magazine, still lusting after the silk corsages and pastel glimmery frocks.

'The ghosts are white and creepy and they're really, really sad,' says Millie.

'Why should ghosts be sad?' Blanche asks her, rather wearily.

'Of course they're sad. Because they're dead,' says Millie.

'Of course. Silly me,' says Blanche.

'Blanche—don't be provoking,' I say.

'They have very quiet feet,' says Millie. 'They creep around very softly and you can't hear them coming at all.'

She stands up, tiptoes across the room, stretching out her

arms in front of her, fluttering her fingers like a pantomime ghost. Blanche sighs an eloquent sigh and turns back to her magazine. Millie edges behind Blanche's chair. She puts on a whispery, sinister voice.

'They come nearer and nearer and then they go, *Whooooo*.'

She shrieks in Blanche's ear. Blanche jumps and drops her magazine, though she must have seen this coming.

'Millie. For goodness' sake.' She's cross with her sister for startling her. 'I've had more than enough of your wretched ghosts. Just grow up, will you?' she says.

Millie pays no attention. She goes back to her dolls' house, grave as an owl, all innocence.

'Mum, you've got to speak to her. She's such a little madam,' says Blanche.

'I told you you'd be scared,' says Millie, rather smugly.

When I look in the food-safe the next afternoon, some of the chicken has gone.

An impotent anger surges through me. I think of all the effort that went into making that food—rearing the chicken, feeding it, forcing myself to wring its neck, plucking it and gutting it—all the things I have learnt to do, to make a good meal. And now a whole leg has been taken. Tears fill my eyes, and I try to blink them away.

Then I tell myself it's the cat. That must be the explanation—that I left the door of the food-safe open, and Alphonse found his way in. He's rather wild now, living on birds and rodents, because I don't have much to give him: he'd have jumped at the chance of some easy meat… But if Alphonse took it—why did he take just a leg? And why has the leg been neatly snapped? Why didn't I find the bones scattered?

I feel something edging closer, feel its cold breath on my skin.

★ ★ ★

Millie comes rushing into the house, eyes shining. Burrs have stuck to her jumper, and there is grass in her hair.

'We caught a stickleback,' she says. 'In the stream in the Blancs Bois. He was really big, Mummy. *This* big.' She shows me how big with her hands. 'Then we let him go again…'

She looks up, sees my expression. She frowns.

'What's the matter? Don't you believe me?' she says.

'Some chicken has gone from the safe,' I tell her. 'Did you take it, Millie?'

I almost wish I hadn't asked. The happiness leaks out of her, at my question. Her face is blank, a shut door.

She shakes her head.

'I didn't eat the chicken,' she says, in a flat, stubborn voice.

I kneel down in front of her, hold her face in my hands. Her skin is warm from running.

'Look at me, Millie.'

She looks. I feel her moth-breath on my face.

'Are you really telling the truth?' I say. 'Is that really, really truthful?'

She stares straight into my face. But her eyes are dull, giving nothing away.

'Yes, it is,' she says.

'You know how difficult life is, don't you? When we don't have much food?'

'Yes,' she says.

But I feel I'm not reaching her.

'We have to share it out fairly. This is really important, Millie.'

'I know that,' she says. 'I know we have to share it fairly. I promise, Mummy. I didn't eat it at all.'

I'm left feeling uncertain. Perhaps she didn't take the chicken. I can't quite believe she'd lie to me so brazenly. But maybe I'm wrong—maybe I'm making too many concessions again. I have a defeated feeling. I wonder if I've brought up my daughters unwisely. I hear Evelyn's voice in my mind— rather pious, not quite approving of me. Saying something she's often said: 'Children need plenty of discipline. You're storing up trouble, Vivienne, the way you're so soft with those girls... Trust me, no good will come of it.'

CHAPTER 54

Gunther brings me bread from his ration.

'But are you sure you can spare it?' I say.

'I am happy to,' he tells me.

I'm so grateful. I take it from him, trace my fingers across the cords of his wrists, pull him to me. 'Thank you.' We'll eat it with the chicken soup that I've made.

The next day, when Millie is playing with Simon, I go to my larder, offering up a quick prayer—that all will be as it should be. I pull open the door of the larder, lift the lid of the bread-bin. *No.* Half the loaf is gone. It's been cut—not torn, but cut ineptly, by someone who hasn't yet learnt to use a bread knife properly.

When Millie comes home, I look around for the satchel she takes when she plays. She's dropped it in the passage-way. I unfasten it, feeling the butterfly beat of panic in my stomach: as if I know already before I look inside. A scent of apple hangs about it. I up-end it, and all the treasures she has collected fall out: twigs, little blue stones, a pigeon's feather. Breadcrumbs.

I have a sick feeling—unhappy questions crowding into my mind. Where have I gone wrong? Why isn't my daughter truthful? Is it something I've done? Is it all the stories we've read? Whatever the reason, I've failed in the most important duty of a parent: I have let her live in a fantasy world, and she can't tell right from wrong.

I hear the xylophone ripple of her laughter from the living room. I go in. She's playing with the pram that I used when the girls were babies, trying to persuade Alphonse to lie down in it under a sheet.

'Millie. Some bread has been taken. Did you take the bread?'

Her laughter is torn off.

'No, Mummy?' she says. Her voice has an upward intonation. As though she's trying out the answer to see how it will sound.

The cat slithers out of the pram. She scoops him up: he struggles against her.

'Millie. Put the cat down. You have to listen to me.'

She lets the cat slip away from her; he has left a scratch like a thread of red silk on her wrist, but she doesn't seem to notice. She's a little frightened. I'm not often severe like this.

'You mustn't steal food,' I tell her. 'That's very, very naughty. It's not fair to everyone else.'

'No, it isn't fair.' Her voice is colourless.

'You know how short we are. Food has to be shared out equally.' I'm stern, my voice fierce and high. 'I always give you an apple when you're playing out with Simon. That's all we can spare,' I tell her.

But her expression is opaque. Somehow I'm not getting through.

'I didn't do it,' she tells me. 'I didn't eat the bread.' Speaking defiantly now, as though she has worked out what she should say.

'Millie. I found the crumbs in your satchel.'

'No, you didn't, Mummy,' she says.

I fetch the satchel, show her the breadcrumbs.

'I didn't do it,' she says.

I'm appalled that she just goes on lying like this.

'Millie. You know you have to tell the truth.' I feel I should be angry, should shout at her and smack her. But I see all the misery in her face, and I can't quite do it. 'Lying is wrong,' I tell her.

'Why?' she says.

I try out the answer in my mind. *Because honesty is important. Because we have to trust one another...* Yet my life—my whole happiness—is based on a secret and a lie.

'Some things are just wrong,' I tell her, my voice hollow as the belly of a cave, all the conviction gone from me. 'You must promise me you will never do that again.'

'But I didn't do it,' she says again. 'I didn't eat the bread.'

CHAPTER 55

'Vivienne. Something is worrying you.'

'Yes.'

'Are you going to tell me?'

I prop myself on one elbow, look down at his face on my pillow. Even in the gentling light of the candles in my bedroom, I can see how much he has aged in the time that I have known him—his hair paler and receding, the mesh of lines on his brow. And seeing this, I wonder how I must look in his eyes, how different from that moment when he first saw me in the lane, the scented wind blowing around us: for I know these months and years of war have worn me down, as well.

I clear my throat.

'It's Millie. She's been stealing food. I tell her off, but whatever I say, it doesn't seem to penetrate. I suppose she doesn't understand how serious it is—when we all have so little.'

'It is very hard—for the young to be hungry,' he says.

'And there's more. She makes up stories. She keeps on saying she's seen a ghost in a place where she plays. That the barn where she plays is haunted. It's some complicated make-believe. But she seems to really believe it...'

'Which barn is this?' he asks me.

'It's on Peter Mahy's land. In the field beyond the Blancs Bois. She plays there with Simon, her friend. They have a fantasy game they play there...'

'Many children do that, of course, playing such fantasy games,' he tells me, soothingly.

'But the fantasy seems to be taking over, so it's almost as real to her as the everyday world... I mean, obviously it's an unnatural situation they're in—growing up with a war on. But I've tried to keep their lives as normal as possible.'

'Yes,' he says. 'I know you have.'

'Maybe it's all my fault. Maybe I've read her too many stories.'

He smiles—that smile that I love, that fills his eyes with light.

'A child cannot be read too many stories,' he says. 'That is impossible.'

'And it worries me too that she's telling lies. She took some of that bread you brought us and claimed she didn't eat it. But I found the crumbs in her satchel...'

'I think you shouldn't worry,' he says. 'Millie is still very small. And many children are like her—living at once in this world and in a world of their own.'

'Do you think so? Other children—do you think they believe that their fantasy world is *real*?'

He blows out smoke, the blue soft spirals blurring his face.

'When I was a child,' he says, 'I had an imaginary friend.'

'Oh.' I'm charmed by this.

'This was when I was very small, like Millie. This was before my mother married again,' he says, his face darkening.

'Yes.' I think of what he told me about his cruel stepfather.

I reach out to him and move my hand over his head, loving the naked, vulnerable feel of his close-cropped skin against me. 'So—tell me all about your imaginary friend...'

He flushes slightly. He is a little embarrassed.

'My mother used to have to put a plate for him at the dinner table,' he says.

I'm enchanted.

'Did he have a name, your friend?' I say.

A slight, self-deprecating smile.

'His name was William,' he tells me.

'William?'

'Like your writer William Shakespeare. William was the only English name I knew. I thought it was very sophisticated,' he says.

This makes me smile; but it touches me too. I love to think of him as a little boy. I want to reach back through the years and put my arms around him.

I blow out my candles. I lie with my head on his chest: the smell of his skin is around me, and I can hear the drowsy beat of his heart. I sleep deeply.

I wake when he leaves in the cold of the morning, as the first rook speaks and the first grey light of dawn seeps into the sky. And lying there once he has left me, I feel a vague unease—just a dark moth-flutter in the corners of my mind—and I don't know why I feel this.

CHAPTER 56

September. The autumn term begins, and Millie starts back at school. I'm relieved. With all the brisk everydayness of class—with times-tables, reading books, lists of spellings to learn—she won't be able to spend so much time in the fantasy world she shares with Simon. I cut her hair and let down the hems of both her school frocks: she's grown a lot in the holiday.

On Sunday Blanche will be reading the Lesson in church.

'Mum, I wish you'd come to church sometimes. I wish you could come and hear me,' she says. Her eyes are on me, blue as summer, requiring something of me.

'I'd love to, sweetheart,' I say. 'But I worry about leaving Grandma.'

'It's not just that, though, is it?' she says. 'I know you don't really believe in the Bible any more, with the war and everything. But I wish you would. God has a plan for the world, Mum. It must all be part of his plan.'

'I don't know, sweetheart…' And then, turning to easier things: 'But it's true that I don't like to leave your grandma alone. Except when I really have to.'

'You have to on Sunday,' she says. 'Grandma will be all right on her own for a couple of hours. *Please*, Mum.'

So Millie and I put on our best clothes, and we go to Matins with Blanche.

Though I'm not sure what I think about God, I still enjoy the service, finding a kind of consolation in the familiar words of the prayers. *Oh God, make speed to save us. Oh, Lord, make haste to help us...* And I love the glimmery candles on the altar, and the gilded sunlight falling through the window and laying its jewel colours all over the chancel steps. Most of the service is as it was before the Occupation—though prayers for our country aren't permitted; but we can still pray for our King. We recite the Confession, the muttering of the congregation dragging behind the Rector, the low words rumbling around the echoey nave. *Almighty and most merciful Father, we have erred and strayed from Thy ways like lost sheep. We have followed too much the devices and desires of our own hearts...* Repeating those words, I feel remote from the rest of the congregation, thinking how they might judge my actions—how sinful they'd think my love for Gunther to be.

Blanche goes to the lectern to read the Lesson. She starts off rather shyly, with that slight stutter she sometimes has, then her voice growing stronger, more certain. Seeing her there, apart from me, I'm aware how she is changing—becoming a woman, her body softening, her face more clearly defined. I know she still regrets that we didn't go to London, believing her hope of happiness to lie a long way away—far off in the future, or over the Channel, anywhere but here. My eyes fill up as I watch her—sensing that yearning in her, for all the things she can't have because she is growing up in wartime. I wonder if she'll ever find what she is looking for.

She comes back to join us in our pew, bright colour staining her cheeks, at once pleased and embarrassed. We settle
down for the sermon, which is all about Heaven and Hell.
They're not real places, the Rector says—at least, not in the
sense that St Peter Port is a place: Heaven and Hell are states
of being. In Heaven, we are for ever in God's presence, and
worse than the myriad torments of Hell is the terrible absence
of God.

After the service, I chat with Susan Gallienne, who com-
pliments me on Blanche's reading. Susan is elegant as ever,
in a dress of coral linen; though there's something about her
smile, sweet as icing, that sets my teeth slightly on edge.
While Susan and I are talking, the girls walk on ahead of
me.

I say goodbye as soon as I decently can, and catch up with
Millie and Blanche. They're deep in conversation, heads
close together in the gold dappling light of the lane, a cool
lacework of branches above them. They're talking about the
sermon: I'm surprised they were paying attention.

'I know about Hell,' Millie is saying. 'That's where my
ghost comes from.' Very matter-of-fact.

'And how do you know that exactly?' says Blanche.

'Because he told us, stupid. That's where he lives. He lives
in Hell,' she says.

Blanche turns to face her. I think she's going to tell her
sister off for calling her stupid. But she's suddenly earnest—
made serious by the service and her role in it, and rather
troubled by what Millie said.

'Millie. You shouldn't go making up stories like that, about
Hell.'

'I'm *not* making up stories,' says Millie: robust, emphatic.

'I mean it, Millie. It's not a thing to joke about. People go to Hell if they're wicked and don't believe in Jesus.'

Blanche is intent and solemn, concerned for her sister's soul.

'My ghost is a good ghost,' says Millie.

'No, Millie. He must be bad if he lives in Hell,' says Blanche. 'He must have been bad in his earthly life.'

'He isn't bad,' says Millie.

Blanche purses her lips. She has that look of exasperation that always comes in her face, when Millie talks like this.

'Anyway—Hell's not a place you can just dip in and out of,' she says. 'People never come back from Hell. If you go to Hell, you're stuck there. That's what the Bible says. You ought to know that.'

'They do. They do come back. *Sometimes* they do,' says Millie, uncertainty creeping into her voice. I see that her lip is trembling.

I join them, reach to take her hand—but she pulls away from my touch. She breaks off a stick from the hedgebank. As we walk along, she swishes the stick, hitting the plants that we pass, turned away from me and her sister. Her eyes are shiny with tears, and she doesn't want us to see.

CHAPTER 57

Gunther is going on leave for a fortnight.

The night before he is due to go, he follows me up to my room. I close the door, turn to him, but he doesn't immediately hold me or touch me. He sits down heavily on my bed. He has a serious look. I wonder what is coming.

'There is something I need to tell you,' he says. 'Something that I have just heard. There are plans to deport people who are not native islanders—people who were not born here.'

'People like me. I wasn't born here,' I say.

'Yes. People like you,' he tells me.

I'm struggling to make sense of this. There's a shrill, febrile voice in my head that seeks to make everything all right, to make it all go away. They surely wouldn't do this to people who don't make any trouble—especially mothers with young children. They couldn't do that—it wouldn't make any sense, they have to be reasonable, children need their mothers, everybody knows that… And if they *did* send people away, they'd certainly just be sent to France: maybe just for a month or two. Islanders have gone there to prison: they say it isn't too terrible; mostly they come home again…

'Deported to where?' I ask him.

'To internment camps in Germany,' he tells me. 'Until the war is over.'

The ground splits open in front of my feet.

'No,' I say. *'No.'* I can't believe that he is so calm, so untroubled, telling me this. Fear floods me. 'But what will happen to my children?'

There's a sob in my voice. I see it rushing towards me, the thing I have always most feared—that they will be torn away from me. I remember the sickroom, my mother's altered face, the sore-throat smell of disinfectant: the wrenching sadness of parting—that I didn't feel in that moment, when I was only three; that I have felt for the rest of my life. The sadness I would do anything to protect my children from.

'Vivienne.'

He puts his hand on my arm. I feel all the comfort in his touch. The world steadies. And at once I understand why he is so untroubled by this.

'You can do something? You can help us?' I say.

He nods.

'I will do what I can,' he tells me. 'Perhaps some names will not appear on the lists.'

'Could you do that? Could you really?'

'I think so. I think there will be some concessions. But you must be very secret about this. Don't talk about it to anyone,' he tells me.

'No. Of course not.'

That is easy for me. I am used to secrecy.

When he leaves me in the early morning, when I take him to the door, the poignancy of parting suddenly overwhelms me. I can't let go: I cling to him.

He peels my fingers from his arms, he kisses my hands.

'It is only two weeks, and then I will be back with you,' he tells me.

'Two weeks is a long time in wartime. Anything could happen.'

'Vivienne. I will come back to you. I promise.'

I watch him as he crosses my yard in the grey pale light of sunrise. The sky is high and remote, and softly gleaming, like a pearl.

I go back to my bedroom, but my bed feels so empty without him. I'm missing him already—as though a part of me has gone.

The evening after Gunther leaves, I decide I will go blackberrying. Celeste is seeing Tomas her boyfriend, so Blanche is staying home; and I leave her to keep an eye on things, and cycle up to the clifftop, where there are great stands of blackberry bushes.

I leave my bicycle in a gateway and walk along the lane. The hedges are low here: beyond them, the fields slope down to the cliff, where the land drops sharply to Les Tielles, and there's a wide view of the sea, which today is silky with evening and filled with daffodil light. There's a kestrel high above me, poised and vigilant, sooty black against the sky dazzle, hovering on the up-current where the cooler air sweeps off the sea. The wind has died, the land seems vast and empty: I feel as though I am the only person in the world. A deep peacefulness settles on my shoulders like a shawl.

The hedges are rich with berries, many now dark and glossily ripe. I start to pick; the tips of my fingers are coloured with the berries' vivid indigos. I suck the tart taste from my skin. It's so quiet I can hear my shoes creak as I move, and the rustle of the bramble leaves is loud against my hand, like something tearing. Soon, I have enough ripe berries to make a couple of pies, and I feel that brief soaring sense of triumph that always seems to come when I find food for my family.

At last I turn to go home, a little reluctant to leave the peace of this place, pausing for a moment to look out again over the sea. The sun is setting amid thick cotton-wool streaks of cloud, which soak up the radiance like a stain. All the yellow is gone from the water now; the sea heaves and stirs like some grey scaly beast that is restless and moves in its sleep. The kestrel still hovers above me; then folds its wings and plummets like a dropped stone.

A sudden noise startles me—a German voice, abrupt, steely, shouting an order. I'm still, my heart thuds in my chest: I know what this means—a gang of slave-workers coming back from their work. The thing I saw before rushes through me—that terrible casual savagery that I have tried so hard to put from my mind. I have no time to hide away. I press myself into the hedge.

The work-gang comes into view around the bend in the lane. They must have been building Hitler's ring of concrete at the clifftop. They are guarded by two OT workers, who have swastika armbands and guns.

I stare at the slave-workers. The world tilts around me.

The prisoners must have been mixing cement—they are covered with it, the greyish powder all over their hair, their skin, their eyelashes, so their faces are blank and whitened, all their colour taken away. Their clothes are rags, and they've covered themselves in the canvas sacks that once held the cement, the canvas tied roughly around their waists with scraps of wire or string, and they have no shoes, and some of them have tied more sacking around their feet. Their heads are bowed from exhaustion, and their bones are sharp through their skin.

In the dimming light they are pale as ghosts, and their feet are utterly silent.

CHAPTER 59

Millie dreams she has swallowed a fishbone, and wakes with a very sore throat. I tell her she'll have to stay home.

'Can I still play with Simon?' she says. 'When he comes home from school?'

'No. Of course not,' I tell her briskly. 'Of course you can't play out if you haven't gone to school.'

Her nose is blocked, and I put some Vick's embrocation in a bowl of steaming water, and get her to breathe in the vapours, with her eyes tight shut and a towel draped over her head. Afterwards she can breathe more easily. I fetch her eiderdown, and make her a bed on the sofa, with her Buckingham Palace jigsaw on a tray. It's the only time I have ever been glad that a child of mine is ill—it makes everything simpler.

About an hour before curfew, when Evelyn is in her bedroom and Blanche is still at Celeste's, I tell Millie I'll be gone for a while. A blackbird is singing his heart out on the gable of Le Colombier, as I cross the lane and walk through my orchard and into the fields. I skirt the edge of the Blancs Bois, pass on through the cool air of evening to Peter Mahy's barn. My heart pounds. I'm alert to every whisper and lisp of the leaves, to every murmur of the countryside around me, to the scrabble of each hidden creature in the seething grass: as if I were a stranger here.

Shadow dense as black river-water laps at the foot of the barn. As I draw nearer, I see that the door is open. I approach softly, look in.

At first I can't make anything out: there's only shadow inside. Perhaps I have been mistaken. Perhaps I jumped to the wrong conclusion. Relief swims through me. I'm about to turn and go back—when I see that the deeper darkness in the corner is a man. He has his side to me, he doesn't see me; I think he is dulled, unaware—from exhaustion, from starvation, from seeing too much. He sits, leaning forward, his bent hunched shadow falling over the floor. Like the men I saw on the clifftop, he is wearing a canvas sack, with wire around his waist and ragged holes torn for his arms. His shoes too are made from sacking. I can't tell what colour his hair is, or what age he might be. All the things that make him himself are erased, by dust and dirt and hunger: his face is almost the face of a skull, the bones so fierce through his skin. I understand why the children believed him to be a visitant, someone from another world: it's the presaging of death in his face. He has a crust of bread in his hand. He tears at it with his teeth, desperate, ravenous.

The world around me is hollow, stilled. All I can hear is the sound that his teeth make ripping the bread, and the soft dull sound of my heart, pounding.

There's a little voice in my head—soft, persuasive, concerned. *Don't look. Keep safe. Go away. Go back to Le Colombier and pretend this never happened. Pretend you didn't see him…* And there's something in me that's desperate to obey the soft little voice—and not only because of the danger. To let myself look is to begin to put myself in his place—hungry, wretched, so abused—and I can't bear that. But my daughter has come and looked at him: Millie, who is six now, and not afraid of the dark. Millie has come and looked and not turned away.

When I get back, she is still under her eiderdown on the sofa, doing her jigsaw. The bracing smell of menthol and eucalyptus hangs in the room, and makes my eyes sting.

I kneel on the floor beside her.

'Millie. I saw your ghost. In Mr Mahy's barn.'

She goes quite still, her face set as a mask, her hand poised over the jigsaw. Between her finger and thumb she holds a little piece of sky.

'I know you took the food,' I say.

She puts the jigsaw piece down on the tray, delicately, with a small clear click, like the breaking of a tiny bone.

'He was hungry.' Defiantly. 'We had food and he didn't. That isn't fair,' she says.

'No, it isn't,' I say.

She has a slight fever: a strand of hair sticks to her red damp face. She pushes at the hair, as though she is angry with it.

'You mustn't be cross with me, Mummy.'

'I'm not cross, sweetheart. I'm not cross with you.'

'He was hungry, and we fed him,' she says. Her hands are balled into fists. She's concentrating so hard, trying to explain to me.

'Yes. I know why you did it…'

'He came from Hell. That's where he lives. He lives in Hell. He told us.'

'Millie…'

'And it isn't like the Rector said. The Rector is wrong

when he says that Hell isn't a place. My ghost says that Hell is a real place. I know you don't believe me...'

'I do believe you,' I say.

Her eyes widen with surprise.

I reach out, put my arms around her. She's rigid, holding back from me—not sure what to make of me, still not sure what I think.

'But I don't want you to do it any more, sweetheart,' I say. 'It's far too dangerous for you.'

'No, you're wrong.' Protesting. 'You're saying that just because you don't know him. The ghost is kind. The ghost wouldn't hurt us,' she says.

'No, I'm sure he wouldn't.'

'I only said those things to frighten Blanche,' she says. 'When I said he was scary. I was fibbing when I said that. I did it because she was being a pain. I wanted to give her a fright.'

'That isn't what I mean. I know he wouldn't hurt you. But if the Germans found out, they would be very angry,' I say.

'Would they put us in prison?'

'Yes. In prison or...' I remember what Vera said at the school gate—about the woman on Jersey, who took a slave-worker into her home. How she was shot. I push the thought away. 'The thing is—they mustn't find out. Not ever.'

'But somebody's got to feed him,' she says. 'If me and Simon don't do it, who will? He'll *starve*.'

'It should be grownups who do these things, Millie,' I tell her. 'It isn't safe for children. I want you to tell Simon that you can't go to the barn any more. Will you do that?'

She's frowning. She doesn't say anything.

'He won't starve, Millie. Trust me.'

She looks at me doubtfully.

'I need you to promise,' I tell her.

'All right,' she says. Reluctantly.

'And, sweetheart, something else. This has to be a secret. We won't tell anyone. Not even Grandma or Blanche...'

This pleases her. I see her quicksilver smile.

'Yes. It's our secret,' she says. 'It's a really big secret, isn't it?'

And I think, with a little lurch of my heart: *Yes, it's a really big secret.*

I wake abruptly in the night. It's surprising to find myself alone: I've grown so used to sleeping with Gunther wrapped around me. The bed feels too big and empty without him. The silence in the house around me is deep, complete, but my heart is racing as though some sudden sound disturbed me. I don't know what can have woken me.

I get up, go to the window, look out across my dark yard, resting my forehead against the cool glass. There's a little tentative moonlight: a gusty wind is pushing rags of cloud across the moon. The hollyhocks in the garden of Les Vinaires look spectral, unreal, in the moonlight—as white and luminous as ice. And immediately the thought is there in my head—as though this realisation came to me in my dream, as though this is what woke me. *I told Gunther. I told him about Millie's ghost...* I try to remember how he reacted when I told him. He was reassuring, I think: he talked about his own childhood. But maybe he was just humouring me. Maybe he guessed who Millie's ghost really was: maybe he knew all this time... The thought appals me. It doesn't change my resolve, but it fills me with fear. What will happen to her, to us?

The rest of the night I don't sleep.

CHAPTER 60

I make a thick soup with some of the potatoes Johnnie brought, the day I slaughtered the chicken. I add plenty of milk to the soup. I taste a spoonful. It's creamy, warming—I hope it will be easy to digest.

All is as it should be: Blanche at Celeste's house, Evelyn safe in her room. Millie is on the sofa, with her cut-out dolls on the tray; she likes to dress them up in cardboard clothes that fix to them with little tabs. When I tell her that I'm going out, she gives me a quick knowing smile.

It's a beautiful evening, with low smudged clouds and a golden light on the land. I walk quickly through the fields, my heart juddering.

He is there, just as yesterday, hunched on the floor of the barn, rocking slightly as he sits there. I slip in through the open door. I think he will notice my shadow falling across the ground in front of him: but he doesn't turn, doesn't see me.

I stand there for a long moment. My heart is beating so hard it shakes the fabric of my blouse. I tell myself I could go, I could still turn and leave. Everything flashes before me, spooling out in my mind—vivid, precise, incandescent with disaster. The Germans will see us, I will be shot, my children will be left motherless—the worst thing, the thing I had always vowed must never happen to them.

My throat is narrow as a needle's eye.

'Excuse me,' I say.

My voice sounds odd, as though it isn't my voice. I think, What an utterly stupid thing to say. Knowing he won't understand me.

He turns, slowly. I don't think he heard me coming: perhaps my voice has startled him. I'm about to say, *Don't be frightened*, but I see he isn't afraid; perhaps he has left all everyday fears behind him. His eyes are black as sloe-berries and fringed with whitened lashes. His gaze, without curiosity, rests on my face.

'I am Millie's mother. Millie, the little girl…'

I put out my hand to show how small she is. I mime reaching out to take the hand of a child.

I feel hugely awkward, as though my body is fixed together wrongly: amid all the danger, the risk, feeling above all a kind of social embarrassment, that I don't know how to do this—how to talk to someone who doesn't speak the same language as me.

He looks at me, his eyes too dark for the chalky pallor of his face. I think I see a gleam of understanding in his gaze.

'I have food,' I say.

He watches me. He doesn't move.

I trace out a bowl in the air with my hand, mime spooning food into my mouth.

'Come with me,' I say.

I beckon.

'The children are good children. The children are my friends,' he says, in perfect, lightly accented English.

I hear my quick in-breath.

'You can speak English?'

'Yes. I speak English. The children and I can talk together,' he says.

His voice is too high for a man. I remember what Angie told me, about people who are starving—how their voices have a sound like the voices of birds.

'How did you learn?' I ask him.

'A man in my village taught me English,' he says. 'And also Polish. He worked on a farm in my village, but he had worked at a university once. He taught me many things...'

'Oh,' I say.

I can't imagine where he comes from; or why in his country such a teacher might have to work on a farm. I know nothing. I feel a jolt of surprise—that this man, with his rags, his wretchedness, is better schooled than me. Nothing is as I'd thought it was.

'My name is Vivienne,' I say then.

'I am Kirill,' he says.

He points to his chest, using his second finger, not his index finger. I see that part of his index finger is missing, that the finger ends in an ugly, purpled stub of flesh.

'We will go to my house, Kirill,' I tell him.

'Yes. Thank you.'

I lead him through the fields, keeping close to the hedge. He walks silently behind me. He shuffles; he scarcely has the strength to lift his feet from the ground. He has a musty smell, not quite human, like something old, neglected. I don't feel scared, just unreal—as though I am watching myself from a great height.

We reach the lane. I look around, wary, but everywhere is quiet. I take him through my back gate, the little wicket gate in the hedgebank that leads into my garden, and through the back door of my house, the door I rarely use, that cannot be seen from Les Vinaires. I lead him through to the kitchen.

His eyes widen. I see that to find himself here in this room is astonishing to him: that for him my simple kitchen is a place of enchantment, a fairytale castle, removed, encircled by thorns.

I pull out a chair and seat him at the table. He is a big man—or would have been big, before the flesh fell off him. He moves cautiously, as a big man will move in a small enclosed space, as though afraid of breaking something.

The room is full of the scent of the soup that is simmering on the stove. I ladle some into a bowl, put it in front of him.

'This is for you,' I tell him.

He picks up the spoon, and bends low over the bowl. I see that his hands have a tremor. He eats, absolutely intent.

I let him eat. I don't talk.

As he eats, I'm startled by a sensation I didn't expect. A warm elation floods me. That his need is so great and I can fulfil that need: that I can feed him. It's like the way you can feel when a child is sick and needing you completely, this perfect, simple imperative—all conflict wiped away, your purpose clear as ink on white paper.

Millie has heard us. She slips into the room with us. She has a slight pleased smile.

He looks up from the soup.

'Millie,' he says, and a little light comes in his face.

She sits beside him, folds her hands fastidiously in front of her. She's on her best behaviour for him.

I refill the bowl. He eats that too. He sits back with a sigh.

'Thank you. Thank you,' he says.

I find a clean towel for him.

'You can wash your face if you want,' I say.

He turns on the tap, lets the water splash on his hands. The water drops glitter, holding the gilded evening light that falls all over the room. He watches the swollen radiant droplets for a moment, as though this is a miracle unfolding between his hands, then he lowers his head and plunges under the tap. As the water sluices the dirt from his face, he becomes himself again, emerging from his cocoon of grime, so we can see who he is. He's young, not much older than Blanche—so young, he could be my son. His youthfulness catches at my heart. His hair and beard and eyebrows are dark, and his skin is brown and weather-beaten under the dust and the dirt. You can see all the scars and cuts on his skin that were hidden by the cement dust.

When he has washed, he sits at my table again. I take out two cigarettes, light them, pass one to him. He takes a deep, grateful drag, the glowing tip reflecting redly in the dark of his eyes. The illusory brightness makes him seem more vividly alive, more present.

'Kirill. How do you get out of the camp?' I ask him.

'There is a hole in the wire,' he says. 'There are guards who will not notice if we leave the camp at night. They look in the other direction. If we are there for the morning roll-call, some of them turn a blind eye. There is little food in the camp. They give us only water with a bit of turnip in it.'

'You can't possibly live on that,' I say.

'I think they let us go out so they don't have to feed us,' he says. 'We steal. There is no other way. Before the children fed me, I had to steal to survive.'

'Yes. Of course,' I say.

'And we know where the rubbish tips are. We eat off the rubbish tips.'

'That's terrible,' I say.

'No, it is good,' he tells me. 'I can say, the rubbish tips are life to us. It is the camp that is terrible. The work is hard, and we are beaten. Many people have died there. For those of us who still live, it is our hatred that keeps us alive.'

His clever, sloe-dark eyes on mine.

'You can eat here for this week,' I tell him. 'But we will have to be careful. There are German soldiers living in the house next door. You must wait in the barn tomorrow and I'll come and meet you there...'

It's nearly time for curfew—I know I have to take him back.

'Millie, Kirill is going now,' I tell her. 'You have to say goodbye.'

She waves to him, happily.

I take him out through the back door.

'Thank you, Vivienne. You are very kind.'

Under the hedgebank the shadows are dark as wet walnuts. He crosses to my orchard, and vanishes in the sepia gloom on the other side of the lane, as silent as the night breeze.

'He liked the soup, didn't he?' says Millie, when I get back.

'Yes.'

Her face shines.

'He *really*, *really* liked it,' she says. 'Can he always come to our house?'

'He can come here for a few days,' I tell her. 'After that, I don't know, sweetheart. I'll have to work something out.'

'Yes. You'll have to, Mummy.'

I notice she doesn't talk about him as a ghost any more: that it didn't surprise her to see him in the everydayness of our kitchen. Perhaps it's just as Gunther said—that she lives at once in this world and a world of her own, moving easily between these worlds.

'Millie—we have to be very secret,' I say. 'Nobody must know. Nobody. Can you do that—be very secret?'

'Yes, of course,' she says.

I wash the bowl he ate from. There's a sifting of pale cement dust under the table, and dirt in the sink from when he washed his face and his hair. I clean the sink, and brush up all the cement dust very meticulously.

'Vivienne.'

I jump. Dust from the dustpan spills like a gritty grey flour on the floor. It gets everywhere.

Evelyn is there, in the doorway.

Thank God, I think. *Thank God she didn't come down before.*

'I need my Bible, Vivienne. I want to read my Bible. I can't find my Bible, Vivienne.'

The towel Kirill used is lying on the draining board. He couldn't wash off all the dirt, and the fabric holds smudges of grime, in a blurry photographer's negative, tracing the lines of his face. I fold it up quickly.

'Your Bible is on your bedside table,' I say.

'Is it, Vivienne?'

'Yes. I saw it there.'

But she has a perplexed look, as though she still feels that something is lost or taken away.

Her eyes fall on Millie.

'You shouldn't be up, young lady.' This at least she is certain about. 'It's long past your bedtime.'

Millie darts a complicit look at me. I give her a slight warning frown. To my relief, she doesn't try to explain.

'I'm going to bed now, Grandma,' she says, demurely.

'Come back upstairs,' I say to Evelyn.

But Evelyn stands there, unmoving.

'You've got dirty hands, Vivienne.'

'Yes. I've been sweeping up…'

This doesn't satisfy her. Her puzzlement gathers between her eyes, in a faint, perplexed fleur-de-lys.

'Vivienne. Somebody's been here. Something smells different. I can smell it.'

'Don't worry, Evelyn, it's nothing.'

'Somebody's been here. A stranger's been here. Someone who doesn't belong.'

'No, Evelyn. Not a stranger.'

'Is it one of your friends, then, Vivienne?'

'Yes. Just one of my friends,' I say. 'It's nothing to worry about.'

'You and your friends. So many comings and goings.' She shakes her head, disapproving. 'Why can't we have a bit of peace?' she says.

'These aren't peaceful times we live in,' I tell her, vaguely.

I take her up to her room, find her Bible for her. But she's too tired to read now. She lies in her bed, and I tuck her up like a child. Her head is so small on her pillow, her scalp pink and vulnerable through the frail white fuzz of her hair. Her eyes gleam in the light of her bedside lamp. She's staring over my shoulder and I wonder what she sees.

I find myself wondering what it is like to be old, as old as Evelyn—to look back over your lifetime, to reflect on the choices you made. I think of the words of the Confession. *We have left undone those things which we ought to have done;*

And we have done those things which we ought not to have done...
I wonder what causes you most regret, in the final years of
your life: the undone things—or the things you did, that
you ought not to have done.

I turn off her lamp, and leave her.

CHAPTER 61

'Vivienne.' Ruthie Duquemin smiles warmly at me. 'How lovely to see you,' she says.

But I can tell she's anxious, wondering what's brought me. Her eyes, gentle, full of inquiry, green as hart's tongue fern, rest on me. She pushes her hand through her mass of pale disorderly hair.

She ushers me into her kitchen, which is cluttered and busy and cheerful, with lots of children's drawings pinned to the walls—sketches of Hurricanes and Spitfires. It must be very different, having boys: Millie only ever draws cats and beribboned princesses. I think briefly, as I sometimes do, how I'd love to have a son. The room has a scent of laundry soap; dishcloths are boiling on the stove, and a slippery froth is slithering down the side of the pan. Ruthie stirs the pan with a wooden spoon.

'I haven't got anything to offer you. Well, only water,' she says. 'I'm so sorry.'

'Water will be fine,' I say.

I sit at her well-scrubbed table. She fills two glasses at the tap. I don't know how to begin.

'I've come about Simon—well, Millie and Simon, really,' I say.

'I thought it might be something like that.' She smiles a

rueful smile. 'The thing is, with Simon, I never know what he'll do next. You know, I love my boys to bits. But girls aren't so much trouble. Sometimes I really envy mothers like you who only have girls…'

'It's nothing bad at all,' I say quickly, wanting to reassure her. 'It's just this thing I found out…' Then, seeing how anxious she looks, 'Simon's such a good friend to Millie. They're so sweet together…'

'Simon loves Millie,' she tells me.

Her voice is tentative, uncertain. Standing there, she's caught in the sunlight that streams through the window behind her: she's a dishevelled, harassed angel with a golden halo of hair.

'Has he told you what they've been doing?' I ask.

'He never tells me anything.' She smiles. 'Just that he's going to marry Millie…'

'Did he tell you about the ghost?' I say.

She goes very still. The smile is wiped from her face.

'No, he didn't,' she says.

'Millie was talking about a ghost, in Peter Mahy's barn,' I say. 'That they had met a ghost there.'

Ruthie's eyes widen. I know she understands at once. She sits down abruptly at the table.

'And you went to look, and he wasn't a ghost? He was one of those poor, poor men?' she says.

I nod.

I see all the warring feelings that pass rapidly over her face—curiosity, fear: perhaps a kind of wonder.

'They've been befriending him—giving him food,' I tell her.

'Oh, my God. I had no idea… Oh, my God. I did have to tell Simon off, though, because some bread went missing. But

I thought he was eating it himself...' She looks remorseful. 'I wouldn't have scolded him if I'd known. That makes me feel so awful—that he was trying to do something good, and all he got was a smack...'

'I've told Millie they mustn't do it again,' I say. 'And I've told her to tell Simon that. I'm feeding the man myself now. It isn't safe for children.'

A shadow moves over her face.

'Or for you, come to that,' she says. She reaches across the table, touches my arm with one warm finger. 'Be careful, Vivienne. I mean, don't you have Germans next door? Simon told me.'

'Yes.'

'Watch your back. For goodness' sake...'

It enters my mind that her warning is just like the warnings I give to Johnnie. Thinking this, I feel a little creep of cold on my skin.

'I'll do my best,' I say lightly.

'Well, thanks so much for coming to see me,' says Ruthie. 'I'll speak to him about it. To be honest, I was ever so worried when I saw you here. I thought you'd say you didn't want them playing any more.' She moves her hand abstractedly through her bright aureole of hair. 'Simon would have been heartbroken.'

'Well—he doesn't need to be...'

'I never know what he'll get up to next,' she tells me. 'He used to be friends with little Jenny Le Page. She was always really nicely turned out, and she managed to fall in the soot pile wearing her Sunday-best frock.' A slight grin sneaks into her face. 'He tried to clean up her frock by washing it under the tap... Well, that was that, of course. Her mother wouldn't let them ever play together again.'

'I love them playing together,' I say.

'You know,' she says, thoughtfully, 'I feel a little proud of them, don't you? For trying to help like that. Their hearts must be in the right place... We've tried to teach Simon to be kind. That's the best you can do really, don't you think? The world is so full of terrible things. All you can do is be kind... Now, just you be careful, Vivienne.'

CHAPTER 62

He is waiting for me: he stands up as he sees me.

'Vivienne. You came.'

'Yes.' I put my hand on his arm. 'Of course I did,' I say.

We walk silently through the fields to Le Colombier. There's an operatic sunset, the backdrop of the sky painted over with scarlet and gilt, but darkness is gathering in the wood, and in the hidden places under the hedge.

He washes his face and hands at my sink, and eats the soup I have made, while Millie and I sit with him.

When he's almost finished his second serving, he picks up the bowl and puts his head back and tips it into his mouth, so as not to waste a single drop. He puts the bowl down, sighing deeply.

'Thank you. Thank you, Vivienne.'

I light two cigarettes, give him one. There's still a little time to talk, before he has to go back.

'Where do you come from, Kirill? Where is your home?' I ask him.

'I come from far away,' he says. 'My country is called Belorussia. It has a border with Russia. Perhaps you have heard of it?'

I haven't, but it wouldn't be polite to say so. I nod.

'I lived in a village there. I dream of it always,' he says.

We sit for a while in silence, the sunset light falling over us. Little sounds brush at the edge of the stillness—a gauzy-winged fly at the window, the insistent tick of the clock.

'What is your country like? Tell us about it,' I say.

'There is a forest with many birch trees.' He speaks slowly, searching for the words, in that strange, high, hungry voice he has. 'There are birch trees and little rivers. It is very quiet there. Our houses are all made of wood and storks nest on the roofs of the houses…' There is a distant look in his eyes, as though he can see these things as he talks. 'There my heart is always,' he says.

'It sounds a lovely place,' I say.

He nods.

'But, I can say, this was not a perfect life,' he tells us. 'When I was a child, we were often hungry.' He blows out smoke, remembering. 'February was a difficult month. Sometimes we only had old potatoes to eat for a week at a time. The first sign of spring was the coming up of the sorrel. My mother would send me and my brother to gather the sorrel for soup. The next sign was the new potatoes, and only then did you start living again…'

He is silent for a moment.

'Leaving that place was like darkness to me,' he says.

'Yes,' I say.

'Sometimes the pictures fade for me. But talking to you I can see it so clearly,' he says.

The thought comes to me that he is talking only about his childhood—rather like Gunther and me, when Gunther first came to my bed. And perhaps for the very same reason: the past, whatever its rigours, is a safer place than today.

'Tell us about your mother and brother,' I say. 'Tell us about your family.'

'My family all play music,' he tells us. 'I was a violin-maker, in the life that I had. By day I would work on the farm, but at night I would make my violins. My father also did this. He taught me.'

This startles me. I didn't expect him to have such a rich life, such a skill. Perhaps I'd believed that his rags, his hunger, said something that mattered about him—that his wretched-ness could tell me about the person he was. But I was wrong: his wretchedness tells me nothing.

'When I was a child, the party encouraged all music,' he says. 'The music for weddings and festivals, the costumes and the dancing. All those good things that were always part of our life… In these last few years, under Stalin, these things were not encouraged. But I went on making my violins in a little workshop I had, in a room at the back of my house.'

I'm trying to understand. What does he mean by the party? Is Belorussia ruled by Stalin, by Russia? Was it part of the Bolshevik republic before the Germans marched in? I think of so often how little I understand about the world. And I'm curious about this music they played. Wondering whether it has that wildness of much East European folk music—rather like the melancholic Chopin mazurkas I love.

I glance at Millie. She's listening intently, scarcely blink-ing: it's the look she has when I read from her fairytale books.

'I loved my violins,' Kirill tells us. Pride briefly fattens his voice. 'I loved them too much, perhaps. My wife would say that I was married to them… My wife would complain about it. Other women might say that their husbands drink too much vodka. But my wife would complain that I spent too long at that work…'

'You're *married*?' I'm surprised. He seems too young to have a wife.

There's just a sliver of quiet. His face darkens.

'Her name was Danya,' he says.

I hear the past tense: a little current of fear moves through me. I'm scared to ask more about her. Later, perhaps. Not today.

'I had a friend here on Guernsey who played the violin,' I say. 'We used to play duets. He went on the boat to England. I've always loved the violin…'

There's a gleam in his face, when I say that.

'To make a violin is a beautiful thing,' he tells us.

'Yes. It must be.'

'So much care goes into the making of it. It is such a small thing, so fragile, so easy to break. But it sings out so clearly,' he says.

I think of Nathan Isaacs and the music we played— Beethoven's Spring Sonata, the clear high notes, like a human voice, but truer.

'It must be wonderful—to have such a skill,' I say.

The shadows are black in the hollows under his eyes.

'Even if I return to my home, I will never make my violins again. That life is over for me.'

He holds out his injured, shaking hands. I see again that part of his right index finger is missing, see the stump of mutilated flesh. A thrill of loss goes through me. I don't say anything.

CHAPTER 63

I make some soup from leeks and peas, and boil a joint of ham. When the soup is thoroughly cooked, I will add some meat from the joint, cutting it wafer-thin so it will be easy to eat.

While the soup is simmering, I take an old globe from the kitchen cupboard. I bought it for Blanche, to try and help her with geography lessons at school; she always hated geography. I peer at the globe, at the tangle of countries with unpronounceable names that all seem to be part of Russia now.

Millie comes up with her ragdoll, dragging the doll by the hair.

'Mummy, are you looking for Kirill's country?' she says.

'Yes. I've found it. Look...'

It's much bigger than I thought, at least as big as the British Isles. This surprises me. It has no coast, and looks empty, with hardly any cities or towns.

Millie peers at the globe.

'Where's St Peter Port?' she asks me.

I show her.

'England is here—and Guernsey is here, but it's far too small to see clearly...'

I put my finger over the place.

She frowns.

'You're wrong, Mummy. It can't be. Guernsey is really big,' she tells me, very definitely.

I remember those moments from childhood—the moments when you begin to get the measure of the world, to have some fleeting sense of its vastness. How that vastness takes your breath away.

'If you look really close you can see it,' I tell her. 'It's just that tiny pink speck.'

She lets the ragdoll fall to the floor. She touches Guernsey— her finger also covering half of France. She stretches out her hand, encompassing the distance from here to Belorussia in a handspan.

'Kirill's country isn't really very far away,' she says.

'It is though, Millie. It's a very long way. His home must seem as remote now as the moon and stars to him.'

'Will he ever get back there?'

'I don't know, sweetheart.'

She cups the globe in her hands, then sends it spinning. The colours bleed together, the whole world a dizzying whirl of colour, a vivid, giddy kaleidoscope of greens and browns and pinks. It moves so fast you feel all the lands of the world might spin right off it—flying up high in the air, then settling again as it slows, all shaken about and landing each in a different place. A wrong place.

The door is flung open: Blanche is home from Mrs Sebire's. She walks crisply into the house. She pulls off her chiffony headscarf, runs her hand through her toffee-blonde hair.

'Mmm.'

She sniffs the air with relish, goes to peer in the pot on the stove.

'That's a really nice soup,' she says. 'I'm looking forward to that.'

I see how she swallows as her mouth waters. I feel a flicker of guilt.

'Blanche—I'm sorry, but I'm keeping the soup for someone else,' I tell her.

'But I'm really hungry, Mum.' Her voice is tight with protest.

'I know you must be. I'm sorry, sweetheart. There's macaroni for tea.'

'You *know* I don't like macaroni... So who is this special someone who gets the nicest soup?'

'A visitor,' I say.

'And why is this someone else more important than Millie and me?' she says, aggrieved.

'It's not someone more important than you—it's just someone who needs it more than you... Look—you can have some if there's any left, when you come back from Celeste's.'

'But why all the mystery?' she says.

'It's just someone who's coming by. You don't know the person,' I tell her.

She studies my face for a moment, trying to read me.

There's a small, awkward silence between us. Her blue eyes narrow, harden. I feel my mouth turn to blotting-paper. I wonder if she thinks this person is my lover: I wonder if she suspects about Gunther and me, and this soup kept for someone special serves to confirm all her suspicions. I've always protected her from knowing how unhappy we were, her father and me—from her father's long love affair, from Monica Charles. I think how she must hate me, if she suspects me. Yet it's safer for her to think this soup is for my lover, than to know the truth—that I am feeding Kirill.

Then she turns away from me, shrugging slightly. I let myself breathe out. The moment has passed, and I wonder if I misread her.

'Honestly, Mum, you're starting to sound like Millie,' she says. 'You're always clamming up, both of you…'

She puts her handbag down on the table: her gaze falls on the globe.

'And why on earth have you got that thing out? Millie doesn't need to bother with all that yet,' she says. There's an edge of outrage in her voice. 'Miss Delaney can't be teaching her geography *already*. She can't be that *cruel*.'

'We're looking for a country,' says Millie, very solemn and important.

'It's awful being a child,' says Blanche. 'One day you're having a nice time catching sticklebacks, and the next you're having to learn all about tornados and things…'

'It's a secret,' says Millie. 'It's nothing to do with school.' She presses her lips tight together.

'You and your secrets,' says Blanche.

She turns to me, raising her eyebrows, as though to say, *She's off again*.

Millie puts the globe away in the cupboard. She shuts the cupboard door with a small significant crack, like the sound ice makes splintering.

CHAPTER 64

Kirill sits at my table, drinks the last drops from the bowl.

'Thank you, Vivienne. Thank you.'

I light our cigarettes. He leans back in his chair, with a sigh.

There's a question I feel a little frightened to ask: yet something in me knows he wants to tell his story.

'How did you come here, Kirill? Tell us what happened,' I say.

For a moment he is quiet. The liquid whistle of birds floats in through my open window, and the languorous scent of my roses, that smell so sweet you can never smell them enough.

He clears his throat.

'I lived in a village in the forest, as I told you,' he says slowly, in his high, starved voice.

'Yes.'

Millie pulls her chair closer to mine, presses up against me, as she does when I'm reading to her: it sounds like the start of a story from one of our fairytale books.

Kirill's gaze is on us—but I'm not sure how clearly he sees us. His eyes burn, as though with a fever.

'One morning in the darkness, the Germans broke down

our door. It was four o'clock. They shook me and Danya, my wife, awake. They dragged us outside, and onto the road that led to the next village. Then we were tied together like this…'

He reaches out, presses the back of his hand against mine. His skin is so cold, his touch startles me.

'Hand to hand?' I say.

He nods.

'We were tied together hand to hand, and they made us spread out in a line across the width of the road. We were told to start walking, taking very small steps… My wife, who came there after me, was at the end of the line…'

I hear the rawness in his voice. A judder of fear goes through me. I know this matters somehow, that his wife was walking at the end of the line.

I glance at Millie. Her eyes are fixed on his face. I wonder if I should tell her to leave us, if I should protect her from hearing this. But something stops me—some sense of the strength of their friendship: a sense that Millie has the right to hear the story he tells.

'We walked, and the Germans followed some distance behind,' he tells us.

I can picture it—but I don't understand, don't know what causes the horror I see in his face.

'The Red Army partisans were fighting the Germans,' he tells us. 'They lived in the woods around us. The partisans had been planting mines.'

Millie frowns.

'I don't know what a mine is,' she whispers to me.

Kirill answers her.

'A mine is a secret weapon that is hidden under the earth. If you step on a mine…' He throws his hands in the air, to mime an explosion. 'If you do that, it is over for you,' he says.

Millie's eyes widen.

'The Germans were using us to search for mines,' he tells us. 'Whatever we did, we would die. We would die if we stepped on a mine. And if we stepped over a mine, and the German behind us blew up, they would shoot us because we had missed the mine. So we walked without hope, because either way you would die.

'We did the little we could. We walked in the tracks of horses. We tried to avoid those places where the earth had been disturbed. Because death by explosion seemed worse than death by shooting. From fear, my mouth dried up. I was weeping, all of us wept. Our tears falling half blinded us. That was what it was like...'

He is silent for a moment. I can feel my heart pounding. Millie sits quite still, very pale, her wide eyes on his face.

'I remember the sudden shake, the noise. I had never heard such a sound. We were thrown to the earth,' he tells us. 'Then afterwards, the silence. For a little while, our ears were stopped, we could hear nothing at all. There was blood and soil all over us. I knew even before I turned, I knew that Danya was dead. She lay still, her body torn open. The Germans cut the rope on her hands that tied her to the next person. They left her lying. They made those of us who were still alive walk on along the road...'

His voice fades.

I look at him, but I can't see his face any more. While he has been talking, dusk has come to my room, and the shape of him is black against the window. Behind him, the sky is a profound blue, and in the Blancs Bois a nightingale is singing its rapturous song. I don't understand how these things can exist in the same universe—the nightingale, the soft blue of dusk: and the pain that drenches his voice.

'I'm so sorry,' I say, but my words sound all wrong, too loud for the small, quiet room. 'I'm so sorry about Danya.'

He nods slightly.

'That night,' he says, 'they locked us in a store room in the village. I wept for my wife. I thought that it should have been me at the end of the line, that I should have died, not Danya. That it was my fault. That if I had let her join the line first, then she would not have died. I still think this...'

I open my mouth. I'm about to say, *It's not your fault, you couldn't have stopped any of it...* But I know that wouldn't comfort him. There is no comfort for him.

'The night before she died, we had quarrelled. She said that I was always working and had no time for her.' There's a choke in his voice—I have to lean forward to hear. 'I was not always a good husband to her. I was not a good man. My last words to her had been angry words.'

I can tell from the anguish in his voice, that this torments him above everything, all the brokenness, the unfinished business of their parting.

'I would have died to save her,' he says. 'But I wasn't given the choice.'

I have heard how people will blame themselves, if others die around them and they are left alive. Of the guilt you can feel for having lived. I see this written in his face.

'There was nothing you could do,' I say. 'Nothing.'

My words are empty.

He sits there for a long while, his cigarette held in front of his face, not speaking.

Millie pulls my head down towards her and whispers to me.

'I want to know what happened next.'

As though, after what she has heard, she's become suddenly frightened of him, afraid to speak to him directly.

He hears her, and stirs.

'I will tell you the rest now,' he says. 'The next day we were taken by lorry to Minsk. That is our capital city. From Minsk we were sent to Germany. There was a big centre at Wuppertal, where there were many prisoners. The old and the weak were led outside, and we never saw them again.'

Millie looks up at me. A question floats in her eye.

'What happened to them? To all the old people. What happened?'

'Shh.' I put my arm round her. 'Shh.'

'Then we were taken to a place by the sea. We were put on a ship to come here. I had never seen the sea before,' he tells us.

Millie murmurs to me, amazed.

'But the sea is *everywhere*.'

I hold her close against me.

'The ship did not sail for a very long time,' he says. 'We had no food, and many died. The Germans poured water into the hold for the prisoners. We had to do this to catch the drops…. '

He shows us—holding his mouth open, tilting back his head, cupping his hands as though to catch water.

'Then we sailed here,' he tells me. 'That is how I came here.'

He stubs out his cigarette in the ashtray. He leans forward on the table, resting his head in his hands. He is exhausted: telling his story has used up what little strength he had.

We sit quietly for a long time. The clock ticks, the shadows reach out towards us. All words are taken from me.

'You should go back now,' I say at last.

'Yes,' he says.

I take him through the back door, and out through the garden to the lane.

'Come to the barn tomorrow,' I say.

'Yes, Vivienne. Thank you.'

He vanishes into the blue dusk.

When I get back to the house, Millie is still sitting in the twilight of the kitchen.

'You need to go to bed now, sweetheart,' I tell her.

She doesn't say anything.

I turn on the lamp.

She looks up at me, blinks in the sudden light. She's been crying: her pale face gleams with the shiny tracks of her tears.

I put my arms round her. I hold her so close I can feel the fizz of her heart.

I'm expecting questions to tumble out of her. Why did these things happen to him? Why were they so cruel to him? Why did his wife have to die? So many questions to which there are no answers.

But she presses into me, and says nothing.

CHAPTER 65

That night I lie awake for a long time. And when at last I sink into a restless, fractured sleep, I dream about what Kirill told us.

In the dream, I'm walking along a lane between fields, the lane that leads to Elm Tree Farm. The trees in the hedgebank are leaning in, almost meeting over our heads. There's a line of us tied together, stretched out across the lane—Millie and Blanche and Evelyn, and women from the school gate. I feel no emotion. There's no fear at all in the dream—I just accept what is happening, don't question it. All the colours are heightened—vivid, carnival colours—the sunlight yellow and sulphurous, the sky a clear, bright, suffocating blue. It's very quiet.

There are soldiers walking behind us. I know they're there, sense their presence: I can hear their voices, the click of their booted feet on the road. But I try not to look behind me. This is the one thing I know, that I mustn't look back.

It comes to me that I recognise the voice of one of the soldiers. There is a sense of utter inevitability about this, that his presence here is confirming something that I have always known. In the end, I can't stop myself. I turn, and see it is Gunther. This is entirely unsurprising to me.

I wake, with a start. I sit up sharply, gasping: it's hard to breathe, as though some great weight is pressing down into my chest. The first light of dawn is leaking under my curtains. I stare around at my room, trying to ground myself in all the solid, familiar things, the sturdy furniture, the cloistering walls of my home: struggling to leave the world of the dream behind me, to push away its meaning. *It was just a dream*, I tell myself. *It didn't mean anything*. But the horror of it stays with me, like a stain.

CHAPTER 66

It's the day before Gunther is due back from leave. A storm is brewing: the sky is dark as a bruise. As I walk through the fields, a sudden wind pushes my hair in my mouth, and makes quick, small whirlwinds of the dust and dry leaves on the track.

Today Kirill has something for me—some hedgerow flowers he has picked, herb robert and toadflax tied together with wire, to make a posy.

He holds the flowers out to me, with a small, courteous bow.

'For you,' he says. 'I have no other way to say thank you.'

'They're lovely.'

I press the flowers to my face. They have a green polleny smell. I'm so touched—that out of all his poverty, he has found a way to give me a gift. And I know that this will matter to him—that he is a proud man. That his terrible neediness is hateful to him.

I take him back to my house, and Millie joins us in the kitchen. I feed him with soup I have made. As he eats, I put the flowers in a glass tumbler on the windowsill. They're so pretty, but fading already, their pinks and purples browning at the edges. Once picked, hedgerow flowers have only a short time to live.

When he has eaten, I sit with him at the table. Millie has her chair pushed close to mine; I put my arm around her.

Tonight, he talks again about his birthplace—the birch forest, the gentle rivers; the workshop where he made his violins. I imagine him—younger, his face not yet marked by suffering, his head bowed over his work, intent. I think of the complexity, the delicacy, of that work. As I imagine it, his hands are whole and healed again.

'I will go back one day,' he says.

'Yes,' I say. 'Yes, you will, of course you will.'

And then we sit in the quiet—companionable, as though we have known one another a very long time.

As we leave, he glances at the picture that hangs on the wall of my kitchen, the Margaret Tarrant devotional print— the Christ Child in his crib, with angels all around, their wings vast and intricate, and coloured the soft, matt blue of bluebells.

'Do you believe in all this?' he asks me, pointing to the picture.

I don't know how to answer. Do I? Not in the way that Blanche does. I remember what she said—*It must all be part of God's plan. There must be a purpose to it.* But I can't see it like that. Can't see the purpose.

'In a way,' I tell him. 'Some of it.'

'My mother still believes—she keeps the family icons secretly in her attic,' he tells me. 'But I don't believe any more.' His voice is weary. 'None of us in the camp believe. None of us. None who have seen what we have seen. You cannot suffer as we have suffered and still have faith,' he says.

There's nothing I can say to that.

'I don't believe in God, but I still feel angry with him,'

he says. He smiles slightly. 'That makes no sense, does it, Vivienne?'

I take him out through my garden. A few brown leaves are falling, and the sound of the wind in the trees is like the sea, like the surge of shingle: the sound that Angie has told me presages rain.

In the shadow of the hedgebank, I put my hand on his arm.

'Kirill—there's something I need to tell you. I didn't want to say this in front of Millie. But after today, it won't be safe for you to come here any more.' It hurts, telling him this— knowing what it must mean to him, to come and sit in our home. 'One of the Germans at the house next door is coming back from leave. He comes to this house sometimes.'

I wonder if Kirill will be appalled that a German visits my house. If he will question me. If he will doubt me. But he just nods.

'I'm so sorry,' I tell him. 'But I'll bring you food in the barn, like Millie and Simon used to do. If you aren't there, I will leave it under the tractor.'

'Thank you, Vivienne,' he says.

'Take care,' I tell him.

'And you, Vivienne.' He bows a little. 'I am so grateful,' he says.

He turns from me, passes into my darkening orchard. The bruised cloud presses down on the land. Soon the rain will begin.

CHAPTER 67

S aturday. I wake with a surge of happiness, the shiny
festive feeling rushing in before the thought, before
I know why I am happy. Then at once I remember
why I feel this: Gunther is back from leave today. And with
the realisation comes a little apprehension, misting over
the gleaming surface of my mood, like breath that blurs a
mirror. What would he do if he knew about me feeding
Kirill? Would he betray us—Kirill and Millie and me? What
would he do? I tell myself, Of course he wouldn't betray
us. He is a good man. I know him to be a kind man... But
I hear Blanche's voice in my mind. *How can you ever really
know someone? How can you ever be sure what they're like?* Her
disingenuous blue eyes on me, searching my face.

When I'm out in my yard, I glance up at the big bay
window of Les Vinaires, hoping for a glimpse of him. And
now and then I go up to my bedroom and look out over
their front garden. The world is bright and glittery, washed
clean by last night's storm, everything radiant, hopeful. But
I don't see him.

A good while before curfew, I take some food to Peter
Mahy's barn—bread and ham and apples, wrapped in a
tea-towel in a basket. Kirill is waiting. He takes the food
from me.

'Thank you, Vivienne. Thank you so much.'

I don't wait with him while he eats: it's too risky being out here with him. I don't want to draw any attention to us. What if someone saw me, wondered where I was going—followed me, even? But I feel a little tug of sadness, leaving him there.

I hear Millie's prayers and tuck her blankets in. She reaches up, pulls my head down urgently towards her. She presses her mouth to my ear; her soft breath feathers my skin.

'Kirill didn't come,' she says.

'No, sweetheart. But I've fed him. I took his food to the barn. From now on, I'm going to have to do that.'

Lamplight bright as marigolds spills across her. As I bend down towards her, my shadow blots out her face.

'Can't he come here any more?'

'No, I don't think he can. It isn't safe here now. And I don't want you to come with me when I go to the barn—just in case somebody sees us.' Moving on quickly, because I'm afraid of what she will ask.

'But I really want to come with you.' She's outraged. 'He's my friend too. He was my friend *first*, Mummy.'

'I know. But we have to be careful—you know that. We could be in danger, Millie. You have to do as I say.'

She frowns. She's wondering whether it's worth protesting—wondering if I'll give in.

'Anyway, your cold's better now,' I tell her. 'You'll be able to play with Simon again, after school.'

Doubt swims in the dark of her eye like a little fish. I feel my blood flow faster. I'm waiting for her to ask, But *why*, Mummy? *Why* can't Kirill come here?

Her frown deepens, as though someone has drawn on her brow with blue indelible pencil.

'I wish he could still come to our kitchen,' she says.

'I know, sweetheart. So do I. But the thing is, we don't want to put him in danger,' I say.

She accepts this. She yawns as wide as a cat, stretches extravagantly, settles back on her pillows. She pulls her blanket up to her face.

'Well—see you take good care of him, Mummy,' she says.

At ten o'clock I hear a soft knock on the door to my yard. My heart pounds.

I open the door. Gunther is dark against the moonlight outside.

He has a bottle of brandy for us. I go to my kitchen to find glasses. He follows me. I feel suddenly awkward with him. It's as though we've forgotten how to be with one another—as though there's a rhythm we used to know, that we have to learn over again.

'So how was everything in Berlin?' I ask him.

It's the kind of question you ask when someone has been away. But the question is fraught, complicated. My body feels clumsy, a bit too big for the room.

'Berlin was much as usual. But in Cologne and Lübeck the bombing has been terrible. So much destroyed. I can't talk about it,' he says.

I don't know what to think. Isn't this what I should want? For German cities to be destroyed? But I see the distress in his face and I can't feel any triumph—just a confused sadness. I don't say anything.

'This is a terrible world we live in, Vivienne,' he says.

'Yes.'

That at least I can agree with.

I ask about Ilse, his wife.

'She is the same as ever,' he says. 'She always keeps the house well. Though daily life is difficult, of course…'

I think how strange it is to be asking these things. Our love had seemed so natural before he went on leave—easy as air, as though it were the element I lived in. Now there's a shift, a disruption.

'Did you see Hermann?' I ask him.

His face softens, hearing his son's name. But he shakes his head.

'No,' he tells me. 'He is in Africa, with Rommel.'

There's a thread of fear wrapped round his voice. He turns from me, to hide the feeling—and his gaze falls on the flowers that Kirill picked for me, that are in a glass on my windowsill. The flowers are almost dead now, the petals crinkled like scraps of brown paper; but they were such a precious gift I can't bear to throw them away.

'Someone gave you flowers?' he says.

There's a slight edge to his voice. I realise he might think that I have another admirer.

'Oh—that was just Millie,' I tell him, with a little throw-away laugh.

But it comes out wrong: the laugh sounds forced. A shiver goes through me, cold crawling over my skin. For a brief, panicked moment, I fear he will read my secret in my face.

But then his mouth is on mine and his arms are all around me, and I feel myself open up to him as I always do. I have been so hungry for him.

I take him up to my bedroom. He has a bag of gifts for me; he shows me what he has brought. Silk stockings; French cigarettes; Guerlain L'Heure Bleu, in a cut-glass bottle that dazzles and catches the light. I open the bottle, breathe in deeply: the scent is wonderful, profound, smelling of almonds and melancholy. I touch the stockings delicately, feel their cobwebby fragility, afraid that they'll be laddered by the calluses on my hands. I'll have to wear gloves to pull them on. I wonder if these gifts are all too glamorous for me—if I'm too worn out, too used-up for such luxury now.

In his arms, I think of nothing but him. I feel the rightness, the sweetness, of having him here in my bed, where he should be. But afterwards the questions are there, insistent wings that beat at the darkened window-panes of my mind.

He can tell, of course.

'You seem preoccupied, darling,' he says. 'Is something the matter?'

'Don't worry, it's nothing,' I say.

He traces out the side of my face with one warm finger.

'I know there's something,' he says.

'Well—just the usual things. You know—keeping everything going. With all the shortages. With Evelyn not quite right in her head...'

Kirill's story is in my mind—the villagers tied together in the forest. I want to ask him how such things could happen, how people could be treated as nothing—used, discarded, thrown away. To see whether Gunther has ever heard of such inhumanity. But I can't ask: because if I asked, he would wonder at once where I had heard this story.

'And what about young Millie? Are you still worried about her?' he says.

I wish he hadn't said that. It's too close to the things that weigh on me. I turn a little away from him, so he can't quite see my face.

'No, she seems fine. She's settled down,' I tell him.

'No more ghosts?' he asks me.

'No, she doesn't talk about all those things any more.'

'It was just a stage. All children go through stages,' he says.

'Yes, I expect so.'

He exhales deeply, stretches, wraps his arms around me again. I rest my head on his chest. I can feel his heart beating.

'It's so good to be home,' he tells me.

I can't believe he meant that—when he called my bedroom 'home'. I tell myself it's just a slip of the tongue. But I still feel happy that he said it.

CHAPTER 68

Every evening that week, I take some food to the barn. Kirill is there, waiting for me. I never stay long: we speak briefly, but it doesn't feel safe to talk like we did when he sat at my kitchen table. This saddens me: I feel that we're withdrawing from one another a little, and I'm so glad we had that time together, safe in my house. I no longer feel afraid when I do this, though I am always wary. It becomes a routine with me, something I grow accustomed to. To take the food to the barn, to speak to Kirill: then to come back home and wait for Gunther. Moving from one world to another.

On Friday evening I go as usual; but Kirill isn't there. I sit in the barn doorway, feeling the soft dull thuds of my heart. At last, I think I hear a quiet footfall; and relief swims through me. I turn quickly. But there is nothing behind me—only rustling grasses and leaves and the shadows of leaves. I wait for a long time. I don't like leaving Evelyn and Millie; but I can't go till I've seen him. The sun begins to set in a blaze of pink and amber and gold. I sit so still that rabbits come right up to me, moving utterly silently through the pale ruffled grass. There's a chalky crescent moon in the deepening sky, like a nail-paring. When it's almost curfew time, I head back home.

I tell myself that anything could have happened. Perhaps the prisoners have been forced to mend the hole in the fence. There could be a different guard on, who doesn't turn a blind eye. I tell myself he will be there tomorrow. But I have a cold, sick feeling.

'You have that little frown,' says Gunther. He runs one finger down between my eyebrows, as though to wipe the frown away. 'Is it Millie?'

'No, it isn't Millie. It's nothing. Really,' I tell him.

I can tell he doesn't believe me—but he doesn't say anything more, and that worries me, that he doesn't question me further. As though he knows I may not tell him the truth. I wonder if he suspects me.

The next day, when I go to the barn, the things I left are still there under the tractor, the basket and tea-towel scattered, the food strewn around and gnawed at. It looks as though rats have been there.

I feel a chill. I think of the horror of what I saw by Harry Tostevin's land, all those months ago now—the man who was beaten and kicked to death. I can't bear to think what may have happened, in the hell that Kirill inhabits.

I return every evening, hoping: but Kirill isn't there, and the food is untouched where I left it, or has been spoiled by animals. I know I will have to stop doing this. I can't really spare the food, if nobody is eating it. So I only go on alternate days, and then I stop going at all.

I don't know what to tell Millie. I decide to say nothing. She inhabits the present tense of childhood; she's always out with Simon, battling with conkers, roaming the Blancs Bois, fishing for sticklebacks in the streams. Maybe she scarcely thinks about Kirill now.

One day I make a treat for tea—some apple charlotte with apples from our orchard, Bramleys that are good for cooking. I sweeten them with Gwen's honey, and make a crunchy topping from some precious crusts of stale bread. Millie watches. She loves to see me prepare the apples, how I cut from each a single gleaming spiralling ribbon of peel.

She comes back into the kitchen as I take the pudding out of the oven. Delicious scents float on the air—caramel, apples, toasted bread.

'Mmm. That smells really nice. Kirill will like that,' she says.

I don't say anything. I have my back to her. I feel her questioning gaze on me.

'What's the matter, Mummy? Is Kirill all right?' she asks me.

I know I have to tell her, to be honest. I owe her that. He was her friend first, as she said.

'I don't know, sweetheart. I'm worried about him. He hasn't been to the barn. I haven't seen him for a while.'

Her small face darkens. She says nothing for a moment. A cranefly skitters across the window, gangly, grey as rain. Outside, there's a blustering wind that scuffs at the drifts of coloured leaves, and more leaves fall past our window: the season ending, everything falling apart.

'What's happened to him?' she asks me.

'Maybe he hasn't been able to leave the work camp in the evening. Or maybe they've moved him somewhere else. He might even be in a different country,' I say.

But I don't know if that can happen—whether they move the slave-workers from one country to another, or whether once they're here on Guernsey, they stay.

'Has he died?' she asks me.

The words shake me, coming from her.

I have such an urge to reassure her, as you do when a child has a nightmare—soothing them, telling them all is well with the world. But it feels wrong to do that.

'I don't know, Millie... Sweetheart—you will always remember this has to be a secret, won't you? Kirill being our friend? That we fed him?' I take her face in my hands, look into her eyes, see the gold flecks in the darkness of them. 'We mustn't tell anyone, ever. Even if we never see him again.'

She looks straight back at me. Her gaze is sepia-brown and luminous.

'I *know* that, Mummy. You've *told* me.' She's a bit cross, impatient, because I keep repeating this. 'I promised. It's our secret, isn't it? Our really big secret.'

And I think, with that little lurch of the heart, *Yes, it's our really big secret.*

PART V:

DECEMBER 1942 - NOVEMBER 1943

Winter comes—the third winter of the Occupation: everything closed down, retreating, my garden full of barren white stalks like little bones. It's cold. We rarely have frosts on Guernsey—but a vicious wind blows that chills everywhere it touches. From the lane past Harry Tostevin's fields, you can see the sea, pale and ferocious, how it beats and batters the land, the plumes of white spray flying. I ration our wood very carefully. When a fire has been lit in our living room, I tell the girls off severely if they forget to shut the door and let a little heat escape. If the war goes on for another year, I don't know where our fuel will come from. I may have to fell the trees in my orchard—though whenever I think this, sadness tugs at my sleeve.

One day, Blanche comes to find me in my bedroom. Vivid spots of embarrassment flare in her cheeks. I feel a flicker of apprehension.

'Mum.' Her voice is hushed and ashamed. 'I wanted to ask you something… The thing is… It's the curse. It hasn't come.'

'Blanche. *No*.' I'm appalled. Our hunger, the shortages, and now *this*: another mouth to feed.

She flinches.

'Don't be cross, Mum. *Please.*'

'Why on earth shouldn't I be? How many months have you missed?'

'Just one. Mum, you don't understand. I haven't...' She can't quite say it. 'I mean, honestly, it's not that. You know that, Mum, you know I don't even have a boyfriend. The thing is, I wouldn't *think* of going out with one of the island boys. They're all so boring... And even if I did—of course I wouldn't—you know... Mum, I do as the Bible says. Why don't you trust me?'

I look into the summer blue of her eyes. She doesn't flinch from my gaze.

'You're really telling the truth?'

'Yes. I promise.'

My anger seeps away.

'Sweetheart—I'm sorry. I was worried...'

She doesn't say anything. I know she won't readily forgive me for doubting her.

'I think it could be happening because you're hungry,' I tell her. 'If you get too thin, your system all closes down. I've read that somewhere.'

'Oh. Are you absolutely sure?'

'Yes. It doesn't mean that there's anything wrong,' I tell her.

I think how my own cycle has been erratic too. I feel bad that I was so cross with her.

'Will I still be able to be a mother when I get married?' she says.

'Yes, of course,' I tell her. 'It'll all go back to normal when we have a bit more to eat.'

I put my arm around her. Her body is stiff, resisting. She's still cross that I didn't trust her.

★ ★ ★

Our clothes are all worn through. It's not so bad for Millie: she's able to wear all Blanche's old things, so she still has plenty of clothes—a tartan kilt, a Fair Isle jumper, a dress of white organdie with a sash of cherry-red ribbon. Anyway, she's still only six—she doesn't care what she wears. But Blanche is desperate. She stares at the pictures in her magazines, and yearns for glamorous clothes.

One day I'm using my sewing machine; some of our sheets are wearing through, and I'm turning them sides-to-middle. Blanche watches me thoughtfully.

'Mum. Could I do some sewing? Could I make myself something new? I look so frumpy nowadays.'

'Of course you don't, sweetheart, you always look lovely...'

'You're only saying that because you're my mother,' she says. 'Really. I mean it.'

'I could have a look in St Peter Port. But there's hardly any material in the shops now,' I tell her. 'Only the ends of rolls that nobody wants.'

'Celeste made a skirt from old curtains,' she says. 'She looks so stylish in it. She really looks the part... There must be a bit of material in the house I could use.'

I go up to the back attic, determined to find her something.

The attic feels separate, sequestered, the only sound the shuffle and murmur of pigeons up on the roof that seem loud in here, as though the air is breathing. Through the dormer windows you can see the high winter sky, as grey as tin and shining.

I open a big old blanket chest, the camphor smell tickling my nose. I find pillowslips and tablecloths that I brought here

when I was married—linens too good for everyday use, and
so somehow never used. I'd forgotten all about them. At the
bottom of the chest, I find a green velvet curtain that used
to hang inside the front door to keep out the draughts. I
shake it out, hold it up. It's a rich jade colour, like deep sea-
water on a hot summer's day, like the sea at Petit Bôt where
it laps at the foot of the cliffs. The shade would be perfect
for Blanche. I'm sure she could make this into something.
Myself, I'm hopeless at sewing: any length of fabric will feel
recalcitrant in my hand, as though it has a life of its own.
But Blanche is a natural seamstress.

I take the curtain downstairs, hold it up to her face.

'The colour looks beautiful on you,' I say.

'Could I use it? Really, really?'

'Yes, of course. I'll hang it out to get rid of the smell of
mothballs…'

'But what should I make?' she asks me.

We look in my sewing cupboard in the dresser. We poke
around among the entangled, lavish colours, the skeins of
thread and scraps of vivid wool, and find a Simplicity pattern
that I bought and never used, for a sleek fitted jacket. The
woman in the sketch on the packet has a sheen to her; she
looks as wealthy young women used to look before the war.
She has a hat of damson velvet pulled flirtily over one eye,
and her shoes are spindly and delicate. You can picture her
in the Palm Court of an opulent hotel, perched louchely on
a bar stool, with a cigarette in a long holder and a Side Car
in her hand.

Blanche peers over my shoulder.

'That's *exactly* what I want to look like,' she says.

Blanche sews assiduously every evening. In five days the
jacket is ready, and she puts it on to go up to Celeste's house.

The colour sets off the caramel blonde of her hair, and the fit is perfect. She suddenly looks so much older—not just a girl any more. Her loveliness dazzles me.

'That looks gorgeous,' I say.

'Yes,' she says, accepting this.

As she's leaving, we hear the ringing of a bicycle bell in our yard. I go to open the door: it's Johnnie with a present from Gwen, a bag of cabbages and curly kale. He's rushing, as usual. He almost bumps into Blanche as she slips out through the door.

'Oh,' he says.

I see the way he looks at her—eyes widening, as though she startles him, as though he's never really seen her clearly before. She's aware of his look: she's shy, a little embarrassed, with this boy she used to play with. A bright blush spreads all over her face and her neck. Neither of them says anything; neither of them smiles.

Later, when she comes home just before curfew, I remember the little incident.

'It's a shame you never see Johnnie now,' I say to her, not thinking. 'Remember when you were children, how the two of you used to play? You'd be off in the woods for hours and hours. And I'll never forget that afternoon you tried racing snails on the terrace… You were just like Millie and Simon…'

She gives me a rather hard look, unsmiling. I know that I've struck the wrong note.

'That was an awfully long time ago now, Mum,' she tells me, coolly.

She still has the jacket on. She goes to look at herself in the mirror in the living room. She holds up her hair with her hands, seeing how it might look swept high up on her head, revealing her graceful pale neck, a few stray blonde curls hanging down. She's like a yellow flower on a willowy stalk that tilts its face to the sun. She smiles at her reflection, striking a pose. She strokes the lapel of the jacket.

'A week ago this was just an old curtain,' she says.

I admire her—the way she's made something so lovely from a thing so long forgotten.

Gunther still comes to my house. His close-cropped hair is white now. When I notice this—as always when I'm aware how the years have marked him—I wonder what he is seeing when he looks at me. My hair is still dark, free of grey; but if I catch sight of myself in the mirror, when I'm unaware, not smiling, I see a new severity in my face—my lips are tight, my forehead creased in a frown—as though I'm surrounded by things I need to defend myself against. So I try not to look in the mirror. Our love has become a quieter, gentler thing now: sometimes we just fall asleep in one another's arms, like a long-married couple. I feel a deep gratitude for him—for his presence in my life, in my bed. It makes everything bearable.

We still get news of the war, from the wireless that Celeste's mother has hidden in one of Mr Ozanne's coffins. Blanche tells us about the siege of Stalingrad. The Germans are in the city: the German army is cut off, surrounded, but they will not give in.

I ask Gunther about it.

'What's happening in Stalingrad?'

I see how his face tightens, the hardening of the muscles round his mouth.

'It's Hell on earth there,' he says. I hear the splinter of fear that is always there in his voice, when he speaks about Russia.

'The dogs and rats flee the city, only the people remain... Even the river burns, they say. There is nothing but fire and death there...' He stumbles: as though there are no words in either his language or mine that could express the horror of it. 'They are calling it the mass grave of the Wehrmacht,' he says.

We welcome the coming of spring—the tremulous catkins, the flowering in the hedgebanks, the hope that comes with the softening air, the lengthening light. On daffodil-yellow mornings, when the breeze has a scent of blossom and last night's rain still wet on the grass, you can believe for a while that things don't have to be this way, don't have to be such a struggle. That there could be an end to this: that we could be living a different life.

Spring gives way to summer. The swallows come: I love to watch their darting flight over the fields, the warp and weft of their movement, as though they are weaving some gossamer fabric in the blue wide air. The roses in my garden bloom, the Blancs Bois is full of singing birds, and secret under its gorgeous canopy of green. The world turns on in all its loveliness, oblivious to us: whatever is done to us, whatever we suffer, whatever choices we make.

CHAPTER 70

It happens in high summer.

One evening, when the girls are in bed, an hour before Gunther will come, I'm sitting alone in my living room with a load of darning to do. I hear a soft dull thud on the door at the back of the house. I jump up. My first thought is that some large animal has bumped against the door—that maybe a horse or a cow has broken into my garden. I go to the door, my pulse skittering, open it cautiously.

I can only move it a little way: something is pushing it shut. I peer through the crack. For a brief, muddled moment, unable to make sense of what I see, I think that a heap of filthy grey rags has been flung down on my doorstep. I stare. *Oh God.* The bundle of rags is a man. He's on his front, his face hidden. As I look, he raises his head.

'Oh God. Kirill.'

His eyes flicker open.

Please God, I think. *Please God, that nobody saw...*

'Vivienne. I came back.' His voice is a rasping whisper.

The change in him appals me. He was wretched, ragged, starved, before; but now there's such fragility to him, almost a translucence. His face is hollow, the skeleton looms through the skin: you can see how he will look in death. There are shadows like bruising around his mouth, his eyes. He coughs;

and the cough is a predatory creature, scrabbling at him, almost destroying him.

He moves, just enough to let me open the door. I slip out.

'Can you get up?' I ask him.

I put out my hand. He grasps it, struggles to his feet. I bring him into my house.

I give him what food I have, cold potatoes and soup. He eats slowly; he has to struggle to swallow, the action takes all his will. I remember how eagerly, hungrily, he used to eat my food. I'm glad that Millie is sleeping, that she doesn't have to see him like this.

'You stopped coming to the barn,' I say.

'There were different guards,' he tells me.

But perhaps that's not the real reason. Perhaps it was because I'd said that a German visits my house.

I light our cigarettes, hand him his. He sits at my table, resting his head in his hand. I look at him, at the shadows blue as ash in his face. I remember my mother on her sickbed, the imminence of death in her. I know he has only a few days left. Yet he came here to find me. Something in him still clings to life, something will not let go: not yet. He came here.

In that instant, thinking this, I know just what I must do. I see this with perfect clarity, the absolute necessity of it, the weight of the moment falling on me, sudden, drenching as rain. But I flinch from it. Everything's happening so quickly: I'm not prepared—not ready. This isn't the way I do things—so instantly, impulsively. I would like to think it through—I would like to weigh everything up. But there's no time for any of that.

I swallow hard. My throat is thick with fear. It's the moment I can't go back from.

'Kirill.' My voice sounds almost normal—just a little too high. 'If there was a way to get out—if I could find someone to help you escape—would you want that?'

I see a brief light in his eyes.

'Yes,' he says. 'Yes, Vivienne.'

Panic grips me, now I've said it—fear for him, and for me.

'Think about it,' I tell him. 'You've got to think about it carefully. If you try to escape and they find you they will shoot you in a heartbeat. You know that.'

He starts to reply, but his cough drowns out his words. It masters him, has its claws in him. He struggles to speak, as though this has to be said, as though he is running out of time: but he has no breath.

At last the coughing subsides.

'Vivienne. If I stay in the camp, I will not live,' he tells me.

'I can't keep you with me now,' I say. 'I'll have to work out how to do this. There's someone I need to talk to.'

He nods.

'Come to the barn tomorrow,' I tell him. 'I'll meet you there. I'll see what I can do.'

I take him over the lane. The food—or my promise to him—has given him a little strength: he can walk now. He shivers, yet a thin heat comes off his body. His hand is as light as the brush of a falling feather on my arm.

CHAPTER 71

Gwen's kitchen door is open: she's at her sink, peeling potatoes. She turns, takes one look at my face. Her own face darkens. She puts down her scraper and lifts up her apron, wiping her hands.

'Viv—what is it? What's happened?'

'Gwen—I need to see Johnnie,' I say.

A frown comes in her forehead.

'He's trying to fix the tractor,' she says. 'Up past the hayfield. Viv—can I do anything?'

'I just need to have a word with him,' I tell her.

She reaches out to me, puts her damp, urgent hand on my arm.

'Don't get him involved in anything, Vivienne.' She knows me so well: perhaps she can read something of my purpose in my face. Her voice has a high note of pleading.

'There's something I have to ask him,' I tell her.

She isn't reassured. But she doesn't try to stop me. She leans against her sink and watches me as I go, her arms wrapped tight around her body.

I walk round the back of the farmhouse, past the glasshouses that have a warm scent of tomatoes, past a field of grass grown for hay that ruffles and parts in the wind, as though a hand is stroking it.

I see the tractor on the track by the hedge. Johnnie has his head in the engine. He looks up, startled to see me.

'Auntie Viv?'

He straightens. His fingers are blackly stained with oil; he rubs his hands on a rag, distracted, his face a question.

'There's something I wanted to ask…' My voice is creaky, thin. 'I've got a problem, Johnnie.'

I'm speaking very softly, though there's no one to hear. The wind whispers at the ragged edge of the hayfield. Johnnie takes a step closer, waits for me.

'There's a man from the work camp. Kirill—his name is Kirill.' I think how I don't know his surname, and had never thought to ask. 'He comes from Belorussia. We're friends. Last year he would come to my house for a while, and I would give him a meal.'

Johnnie's eyes widen. He says nothing.

'Then for a long time I didn't see him,' I say. 'I worried what might have happened. I mean, you know what those places are like…' My voice is serrated with panic: the words spill out, tumbling over one another. 'He came back yesterday evening. He's ill, he's terribly ill. I'm so frightened for him. If he stays in the camp, he'll die. I know that. You can just tell that… Johnnie, I can't let him die…'

I realise my face is wet.

Johnnie is embarrassed.

'Don't cry, Auntie,' he says, helplessly.

He pulls a handkerchief out of his pocket, hands it to me. I scrub at my face, but the tears still fall.

'Johnnie. Can you help us?'

For a moment he says nothing. There is utter silence between us and in the land around us, all still and empty, the fields, the lanes, the woods: depth on depth of quiet. I hear the shushing sound the wind makes in the field of tall grass.

Johnnie's face works.

'I might be able to.' He looks wary.

I'd hoped for something definite, something practical and clear.

'You said you had plans to help some slave-workers escape.' My voice is shrill, and rather accusing. 'You said you might have safe houses.'

'We're getting there,' he says. 'But we're not very organised yet. On Jersey they've got a whole network...'

'So could you help us?' I say again. Still wanting a different answer.

'Maybe.'

'The thing is—Kirill speaks very good English. A man in his village taught him. Someone who'd worked in a university...'

Something new comes into Johnnie's face when I say that, as though this changes everything.

'Good enough that he could pass for an islander?' he says.

'Yes.'

'That makes all the difference,' he tells me, his face brightening. 'If he could live as one of us...'

'He could. I'm sure he could. I mean, islanders would know, of course. They'd hear his accent—he has a bit of an accent. But I think the Germans wouldn't be able to tell.'

'It's what they do on Jersey,' says Johnnie. 'There's a handful there who've escaped. They don't try to hide them, they live in plain sight, as farm labourers... It's the only way.'

He's tracing random crescents in the mud with the toe of his boot: planning, puzzling, working it out.

'It would be best to keep him hidden for a while,' he tells me. 'He'll need an identity card, of course, and that takes time to make. There's a man in town who does them. And there's somebody up in St Sampson who I think would take him in. Better really if you don't know the exact details...'

'He's coming back to my house tonight. You could come and take him then,' I say.

But Johnnie shakes his head. Seeing that, I feel the world lurch around me.

'No, not tonight, Auntie. We'll have to move him in the daytime,' he says.

'Why? Why in the daytime?' My heart cantering off.

'For a start, we can't risk being out after curfew. And it'll take a while to get him where he needs to be.'

'Oh.'

'Anyway, like I said, it's best to do these things in plain sight. Bang in the middle of the working day. Jerry's much more likely to stop you in the evening. He'll reckon you're up to something.'

I clasp my hands tight together, so Johnnie won't see the trembling that passes through me.

'Auntie. Could you keep him with you for just one night?' he says.

Oh God.

'There are Germans next door,' I tell him. But I can scarcely speak above the hard dull thumps of my heart.

'That shouldn't be a problem,' he says. 'I mean—it's not as though they're going to actually come in your house...'

I don't say anything.

'In a funny way it helps that they're there,' he tells me. 'It works to our advantage. No one would think you would

take the risk. They'd never suspect you of harbouring someone—not with the Germans that close.'

I can't tell him how close they really are: can't tell him
about Gunther and just how perilous this is. I know this is
unfair to Johnnie—if he's going to help me, he needs to fully
understand the risk. But I can't do it.

'Do you have anywhere you could hide him?' he asks me.
'Some kind of nook in the house?'

I think of the attic where Millie and Simon sometimes
play.

'We have a little back attic—it has a different stair. It's not
properly secret, but it's not immediately obvious…' I try to
remember whether he used to play there with Blanche; but
those times are a far country, an image glimpsed through
a prism—tiny, rainbow-coloured, remote. 'I don't know if
you've ever been up there…'

'And do you have clothes he could wear?'

His eyes are ardent and gleaming now. This thrills him—
putting the jigsaw together, fitting in all the pieces. I see,
with a jolt of misgiving, that this is still a game to him.

'He could have some old clothes of Eugene's. They'll be
too baggy on him—but they'd be about the right height,' I
tell him.

He nods.

'Nobody must know,' he says. 'Not Blanche. Not Millie.
Nobody. That's the safest way for everyone.'

'Yes. Of course.'

His eager gaze on me.

'So can you do that, Auntie?'

I think of all the danger—to my family, to Johnnie—
edging out like ripples where a stone is dropped into a pool—

stealthily, secretly. But then I think of Kirill: how he came to find me.

'Yes, I can do that.'

'Keep him tonight, and I'll be with you first thing in the morning. I'll have to bring the horse and cart—this tractor's on its last legs… I'll find something to hide him under. I'll be there as soon as I can. I promise.'

It's real, suddenly. All the panic I've been pushing away from me presses into my chest, so hard I can't breathe.

'I'll go and see my contact right away.' A sudden grin unfurls across Johnnie's face. 'You're a bit of a dark horse, aren't you, Auntie? I'd never have thought it of you. Well, good for you,' he says.

Walking home, I have a constant urge to look behind me. Like on those summer days before the Occupation, walking along the causeway from Lihou Island with the girls: always that fear at your back, that the water might overtake you.

CHAPTER 72

From the wardrobe in my bedroom, I sort out some clothes of Eugene's—trousers, a couple of linen shirts, some strong leather shoes. With my arms full of the clothes, I go to the stairway by Blanche's door that leads to the back attic.

I hear a door open behind me. Evelyn comes out of her room. Everything slumps inside me. I don't want to have to explain to her.

She stares at the clothes in my arms, at the shoes.

'What are you doing, Vivienne?'

'It's nothing—don't worry,' I say.

'Vivienne—why do you have his clothes? Is he coming back?' she asks me.

'No, not today. I'm just doing a bit of sorting,' I say. 'Tidying up the wardrobe. Making a bit more space.'

She doesn't seem to hear me.

'He's coming home, isn't he, Vivienne?'

Her face is suddenly vivid with a desperate hopefulness. Sadness snares me, as it does so often, because of the way she constantly rediscovers the harshness of things, and the terrible fact of her son's absence.

'No. Eugene's not coming back yet. Eugene's still away, Evelyn,' I say.

'Are you telling me the truth?' she says.

'Yes, of course.' Feeling guilty about so many things, as I say this. 'I'm so sorry, Evelyn…'

I wait at the barn, my pulse racing. He's late, and I wonder if he has died already; and there's a tiny, shameful part of me, hunched up like a mouse in a secret corner of my mind, that is almost relieved when I think this. Because if he didn't come, I wouldn't have to do this thing.

I hear a shuffle behind me. I turn—Kirill is there. He's so weak he can scarcely walk, and I take his arm and help him. It's a beautiful summer evening and there's still some warmth in the sun, but he's shivering. We walk through the fields and over the lane, moving from shadow to shadow. He moves so slowly, it seems to take for ever. I only let myself breathe out once I have him through my back door.

I seat him at my kitchen table. There's a dulled, remote look in his eyes. I wonder how real all this is to him—my room, the plans we have made. Whether it's all receding from him, the world becoming insubstantial—a place of mist and memory, fading. Whether all this seems a dream to him.

'Kirill. Do you still feel the same—that you want to escape? That you'll take that risk? I have to be certain,' I say.

He tries to speak, but coughing shakes him, racks him.

'Yes,' he mouths through the coughing, forcing out the words—as if he has to seize the moment, daren't let it pass. 'Yes.'

The coughing is over; he rests his head on his folded arms on the table, as though his head is too heavy for him and cannot be held up.

'Then here's what we'll do. You can stay here tonight. You can sleep in my attic,' I tell him.

'Thank you, Vivienne.'

'Someone will come in the morning and take you to a safe house. Until they get papers for you. After that you'll live as an islander. We'll find a place for you to live,' I say.

He reaches out, clings to my hand.

'Thank you,' he says. 'Thank you.'

When he has washed and eaten, I take him up to the back attic. My heart beats in my throat; but the whole house is quiet, the girls both in their rooms, Evelyn safely sleeping.

The attic is ready for him. I have put up an old camp bed, and piled it with warm blankets; and there are the clothes of Eugene's, a candle, and water to drink in the night.

He sighs a little when he sees this—as though at last he can breathe freely.

'Thank you for all your kindness,' he says.

I close the attic door behind me. Triumph surges through me—that we have got this far: that I can look after him here tonight, that he doesn't have to return to the hell of the camp. I feel all the glowing righteousness of having him here in my house: the feeling moves through me, warm as fever.

I go down to my bedroom to make myself ready for Gunther—to brush my hair, put on a little of the scent he gave me. Around me I hear the familiar rustles and creaks of my house, as it cools and settles for the night. Then all at once the tenuous sense of triumph leaves me. My palms are suddenly clammy with sweat, the hairbrush slides from my grasp. Down here in my bedroom, I can still hear Kirill's coughing.

It's ten o'clock, and Gunther knocks at the door.

'Vivienne.' That way he has of saying my name, as though it is the answer to a question.

I take him up to my room.

He kisses me: then pulls back, frowns slightly, looking into my face.

'What is it?' he says.

'It's nothing.'

He won't accept this.

'You seem rather nervous, darling. Tell me what the matter is.'

'It's nothing. Really,' I say. 'Well, just the usual things.' I grab at the first explanation I can think of. 'You know, feeding everyone. We're very short at the moment...'

'I'll see what I can do.' He starts to kiss me again.

I try to lose myself in him, but it's impossible. I feel as though I am balancing in a difficult, treacherous place—on a high narrow ledge, the wind whistling perilously about me.

'That was as good for you as usual?' he asks me afterwards, concerned.

'Yes, it was lovely. It always is.'

As I lie with my head on his shoulder, I hear Kirill starting to cough. I will him to stop, but the coughing goes on and on endlessly. It's hard not to flinch when I hear it: this takes all the strength that I have.

Gunther frowns, listening.

'Your mother-in-law has a terrible cough,' he says.

'Yes, it is quite bad.'

I hate lying to him.

'I can tell how it worries you,' he says. 'You become very tense when she coughs.'

'Well, she's quite frail now...'

'Would you like Max to come and examine her?' he asks me.

'It's better not,' I tell him.

The cold wind whistling around me: trying not to look down.

'Max really wouldn't mind,' he says.

'No, I know he wouldn't. He was so kind to Millie when she was hurt… It's just—I don't think she'd accept his help. Evelyn is very correct. She'd see it as fraternising, and she wouldn't approve.'

'Well—if you're sure. But the offer is there. I know he'd be happy to help her…'

We both listen to the coughing for a moment. Gunther makes a slight clicking noise in his throat, disapproving.

'It sounds very bad,' he says. 'You shouldn't let her continue like that. You need to get some help for her.'

'Yes, I will…'

For the first time since we've been lovers, I'm desperate for him to go.

It's still dark when he stirs and wakes. I take him downstairs and stand on my doorstep, watching him as he leaves. There's a silver spill of moonlight over the yard, but at the foot of the hedgebank the darkness is dense and complete. Gunther's body is black against the gravel, so he and his shadow make one indivisible whole. I watch as he moves through the silver and black of my yard: moving through darkness and light, away from me. A story comes to my mind—a story I read to Millie, from Angie's folktale book, about the fairy invaders who came from far-off countries, and married island women: how, in spite of their marrying, they were bound by a contract written in blood, so the women never knew when the men they loved would leave them; and sail towards the thin blue line at the edge of the world, in their boats that could shrink as small as a pebble or the delicate bone of a bird.

When Gunther is gone, I go up to the attic.

Kirill is asleep now. White moonlight through the uncurtained windows falls across him, and his skin seems pellucid, translucent. His hands are clutching at the blanket even in sleep, as though it is a precious thing that might be torn away from him. I can hear a high-pitched, dangerous note in his breath. But there's a stillness—a peacefulness, even—about his face as he sleeps. I wonder if he is dreaming of his homeland, of the place where his heart is—of the birch forest, the quiet rivers.

I stand there for a long time, watching him sleep. I feel a sudden, precarious happiness. I know I am doing the right thing, in keeping him here.

I sleep deeply, and my dreams are sweet and untroubled. I have a dream of flight—I am flying towards the morning over the sea, the dark sky above me, the dark sea below, and before me all the golden glory and flaming splendours of light.

CHAPTER 73

'Mum, why are we having porridge?' says Blanche.

'I had a bit of oatmeal left. I thought we might as well eat it up,' I tell her vaguely.

'Mmm. I like porridge. D'you remember before the Occupation, when we used to have porridge every day?' she asks me.

But it's becoming harder to remember that time—before the Occupation.

When Blanche has gone to work, and Millie is playing in the garden, and Evelyn is knitting in the living room, I fetch a tray and put out food for Kirill. To pour on the porridge, there's creamy milk in a jug, and I'm going to give him some Golden Syrup I've saved. I'd been keeping it for Millie, in case she ever had to take some bitter medicine; there's just a scraping at the bottom of the tin. I spoon it out, and watch as it falls in the bowl, gorgeously sticky and gilded. All the time I'm listening out for the horse and cart, for Johnnie.

There's a knock at my front door—then someone walks straight in, not waiting for me to answer. Relief floods me. It must be Johnnie. I'm surprised I didn't hear the cart: he must have thought it safest to leave it further down the lane.

I put the tray down on the kitchen table. I come out of my kitchen, step into my passageway.

Gunther is there. He has a loaf of bread in his hand. He looks immediately uncertain—reading something in me.

'I didn't wait for you to come to the door,' he tells me, in a lowered voice. He's studying my face—worrying that he's done the wrong thing and upset me. 'There was a woman walking her dog in the lane.'

Probably Clemmie Renouf, I think. Long, long ago, in another life, I might have been alarmed.

'I know you would prefer she didn't see me at your door,' he says.

'Yes. Thank you.'

'Vivienne. I know you don't like me coming here in the day. But I was worried about you...'

I wish he wouldn't keep apologising like this.

'You don't need to worry about us. But that's very thoughtful,' I say.

My voice sounds unfamiliar to me, as though it is someone else's voice.

He comes into the kitchen, puts the bread down on the table.

'You said you were short of food, and I thought this might help,' he tells me.

There's a sliver of doubt in his voice. I see his gaze falling on all the food on the tray.

'That's so kind of you,' I say again.

My tone is all wrong—formal, constrained. As though I scarcely know him. As though our loving was just a dream that I'd had.

'Are you sure you're all right, Vivienne?' he asks me.

'Yes, I'm fine,' I tell him.

My hands are shaking: I push them into my apron pockets, hide them.

'How is your mother-in-law?' he says.

'She's much the same. Thank you for asking.'

He's still staring quizzically at the tray. I know I have to explain.

'I was just taking some breakfast up to her bedroom for her,' I say.

'I hope she feels better soon. I do think you should ask a doctor to examine her.'

'Yes. I will.'

'Darling.' Speaking very softly now. 'There was something else. I'm afraid I can't come 'round tonight—I have a late meeting,' he says.

I nod. I hope he can't read my relief in my face.

'Well—thank you so much for the bread,' I say.

'My pleasure,' he says.

I follow him out to my door. He leaves quickly. I close the door behind him.

I turn; and feel the drumbeats of disaster through my body. I stand transfixed in the passageway. I try to recall just where he was standing, when first he stepped through my door—try so desperately to remember. Could he have seen straight past me? Did he see into the living room? Did he see Evelyn there, knitting briskly, looking perfectly well?

CHAPTER 74

Kirill stirs as I go in. Sunlight slants through the uncurtained dormer windows, golden and thick as honey and dense with motes of dust, looking as though it might feel solid if you touched it; while the substantial things in the attic have an indistinct, unreal look—the blanket chest, the bed, the man who lies in the bed.

He stares around him. At first he has a look of utter confusion.

'Kirill. It's Vivienne,' I say gently. 'You're staying with me now, remember? You're not in the camp any more.'

I sit on the blanket chest and wait for him to wake properly. In the brightness of the morning light, I can see a den that Millie and Simon have made, with a moth-eaten curtain I found for them, draped across a clothes-horse; and there's a broken old doll that's been put to bed in a box—this looks like Millie's handiwork. I wonder whether Millie sometimes comes here to play on her own. I know I will have to speak to her.

Kirill sits up shakily. I prop the pillows behind him.

'You are so kind, Vivienne.'

I see the lilac stains of illness around his mouth and his eyes.

'I've brought you some breakfast,' I tell him.

I spoon treacle onto his porridge, pour milk.

He watches the swirl of milk on the porridge, the opulence of the syrup.

'Is he here yet, Vivienne?'

'No. Not yet. But he'll come,' I say. 'I trust him. I've known him for years.'

'I thought someone came,' he says. 'When I was still sleeping. I thought your friend had come then.'

'It was someone else,' I tell him. 'But don't worry. You'll be safe here.'

'I don't want to put you in danger,' he says. 'When you have been so kind to me.'

'You just rest and get yourself well again. Don't worry about us,' I say.

Millie is in the garden, skipping and chanting breathily.

'Miss Lucy had a baby
She called him Tiny Tim
She put him in the bathtub
To see if he could swim…'

The lawn needs cutting; the long grass is lustrous with dew, and so are all the flowering weeds that grow there— yarrow, dandelion, white clover. Everything is glittering.

'Millie.'

I startle her, break her concentration. She stumbles over the rope.

'*Mummy.* You made me trip.' Accusingly. Her face is flushed, her voice is full of breath. Her brown hair shines like a seal's pelt in the brightness.

'Sorry, sweetheart. But I need to tell you something important.'

She waits, the skipping rope trailing from her hand, still resentful that I broke her rhythm. She's wearing her summer sandals and the straps are dark with wet. Around her, I can see the cross-stitch patterning of her footprints, where with all her skipping and jumping she's crushed the brilliant grass.

I bend to her, speaking very quietly.

'Millie. I don't want you playing in the back attic today.'

She's puzzled.

'I wasn't going to anyway, Mummy,' she says.

'All right. But just promise me anyway.'

'I promise,' she says.

Behind her, climbing nasturtiums flare on the walls of my house, orange as tongues of flame, as though little fires have been set there.

'And it has to be a secret,' I tell her. 'Just do as I say. Don't tell Blanche or Evelyn or anyone.'

A small smile plays on her lips.

'One of *those* secrets, Mummy? Just you and me?' she says.

'Yes.'

But I wonder if I have misjudged this. I know that she suspects that this is something to do with Kirill. Perhaps I should have kept quiet and hoped for the best; or perhaps I should have been open, told her everything. I don't know what the right path is. I don't know how to keep her safe any more.

CHAPTER 75

I listen out for the horse and cart all morning, my hearing acute, missing nothing; but Johnnie doesn't come. The morning stretches on for ever. My heart is pounding, pounding. I can't settle to anything. I busy myself preparing lunch; but the smell of boiling vegetables makes me feel sick.

Around noon, I hear footsteps coming rapidly up to my door, crunching in the gravel. Relief floods me. I'm sure, so sure, it's Johnnie. I rush to open the door.

'Oh,' I say.

It's Piers Falla. I stare at him—his twisted body, his eyes that see right into you. I can tell he's been rushing—his black hair is glued to his forehead, his face is glossy with sweat.

'Piers. What are you doing here?'

But I know. I can tell from his face: which is at once hard and stricken.

'It's Johnnie. The bastards have got him. He's been arrested,' he says.

My heart leaps into my throat.

'Oh God.'

My first thought is that this is my doing—because I asked Johnnie for help. That this disaster is all my fault.

'They came yesterday evening.' Piers' voice is bitter. He

turns a little away from me, wanting to hide what he feels. I see his face in profile, the fierce shape of his nose and his brow that makes me think of a bird of prey. 'They found that shotgun of Brian's.'

I stare at him. It's not as I thought. For a moment I don't understand.

'There was this gun that belonged to his brother,' says Piers. 'They're having a clampdown on wirelesses. Some two-faced rat must have tipped them off. Someone must have told them there was a wireless at Elm Tree Farm. So the bastards came to his house, and they ransacked his room.'

'I thought he'd buried the gun,' I say. 'Gwen talked about it. She said she'd make sure he buried it.'

Piers shakes his head, despairing.

'He'd hidden it under his bed. He kept all Brian's things with him. Johnnie can be such a bloody idiot at times.'

His voice is striped with scars. I can hear just how much he loves Johnnie.

'What happened?' I say. 'Did they hurt him?' Not meaning that exactly: meaning more than that. My heart thudding, hurting my chest.

'He's in the prison at St Peter Port,' Piers tells me.

I feel a rush of relief, that at least he's still alive.

'But—what will they do?' My throat seals shut. I can scarcely form the words. 'Piers—will they shoot him?'

'Depends,' says Piers curtly.

'It depends on what?'

He makes a slight gesture that would be a shrug, if it weren't for all the pain behind it.

'And Gwen? Is Gwen all right?' I ask.

He gives me a small cold look. I can tell he despises me, that I am asking all these stupid questions.

'Well—what do you think?' he asks me.

I'm desperate to see her—but I can't go, I can't leave the house.

I reach my hand a little way across the space between us, as a drowning person might reach, in a scrabbling, desperate gesture.

'Piers.' I lower my voice to a whisper. 'I've got Kirill here. Kirill from the work camp. I've got him in my attic.'

'That's what I've come about. You'll have to keep him,' he says.

There's an edge of steel in his voice. Behind him, I hear the insects around the fruit on my pear tree, buzzing and crackling, like sugar overheating in a pan. Everything sounds dangerous to me.

'Johnnie said—just for one night.' I hear the tremor in my voice. 'He said you'd need to move him on, to your safe house in St Sampson.'

He shakes his head briefly.

'We can't possibly move him now,' he says. 'Not when they've got their eye on us.'

In the glimmery silence between us, I hear Millie from the garden round the back of the house:

'In came the doctor, in came the nurse,
In came the lady with the alligator purse…'

Her voice rises up like a bright balloon.

A chill passes through me, in spite of all the lavish warmth of the sun.

'Piers—I've got children,' I say.

'You wanted to help Kirill.' His mouth is set in a thin line, unrelenting.

'Of course I did. Of course I do.'

'Well, then.'

This lad is all I have—the only one who can help me: this harsh boy, with the face of a kestrel, who scarcely knows me but guessed the truth about me. This boy who would have painted a swastika on the wall of my house.

'But I don't do things like this. I'm not a hero,' I say.

My voice seems to echo in the hollow rooms of my memory. I think how Gunther once spoke the very same words.

'Well, maybe you're going to have to be one,' says Piers, dryly. 'Just keep him. Someone will come.'

'When? When will someone come?'

'It could be a week,' he tells me.

'I'm frightened,' I say. And immediately regret that I said that. Whatever this boy is, he isn't weak. I don't think he understands weakness.

'Live with it, Mrs de la Mare.' His voice is rough as sand-paper, scraping my skin. 'All across the world now, people are bleeding and dying. You can put up with being a little bit *frightened*.'

I don't say anything.

'You know what to do,' he tells me.

Then, as though he's ashamed of his outburst, he reaches towards me and puts a hand on my arm. I feel all his warmth through the flimsy sleeve of my blouse.

'You're stronger than you think,' he says. 'Just keep him. Someone will come.'

He turns and leaves me.

Kirill is in the bed, half asleep, the blankets pressed to his face.

I kneel on the floor beside him.

'Kirill.'

He opens his eyes, sees me.

'There's something you need to know. There's been a change of plan,' I tell him. 'That boy who was coming—the boy I knew—he isn't coming today.'

I notice how I've used the past tense—*the boy I knew.*

'Has something gone wrong, Vivienne?' he asks me.

'It's nothing to worry about,' I say. 'They'll just have to send someone else.'

'When, Vivienne? When will it be?'

'We don't know exactly,' I tell him. 'It might take a few days. You'll be safe here...'

I see something surprising in his face—not the fear I was expecting, but a letting-go, an overwhelming relief. Yet at once I understand why he feels this—knowing he won't have to stir from this bed, that he can just stay here, dozing in the slanting beams of sunlight. That he is at peace for the first time since the Germans broke into his house—long, long ago, in another world, in the early morning dark of Belorussia. That he doesn't have to fight each moment just to stay alive, that he can lie here and listen to the murmur of the pigeons on the rooftop, and dream of his forests, his rivers, of the wooden houses where the storks make their nests.

'Thank you, Vivienne.'

He sighs, leans back on the pillows. Sleep comes to him abruptly, like the closing of a door.

CHAPTER 76

Sunday. I make breakfast for Evelyn and the girls; I take some food to Kirill.

After breakfast, Blanche goes off to Matins at St Peter's, elegant in the velvet jacket she made. Evelyn and Millie are in the living room—Evelyn is reading her Bible, Millie has her cardboard dolls with the sets of cut-out clothes. I open my kitchen window. It's a perfect summer morning, with a slight silver haze above us, as though all the blue of the sky is covered over with gauze. Through my open window, a polleny green air floats in, and a ripple of song from a blackbird in my pear tree. I listen for a moment.

Another sound comes—an engine. It must be the person that Piers is sending, sooner than he said. Johnnie had said they'd bring a horse and cart, but it sounds like they've got a tractor. *Thank God*, I think. *Thank God for that...*

The engine noise comes nearer. It's moving too fast for a tractor. It stops with a scream of brakes in the lane by the gate to my yard. I hear footsteps crunching in the gravel, coming up to my house. Many footsteps.

There's a noisy banging at the door, that echoes in the silent house. My heart sucks at my ribs. I go to open the door.

The man who stands there is wearing the brown OT

uniform. He's short, fleshy, intense; he has little wire-rimmed glasses and stony, light-coloured eyes. There are three other OT men behind him. They all have red swastika armbands.

'Mrs de la Mare?'

'Yes.'

I feel unreal, as though I am floating high above my body. As though it's someone else's heart that is thudding in my chest.

'I am going to search your house,' he says. He has a heavy accent. But I understand him perfectly. 'You must come out of your house. You, and anyone else who lives here.'

I rush into the living room.

'Millie, go out to the yard.'

She obeys at once, hearing my voice. She still has one of the cardboard dolls in her hand.

Evelyn doesn't move.

'We have to sit out in the yard for a while,' I tell her.

She looks up at me, puzzled.

'I don't see why, Vivienne. I'm perfectly comfortable here.'

'We've been told to. We have to. *Now,*' I say.

She frowns.

'Well, whoever it was should wait awhile. They should know I don't like to be rushed. They should show a little consideration,' she says.

I pull her abruptly to her feet. She comes with me, but reluctantly; she's heavy on my arm. I seat her at the table in the shadow of the pear tree. She stares at the soldiers.

'What are these men doing, Vivienne?'

'They've just come to have a look 'round,' I tell her. 'There's nothing to be frightened of.' Lying to her.

She sits on the edge of her chair, her back straight and thin as a flowerstalk. Her blouse has come open in front, from when I pulled her up from her chair: you can see the lace trim of her slip, and I feel embarrassed for her. But I have to leave it: I know I'd mortify her if I went to button it up.

I stand behind her, reach for Millie. I'm no longer afraid: I feel nothing, I'm quite cold and calm and controlled; but I have Millie's hand clutched very tightly in mine.

Millie hisses at me.

'My doll. You've creased it.' She pulls her hand away from mine, tries to smooth out the doll she was holding. 'It's ruined. *And* you were pinching, Mummy,' she says.

The captain stands there watching us. He has his gun out of its holster—not exactly pointed at us, but ready in his hand. The other soldiers go into the house.

All the time there's a voice in my head, an icy, sensible, terrible voice: logical, rational, spelling everything out. *Gunther heard someone coughing. He saw me with the tray of food I was going to take up to somebody, he knew it wasn't for Evelyn, he could see her in her chair. Gunther knew I had a secret...*

I can hear them slamming around in my house, drawers thrown open, doors flung back. I still feel unreal, as though I am watching all this from a height; but my body is utterly fragile, like Millie's cardboard cut-out doll: the slightest breath of wind could blow me away. They're beginning their search in the downstairs rooms. I hear them in the kitchen, then moving into the passageway; hear how the noise they make changes when it comes from different rooms: how their booted feet bang and clatter, going up the wooden stair. It's just a matter of time now.

The captain is still watching us. He has his back to the house. I can see out over his shoulders; I can see the wall of my house, the wicket gate to my garden, the leaf-shadowed lane. Behind him, I see a shadowy shape that creeps round the corner of my house, then through the little wicket gate and out into the lane. *Kirill.* My heart seems to stop. All the pent-up fear rushes through me. He must have slipped down the staircase from the attic, and out through Blanche's window and onto the roof of the shed. He steps softly into the lane, crosses to the further hedge and into the shade of my orchard, a shadow among shadows.

A sudden wild hopefulness seizes me, hot and thrilling as fever. Perhaps we will all be saved from disaster. Perhaps Kirill will escape.

I drag my eyes away from him, not wanting to let the captain read anything in my face. But he must have heard something—a footfall, the slightest wheezy breath.

He turns. He curses in German, runs out into the lane.

I wrench Millie against me, press my hand over her eyes.

'Stop it, you're *hurting*,' she says.

She tries to struggle free, but I keep my hand sealed to her face.

Kirill moves forward under the apple trees: walking on, not looking back.

The captain raises his gun. One shot. The shock of it goes through me. Kirill falls: there's no shudder, no struggle, nothing—he drops like a fruit from a tree. The speed of it, the lack of struggle, are an obscenity to me. I can see where his body lies in my orchard, so still in the long straggling grass, like a heap of clothes thrown down there.

The captain lowers his gun, walks back to us. He has a casual air, as though this is nothing to him. I think of something Gunther once said. *It is very easy to kill. To start*

with, maybe not so easy. But after a while it is very easy to kill.
I suddenly hear the blackbird in my pear tree: it must have
gone on singing all this time. Yet everything seems to have
taken place in an absolute empty silence.

Evelyn is sobbing, tears spilling over her face.

'Oh God—oh God—oh God…'

She tries to get up. I put my hands on her shoulders.

'Evelyn—you've got to stay here.'

'But it's Eugene. They shot Eugene.' She reaches out,
claws at my arm. 'You've got to let me go to him, you've
got to…'

I try to push her back down into her chair.

'It's nothing to do with Eugene,' I tell her. 'Eugene isn't
here.'

'My boy. My darling boy.' Her tears fall, make glimmery
tracks on her face. She hits out at me weakly. 'You should
have let me go to him, Vivienne.'

'It isn't Eugene.'

'Of course it's Eugene. I'd know that nice shirt of his
anywhere.'

I put my arm around her. I pray the captain didn't hear.

The captain slips his gun back in its holster. He takes off
his glasses and wipes his face on his sleeve: he's a fleshy man
and all the action has made the sweat pour off him. His eyes
seem too small without his glasses, like little pale stones.

I hear the clock chime in my kitchen. It's time for the
service. Up at St Peter's, the late-comers will be shuffling
into their seats. Blanche will be sitting ready, her prayerbook
open at the Confession: *Almighty and most merciful Father, we
have erred and strayed from Thy ways like lost sheep…* Soon the
choir and the Rector will start to process up the nave. I think
about these things: cling to them.

The man puts his glasses back on. He takes out a cigarette, lights it, his pale eyes fixed on my face. He has an eccentric way of smoking, cradling the cigarette in the hollow of his hand. He inhales deeply, thoughtfully. He is taking his time.

'When the scum ran across the road behind us,' he says, 'I think he came out of the back door of your house, Mrs de la Mare.'

'He can't have,' I say. 'He can't have done. Why would he do that?'

'Perhaps you can tell me that,' he says.

'It's nothing to do with me,' I say. 'I've never seen him before.'

The captain goes to the door of my house, shouts a name. One of the other men comes out. The captain speaks to him briefly in German. The man crosses the lane to my orchard. I keep Millie pressed against me, try to stop her from seeing. But she won't be held: she rams her fists against me, pushes me away. The soldier takes Kirill's feet and drags him through the long grass, so lightly, easily, as though there is no substance to his body. I can scarcely bear to watch this—but I make myself look. I feel I owe him that—to look. I think how wet his body will be, from all the dew on the grass, and this troubles me profoundly—as though the damp could harm him. They fling his body into the back of the lorry. I wonder if they will drive to the clifftop and throw him into the sea, like all the poor souls whose bodies rot in Alderney harbour.

The meaning of what he did presses down on me, floods through me. As I think this, there's a hard knot of tears in my throat. He did what he did to save us. He knew he would die—every step he took, he knew he was walking on to his death, that they would see him, that nothing could save him. While he stayed in my house, he had hope: they might not have found him, or, finding him, might have taken him back to the camp. There was still the smallest sliver of hope—they're capricious, they could do anything. But he knew what would happen to us, to my daughters and me, if he were found in our house. And he wouldn't let that happen. He couldn't die to save Danya his wife, but my children and me he could save. He gave his life for us.

I think of him coming down the staircase, crossing the lane. Knowing. Choosing.

One of the other OT soldiers comes out of the house. He speaks to the captain; as he speaks, the captain keeps glancing at me. They're talking softly in German, but I can imagine their words.

'Mrs de la Mare,' the captain says then. He shakes his head mournfully, as though saddened by human weakness. 'We have found a hidden room at the back of your house, at the top.'

'Yes,' I say.

'There are certain things in that room—a bed, the remains of a meal that was recently eaten. Anybody might think that you had been hiding somebody there.'

His tone is almost regretful.

'I have a young daughter,' I tell him. I take Millie's hand in mine. 'She likes to play house in that room.'

I wonder if he will see my heart beating under my blouse—the way it shakes the fabric.

'And the old woman seemed to know the scum,' he says.

'My mother-in-law misses her son. Her son is away with

the army. Sometimes she thinks she sees him when he isn't there,' I say.

He considers this.

'The scum had new clothes,' he tells me.

'Perhaps he stole them,' I say. 'How would I know where he got them?'

He is silent for a moment, cradling his cigarette in his hand.

'Also, I notice that you seem very upset.' His eyes on me, appraising me.

I try to make myself still. I think of Blanche at the service—make myself think of the prayers, say them over and over inside me. *O, God, make speed to save us. O, Lord, make haste to help us...* I cling to the words: they are bits of driftwood in a stormy sea: they keep me from going under.

'You were very upset when we shot the scum,' he says again. 'I have to ask myself why.'

'It was a shock,' I tell him.

'This is war, Mrs de la Mare,' he says, wearily. 'We are at war. These things happen.'

'He was helpless.' My voice is a tiny piping, blown away on the breeze. 'He couldn't defend himself. You shouldn't have shot him.'

The man shrugs.

'The scum was an escaped prisoner,' he says. 'He was no use to anyone... These men are all sub-human. They are not like you or me. You don't need to concern yourself about them...'

It's too close to what Gunther once said. *You mustn't think about it. You must try not to dwell on it.*

He smokes his cigarette, his eyes moving over my body: he's wondering what to do next. I feel my throat close like a fist, as I see where his gaze falls.

CHAPTER 77

'So, little girl—what is your name?'

'Millie de la Mare,' she says.

'Come here, Millie de la Mare.'

He speaks her name elaborately, each syllable exact, as though relishing its foreignness.

He beckons her to come forward, where she can't so easily see my face. Before she moves, she gives me a questioning glance. I nod. She steps towards him.

He is easy with children, I can tell that. He crouches down to talk to her, so his face is level with hers, so he's not talking down to her. It occurs to me that he must have children of his own, that he will have rocked those children tenderly in his arms—this man who has just shot down my friend Kirill like an animal.

'Do you like chocolate, Millie?'

She doesn't know what the right answer is. She half turns to me; I nod slightly.

'You shouldn't look at your mother when you answer my questions,' he says. 'Or I won't know which of you is answering...' The voice is perfectly reasonable, but I can hear the threat in it. 'So—I ask again—do you like chocolate?'

'Yes, I like chocolate,' she says.

He holds his cigarette in his mouth. He takes some

chocolate out of his pocket, unwraps it. In the silence, the rustle of silver paper sounds unnervingly loud. He breaks some off, gives it to her. I see how it softens immediately in the warmth of her hand.

'Can I eat it?' she says.

She's trying so hard to be good—but she doesn't know what the rules are.

'Yes, of course.' He smiles. 'It's for you, Millie de la Mare.'

She eats, and licks the smear of melted chocolate from her palm, so her mouth is smudged with it. I have a stupid urge to tell her to wipe the smudge from her face.

He's still crouching there, his face on a level with hers.

'I can tell you're a good girl,' he says to her. 'That you don't tell lies. That you always tell the truth. That is right, isn't it?'

'Yes,' she says.

'Telling the truth is very important, isn't it?' he says.

'Yes.'

'I'm sure your mother has told you that you should always tell the truth.'

She nods.

'We have searched your house. It is a big house. You have certain secret places and hiding places,' he says.

She doesn't say anything. Even from behind her, I can tell how tense she is, how warily she watches him.

Fear has me by the throat. I'm terribly afraid for her— because she will be left without me, when I am taken away. I tell myself that Blanche will manage—that Blanche is almost a woman, Blanche can look after herself. But Millie is so small still—too small to lose her mother.

'There is a room at the top of your house at the back,'

he says to her. 'A secret place that you go to up a narrow stair.'

'Yes,' she says, uncertain, wondering what is coming. 'Mummy calls it the back attic.'

I can't see her face, but I sense the confusion in her—she knows that this is important, but she doesn't know what she should say.

'The back attic.' He repeats the words, as though they are unfamiliar to him. 'I think the back attic must be a good place to play,' he says.

Here at last is something she can respond to.

'Yes, it's very nice,' she says. Her voice eager, helpful.

He takes a long drag on his cigarette, his eyes never leaving her face.

'When did you last play in your attic, Millie?' he says.

She's trying to think, so hard: I know how her face will look, creased up with trying, with thinking, the little frown drawn with blue indelible pencil on her brow.

'I like to play in the attic,' she says carefully.

'Did you play in your attic today, or yesterday?' he says.

I hold my breath. I know what she will say. I remember exactly what I told her. *Mummy said I shouldn't go there. Yesterday, Mummy said I mustn't play there any more. She said it was our secret. Our big secret...* I'm so sure she will say this—it's almost as though I can hear the words already, spilling out like water drops, innocent and shining and pregnant with disaster.

He is watching me. As he speaks to her, he keeps raising his eyes to me, studying me. I clasp my hands fiercely together. I know that he can see the trembling that goes through me.

Millie still hesitates.

'Did you?' he says. 'Did you play there today, or yesterday?' His voice is stern, insistent.

'I play in the attic every day,' she tells him.

'Now, I think that you aren't alone when you play in the attic,' he says. 'Who do you play in the attic with?'

'I play there with my friend,' she says.

The man's eyes have a hard gleam.

'And who is your friend?' he asks her.

She thinks for a moment. I sense the fog of anxiety that comes off her—as though it has a sulphurous edge that I can taste on the air. Then she clasps her hands and puts her feet neatly together. I see she has made a decision. I know, with a cold, sick certainty, that she is going to tell him that Kirill was here.

'My friend is called Simon. He's nearly nine,' she says. Her voice is measured, precise, and just a little too high.

All this time, the man watches me. I keep my face utterly still; but all the breath I didn't know I was holding rushes out of my mouth. I pray he doesn't hear this.

He stares at her a moment more, then he shrugs slightly, straightens. He drops his half-smoked cigarette and grinds it under his heel, as though it holds no more interest for him.

He goes to the door of my house, shouts an order. The other men come out of the house, move rapidly off to the lorry. One climbs in the cab, the others clamber up into the back. One of them kicks at something, and I know it will be Kirill's body: that he's kicking Kirill's body aside, to make more room for his feet.

'I will be watching you, Mrs de la Mare,' the captain shouts at me as he goes.

He climbs up into the passenger seat of the cab. The engine bursts into life; they drive off.

The shock of their sudden leaving unravels me. The world is spinning around me; I lean on the table and wait till it comes to a stop.

Evelyn is still weeping, not even trying to wipe away the tears as they fall.

'They killed him, didn't they?' she says.

I kneel beside her on the gravel.

'It's nothing to do with Eugene,' I tell her.

'They shot him. You saw. My boy, my darling boy.'

'Eugene isn't here,' I say. 'It wasn't Eugene who died.'

'He couldn't defend himself,' she says. 'They shot him in the back. They're such cowards. You should have let me go to him, Vivienne.'

'It wasn't Eugene, it was someone else,' I say.

'How can you say that, Vivienne? He was wearing Eugene's clothes.'

'It wasn't Eugene they shot,' I say again.

'That's such a sad death, Vivienne. He died all alone, there was no one to give him comfort. My poor, sweet boy. Such a sad, sad death,' she says.

I hold one of her hands in mine. Her hand is cold: her skin feels like fabric, not flesh.

'Eugene's away with the army, remember, Evelyn?' I say.

'Why do you lie to me, Vivienne? Why don't you ever tell me the truth?' she asks me.

'You should come to bed now,' I tell her. I pull her gently to her feet; she staggers. 'You can have a nice little sleep. We all need a rest now,' I say.

I take her into the house. She cries soundlessly, desolate,

hanging onto my arm. I take her upstairs and help her into her bed.

When I go back down to the kitchen, Millie is waiting for me. Her eyes are raw holes in her white face.

'Did I answer the questions right?' she says.

'Yes, sweetheart. You were very brave.'

I put my arms around her. Her body is rigid.

'Will Simon get into trouble?' she says.

'No, he won't get into trouble. You said the right thing.'

'But what if the Germans put Simon in prison?' she says.

'They won't, I promise. Simon hasn't done anything wrong.'

'But Kirill didn't do anything wrong and they still shot him,' she says.

My throat is constricted with tears, and for a moment it's hard to speak.

'Trust me, sweetheart,' I say then. 'Simon will be all right. The Germans aren't bothered with Simon.'

She pulls me down to her, holding my face close to hers. Her breath has a sickly-sweet smell from the chocolate the man gave her. She speaks into my ear, her whispered words brushing my skin.

'I know that Kirill was in the back attic,' she says. 'I heard him coughing. That was our secret, wasn't it? The secret you told me about? When you told me not to play there?'

'Yes.'

'I didn't tell the secret. Was that right?' she says.

'Yes, that was right,' I tell her.

'I didn't know what to say. I knew they'd be angry with us if they found Kirill had been here—but I didn't want to get Simon into trouble. It was really hard,' she says.

'Yes, I know,' I tell her.

'Mummy. Kirill is dead, isn't he? They killed him, didn't they?'

I think of the soothing things we say to comfort children. *Everything's all right, there's nothing to be frightened of. Those terrible things you saw weren't real—they were just a nightmare, a dream. There are no monsters, there's nothing there in the dark. Go to sleep now...* There's nothing I can say to her.

Later, we go to pick flowers.

There isn't much blooming in my garden now, because of all the vegetables, so we pick wildflowers from the hedge-bank—speedwell and red valerian—and tie the flower stalks together with string. I think of the posy that Kirill once gave to me. We cross the lane into my orchard. Around us, the summer morning is as it was before—the hazy, silvery sun-light and all the singing of birds. But everything is changed now. I can't live the way I did before. I can't be the person I was.

The grass is crushed where his body fell, and there's a dark stain on the ground, where his blood sank rapidly into the earth, and the trunk of the tree where I once stood with Gunther is spattered with darkening drops. Millie is poised and still, but her face is absolutely white. I think, He will never see them again, all those places he told us about, all the things he longed for—the birch forest, the quiet rivers. He will never go back to the workshop where he made his violins—that are made with so much care, that are so small, so fragile, so very easy to break; and yet sing out so clearly.

'Shall we say a prayer?' says Millie.

But I don't feel able to pray.

'We'll say a prayer inside our heads,' I tell her.

We place the flowers of speedwell there, on the stained earth.

CHAPTER 78

At night, when the girls are in bed, I sit at my kitchen table. I go through it all again and again, and the questions slice through me like blades. Was it Gunther who betrayed us? Could he have done such a thing, in spite of all that has passed between us—all the loving, the tenderness, all that we have shared? Is he capable of such treachery?

As I think these things, I draw in breath as though I'm drowning.

At ten o'clock, I hear the familiar soft knock at my door.

He comes in and I shut the door behind him. We stand looking at one another. Usually we will kiss, and then I will take him up to my room. But he doesn't move. Perhaps he immediately reads something in my face, something that troubles him. He doesn't bend down to touch me or kiss me, just stands there. He looks different, in a way that I can't quite define or express.

'You seem so tired,' I say, noticing this.

'Yes. I am tired.'

He rubs a hand over his face. His hand moves jerkily—as though his body isn't fluent any more.

He clears his throat, as if to say something.

'Vivienne...'

He swallows, as though this thing is too hard for him to say.

I know I have to be the one to say it.

'Something happened here today, in my orchard,' I tell him.

'Yes,' he says.

But his tone is somehow dismissive. An icy sliver of doubt runs through me, hearing this.

'A man was killed,' I say. 'Shot. One of the slave-workers.'

'Yes, I heard,' he says. Nothing more.

His awkwardness, his reticence, tell me all I need to know. That he knew about Kirill, that he realised. How could he not have known—hearing the coughing, seeing me with the breakfast tray, knowing I wasn't telling the truth when I said that Evelyn was ill? That he realised, and just did his job. That it was a difficult choice, but his duty was to his country. Bad things happen in wartime. You have to be careful, you don't want to step out of line. Killing is easy—to start with, maybe not so easy. But after a while, it is very easy to kill...

And in that moment I decide.

'Gunther,' I say, in a shred of a voice. 'I need to tell you something.'

He nods, just a slight, curt movement of his head. His face is serious, resigned. As though he has given up somehow. As though something has died in him. It's almost as if he expected this—it is all pre-ordained, he knows it and expects it, he just has to make his way through it.

'Gunther. I don't think I can do this any more. I'm so sorry...'

He says nothing. His silence is terrible.

'It's too difficult. Too confusing,' I say. There's a pain in my throat, as though saying this has hurt me.

I'm willing him to read my mind, to put everything back as it was. I want him to know why I am saying these things. I want him to explain that it was nothing to do with him: that what happened to Kirill wasn't his fault—that he wasn't the one who betrayed us. But I can't ask directly: because to ask him if he knew and told would be to reveal too much—to reveal that I harboured Kirill here. The fact that could put me and my children in danger—the fact that Kirill gave his life to conceal.

'I'm sorry,' I say again, helplessly.

With him standing so close, I feel the two things at once— the need to push him away from me; and the yearning for his touch, so familiar, so sweet. He was my refuge from all the fear and horror of these times—the place where I hid, the place where the war didn't come. But now the war is here between us: Kirill's terrible death is here between us.

'If that is what you want…' he says.

His voice is clear, but sounds as though it comes from far away, like a voice heard over water. He shrugs slightly. His eyes are blank. As though he has withdrawn from me already. I can't bear the coldness, the distance, in his face.

I nearly say, *No, it's not what I want. It's what has to happen, but of course it's not what I want.* But I don't say anything.

I reach out, needing to touch his arm, to soften the harshness of this: and he steps away, as though he can't bear my closeness.

I want him to protest. I want raised voices—for our parting to be messy, full of overt pain: for accusations, a sound of things tearing apart. Not just withdrawal and restraint. It seems all wrong that it ends like this—with this silence, this absence.

He bows briefly, with that old-fashioned courtesy he has, and turns from me.

But as he goes, he stumbles and stubs his foot on the sill of the door. He curses under his breath—a quick, hushed, furious torrent of curses in his own language. His hands are balled into fists; I see how the veins stand out like knotted string on the backs of his hands. Then he goes to the door and closes it quite quietly behind him.

Even as I hear the click of the door, I feel the loss surge through me.

I sit at my kitchen table. I tell myself that this pain will lessen, diminish. That this is the very worst moment. That one day it won't hurt so much. But I can't imagine how that could ever happen.

On Monday evening, Blanche comes home with some peaches, a treat from Mrs Sebire. I remember the first time she did this, in the early days of the Occupation, when she was just beginning her job at the shop. I was a different person then.

She puts the fruit down on the kitchen table.

'Why are there flowers in the orchard?' she asks me, rather accusingly.

I turn to her. She was sure to notice them some time, but, stupidly, I haven't worked out what to say.

'Mum, haven't you seen them? Somebody's put some flowers under a tree. I just noticed.'

Her quizzical stare, blue as summer, is on me.

'And there are black spots all over the tree trunk,' she says. 'How long has all that been there?'

'I put the flowers there,' I say.

She waits for more.

'Why?' she asks, when I say nothing.

'Something sad happened,' I say. 'Yesterday, when you were at church. One of the slave-workers was shot there.'

'What?' she says. 'But that's awful. Why didn't you tell me before?'

'I thought—the less you knew about it the better,' I say.

Her eyes are bright and curious. She's feeling both the sadness and the drama of this.

'Mum—this wasn't all something to do with Millie's ghost, was it?' she says. 'That ghost she used to talk about last summer?'

'Blanche—I don't want to tell you more than that. Trust me. It's safer that way.'

'That means yes,' she says. 'All right, Mum, don't worry. But I did start to wonder about Millie's ghost—whether he was one of the men from one of those horrible camps.'

'Blanche—we have to keep this to ourselves. I mean it.'

She gives me a slight complicit smile.

'I'll forget you ever told me,' she says. 'I won't say a word to anyone.'

She turns from me, unbuttons her cardigan, flings it down on a chair. She's too casual, too unconcerned.

'It's important, Blanche.'

'It's all right, Mum. I understand.'

I'm still worried I'm not getting through, that she doesn't understand how secret we have to be, how careful. Perhaps when I say what happened to Johnnie, she will see.

'There's something else you need to know,' I tell her. 'Johnnie's been arrested.'

She whirls round to face me.

'Johnnie?' Her voice is hoarse. Her face crumples. Her reaction startles me: I didn't expect that this news would upset her so much. I was careless: I wish I'd found a way to break it to her more gently.

I put my arms around her. I can feel her agitation, everything inside her spinning round like a top.

'He's in prison in St Peter Port,' I tell her. 'People think it'll be all right—he'll probably just be sent to prison in France.'

'Was it one of his stupid, stupid schemes?' she says.

'They found Brian's gun in his room,' I tell her.

'Johnnie's such an idiot.' Her voice blazes with anger. 'How could he be so stupid? Why doesn't he realise that he matters to people?' she says.

'Blanche—I didn't know you saw him…'

'Well, I don't. Not really… Well, just sometimes,' she says. 'Why did he let that happen? Why didn't he see?'

Later I hear her crying in her room. She doesn't often cry. I knock and go straight in. She's sprawled out on the bed, as though she were flung from a height. Her face is distorted with weeping, a soaked handkerchief balled in her fist. I sit beside her, put my hand on her arm.

'Blanche, he'll be all right. I really think he will. It's happened to other Guernsey people. They've come safe home again… And you know how upbeat Johnnie is—how nothing gets him down…'

She sits up. I put my arms around her and she clings to me for a moment. Her face is damp, her eyelashes clumped together. Then she pulls away and scrubs at her face with the handkerchief.

'Sorry to be so pathetic,' she says.

'Sweetheart. You don't have to say sorry for being sad,' I tell her.

She blows her nose.

'Bother. I bet I've gone all red,' she says.

I push back a strand of hair that has fallen over her face. It's wet with her tears, like drowned hair.

'The thing is, Mum,' she says then. 'It's just that sometimes somebody goes. And you realise just how much you're going to miss them. That you won't know quite how to keep going when the person isn't there… Mum, what is it?' She stares at me, eyes widening, alarmed. 'Don't do that. *Please*.' Her voice shrill. 'You're my mum. You mustn't cry. I hate it when you do that.'

The days shorten. The land is mellow and fruitful, the hedgebanks heavy and rich with rosehips, blackberries, elderberries. The Brent geese fly in from Siberia and graze in the fields near the shore: you can hear their strange creaking cries in the night. The apples in my orchard swell. There are figs on the fig tree on my terrace, and mulberries on my mulberry tree that darken to a luscious red so deep that it is almost black. The mulberries are easy to crush and we eat them straight from the tree, so Millie's lips have a permanent stain of vivid, wine-dark juice. The island is full of ripeness, of completion.

I still see him around, as summer sifts down into autumn. I'll glimpse him from my bedroom window, walking up the path between the borders at Les Vinaires; or when I'm tending the chickens I might see him talking with Max or Hans in the garden. A couple of times I pass him in the lane. My heart pounds. I don't know what will happen. But it's easy—too easy. He nods politely, and then avoids my gaze—it's as though we are almost strangers, people who just know each other by sight, people who happen to live in next-door houses. As though we never loved one another at all. Once I glimpse him through the window in the darkening evening, sitting at the table, writing a letter by candle-

light—for we have no electricity in the evenings now. He's
deep in thought, his sleeves rolled up. I wonder what he is
thinking: I feel something is withdrawn in him, that he is
not entirely present. I wonder if in his mind he has retreated
to Bavaria, to the stillness of that mountain landscape he
loves, where he would paint and have a whole day of quiet:
where he could shape his picture precisely as he wanted it,
everything flowing like water, the scene forming under his
hand.

Evelyn worries me more than ever. She spends so much of
her day asleep now, or in the hinterland between wakeful-
ness and dream, and sometimes I wonder what she sees in
her sleep—if the past is more real, more vivid to her than
the present; if she sees all the people and scenes of her past,
all crowding into the house. Then at night-time sleep will
elude her, and I'll find her wandering in the house or garden
in her night clothes, and I'll take her hand and guide her
back to her bed.

One day when I'm cleaning the living room, she suddenly
looks up at me. Her face is thoughtful and alert, as though
she sees me clear.

'So, Vivienne, my dear,' she says. As though something
has just occurred to her. Almost as though she's continuing
a conversation we've had. 'Eugene's away at war, you say?'

'Yes.'

'So you've been on your own all this time?'

There's tenderness in her voice. Her eyes on me are sweet
and blue as a child's.

I nod.

I suddenly remember what she was like when she was
younger, before old age began to dull and fracture her mind,

to steal so much away from her. How she was brisk, sometimes acerbic, but her forthrightness always tempered with
a practical down-to-earth kindliness.

I kneel beside her chair.

'It must be lonely,' she says. 'So lonely for you without
him. What a struggle for you. Bringing up Blanche and
little Millie and looking after me... And in wartime too...
And, my dear, I know I'm not always the easiest person in
the world...'

I try to speak, but my throat is tight with tears.

'I'm so sorry, my dear. That you've been so lonely like
this... And maybe even when Eugene was here... Well, I
saw it sometimes, Vivienne. That he wasn't always as good
to you as he could have been,' she says.

I'm amazed. I suddenly wonder if she knew about Monica
Charles.

She puts her hand on mine, and her touch is gentle, a
mother's touch.

'Maybe I haven't always understood. I'm so sorry,
Vivienne... So sorry for everything...'

And then there's a blurred look in her eyes again, their
clarity clouding over like an end-of-summer sky, and she
drifts off to some other place.

I wrap her blanket around her, trying to swallow down
my tears, so they don't fall on her.

Johnnie, as Piers predicted, is sent to prison in France for
a year.

I visit Gwen often. Her kitchen is cleaner than ever, everything polished, scrubbed, scoured. She's always so busy
and driven—as though with all her striving she could make
everything turn out well.

'He's been lucky—I know he's been lucky,' she says.

She rubs her hand over her face. She has a new, dramatic streak of white in her hair.

'Well, yes—in a way,' I tell her.

On the table between us, there's a vase of chrysanthemums, in those dusty colours they have, that always look a little forlorn. She moves her hands on the table top, tracing random pathways through the petals that have fallen there. She makes me think of Johnnie, the way she can't keep still. It's as if she has taken his restlessness into herself.

'I really think that, Viv. We've all been lucky,' she says. 'People have been shot for less, I know that. But, my God, I miss him. It's like losing part of myself. The best part…'

I put my hand on her arm.

'It's less than a year to go now,' I say. 'I know it seems like for ever, but it isn't really.'

She nods.

'That's what I keep telling myself. The thing is—I can talk to Johnnie like nobody else,' she says. 'Ernie's my rock. He's such a good man. Hard-working. But you know what men can be like—he doesn't really *talk* to me. But Johnnie would talk, we would talk for hours… I want him back,' she says.

It's dark in the evenings now, and Millie and Simon can't play outside any more. After school, they play in Millie's bedroom. Millie adamantly refuses to play in the attic. She has a fixed idea that she'll get Simon into trouble with the Germans if they go there—and nothing I say can reassure her.

We pick the apples in my orchard. The girls help me, a little wary, watching out for wasps. We sort through the apples meticulously, removing all the blemished ones that won't keep: these I will bake in the oven with some of Gwen's clover honey. I lay out the rest of the apples on cardboard trays in the shed, where it's cool and they will keep well. Each one is precious.

When the fruit have all been picked, Harry Tostevin comes with his saw to fell my apple trees. We'll need this wood for fuel, to see us through the winter months. Everywhere, people are doing the same, cutting down the trees that made our island so beautiful. I watch as Harry fells the first tree: there's a tearing sound as its branches catch on the other trees as it topples, then a deep dull thud as it hits the ground, and its many soft brown leaves shiver on for a long time after its fall. After that I can't bear to watch any more, as he cuts down the tree under which I first talked to Gunther—the tree where Kirill died, that was splashed with drops of his blood. But I can't escape the sound of it. I think of all the stories of Guernsey ghosts I've read to Millie: I wonder what spirits will haunt our island in generations to come. Will Kirill haunt my orchard, restless and troubled in this faraway place, forever trying to find a way back to the homeland he loved?

Afterwards, the land where my orchard grew is ugly—scarred with stumps, where once there was so much blossom and fruit. Harry chops the wood into logs and we store them in my garden shed. At least we have fuel for the winter now.

You do what you have to do.

I can't hear the click of Evelyn's needles. I look in on her, but she isn't asleep. She's unravelling her knitting. She slides the needles out of the stitches and pulls on the strand of wool. She does this as carefully, as assiduously, as when she is making something.

I go to her. I put my hand gently on hers. She moves her hand away from mine. She goes on pulling at the wool, undoing her work. It's so horribly easy to do: the wool is still crimped where the stitches were, but it's rapidly losing its shape, like something melting.

'You don't want to do that, Evelyn. After putting in all that work,' I say.

'But I have to, you see, my dear. I have to…'

I can't bear to see her do this. I'd like to take the knitting from her, to save what she has made. But I can't remove it from her by force.

She pulls and pulls at the wool. At last there's just a messy heap of crinkled wool in her lap.

She gives a little sigh, as though something has been completed.

'There,' she says. 'It's all done now.'

Her voice is calm, her movements measured; there's none of that agitation that so often hangs about her.

I don't know what to do now, whether to take the wool from her. But she holds the heap of it out to me. There's a surprising, unfamiliar peacefulness in her face.

'There you are then, Vivienne,' she says.

In the daytime I keep busy, I try not to think. I make sausages from haricot beans and a cake with grated carrot. I look after my chickens and tend my vegetable patch: I pick onions and leeks, and the first Brussels sprouts of the year. I clean the house and darn our clothes, and take up the hems of some of Blanche's old frocks for Millie—keeping everything going. And all the time I long for him—that longing that is just a fact of the body, like a sickness.

I sleep a lot, even during the day. I have such a hunger for sleep. When Millie is at school, and Evelyn is sitting quietly, and for a while nobody needs me, I creep up to my bedroom. I kick off my shoes and lie down under the covers. My head just touches the pillow and I immediately fall asleep, the drowsiness like a drug in me. I've heard that sadness can take you like that.

I make an oil lamp from an old Brasso can. Every evening, by the light of the lamp, I read a story to Millie from Angie's book of Guernsey tales. I read about healing wells and ghostly funeral processions. I read about hearth fairies, and the duty we have to tell family news to the bees. I read how cobwebs can staunch bleeding, and how the seagull is viewed with mingled awe and suspicion, for in its wide-ranging flight it perceives many mysteries that are hidden from men; and how a cloud of midges over water signifies rain.

And I read the story I first read when I was falling in love with Gunther, the story about the man who took the boat to Sark, and shot at the duck who was really a girl. How she was wounded.

C H A P T E R **81**

One Friday morning, once I'm back from Millie's school, I take Evelyn's toast and cup of tea up to her room. I open her door; and see at once that something is wrong. I usually find her sitting up, wearing her tea-rose silk bed-jacket; but today she still seems to be sleeping. Her body is sprawled across her bed, as though she tried to get up and fell back. Her breathing is noisy, her mouth gaping open; the bones in her face seem too clear.

'Evelyn,' I say. Then louder, frightened: '*Evelyn*.'

She doesn't stir.

I put my hand on hers. I shake her slightly. I can't wake her. There's something troubling about the look of her wide-open mouth.

It could take hours to get the doctor to come. I'd have to cycle up to his house on the main road, or I could ring him from the nearest phone box, but that would take almost as long. I remember what Gunther said to me, when he thought it was Evelyn coughing—that Max would come and examine her if ever she was ill. I remember how kind Max was to Millie.

I go out into the chilly brightness of the morning. I run round to Les Vinaires, rush up the path between the flower borders. Michaelmas daisies are growing there, tatty and straggly as weeds; they snatch at my legs as I pass them.

Hans Schmidt answers the door. He must have been eating breakfast: his lips are glossy with grease. He speaks before I can open my mouth.

'You wish to see Captain Lehmann?' he says.

I realise they must all know about our affair. Well, of course they would. It's not important.

'No. Captain Richter,' I say.

Hans goes to fetch him. I'm aware that I am listening out for Gunther's voice. There's a burst of loud male laughter from the back of the house: I think one of the voices could be Gunther's but I can't be certain—he never laughed in that noisy, raucous way when he was with me. I remember what I once said to him: *What are you like when you're not with me?* How he smiled and said that of course I couldn't know that.

Max comes into the hall. He's in his shirtsleeves.

'Mrs de la Mare.' Reading my face: solicitous, concerned.

I'm so glad to see him. I remember when he first came to my door, how I refused to shake his hand. How that seemed a matter of principle, seemed the right thing to do—the *good* thing. It's all so long ago now.

'I'm sorry to bother you,' I say. 'It's my mother-in-law. I think…' I hear the catch in my voice. 'I think she may be dying. I wondered if…?'

'I'll come at once,' he says. He doesn't bother to fetch his jacket, but comes as he is, in his shirtsleeves.

He moves very softly in Evelyn's room, speaking with a hushed voice. I can tell how he eases back into being a doctor again, how the part suits him. He takes her pulse, tests her reflexes, pulls back an eyelid and looks into her eye.

'I think you are right,' he tells me, speaking very quietly. 'I think it won't be long. She has had a stroke. There is no treatment. I'm very sorry.'

I nod.

'I thought it was something like that. Well, thank you so much for coming.'

'Is there anything else I can do for you?' he asks me.

'It's kind of you to offer, but I think I'll be all right,' I say.

'I'll see myself out,' he tells me. 'You must call again if you need me.'

'Yes, I will. Thank you…'

I sit with Evelyn and hold her hand. Her skin is dry and cold against me; her body moves very slightly with her noisy, laboured breath. I stay like that for a long time. I listen to the tick of the clock, to the tiny settlings of my house. Slow brown leaves drift past the window, and woodpigeons huddle on the sill, their small eyes pink and vacant—untroubled by our presence, as though there were no one here at all. The morning is very long. Evelyn's face is expressionless, and white as the pillow she lies on.

Towards noon she stirs and opens her eyes. She looks straight at me, as though she sees me clear, and that at least I am grateful for—that for this moment she is herself, not blurred and diminished by age.

She's trying to speak. I bend down to her, desperate to hear. She murmurs something, but her mouth won't move properly. I think she says 'Eugene', but I can't be sure. A shudder passes through her, into my hand; and then nothing.

I close her eyelids, and fold her hands on her chest. I think

how I can't reach Eugene, to tell him his mother is gone—
how one day he will come home from fighting and find his
mother buried. How sad he will be that he wasn't here to
grieve for her when she died.

I cry for her, yet I'm glad that she could slip away so
gently. This at least was a quiet death, a death in the fullness
of time.

Later that afternoon, Max comes back to my door. Perhaps
he's noticed the other people who've called at my house
through the day—the local doctor confirming the death,
and Mr Ozanne with his horse-drawn cart, to take the body
away.

'Mrs de la Mare.' He has a look like a question.

I nod slightly.

'My mother-in-law has died,' I say.

His face is serious.

'Then may I offer you my condolences,' he says.

'Thank you for coming to see her,' I say.

He shrugs slightly, as though to say this was nothing.

He hesitates for a moment, his eyes on me, trying to read
me. As though I'm some wild, timid creature he doesn't want
to scare off.

'There's something I need to tell you,' he says, rather
quietly. 'We are leaving your island—Gunther and I.'

My heart judders. Somehow I never expected this: it's
as though I'd believed that Gunther would always be here.
Maybe I'd thought, deep inside, that I could always change
my decision. That there was time. That there would always
be time.

'Leaving?' I say stupidly.

'Yes.'

'Where are they sending you?'

He has a slight rueful smile.

'The Eastern Front, unfortunately. This is not good news for us. Also, winter is coming.'

I remember what Gunther had said—about the carnage there, about the immensity of Russia and her armies: about Stalingrad that they called the mass grave of the Wehrmacht: about the cold, everything turned to ice—the lubricant in the tanks and guns; the lifeblood of men.

I swallow hard.

'Oh. When are you going?'

We're both very cautious, very formal.

'We leave on Monday,' he says.

'So soon?' I say.

'Yes, so soon. But whenever it was, it would be too soon for us.'

'Thank you for telling me,' I say.

I expect him to go then, but he doesn't. I see his throat move as he swallows.

'There is something else that I think I should tell you.' He is speaking so carefully. I know he has thought deeply about whether to say this to me. 'Gunther has heard that his son has been killed. His son Hermann.'

The world tilts. The words hang in the air, like sharpened blades. If I put out my hand they will cut me.

He watches me. He nods slightly.

'I thought as much,' he says. 'I thought he hadn't told you. Gunther is a private person. He keeps many things inside himself…'

Neither of us says anything for a moment. In the silence between us, I hear a far-off torrent, the rush of water that comes with the turn of the tide. Soon it will overwhelm me.

'When?' My voice is distant, muffled. 'When did he hear this?'

But even as I ask the question, I know what Max will say.

'It was six weeks ago. It was about the same time that there was that unfortunate incident in your orchard—the shooting of the escaped prisoner... I thought you should know,' he tells me.

'Yes. Thank you,' I say.

CHAPTER 82

On Monday morning, after I've taken Millie up to school, I set about cleaning the house for the funeral tea.

It's strange to be alone here. This hasn't happened for an age—not since Evelyn stopped going out. There's a different quality of stillness to a house that's empty—a sense of release, a flat calm quiet, almost as though the house itself is letting out its breath. There's no sound but the rasp of Alphonse's tongue on his fur, as he sits on the windowsill in a circle of thin gilded sun. The weekend has been busy—with Blanche and Millie distraught about their grandmother's death, with the funeral to organise. But now, in the silent house, I feel an unexpected clarity: as if a sound in my head, a constant insect-buzzing like static on a wireless, has been suddenly switched off.

In the unfamiliar stillness, there's one thought at the front of my mind. *It's Monday and Gunther is leaving.* And, thinking that, I return again to the terrible thing Max told me—how Gunther's son had been killed. The shiny ribbon of the past, that had seemed so neatly tied up, unknots and spools out in front of me. My mind is full of questions. Did I read everything wrong? Was that why he seemed so remote, so withdrawn—when I saw him that evening after Kirill had been shot? What if it wasn't Gunther who betrayed us? What if he had nothing at all to do with the death of Kirill? What if I pushed him away for nothing?

There are no answers to these questions.

There's a grey bloom of dust on the books in the bookcase, where I rarely clean. I pull out a handful of books to dust them, and something drifts to the floor, a piece of thick folded paper. I pick it up, open it, smooth out the creases. It's the drawing Gunther made of me that first evening we spent together: I'd tucked it in between the books where nobody could see.

I stare at it, the way it's so accurate, not very flattering really—yet revealing something, showing me as I am. I remember how we looked at the drawing together—how, as we looked, he ran his finger down the curve of my cheek. My body is suddenly weak. I sit down abruptly on the sofa: my hand goes limp and the paper falls to the floor. Everything seems illuminated—so simple, so dazzlingly clear. I have to say goodbye to him: I have to hold him once more. Why didn't I see that? Why has it taken so long to understand? Suddenly, this is the only thing in my entire world that matters.

I pull off my apron, rush out of the door, race round to Les Vinaires. I notice that the black Bentley that Gunther uses has gone. I knock at the door. It hurts to breathe.

A thickset man with hooded eyes answers the door. I don't recognise him.

'I'm looking for Captain Lehmann,' I say.

He shakes his head.

'They have gone already,' he says.

'To St Peter Port?'

It's as though a heavy boulder is pressing into my chest.

I could never get to town in time—it takes an age to cycle there.

He shakes his head.

'Not to the port. To the airfield.'

I feel a surge of joy. With this news, he has handed me a gift: the airfield is easy to get to, just up the hill and along the main road.

'Thank you,' I say. 'Thank you so much.'

He frowns slightly, perplexed by my excessive gratitude.

I run to get my bicycle. I'm full of a frenzied energy. I seem to ride so effortlessly up the hill—though I have to hold tight, my hands are damp and slippery and slide around on the handlebars as though they aren't really mine.

The airport is full of commotion and shouting and pur-pose, German soldiers everywhere, and lorries, motorbikes, Jeeps—all the teeming, solemn, elaborate apparatus of war that I am so ignorant of. A plane takes off as I approach, the roar of it filling the world, making my ears thrum. Some great movement of troops is happening. Something shrivels inside me. I was so intent on getting here, I hadn't thought through what I'd do—just had this hope, this certainty, that I'd somehow find him, that this was meant to happen.

As I cycle up the approach road, I notice the black Bentley, parked with some other civilian cars on the kerb. My heart lifts. But there is nobody in it.

I jump off my bicycle, leave it lying at the side of the road. Out of nowhere, a wave of nausea breaks over me. My body convulses; I retch up a little clear bile. It must be because of all the stress of the day, the exertion of the ride here. I wipe my face. I'm embarrassed, I hope that nobody saw. But I feel lighter, clearer, now.

Three soldiers are standing near me, smoking; they're casual, talking, laughing. They quiet as I approach.

'Excuse me. I'm looking for someone, I wonder if you could help,' I say.

They shake their heads, make small helpless gestures, shrugging—that universal language that says that you don't understand.

'I'm looking for Captain Lehmann. It's important,' I say.

Perhaps they will at least recognise his name. But they glance briefly at one another, then shake their heads again. As I turn away, one of them murmurs something in German, staring at me: the other men laugh loudly. I feel my face go hot.

I walk boldly up to the barrier that controls traffic into the airport. A soldier standing there stops me.

'You should not be here,' he tells me. 'You cannot come through.'

At least this man speaks English. I'm so grateful for this, so warmly, deeply grateful.

'Perhaps you could help me,' I say. 'I'm looking for Captain Lehmann.'

'Could you repeat the name?' he says.

I tell him again.

A sliver of recognition comes in his face.

'Captain Gunther Lehmann?'

'Yes.'

'I know Captain Lehmann,' he says.

I feel a hot rush of gratitude. This is all playing out as it was intended to do, everything happening as it was meant to happen. I could fling my arms around the man.

'I'm so glad,' I say. 'Could you tell me where to find him? I'd be so grateful.'

'The Captain has gone. You cannot see him,' he says.

I shake my head. I'm almost laughing, that he is so wrong about everything.

'You're not serious, are you? You're having me on,' I say, smiling, sharing the joke: sustained by my absolute certainty that this is meant to be.

The phrase makes no sense to him. He frowns.

'I don't understand you,' he says.

'You're joking, aren't you? You don't mean it.' I'm so confident, so certain. Though my voice is a little too shrill. 'You don't mean that he's gone. He *can't* have gone…'

The man says nothing, points upwards.

I look up there, where he is pointing. I see the black fleck of a climbing plane that as I watch is lost and gone in the empty shine of the sky.

CHAPTER 83

October is cold, with a wind that blusters through the wreck of my orchard, the boughs in the lanes bare and blackened with wet, above us a white rushing sky. Our daily lives take so much thought and planning and care: there's even less food in the shops now. I'm permanently exhausted, my body heavy and slow. Yet in a way I'm grateful for all the demands of this life, which leave me little time to think. I try to keep cheerful for Blanche and Millie. I only let myself cry in the evening, when they are up in their rooms; or at night when I wake in my empty bed, and press my face into my pillow.

One late afternoon in November, I'm making tea in the kitchen when there's a knock at the door. An assertive male knock. I think for a half-crazed moment that my desperate prayers have been answered—that he has been given back to me. I open the door.

I feel a sense of disappointment, shading into dislike. It's Piers Falla.

'Hello, Piers.'

'Mrs de la Mare. I want to show you something,' he says.

He's abrupt, as always. His eyes seem to see right into me,

that look that makes me think of a bird of prey, expecting something of me.

'What do you want to show me?' I ask.

'You'll see. You have to come with me.' And, when I hesitate, 'It'll be worth it, I promise.'

I grab my coat: there's a winter chill in the air. I warn Millie that I'm going out. I follow Piers down the lane, through the dusk that softly settles around us. He turns onto a track that leads up the wooded side of the hill, a path I've never walked before. I follow him through the dull, dormant woods. The colours of the countryside are muted in the gloom–russet, cinnamon, nutmeg, like the hides of animals. There's a slight wind in the branches, and our footsteps rustle on the path that is deeply drifted with leaves.

The silence between us is awkward. Piers is not an easy person.

'You must miss Johnnie,' I say, to break the silence.

'Yes,' he says. 'Yes, I miss him… All those things we did together—I never thought it would end like this. Just because of a stupid mistake…'

'But it isn't such a long sentence,' I say. 'He should be back in July.'

'As long as he doesn't get lost in the system,' says Piers. 'Sent off to some more terrible place.'

'Oh,' I say. 'But surely that can't happen, can it? Surely it's better organised than that?'

'There are rumours that it's happened to others,' he says.

'Oh.' I feel a shiver of fear for Johnnie.

We walk on up the whispering path. A jay breaks cover in front of us; its flash of blue, bright as sapphires, is startling against the sepia gloom of the wood. Around us, we hear the myriad small voices of the streams.

Piers clears his throat; the sound is too loud in the stillness.

'Some of those things we did, Johnnie and me,' he says, out of nowhere, and stops. Then tries again. 'There are things I used to think mattered, that don't matter so much any more. Things that aren't really important...'

I know that he is saying sorry to me.

I glance towards him. His face is working: he's trying to find the right words.

'The way we used to do things, when the Occupation began. We were just kids then. To be honest, we were just playing around,' he tells me.

'You wanted to do what you could,' I say. 'I can understand that.'

He doesn't seem to hear me.

'What I've learnt,' he says. 'It's what a person does when their moment comes. When something is required of them. What they do with the time that is given them. That's what matters... The other things aren't important—who you fall in love with, all of that...'

I feel uncomfortable: I don't know how to respond. Yet at the same time I'm grateful that he said that.

We climb up the steep twisting path through the trees and their tangled shadows, and come out at the top to windy brightness and sky and all the wide air beyond the wood, where there are cornfields and the shine of the sea. The moment that is like a birth—coming up out of the womb of our deep wooded valley and into the light.

I see with a stir of alarm that we have come to the work camp on the clifftop—the camp that Johnnie described, that I never wanted to see. The camp that Kirill came from. I see the high barbed-wire fence, the shacks where the slave-workers sleep, the wooden watchtowers. I think of the things that people say they have witnessed here. Of men left beaten and bleeding. Of a man who was hanged from a tree, and the body left hanging for days.

We move a little closer. I see that the grass in front of the buildings has all been worn away, leaving just bare earth and mud. A bonfire has been made there. Many men sit round the fire; they are thin and ragged and desolate-looking. A guard is watching them vaguely—bored, not very vigilant, absently smoking a cigarette. The men are quiet, scarcely stirring, not even talking together. They have the look that Kirill had, on that long-ago day when I first saw him in Peter Mahy's barn, their faces blank with exhaustion.

But then, as we watch, something moves through the men like a summer wind through wheat—a sudden disturbance, shouts, a slow hand clap. I wonder what will happen. Two men get up from the ground. They have dark hair, sun-browned skin: they could be the gypsies that Johnnie said were among the prisoners here. They stand facing one another, as though they are sparring together, so just for an instant I wonder if they will fight. But they raise their arms above their heads and click their fingers in time; they sway a little and start to dance, stamping their feet on the bare earth, their rags of clothes flying wildly with the swaying of their bodies. The other men cheer, then fall silent. I watch the gestures of the dancers as they beckon, conjure, caress. There is such eloquence in the movements they make: they speak of desire, of solace, of a brief and broken triumph. When they pass in front of the firelight, they seem to hold all that red light and warmth in their hands.

I think of Kirill—of his homeland, the stories he told, all the things he dreamed of. I think: We all have such richness in us—the lives we have lived, the people we have loved, all the things we have longed for. Wherever we go, whatever happens, we carry this richness within us. Whatever is done to us, whatever is taken from us.

And then it ends, as abruptly as it began. Their feet stamp to a close, their hands fall emptily to their sides, they sink to the earth by the fire, their shadows hunched in front of them. The watching men applaud and then are quiet. Silence falls like a leaf. It is all as it was before. Or almost as it was before.

We too are still for a moment.

I turn to Piers. In the dimming light, his kestrel face doesn't look quite as stern as I'd thought.

'Was that what you wanted to show me?' I say then.

'No.'

'But I'm glad that I saw it,' I say.

He nods slightly, acknowledging this.

'This is what I wanted to show you,' he says. 'There's a place in the wire—over there by that ditch…'

I look where he is pointing, to a place where a thicket of hazel trees shades over a ditch and almost reaches the fence. There's a lot of cover. You could get very close and not be seen.

'Yes,' I say.

'There's a rip in the wire there. The prisoners keep it open. You can leave food there. Under those trees, just outside the fence. If you have any food you can spare, you can bring it here and leave it. The best time is just before curfew…'

'What if the guard sees me?' I say.

'It depends who's on duty,' he says. 'Sometimes they turn a blind eye. Some of them aren't bothered, like that man there today. We've had other people do this. With luck, you should be all right… There's always a risk, of course. But then you know that.'

'Yes.'

The shadows are long now, but there are still a few tatters of light in the sky. The brightness reflects in Piers' keen gaze.

'I'm sorry we lost Kirill,' he says. 'But there are others that we can help keep alive.'

'Until the war is over?'

'Until we win,' he tells me. Sounding just like Johnnie.

Will we win? I think. How can we? Is it possible? It seems beyond imagining.

'So what do you think, Mrs de la Mare? Will you do what you can?'

But he already knows my answer.

EPILOGUE:

APRIL 1946

CHAPTER 84

A few months after the end of the war, a postcard comes for me. I cycle to St Peter Port. It's a sunny April afternoon. The town is calm and orderly: the shops are all open, people mill in the streets. Mothers scold their children, people at bus-stops grumble—about the weather, the government, how much everything costs. I think how readily we return to the predictable life of peace-time—those of us who are left, who are lucky: we brush the dust of the past from us, sweep up the fragments, move on.

I leave my bicycle at the foot of the steps that lead up to the tea-shop. Mrs du Barry's has closed now, but this new place has opened. You can sit on the terrace when it's warm, and I thought it would be a good choice.

I climb the steps to the terrace. I glance back over the steep red-tiled roofs, but you can't see the water from here, you wouldn't know you were on an island, except for the quality of the light—that is at once soft and lustrous, and has the silvery clarity of sunlight over the sea.

The place is busy: women meeting their friends and gossiping over tea and *gâche*, men doing business, a nanny with boisterous children. For a moment, I'm confused by all the colour and movement and talk, and I can't see him. Then I spot him, at the table in the corner of the terrace. He's wear-ing a sober business suit and tie. He looks entirely different in civilian clothes—less certain, less authoritative. He sees me and stands as I approach. He takes my hand and gives a little bow.

'Captain Richter,' I say.

Though I'm not sure how to address him. Germany has no army now: presumably he doesn't really have a rank any more.

'Mrs de la Mare. Thank you so much for coming.'

We sit. The waitress comes to our table. He orders tea for both of us.

'You would like something to eat? A cake?'

But I can scarcely swallow, I know I couldn't eat.

'No, thank you.'

When the waitress has gone, he leans across the table towards me. His clear dark eyes are on me. There's such seriousness in his face.

'Mrs de la Mare…'

He stops, clears his throat: as though it's too hard to say the words he has come here to say. Even for this poised, cynical man, who must have seen so many things.

But I can read it all in his eyes.

'He's dead, isn't he?' I say. 'That's what you came to tell me.'

A shadow moves over his face.

'Yes, I'm afraid Gunther died,' he says. 'I'm so sorry.'

'I knew he must be dead, when I got your postcard,' I tell him.

'He asked me to come and find you, when he was dying,' he says. 'I'm keeping my promise to him.'

'Yes. Thank you.'

For a moment we are quiet. The noise of the café around us seems to withdraw, to come from some great distance.

Max takes out two cigarettes, lights them, hands one to me. As I take the cigarette, I see that my hand is trembling.

He leans forward on his elbows, looking into my face.

'There were things he wanted me to tell you,' he says. 'He told me he thought you blamed him for the shooting of that Pole.'

'He wasn't a Pole,' I tell him.

'It doesn't matter now,' he says.

'Yes. It matters.' I'm surprised by the anger that seizes me—that Max talks about him as though he were just some faceless prisoner. 'He came from Belorussia. His name was Kirill. His village was in a birch forest. He was a craftsman, a very skilled man. He made violins.'

My voice is too loud, too intense.

Max leans back slightly and makes a small, soothing gesture with his hands—as though to pacify me.

'Anyway. That man who was shot,' he says.

But the anger is still in me.

'I know to you it was just one incident, one little thing that happened. An unfortunate episode. It wasn't that to me. To me it was all the brutality of war…'

'Yes. Of course,' he says placatingly.

The waitress brings our tea. I try to pour, but my hand is shaking too much.

'You should let me do that,' he says.

'Yes. Thank you.'

He pours. He hands me my cup.

I don't drink. I'm waiting.

He leans towards me again.

'Gunther wanted me to tell you it was nothing to do with him. He knew you were hiding the man in your house.'

'When did he tell you that?' I ask.

'He told me when we were still on your island,' he says. 'That when he came to see you one morning he realised what was happening. He would never have spoken to the OT about it. He wouldn't have put you at risk. He wouldn't ever have hurt you. It wasn't Gunther who betrayed you.'

'How do you know that?' I ask him. 'How can you possibly be sure?'

'I can be sure because I know where the information came from. It came from Hans Schmidt,' he tells me. 'Schmidt saw something in your garden. He went to the OT.'

I remember the fresh-faced blond boy who would sometimes mow the grass at Les Vinaires: the cat-lover.

'Why didn't Gunther tell me?' I say.

'He was a proud man, Mrs de la Mare. As I imagine you know. Once you'd decided your love affair was over, he would never have pleaded with you or begged you to take him back.'

I don't say anything. I know he is right.

We smoke in silence for a moment. Then Max puts his cigarette down, resting it in the ashtray.

'Mrs de la Mare. I have to tell you,' he says, haltingly. 'We didn't know the things that were being done in our name. Many of us who served in the army, believing in our country—that we had to restore our pride, to recover the land we had lost—when we saw what had been done, we wept... Not all of us. But some of us.'

'How could you not have known?' I struggle. There are no words big enough. 'I mean—even here, on Guernsey—you could see the brutality.'

'You do your job,' he says. 'You do what you have to do. You don't always look around you. You don't always think about everything.' And, when I don't say anything: 'You may feel that is wrong,' he says, 'and you would be right to feel that. But that is how people behave. Most of us, most of the time. People behave as they are told to behave, as those around them behave. Generally, this is what happens. It is depressing but true. This is what we are like…'

'You must have known,' I say again.

He opens his mouth as though to speak: but he doesn't say anything.

We are silent for a long time then. The cigarette burns in the ashtray where he has left it. He is utterly still, staring down at his hands.

At last he stirs. He rubs his hand over his face, and looks around him again—at the sunlight, the red-tiled roofs, the bright blowing sky.

'So, Mrs de la Mare. Tell me what your life is like, since the war. Here on your beautiful island.'

I hesitate. What should I tell him? But there's an intimacy between us, because of what he has done for me, in coming here. I'm grateful to him: I am in his debt. I decide I will tell him everything: well, *almost* everything. I owe him that.

'My husband came back from the war,' I say. 'He was lucky, he survived. But we've agreed to live apart now.'

'I am sorry to hear that,' says Max.

'He lives here in town—he bought a flat with some of his mother's money—and I still live at Le Colombier, with the children,' I say. 'I give piano lessons—we get by. We couldn't live together again—after everything that had happened…'

He nods slightly.

'I can see it would be difficult,' he says carefully.

'And Blanche—d'you remember Blanche, my elder daughter?' I say.

'Yes, of course I remember her.'

'Blanche is married now. She married Johnnie—the son of one of my friends. He was sent to prison in France for a while. They found a shotgun in his room...'

Max shakes his head in a tired, resigned way, as at a revelation of stupidity. Perhaps at Johnnie's stupidity in holding onto the shotgun; or at all the pettiness of the rules that governed our lives for so long.

'When he came home they started seeing one another,' I tell him. 'They married just last summer...'

I remember the wedding, picture it. Blanche in the shapely pink suit she'd made, and a little felt hat with a veil. Her blonde hair falling like water and the happiness lighting her face; and the amazed way Johnnie looked at her, as though he couldn't believe his luck; and everyone singing, the sun shining bright, the whole church festive with flowers.

'It was a happy day,' I tell him.

He smiles.

'And Millie is doing so well at school,' I tell him. 'She says she wants to be a doctor. Of course it's a very hard career choice for a girl. But I'd love to see it work out for her...'

His face softens.

'Millie is a beautiful child,' he tells me.

And then we are silent again. And I know it's up to me to break the silence, but for an age I can't do it.

At last, I make myself ask the question.

'How did Gunther die?'

I can scarcely hear my own voice.

Max puts his hand on my sleeve.

'It was in August '44, at Kishinev in Rumania. I was with him,' he tells me. 'He didn't die alone.'

'I'm glad,' I say. 'I'm so glad that you were with him. So glad.' I can't stop saying it.

I notice how he doesn't tell me quite how Gunther died. He doesn't say, It was quick, he didn't suffer.

'I have something to return to you,' he tells me. 'Gunther kept this always...'

He takes something out of his pocket. It's the book of poetry that once I gave to Gunther. I hadn't known that he'd kept it. Max hands it over to me. It has a worn, battered look, and there's a stain on the cover that might be blood.

I flick through. The ribbon still marks the page of my favourite poem. I open the book there.

I have asked to be
Where no storms come...

The words blur. I can't read any more.

I turn to the front of the book, where once I wrote my name. I see that Gunther has written his own name beneath mine, so our two names are together: as lovers will carve their initials together on the bark of a tree.

And then the tears come.

I cry for a long time. The grief possesses me, my body shaking with sobs.

Max sits silently, and waits. I'm so grateful for his quietness.

When at last the crying stops, I'm aware of people glancing at me, disconcerted by so much emotion in this public place. But not surprised: for many of us have grieved.

I am lucky, I keep telling myself. *I have my precious children.*

I am so lucky. But still the pain of it washes through me. I can't imagine how I will ever learn to bear it.

I scrub my face with my handkerchief.

'I have to go now,' I tell him. 'Thank you. Thank you for coming, for making the journey. I don't know how to thank you...'

He shrugs a little.

'I was happy to do this,' he tells me. 'Gunther was my friend.'

We stand. He shakes my hand warmly.

I go down the steps to the street. I undo the lock on my bicycle and set out on the long journey back, as the sunlight mellows with evening and the shadows reach over the road. Going home to Millie; and the little boy who I know will rush into my arms when I get there; whose grey eyes will shine when he looks at me, who will smile with Gunther's smile.

★ ★ ★ ★ ★

If you loved this, read on for an exclusive extract from

THE WINTER GUEST
by Pam Jenoff

Available now

PROLOGUE

New York, 2013

"They're coming around again," Cookie says in a hushed voice. "Knocking on doors and asking questions." I do not answer, but nod as a tightness forms in my throat.

I settle into the worn floral chair and tilt my head back, studying the stucco ceiling, the plaster whipped into waves and points like a frothy meringue. Whoever said, "There's no place like home" has obviously never been to the Westchester Senior Center. One hundred and forty cookie-cutter units over ten floors, each a six hundred and twenty square foot L-shape, interlocking like an enormous dill-scented honeycomb.

Despite my issue with the sameness, it isn't an awful place to live. The food is fresh, if a little bland, with plenty of the fruit and vegetables I still do not take for granted, even after so many years. Outside there's a courtyard with a fountain and walking paths along plush green lawns. And the staff, perhaps better paid than others who perform this type of dirty and patience-trying work, are not unkind.

Like the white-haired black woman who has just finished mopping the kitchen floor and is now rinsing her bucket in the bathtub. "Thank you, Cookie," I say from my seat by the window as she turns off the water and wipes the tub dry. She should be in a place like this with someone caring for her, instead of cleaning for me.

Coming closer, Cookie points to my sturdy brown shoes by the bed. "Walking today?"

"Yes, I am."

Cookie's eyes flicker out the window to the gray November sky, darkening with the almost-promise of a storm. I walk almost every day down to the very edge of the path until one of the aides comes to coax me back. As I stroll beneath the timeless canopy of clouds, the noises of the highway and the planes overhead fade. I am no longer shuffling and bent, but a young woman striding upward through the woods, surrounded by those who once walked with me.

And I keep a set of shoes by the bed all of the time, even when snow or rain forces me to stay indoors. Some habits die hard. "How's Luis?" I ask, shifting topics.

At the mention of her twelve-year-old grandson, Cookie's eyes widen. Most of the residents do not bother to learn the names of the ever-changing staff, much less their families'. She smiles with pride. As she raises a hand to her breast, the bracelet around her wrist jangles like ancient bones. "He made honor roll again. I'm about to go get him, actually, if you don't need anything else..."

When she has gone, I look around the apartment at the bland white walls, the venetian blinds a shade yellower with age. Not bad, but not home. Home was a brownstone in Park Slope, bought before the neighborhood had grown trendy. It had interesting cracks in the ceiling, and walls so close I could touch both sides of our bedroom if I stretched my arms straight out. But there had been stairs, narrow and steep, and when my old-lady hips could no longer manage the climb, I knew it was time to go. Kari and Scott invited me to move into their Chappaqua house; they certainly have the room. But I refused—even a place like this is better than being a burden.

I look across the parkway at a strip mall now past its prime and half-vacant, wondering how to spend the day. The rest of my life rushed by in an instant, but time stretches here, demanding to be filled. There are activities, if one is inclined, knitting and Yiddish and aqua fitness and day trips to see shows. But I prefer to keep my own company. Even back then, I never minded the silence.

One drop, then another, comes from the kitchen faucet that Cookie did not manage to shut. I stand with effort, grimacing at the dull pain that shoots through my thigh, the wound that has never quite healed properly over more than a half century. It hurts more intensely now that the days have grown shorter and chilled.

Outside a siren wails and grows closer, coming for someone here. I cringe. Now, it is not death I fear; each of us will get there soon enough. But the sound takes me back to earlier times, when sirens meant only danger and saving ourselves mattered.

As I start across the room, I catch a glimpse of my reflection in the mirror. My hair has migrated to that short curly style all women my age seem to wear, a fuzzy white football helmet. Ruth would have resisted, I'm sure, keeping hers long and flowing. I smile at the thought. Beauty was always her thing. It was never mine, and certainly not now, though I'm comfortable in my skin in a way that I lacked in my younger years, as if released from an expectation I could never meet. I did feel beautiful once. My eyes travel to the lone photograph on the windowsill of a young man in a crisp army uniform, his dark hair short and expression earnest. It is the only picture I have from that time. But the faces of the others are as fresh in my mind, as though I had seen them yesterday.

A knock at the door jars me from my thoughts. The staff has keys but they do not just walk in, an attempt to maintain the deteriorating charade of autonomy. I'm not expecting anyone, though, and it is too early for lunch. Perhaps Cookie forgot something.

I make my way to the door and look through the peephole, another habit that has never left me. Outside stand a young woman and a uniformed policeman. My stomach tightens. Once the police only meant trouble. But they cannot hurt me here. Do they mean to bring me bad news?

I open the door a few inches. "Yes?"

"Mrs. Nowak?" the policeman asks.

The name slaps me across the cheek like a cold cloth. "No," I blurt.

"Your maiden name was Nowak, wasn't it?" the woman presses gently. I try to place how old she might be. Her low, dishwater ponytail is girlish, but there are faint lines at the corners of her eyes, suggesting years behind her. There is a kind of guardedness that I recognize from myself, a haunted look that says she has known grief.

"Yes," I say finally. There is no reason to hide who I am anymore, nothing that anyone can take from me.

"And you're from a village in southern Poland called… Biekowice?"

"Biekowice," I repeat, reflexively correcting her pronunciation so one can hear the short *e* at the end. The word is as familiar as my own name, though I have not uttered it in decades.

I study the woman's nondescript navy pantsuit, trying to discern what she might do for a living, why she is asking me about a village half a world away that few people ever heard of in the first place. But no one dresses like what they are anymore, the doctors eschewing white coats, other professionals shedding their suits for something called "business casual." Is she a writer perhaps, or one of the filmmakers Cookie referenced? Documentary crews and journalists are not an uncommon site in the lobby and hallways. They come for the stories, picking through our memories like rats through the rubble, trying to find a few morsels in the refuse before the rain washes it all away.

No one has ever come to see me, though, and I have never minded or volunteered. They simply do not know who I am. Mine is not the story of the ghettos and the camps, but of a small village in the hills, a chapel in the darkness of the night. I should write it down, I suppose. The younger ones do not remember, and when I am gone there will be no one else. The history and those who lived it will disappear with the wind. But I cannot. It is not that the memories are too painful—I live them over and over each night, a perennial film in my mind. But I cannot find the words to do justice to the people that lived, and the things that had transpired among us.

No, the filmmakers do not come for me—and they do not bring police escorts.

The woman clears her throat. "So Biekowice—you know of it?"

Every step and path, I want to say. "Yes. Why?" I summon up the courage to ask, half suspecting as I do so that I might not want to know the answer. My accent, buried years ago, seems to have suddenly returned.

"Bones," the policeman interjects.

"I'm sorry..." Though I am uncertain what he means, I grasp the door frame, suddenly light-headed.

The woman shoots the policeman a look, as though she wishes he had not spoken. Then, acknowledging it is too late to turn back, she nods. "Some human bones have been found at a development site near Biekowice," she says. "And we think you might know something about them."

A breathtaking historical novel set in 1930s Vienna, about an ordinary girl living in extraordinary times

When seventeen-year-old Stella Whittaker is offered the chance to study at the Academy of Music in Vienna, it's a dream come true.

Seduced by the elegant beauty of the city, Stella explores the magnificent palaces, gardens and fashionable coffee houses and, after a chance meeting in an art gallery, falls in love with Harri Reznik, a young Jewish doctor.

But, as the threat of war casts a dark shadow over Europe, Stella soon discovers that the city she has come to call home is not as welcoming as it once seemed. And at the dawn of this terrifying new world, no one is safe.

'Stunning and evocative...utterly beguiling'
—Rosamund Lupton

'Margaret Leroy writes with candour and intelligence, capturing the menace of suddenly finding that the world may not be at all as you've thought it'
—Helen Dunmore

Would you reveal a secret that might solve a murder but would ruin your life?

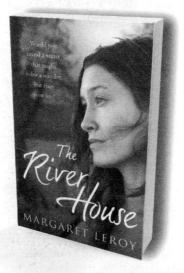

Ginnie Holmes has found something she never intended to find—an overwhelming passion for a man she shouldn't be with.

But when a woman is found murdered by the Thames near where they meet, the lovers' secret becomes a deadly catastrophe. Ginnie finds herself facing the exposure and grief she has feared, and endangering herself and everyone she loves.

www.mirabooks.co.uk

*'I've striven to be the perfect mother,
wanting to create a perfect childhood
for my child. Yet something has
gone wrong...'*

Catriona has the life she's always dreamed of:
a loving husband, a delightful step-daughter
and her own precious little girl, Daisy.

But when Cat is accused of harming eight-year-old
Daisy through Munchausen's Syndrome by Proxy,
Cat begins to realise that the life she has now is
more fragile than she could ever have imagined.

A haunted child.
A desperate mother.
An unspeakable truth.

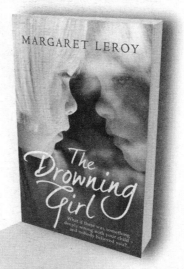

Young single mum Grace is drowning. Her little
girl Sylvie is distant and prone to violent tantrums
which the psychiatrists blame on Grace. But Grace
knows there's more to what's happening to Sylvie.

Travelling from London to the west coast of Ireland,
Grace and Sylvie embark on a journey of shocking
discovery, changing both their lives forever.

POLAND, 1940
A FAMILY TORN APART BY WAR

Life is a constant struggle for sisters Helena and Ruth
as they try desperately to survive the war in a bitter,
remote region of Poland. Every day is a challenge to
find food, to avoid the enemy, to stay alive.
Then Helena finds a Jewish American soldier,
wounded and in need of shelter.

If she helps him, she risks losing everything, including
her sister's love. But, if she stands aside, could
she ever forgive herself?

www.mirabooks.co.uk

'If you will be a great man's mistress, you must pay the price…'

1372. The Savoy. Widow Lady Katherine de Swynford presents herself for a role in the household of merciless royal prince John Plantagenet, Duke of Lancaster, hoping to end her destitution.

Seduced by the glare of royal adoration, Katherine becomes John's mistress. She will leave behind everything she has stood for to play second fiddle to his young wife and ruthless ambition, in the hope of finding a love greater than propriety. But is anything strong enough to face the cries of heresy?

www.mirabooks.co.uk